The L

KATH

Dragon
Moon

Acknowledgments

Once again, I find myself indebted to my family and friends—not just for their unstinting emotional support, but for getting out there and actively promoting me in their various, often amazing ways. Heartfelt thanks to each and every one of these wonderful people. 'They make me go.' I would also like to thank my publisher, Gwen Gades, for her unswerving commitment to the field of fantasy and its lesser known writers, and my editor, Christine Mains, for encouraging me to start this project and helping me to get it right.

God bless us all.

Dedication

This book is dedicated to:

My mother-in-law, Mary.
She loved peonies and porterhouses;
kaloopin', cooking, and Christmas.
She treated me like a daughter;
and I was glad to call her Mom.

And;
to her son, my beloved husband, Les.
May the house of Elrond long endure.

The Dragon Reborn

KATHLEEN H. NELSON

Prologue

*T*wo men sat across from each other with a small, green-tinged fire between them. The smaller of the two was slight of shoulder and clean-shaved, a washed-out Northerner who looked even paler in the loose white travel robes of a Guzzini desert nomad. He had an elaborate serpentine blade in one hand, and an obsidian spur in the other. His peculiar, green-ice eyes were glassy. The rims of his nostrils were white. He was muttering under his breath, and had been for what seemed like hours now. His voice echoed through the underground chamber like an ongoing rumor of ill.

Meanwhile, General Ferman Veeder bided his time—not patiently, for that was not his nature, but with a Granger's unswerving discipline. And he had been a devotee of mighty Grange since the age of ten, from the day his da had dressed him in his first battle kilt and taken him to the temple at Sa'Ba'Nu. His mother had cried that day, begged and pleaded with her husband to consecrate her boy to a more civilized cult, but being the true son of the South that he was, his da cuffed her to silence, then did as he thought right and best. Ferman fingered the tattoos that he'd gotten at his consecration: the burning sword of mighty Grange on his left forearm; the warrior-cult's emblematic sunburst of spears on his right. The hair on the back of his neck prickled as he remembered his first taste of hot needles and ink. Some of the novitiates had sobbed or fainted like women from the pain. But not him. He had taken it in locked-jaw silence, and done his da proud. In the years since then, he had acquired other tattoos: two for each rank he rose to within the cult, and one for each victory he gave to Grange, so many now that his men called him The Painted Man behind his back. He made no effort to discourage this. For while he wasn't a subtle thinker, he did possess a natural ability to inspire like-minded men. Men who believed in tradition and glory. Men who weren't afraid of violence and death. They sought him out like moths to a fire. They fought for him to the death. And, over the course of thirty-one years, they helped him eliminate weaker elements within and without the cult, gutless old men who spoke of reform and the need for Grangers to assume a more ceremonial role in southern society. Now Grange's cult was stronger, fiercer than ever, and he was its undisputed leader. A leader with grand, no—*inspired*—designs.

He glanced once again at the man in front of him. Like many northerners, he went by one name: Seth. Veeder had saved him from a bordertown lynch-mob just over a year ago. Normally, Veeder didn't interfere with such goings-on, especially when a northerner was involved. But that night, he happened to be fresh from a romp with a Cosian whore, and felt as feisty as a game-cock. "What're you hanging him for?" he shouted, as he rode by. "He used sorcery to cheat us at cards," some red-faced farmer shouted back. That didn't sound like a hanging offense to Ferman, so on a whim, he spurred his horse back through the crowd, swept the accused onto his saddle like a bride, and then rode off in a hail of curses.

"So," he said, when they were safely out of cross-bolt range, "tell the truth, worm. Were you fleecing those fine gentlemen?"

"Are sheep good for anything else?" the northerner asked, in a tone as dry as the desert wind.

"Probably not," Ferman said, with an appreciative laugh. "So how is it that they caught you?"

"They didn't actually catch me, my lord. They just got tired of losing."

Ferman laughed again. "You should've let the cards fall as they were dealt from time to time."

"I did, my lord. The whole time. I don't need to use sorcery to fleece farmers."

"But you are a sorcerer," Ferman said, trying to stay one step ahead of confusion.

"Of a sort, my lord," the northerner said. "The lore that I study is somewhat—" He cleared his throat: a half-embarrassed, half-amused sound. "—esoteric. That's what brings me to this part of the world. Rumor has it that there are things out here that may—interest me."

"Is that a fact?"

"It is, my lord," he said, and then gestured at the crossroads that they were fast approaching. "If it's all the same to you, this is where I'd like to get off. My road leads east from here."

Veeder obligingly reined his horse to a stop. The mage slid down from the beast's back, landing on both feet with surprising grace, and then lapsed into a respectful bow. "I am Seth, my lord," he said, "and I owe you a life-debt. That may not seem like much to a great warrior like you, but I offer it nonetheless. Should you ever find yourself in need of my services, all you need do is speak my name three times and I will come to you."

Veeder smirked, unable to imagine any situation where an effete northerner might prove useful. "You're right," he said. "It doesn't seem like much."

Then he had come into his inheritance.

That had happened some six months later in the hills of Na'Pu'e, the place where he and his men had ambushed and then slaughtered a rival faction's forces. That night, as he walked the windswept plains of his dreams, a Voice called out to him. It sounded like thunder, trumpets, and battle-drums. It set his blood afire. His dream-self threw his arms open to the streaming sky and roared, "Destiny! Show me thy face!" An instant later, he was standing on a rocky summit. The southlands spanned below like a dusty, desert-gold mantle. *Yours for the taking,* the voice whispered. But that was merely a fact in need of formalizing. His ambitions were much grander, as grand as the fringe of northern green that now crept over the horizon. He embraced the sight with a grin. An ambitious wish indeed. Only one man had ever held north and south in his mighty hands.

And you shall be the second.

A silver-gray corona shivered into being in the thin air in front of him, then began to shape itself into the aspect of a man. The body was all bones and rotten winding cloth, and a golden death-mask covered its face, but it radiated a sense of majesty so powerful, Veeder could not help but recognize the presence.

"Grange," he breathed, awestruck rather than frightened by this visitation. "I am honored beyond imagining."

"In the moments before death took me, a seer foretold the coming of my heir," the apparition said. *"He was to be a warrior without equal. He was to be a true son of the south. He was to save a mage's life, and kill his brother's lecherous wife.*

"Are you that man, Ferman Veeder?"

"I am," he replied—once in a hopeful whisper, and again as a shout as he realized that he did indeed meet all of the specifications. "I am!"

A jag of lightning tore across the colorless dream sky, then burst into a half-dozen rounds of ball-lightning that danced in the air around Grange's ghost. As Veeder gaped at this fey constellation, the fireballs blistered into strange shapes—glyphs he couldn't quite recognize or name.

"These are tokens of warrior-magic and luck," Grange said. *"He who has them in his possession will take back that which has long been lost and reclaim the glory belonging to the overlord of the whole world."*

Veeder's joy flared as bright as any ball of steeple-fire. He had always known that he was destined for greatness—known it, believed it, pursued it at every bloody turn. But it seemed that not even he had appreciated the extent of his potential. A seer had forecast his existence. Now the ghost of Grange was claiming him as his heir. This was heady, heady stuff.

"I will bear your tokens, mighty Grange," he said, with a fierceness born of pride. "And I will honor the gift with deeds worthy of the giver."

"*Perhaps*," Grange said, in a tone far drier than bone. "*But first you will have to recover them. They have fallen prey to a gaggle of dragons.*"

"I'll recover them," Veeder said, with the off-hand confidence of one of destiny's favorites. "You need only to tell me what they look like."

"*That can be arranged*," the apparition said, and then gestured sharply at Veeder. In response, the fireballs abruptly stopped dancing and collided with his chest. Pain sent his eyes rolling back in their sockets. The reek of seared flesh and open graves rose from him like steam. He clenched his teeth, strangling the cry that swelled up in his throat. He knotted his fists at his sides. As he burned, Grange instructed him.

"*Individually, these tokens will grant you some small power. Together, they will grant you almost anything you desire. One or all, however, you must not try to tap into their potentials firsthand. That is work for a mage.*"

Veeder unclenched his teeth long enough to mouth a word. "Who?"

The apparition shrugged. "*I leave that to you.*"

The pain in his chest subsided, becoming a patchwork of raw aches. Despite his resolve not to, he looked down at himself. Six spanking-new brands glared back at him. The wounds were a meaty color in the center, and crisped like roasted duck skin around the edges. He could tell with one glance that they were going to take a long time to heal. He did not begrudge his maiming, though. These brands were badges of honor, the very highest signs of favor. He was Grange's heir, the One Foreseen.

And he was ready to follow in his adoptive father's footsteps.

Seth, Seth, Seth!

"General!"

The whisper startled Veeder out of his recollections. He blinked, kick-starting his thoughts, then absently rubbed his knuckles over his ever-itchy brands. Seth was looking at or perhaps through him now. His expression remained vacant, almost pained.

"We are ready to proceed."

Veeder grinned. A half-day after he had invoked his name, Seth had turned up at the Granger staging camp. And although his men did not like it, the arrangement between him and the necromage was working out surprisingly well. Seth asked for little enough—a few men to command, a cave for his ceremonies, the title of special advisor. And while it was the life-debt that had drawn Seth here, it was Grange's tokens that had inspired him to stay. As soon as he heard about them, he was hooked. He wanted to study them and learn how they worked. He wanted to see what they could do. Veeder approved of the mage's fascination. It was as good as loyalty—leastwise for a while. It also guaranteed results.

"Take a deep, purifying breath."

But like his men, Veeder held little in the way of affection for Seth. The fact that he was a beardless weakling from the decadent north was one count against him. His scholarly arrogance was another. Then there were his bizarre personal habits. He bathed more often than any decent man ought to, wore a woman's beaded bracelet on his wrist, and included an ironwood coffin among his personal effects. Veeder glanced around the cavern, looking for that body-box, and found it in an out-of-the-way corner, half-hidden beneath a hodgepodge collection of knives, phials, and wilting flowers. Veeder shook his head, thinking, *Degenerate.* But he said nothing, because degenerate or not, he needed a mage.

"Take the knife."

Veeder grasped the dagger's hilt, then snuck a peek at his would-be sacrifice: a fat old farmer whom Veeder's men had snatched during a recent foray across the border. He lay bound and gagged on a crude stone altar. Every time he tried to tear, break, or wriggle free of his bonds, his belly shook like a pan full of pudding. Veeder found that hilarious.

"Take the old man's life," Seth said, in a far-removed voice. "Then return to this fire and sit very still. Do not be afraid of anything you might see."

The altar had been erected on the edge of a great crevasse in the cavern's floor. As Veeder approached it, the farmer began to squirm in earnest. Veeder ran a fingertip along the dagger's edge, then smiled and said, "You Northerners are all the same." The farmer shook his head, an impassioned 'No!' filled with spaniel-eyed grandchildren and doddering friends. Veeder smiled again, then slashed the fellow's throat.

Blood spurted everywhere: over the altar, onto Veeder, into the abyss. He wiped the splatter from his beard with a tattooed forearm, then stepped back to admire his work only to do an immediate double-take. For something was rising out of the chasm now. It looked like smoke. It moved like mist. But mist did not shape itself into distraught faces. And smoke did not cry out in distant, long-dead voices.

"Help me," one phantasm begged, as it drifted past Veeder. *"I do not belong to this world anymore."*

"Have mercy," other apparitions whispered. *"Send us back."*

Veeder whooped aloud, a shout of glee rather than fright. For the doubts that he had harbored about the dew-claw were gone now. It had to be one of Grange's tokens. *Had to.* No mortal had the power to raid the Dreamer's Keep like this, especially not a journeyman necromage like Seth.

But what in Grange's name was he supposed to do with an army of ghosts?

Phantoms continued to issue forth from the chasm. Some disappeared from the chamber immediately. Others formed a swirling, beard-high mass of frigid gloom. One drifted to a stop in front of Veeder and jabbed a boney finger at one of his brands with a despairing shriek. Its touch raised goosepimples on his arms and chest. Its charnel breath turned his stomach.

"Go and slay the red drake who is wreaking havoc with my gold mine," he bade the fright. "Bring me the news of its death afterward."

The apparition scorned him with a death's-head look, then drifted away.

"That's not how it works, General," Seth said. His voice was as washed-out as the rest of him now, but Veeder heard a hint of annoyance in it just the same. "Didn't I tell you to return to the fire and stay still after you performed the sacrifice?"

Veeder shrugged. "What of it?"

Seth responded with a shrug of his own. "You distracted me. I lost concentration. Now the door to the Dreamer's Keep is closed."

Only then did Veeder realize that his ghost army was gone, vanished down to the last vapour. He closed the gap between him and his mage in four angry steps and seized him by the arm.

"So open it again," he said. "You have the token. Use it."

"I cannot," Seth replied. "I have no strength left." Veeder had only to look at him to know that this was true. His normally pale face was a ravaged shade of gray now. His shoulders sagged like an old man's. "And even if it were otherwise," he went on, "I need a sacrifice to find the path to Death's Door. The living are not permitted to know the way."

Veeder let out a frustrated rumble. "Blast you and your excuses, Seth. And what good is an army of the dead anyway, if I can't control it?"

"You may not be able to control it now," Seth said, radiating fatigue and perhaps indifference, "but that will no doubt change as I learn more about the token. Meanwhile, if it pleases you, I can compel those spirits who crossed back into this world today to go north and haunt your enemies and their families."

"Will that kill them?"

"Not directly," Seth said. "But it *will* rob them of sleep, set them on edge, and drive the weakest of them to madness. The resulting chaos will cast the north's defenses into disarray."

Veeder stroked the matted tangles of his beard as he considered the possibilities. As a Granger, he was used to facing his enemies head-on: sword-to-sword, knife-to-knife, even hand-to-hand sometimes. But he *liked* the idea of using ghosts as agitators. They'd need no supplies, no pay, and no supervision. There would be zero attrition among them. And, if they did half of what Seth claimed they would, the north would crumble like a dry cheese when he finally launched his campaign.

"Yes, compel them," he said, and then slapped Seth on the back—a friendly clap that was bit harder than it might've been if the mage hadn't been so easily distracted. As Seth went stiff-shouldered from the blow, he went on to say, "Are we done here? I wish to lead my men in their prayers to Grange tonight."

"Yes, General," he replied, through gritted teeth. "We're done."

"What are you going to do with this?" Veeder asked, nudging the farmer's corpse in passing.

"I'll have Kel bury it."

"I'll save him the trouble," Veeder said, and then booted the body into the chasm. One second, then another passed without a sound. He flashed Seth a savage grin. "Long drop, that. I'd watch my step at night if I were you."

"I will," Seth assured him, with the barest suggestion of a smile. "Thank you for your concern." But what he wanted to say was, *Idiot.* Now his stronghold was going to reek of carrion. Mother of pearl, how he *hated* that smell.

Ah, the things he endured for little Ylana.

He watched through narrowed eyes as the general lumbered toward the chamber's only exit. From the rear, he looked like some well-fed circus bear in a warrior's kilt and sandals. A visitor to the southlands might be tempted to dismiss the man as a buffoon or bully, but that would be a huge mistake. For under his leadership, the Grangers had gone from an obscure warrior-cult to the country's dominant faction. The warrior class—those so-called true sons of the south—had been quick to embrace his brutal philosophies. The rest of society acquiesced to his will simply because it was too weak or too fragmented to do anything else. Securing a land thick with warlords required a fair measure of brains—not the kind Seth appreciated perhaps, but a kind that made General Ferman Veeder very, very dangerous nonetheless. Indeed, if Seth hadn't been desperate, he would never have struck up such a perilous association. But Veeder commanded more men than Seth could ever hope to rally or hire to his cause. Plus, the lord of the Grangers was ambitious.

The combination was too good to pass up.

Seth, Seth, Seth!

If he weren't tired all the way down to his marrow, Seth might've laughed at how gullible the general was when it came to sorcery. Like most men born without magical ability, he assumed too much and not enough, usually at the same time. So it never occurred to him to wonder if that first encounter with Seth had been anything other than chance when in fact Seth had orchestrated the entire event: the lynch-mob, Veeder's intervention, and later, the visit from Grange's ghost.

"The brands were a nice touch."

The voice was soft and fell—a whisper in the dark, murmurings from the abyss. He had first encountered it three years before, in the foothills of the Great Northern Range. He had gone there on the shirt-tails of a rumor, searching for lore that would bring little Ylana back. Poor, dear sister. He should never have left her alone.

"Did you see her?" he asked.

"No. Perhaps next time."

Disappointment struck like a scorpion's sting. Its poison spread through him in a heartbeat, igniting resentment. He did not like this newfound mentor of his. Although he had never seen it, he knew it to be a dark, unsavory thing—a nonborn possibly. *I know many secret things,* it had whispered, from the deepest, darkest shadows. *I can make you strong.* And therein lay the hook. For while Seth did everything he could to appear otherwise, he was not a powerful mage. He could do little things when he had to: raise a ward, charm a crowd, protect his back. But while the potential was there, it was so very hard to unlock. And he had to unlock it if he wanted Ylana back.

"Perhaps there will be no next time." he said, and while he'd said so only in the hope of throwing a scare into the creature, his heart leapt at the possibility nevertheless. Seth wondered what that sensation represented—guilt or pleasure. They felt the same these days. "Perhaps I've gone as far as I can with you."

"I thought you wanted to find your sister."

Guilt then. Heaps of it. Mountains. And his darkling guide knew exactly which stone to dislodge to bring the whole lot avalanching down around his soul. Little Ylana, lost. And it was all his fault.

"Did you not promise your father that you would take care of her?"

He clenched every muscle in his body—a desperate attempt to stop himself from following the voice into the deepest recesses of his mind, a place where he alone had eyes and ears. To no avail. He saw himself, a grimy teenager with a jug ears and a snotty nose standing in front of a bed so rank it made his eyes water. He saw his parents tangled in a tattered doona, slowly but surely drowning in their own infected juices. Their impending deaths filled him with a sense of panic and power.

"Did you not swear it on your life?"

His father seized his hand and held it in a dead-man's grip. *"The elders will burn this place to the ground when we die to keep the disease from spreading,"* he had said. *"If they catch you and Ylana, they will burn you, too. That must not happen, boy. Do you hear? You must get your sister out of here—now. And from this moment on, you must take care of her. Promise me, boy. Swear it on your life!"*

I swear it, father. I swear!

An instant after he said the words, his father went limp. An instant after that, a bloom of fire whooshed to life in the hut's thatched roof. He heard Ylana scream in the next room. The sound impinged on his promise, which triggered his death-primed potential. Without knowing how he did it or why, he set the whole village afire—his first act of death-magic. The next thing he knew, he was running through the woods with Ylana in his arms. His thoughts skipped ahead—past their flight into the foothills, past the weeks of hunger and tears and complaints. All he could see now was an alpine meadow drenched with blood. But he had only left her there for a few minutes, an hour at most—only as long as it took to catch a brace of rabbits. It was so much easier to hunt when she wasn't around to scare the game away with her childish ways.

"Will you now forswear yourself?"

Ah, Ylana! He should have known! Should have guessed. Should have—been there.

"Will you?"

"Noo-o!" The howl erupted from the very root of his bowels, and left his throat raw in passing. "No, damn you." He could not give up now, not when he was so close. He would endure what had to be endured. For Ylana. Because he had promised. "Are you sure you can find her?"

"It is a difficult task at present, for I am much diminished," the voice said, an admission both grudging and frank. *"But I will grow stronger with every token. And with strength comes ease. I will find your sister eventually."*

He snorted, a bitter sound. "You string me along just as I string Veeder."

"Not so. Your arrangement with Veeder benefits only you. Our arrangement benefits us both."

"Not so," he echoed. "As long as Ferman Veeder serves my purposes, I will help him attain his ambitions." He paused for a long moment, then heaved a sigh as heavy as a promise and added, "I just wish there were some other way."

A sound like rat-claws on a stone floor skittered through the chamber: darkling laughter. His loathing for the ghoul returned full-force. It was laughing at him, no doubt. And why not? He had murdered the living and disturbed the dead with its help today—this, without flinching. This, of his own free will. And they both knew that he would do so again and again and again until he found Ylana. His mentor was probably wondering which of them was more the soulless fright. He could not bear the thought. Not tonight. Not in this company. So despite his fatigue, a weariness so pervasive as to have its own mealy copper taste, he got up and started hobbling toward the entryway. On his way out, he muttered, "I hate this. All of it."

"One does what one must," the voice replied.

Chapter 1

*T*he wagon train rolled through the meadow in single file, leaving a fragrant swath of crushed summer grasses in its wake. Despite the creaking of wooden wheels and the squeaking of leather harnesses and the muffled thud of hooves, it was a remarkably quiet procession. Most outsiders mistook this economy of sound for stealth, and stoked their prejudices with it. But to the people of the Wandering Tribe, it was merely a way of life.

One of the wagons ran over a meadow-dog mound and then lurched as the tunnel collapsed. As fleeting as it was, the disturbance jostled Katya out of an uneasy doze.

"What is it, Raffi?" she asked, as she started awake.

"Nothing, Little Mother," her driver replied, in that sweet, patient tone that some men take with old women and dogs. "We hit a bump in the road, is all." He reached into the hamper that occupied the bench-space between them and pulled out a storage-gourd. "Would you like some water?"

"Thank you," she said, as she took the gourd. "The air is very dry today."

She drank deeply, then wet a corner of her sleeve and dabbed at her face. That cooled her down, but did little to refresh her. She was still so very tired. And MerryVale was still so very far away—another six days to the south and east. Her bones would hold every mile against her. Her ankles would swell and her backside would go numb. But as hard as the trip promised to be, she never considered not making it. The Wandering Tribe came together only once a year, and that was at MerryVale at midsummer's eve. And oh, what a eventful gathering it was. The dead would be mourned, lovers would be wed, new children would be introduced to the tribe. There would be food, gossip, and drink; music, dance, and games of chance; contests of might and wit and courage. She, The Wandering Queen, would preside over all of these happenings, and yet—

And yet the prospect did not gladden her heart as much as it should.

That lack of enthusiasm had nothing to do with being old and tired, although one condition seemed to make the other two worse. She had been as excited as a girl on her way to meet her betrothed up until two days ago. Then, in a summery little clearing much like this one, their caravan had happened upon the darkest of portents. The memory of it was so terrible, her mind's eye refused to focus on anything beyond the golden blood and flies. And the threat of tears stung her eyes every time she recalled even that. The rest of her family had been traumatized, too. The youngest ones suffered from night frights now. Their elders had a stunned, hollow-eyed look about them. Katya could almost hear them thinking: *Who would do such a thing? For what possible reason?* As if anyone capable of committing such an atrocity would need something so civilized as a reason. A better question was: What did such an omen mean? And this morning, at last, she finally felt strong enough to scry out an answer.

She drew her pack of fortune cards from a pocket in her skirts and shuffled it until her fingers went numb. Then, concentrating on that memory—*golden blood and flies*—she flipped over the first card and set it down on her lap.

The glyph was of a graveyard at night, its headstones gleaming pale white beneath a full, yellow moon. Katya was not surprised that the Cemetery Card had turned up, for it represented death, and death was certainly an element of this mystery. No, what surprised the Queen of the Wandering Tribe was that the card had turned up reversed. In all of her years as a scryer, she had never seen it that way. What could it signify—a death averted? A close call maybe? She dismissed the possibility with a shake of her head. A close call was good luck. A reversed Cemetery Card was not.

Stuck for an interpretation, she flipped the next card. Sometimes, meaning only came in threes.

The card bore the likeness of a swirling, black funnel-cloud on its face. This was Chaos, straight up, a symbol for upheaval. Yet by itself, it was vague as a halfwit's smile. She set it down alongside the first card, then covered both with a third: the Warrior-King, reversed.

"Worse and worse," she muttered, for a reversed warrior-king usually meant war. And wars were particularly hard on her people. She knew. She bore the scars.

"Are you unwell, Little Mother?" Raffi was quick to ask. "Shall I stop?"

"No, thank you," she replied. "I'm as well as a woman of my years can be. But like most old things, I'm prone to odd sounds at odd moments. Be a dear and pay them no heed."

"As you will, Little Mother," he said, even though they both knew that they would be having this conversation all over again the next time she oohed or ahhed or sneezed.

He turned his attention back to the business of driving the wagon. She turned hers back to the scrying. In the presence of a warrior-king reversed, the other two cards made sudden sense. War bred chaos and near-mortal wounds. War was bad luck and upheaval. By everything that was sacred and sweet! Who was this would-be landwaster? And what need had he for gypsy blood?

Hoping for clues if not outright answers to these questions, she started a new triad. The first card she turned up depicted an upraised hand with an open eye staring forth from the stylized lines of its palm. A groan welled within her like cabbage gas. The Sorcerer's Hand? That meant there was some magical element to this mystery. That in and of itself did not daunt her, for unlike most outsiders, the clans of the wandering tribe held no blind prejudices against arcania. No, what vexed her was the hand's proximity to the reversed warrior-king. That suggested corruption, or perhaps collusion. Neither possibility boded well for gypsies. She flipped the next card with a wish for clarification in her heart. But fortune chose to disappoint her.

"I should've known *you* were involved, Old Fool," she grumbled, as she eyed the Dancing Beggar's glyph. The picture portrayed a grinning, rag-tag old man with a lumpy sack slung across his back. Blind Luck, some called him. Others knew him as Random, or The Dreamer's Consort. Whatever name you assigned him, though, he had the power to reshape the outcome of events that would have been predictable otherwise. Outsiders associated him with gypsies, but while Katya's people welcomed his patronage, they were as often his victims as his beneficiaries. She could not count on him to take their side.

"Babchi! Look!"

The childish cry scuttled Katya's train of thought. She glanced up from the cards to see a slight, black-haired forest sylph with a exultant, gap-toothed smile waving at her from the lead wagon. This was her granddaughter, Mim—her protegee and her favorite, although she would never admit the latter aloud. But where she might have scowled at someone else for interrupting her during a reading, she now responded with an indulgent smile.

"What is it, little one?" she wondered, deftly planting the thought in Mim's mind.

"See what Maman gave me?" the child replied aloud.

She thrust an outstretched fist in her grandmother's direction. Katya squinted, trying to squeeze more sight into her once-sharp eyes, but all she discerned was a faint glimmer of gold and so gave her head a small, sorry shake.

"They're earrings," Mim explained. "For the piercing ceremony. Maman says I am old enough this year."

Katya's smile took a wistful half-turn. She could not remember the last time she had been just 'old enough' for something. These days, she was invariably 'too old'. But she did not share that thought with Mim. Most of life's lessons had to be experienced to be understood. Instead, she replied, *"That's nice, little one. But now you must excuse me so I can return to my scrying."*

"As you wish, Babchi."

Katya took another drink from the gourd, then turned the next card. At the sight of it, the water that she had just swallowed acquired a greasy feel. The Dragon Rampant represented strength and consistency. To gypsies, it was also a symbol of good luck. But how was she supposed to interpret a dragon reversed? Reversals usually portended some sort of corruption or evil. But the skyfolk esteemed truth above all else; they could not be corrupted. And to proclaim a dragon evil was to prove yourself a fool. Evil was a human vice. Evil preyed on men.

As she stared at the second triad, straining for insights that were slow to come, her frustration spiraled. She needed answers, not half-cooked guesses. She needed to know what sort of trouble was afoot before it descended upon her people. In bygone days, she might've taken a horse and gone questing for those answers without so much as a by your leave to her sons. These days, however, that option was beyond her. A horse's back, no matter how well-padded, was more than a match for a crone's brittle bones. And even if it were otherwise, her sons would hold her back. They'd say she was too important to her people, too precious. Which were just alternative ways of saying 'too old'. She glanced at Mim, who was still perched atop of the lead wagon. In the innermost compartment of her heart, a place where she alone had ears, she indulged a moment of mostly benign envy and regret: *oh, to be that strong and healthy again. Oh, to be that young.*

She snorted then, scorning herself for mooncalfing after the impossible. Old or not, she was still The Wandering Queen; and old or not, the welfare of the tribe was in her hands. She needed answers. She needed them now. And since *she* could not go a-questing for them, she must perforce send someone in her stead.

But who?

She could not ask her eldest son, Santana, for he was still nursing the arm that he had snapped in a fall from a green-broke horse. And she would not ask her younger son, Yorgi, for he was not good with outsiders. Her proxy must be nimble of mind *and* body, capable of surviving regardless of the circumstances. He must also be blessed with good luck, because it was clear by the cards that many circumstances were aligned against him already.

A sign, she thought, fingering the deck again. *Give me a sign.*

The tail-end of that wish was shattered by shrill double whistle—Santana's signal to go-to-ground. Out of life-long habit, she glanced skyward for low-flying shadows. As she did so, Raffi whisked her down from her seat as if she were a child and deposited her beneath the wagon.

"What goes on?" she asked.

"Luke returns from the hunt," Raffi replied in fits and starts, as he and one of her many nephews drew a roll of sturdy, camouflaged netting over her wagon and the horses. "He is *running.*"

"Why?"

"I do not know," Raffi said. "It does not look like he is being chased."

Katya hissed. What was the young fool thinking? These hills were famous as a hunting-grounds for dragons. And running one's horse out in the open like that was like ringing a dinner bell. If a dragon *did* show up in the skies overhead, it would not see the caravan thanks to the netting that was now in place. But Luke could lead it right to them, and then the wagons would be as picnic baskets. Fool, she thought again. He had been taught much better.

The drumming of a horse's hooves thundered its way into her hearing. Moments later, she heard a lathered wheeze as well. He must've run the animal for miles without a break, she thought, and added that to his list of crimes. Punishments came to mind: hard labor, a shaming; maybe some time in exile to make him appreciate how much he had put to risk. But before she could decide on the proper course, an anguished shout distracted her.

"Uncle Santana, come quick! I've found another one."

Katya's anger turned to ash in her mouth. At the same time, her stomach knotted, becoming a tangle of grief and dread. She had no doubt as to what it was that her nephew had discovered the grief in his voice was so palpable, and so distinctive, even little Mim would grasp its meaning. She crawled out from her hiding place and then hobbled toward Luke with a thousand apologies in her mouth. He was no fool, simply a soul in shock.

Golden blood and flies.

For what he had found could only be another murdered dragon.

Chapter 2

A mosquito-like buzzing invaded Jamus' wine-soaked dreams. He batted at the air around his ears in his sleep, and then drew a pillow over his head. The buzz became a high-pitched moan that drove him onto the bleary-eyed shores of wakefulness. He slung the pillow onto the floor, then pushed himself up on his elbows. The room was dark. His eyes were slow to focus. For one groggy, netherworld moment, he did not know where he was. Then the moon slipped out from behind a cloud and filled the chamber with soft, white light and shadows. An ironwood settee took shape by the balcony. A gilt-framed mirror loomed large on the far wall. He recognized the decor. This was his home. His bedroom. He was pleasantly surprised. He vaguely recalled starting the night elsewhere.

A whimper floated up from the floor—a pained, abandoned-puppy sound. He rolled in that direction, wincing as his tenderized brains sloshed around in his skull, then glanced over the edge of the bed. There, on the marble tiles, tangled in a bedsheet like a pretty bit of flotsam, he found a woman. Amaranda, her name was. Or something like that. Once upon a time, he had made an effort to remember such details. Nowadays, he rarely bothered. If a woman had a problem with that, well—no one was forcing or even asking her to stay.

A dream-scowl ridged Amaranda's moonlit profile. She looked very young at that moment—as young as she probably was. As Jamus reached down to stroke her midnight hair, she loosed another whimper. The sound grated on his nerves. Instead of petting her as he'd intended, he gave her a poke in the ribs.

"Wake up, sweetling," he said. "You're having a bad dream."

With a petulant whine, she shifted away from him. Now all he could see was her pale white back and buttocks. Desire sparked within him, unthinking reflex. He caressed the round of her hip and whispered, "Ama! Climb back into bed, my sweet."

"Papa, please," she murmured, begging from her dreams. "Lemme be."

Papa? The implications shocked, dismayed, and offended him—an emotional cascade that stirred up decency's dregs even as it smothered his desire. He stroked her back, an apology of sorts. Then, because it was a humid night, and he was wide-awake, he abandoned the bed for the balcony. On the way, he stopped for a short summer robe and a cup of wine. Both were second-rate, a step down from what he had been used to, but he didn't care. Mediocrity suited him these days.

He perched himself on the balcony's railing and stared out at Compara's western reaches. Despite the lateness of the hour, a few spangles of home-fire still flickered in the darkness. One light would be the baker, Jamus supposed, getting his bread dough ready for the oven. Another one would be a scholar, lost in the pages of some dusty old book. And that one lonely light in the far, far distance? That was a man waiting for his beloved to come home. Jamus could imagine him all too well. Some nights, the poor bastard got drunk to dull the ache or pass the time. Other nights, he dallied with strangers, hoping to forget or perhaps remember what it was that he was missing. And some nights, he simply paced, dusk until dawn, driven as a windblown sea. His beloved had been dead for five years now. Even so, he waited for her. He could not stop himself.

As he brooded, a woman's high-pitched shriek shattered the silence. It was a hair-raising sound, all terror and helplessness. "Go away," she screamed. "Someone—please! Help me!"

Candles leapt to life in once-dark windows. Men in rumpled bedclothes appeared in the cobblestone streets below Jamus' balcony. Once upon a former lifetime, he would have been quick to join them in their hunt for the woman's attackers. But tonight, and for many, many evenings now, he was content to let the night-watch handle the matter. After all, that's what they were paid to do.

He guzzled the rest of his wine, then tottered inside for a refill. As he groped for the pitcher, the room took a sudden chill. He looked toward the balcony, wondering if he ought to close the doors. The curtains were still. There was no breeze. And yet the chill seemed to be getting worse. He set down his cup, thinking that maybe he had had enough for the night. A heartbeat later, a pale figure came drifting out of the bedroom and toward him. The beginnings of a smile took hold of his mouth, for he assumed that this was Amaranda, come to wheedle him back into bed. Then, as the figure drew closer, the extent of his mistake became clear. The face he was looking at was heart-shaped, not angular like Amaranda's. And while his young lover possessed many talents, as far as he knew, hovering in mid-air was not one of them.

"Jamus," the apparition whispered, looking right at him.

The hair on his nape and arms stood straight up. At the same time, a strangled croak escaped him. "Liselle."

She stared at him for a long moment. Her spectral face was horribly drawn, as if she were in great pain or sorrow. Her eyes were reproachful hollows. Nevertheless, he wanted to touch her—just once, even if she wasn't real, because it had been so long and he missed her so much and nothing could fill the void that she'd left behind. He croaked her name again, in a voice thick with tears, then extended an arm toward her. As he did so, she drifted just beyond his reach. Although she said nothing, and her expression did not waver, he became suddenly aware that he smelled of cheap wine and another woman.

As a living woman, she had often accused him of being a philanderer.

"Have you returned to torture me, my dear?" he asked, trying to hide his grief and embarrassment behind a bantering tone. "Or are you just checking up on me?"

"I was taken from The Dreamer's side," she replied, all breathless despair. "Now I am compelled to seek out those whom I loved in life." Her image flickered like the stub of a fatty candle, then began to dissipate. Her extremities disappeared first, then her torso from the bottom up. The next thing Jamus knew, he was looking at a disembodied head.

"Don't go," he whispered.

"Find Lathwi," the head said. Then, like a puff of smoke in a wind, it was gone.

For one dazed moment thereafter, all Jamus could do was gape into empty space. Had he really seen what he thought he'd just seen? Had his beloved's ghost just paid him a visit? He pinched himself hard on the underside of his chin—once to make sure he was not dreaming, and then again because he suddenly ached to hurt something.

Find Lathwi?

No bloody way! He would rather be drawn and quartered over a lava bed. He would rather eat glass or someone's sword.

Lathwi was the reason that his heart's desire was dead.

A memory flared unbidden: himself standing next to a disheveled, wild-eyed Liselle, pleading that she stay in Compara where he could protect her—this while the rotting fish stink of dead demon-flesh fouled the air all around them.

"Jamus!" the sorceress had cried. "Weren't you listening to me? I can't stay. My wards are in a shambles and there are demons afoot. Moreover, my enemy may very well be in league with Shadow. Perhaps going off with Lathwi is a goose chase as you say, but right now, it's our only hope. If I don't find out what's going on, you may soon see a day when no one is safe. And that day, my dear, could last forever."

The image in his memory faded—all but Liselle's precious heart-shaped face. Her left eye was a gaping knife wound now. The rest of her was cold, dirty, and blue. "Galza had possessed her, body and mind," Lathwi said, as she laid the feather-light corpse in his unready arms. "But by the power of her Name, she consented to the knife before I threw it."

Jamus howled, then and now, and then pulled hanks of his tangled hair in an effort to drive the memory away. His mind became a cannonade of invectives: bitch, barbarian, *Lathwi*.

"Damn you!" he raged. "You were supposed to protect her."

He swung his fist into the wine pitcher as if it were Lathwi's head. The jug hit the floor with a terra cotta crash. An instant later, dark red wine began to stream across the tiles. That wasn't enough for him, though—not by a wide margin. He had the bitter bit of grief between his teeth now, and he was running wild. He tore the curtains down with a savage jerk, then threw a whole set of wine cups against the wall, one after the other. As he did so, he continued to rant.

"Faithless bitch! Everything has to be your way, doesn't it?"

"Jamie?"

He spun toward the voice to see a pale figure swathed in moonlight. "And you!" he snarled, in the moment before he recognized Amaranda. "You had more faith in her than in me. You still do."

"Jamie, wake up," Amaranda urged. "You're having a bad dream."

He blinked slow and hard to squeeze the sheen of tears from his eyes, then forced himself to focus on the girl. She looked curious and concerned, but a little amused, too—as if she meant to tease him about this incident later, as if she could not see that there was no 'later' for them. She was no Liselle, he thought, as he looked her up and down. But she was here, alive and full of trust, and that's what he wanted right now. So he opened his arms if not his heart to fair Amaranda. And when, on their way back to his bed, she asked, "So who's this Lathwi you were shouting at in your dreams?", he loosed a phony laugh and lied. "No one special, my sweet, just someone I once knew. She's dead now."

Amaranda gasped, then covered her mouth to hide her dismay. "Oh, Jamie! I'm so sorry."

"Don't be," Jamus told her. "She was a blackguard and a thief."

And there was no way he was going to go looking for her. No matter who asked.

೮೦೦೪

"Find Lathwi."

He took a swing at the ghost—a drunken blow from a nearly sober man, a man who could not bear to be mocked from beyond the grave. The specter scattered like fog, leaving wisps of disappointment in its wake. Jamus sagged to his knees, then covered his face with his hands. Mistake. For as soon as he closed his eyes, he found himself back in Liselle's cottage. Although The Rogue had burned it down over five years before during his war against Liselle, Jamus still remembered everything about it:

the stone-hearth that was always lit; the spicy, not entirely wholesome pantry smells; the rocking chair in which she enthroned herself when she was worried. In this memory, he was holding her in his arms and kissing her as a woman should be kissed—for the first and only time. He could still taste her excitement, and her fear. He should've taken her into his custody that night. He would've kept her safe. But had he? No! Against his better judgment, he had let her run away with *Lathwi* instead.

And the dragon-bitch had eventually killed her.

He swiped blindly at the air as if he had the power to strike his former friend from afar. If there was any justice in the world, any at all, Liselle would be making *her* suffer for what she'd done. Instead, she was torturing him—because he loved her. And he'd been told that love was a good thing.

A knock at the door startled him out of his bitter musings. He hurried back to his desk, then dragged a sleeve across his tear-streaked face. In a previous lifetime, he would have combed his hair and straightened out his shirt-front, too, but these days, he preferred the rumpled look.

"Enter," he said.

The door swung open, admitting a young man dressed in the midnight blue regalia of Compara's night watch. He struck Jamus a snappy salute, then came to rigid attention in front of Jamus' desk.

"Well met, Randall," Jamus said, "and please, stand at ease."

Randall opened his stance and tucked his arms behind his back: a slick conversion to parade rest. Jamus had big plans for this tough, loyal man. He'd be commander of the night watch within four years time, and a decent lieutenant governor within seven. Jamus liked the idea of grooming his replacement. He also liked the idea of someone else doing his leg-work for him in the meantime.

"What brings you here tonight, my friend?" he asked.

"You asked me to investigate the recent outbreaks of unrest in the city," Randall said.

"Yes, yes, that's right," Jamus said, and then strolled over to the decanter of wine that his secretary refilled every morning. "Would you care for a drink?" By this hour, the decanter was very nearly empty, but he thought it polite to ask just the same. "Reporting can be thirsty work."

"No thanks, my lord," Randall replied. "I'm on duty tonight. But you might want to pour yourself one."

Jamus glanced sharply over his shoulder at the man. "Why do you say that?"

All at once, Randall looked supremely uncomfortable. "Because I don't think you're going to like what you hear, my lord."

"I see." Jamus dumped what was left in the decanter into a cup, then took a sip to fortify his nerves. For it wasn't like Randall to make such statements. And it wasn't like this was the first bit of bad news that he'd ever borne to this room. He'd said nothing to Jamus ahead of time about the Riverbank Strangler or last year's orphanage fire, two cases where a drink might've helped the news go down. "Well then." He sat down at his desk, stiffly, like a marionette, then made eye contact with Randall. "Let's have it. What have you found?"

Randall swallowed hard, then said, "Ghosts, my lord. A whole plague of them."

For one stunned moment, all Jamus could do was stare at the man and wonder. Was he mocking him? If so, why? Then it hit him. Liselle was part of that plague. He had assumed that his visitations were unique, isolated incidents; incorporeal punishment from the only woman he had ever loved. To learn that he was only one of many sufferers was—disconcerting.

"Why is this the first I'm hearing of this?" he asked.

"We didn't know what was going on at first," Randall said. "And afterward, we didn't grasp the magnitude of the problem. And—" He averted his eyes as if to hide his chagrin. "No one wanted to look the fool by blaming the city's woes on spooks."

Jamus went to take a drink from his goblet only to find that it was already empty. *Drat.* The decanter was empty, too. Why did these things always crop up at the end of the day? A plague of ghosts. Perversely, he felt betrayed, stripped of his special status; *the haunted one.* And it had fit so well.

"I don't suppose there's a quick and easy way to contain this problem," he said.

"I've got men combing the city for a mage," Randall said, "but they've been rarer than hen's teeth in these parts ever since some rogue sorcerer killed a bunch of them off a few years back. Word is, they think the city's cursed."

"They'll get no argument here," Jamus muttered, and then lapsed into a moment's thought. *To do. To do. What to do?* "Extend your men's search into the countryside," he said. "Have them canvass the entire province if necessary." *Find Lathwi.* "And until things return to normal, we're going to need a citywide curfew—absolutely no one on the streets after ten bells. I'm declaring a ban on weapons in public places, too."

"A significant portion of the population isn't going to like having its tavern-time curtailed," Randall said.

"Let them drink at home." Like he did. He glanced at his goblet again. To his dismay, it was still empty. Where did that damn secretary of his stash the wine? "Any other suggestions?"

"None at the moment, my lord."

"Then I won't keep you from your watch any longer. Good night, Randall. And good work."

Randall snapped him a salute, then departed. Jamus would've liked to have gone home then, if for no other reason than the change of scenery. But putting a curfew and a weapons ban into immediate effect meant that the paperwork couldn't wait, so he rolled up his sleeves, pushed back his hair, and went to look for more wine.

℘ ℭ

Liselle hovered above the tiles, cold and unblinking, a hollow-eyed fright. Jamus sobbed at her would-be feet like a man freshly broken.

"Please, Liselle," he said, "I can't bear this anymore. Go away before you drive me insane."

"Find Lathwi," she said, and then melted back into the sauna-room's fog like a bad memory.

For a long time thereafter, he stayed where he was—kneeling like a penitent, or a prisoner on the verge of being executed. His head throbbed. The rest of him ached, as if he had been broadsided by a fully loaded dray. He couldn't continue like this. Could not. Every time she came to him, another piece of him shriveled and died. He couldn't eat, he couldn't sleep. And while he still looked for it at the bottom of every glass, he no longer found sanctuary in drink. His only respite from mind-numbing depression were the fits of rage that struck without warning and then faded away. That had to change. Had to.

So he hauled himself onto his feet and into a robe, then stepped out of the sauna. The attendant gave him a wary once-over as he emerged and then asked, "Are you well, my lord?"

"Fine, just fine," Jamus absently replied.

He left the bath-house in a daze. Although it was a warm summer day, he walked from street to street huddled within his linen jacket. No one got in his way. Indeed, for a market day, there weren't that many people out—not even in the bazaar. And those who were in circulation looked sorely abused. One woman had a black eye. Two others had fresh bruises and split lips. They all snuck nervous glances at the beer cart where a group of scruffy-looking men had gathered. Jamus was on his way to join them for a quick pint when he heard one of them say, "I'm telling you, men—the governor and his flunkies are behind this curse. They called it down on us on so they could take away our freedom to come and go as we please. The next thing you know, they'll be dragging our kids off to labor camps."

Jamus thought about having the man arrested as an agitator, but decided against it. All he was doing, really, was letting off steam. Better that than to bottle it up and up and up until something or someone exploded. The city was *haunted*, for mercy's sake. That qualified as a reason to grumble. Hell, if he thought it would help, he'd grumble, too, this even though he was one of those aforementioned flunkies. So he continued on his way—past the carts and stalls and freelance vendors who hawked their wares from the ground. Everything about the bazaar seemed subdued, even the riot of colors and smells. He was glad to leave it behind for the garrison's reassuring constancy.

His offices were in the governor's retreat, but he did not head there immediately. Instead, he strode across the dusty courtyard and into the enlisted men's barracks. The smells here weren't nearly so subdued. Jamus lifted his sleeve to his nose to escape the stink of unwashed bodies. A moment later, someone behind him sneered at him for doing so.

"How long has it been since you last broke an honest sweat?"

"As a matter of fact, I broke one just last night," he said, and then donned a leer as he turned around. "My companion didn't seem to mind."

His best and oldest friend, Pawl, shook his head in mock exasperation. "Your appetites are going to kill you one of these days, boy-o." Then, turning serious, he gave Jamus a critical once-over. "Maybe sooner than you think. No offense, Jamie, but you look like grilled cat-shit."

The old Jamus would've denied it; danced around it; or made up an excuse. But the new Jamus was running scared, and his only hope for redemption was the truth. "It's Liselle," he said, straining the words past the logjam of pain in his throat. "I can't—take it anymore. She's come back to haunt me."

Pawl's look of concern sagged into one of sympathy. "Aw, man, I'm sorry to hear—"

"Every time she appears, she tells me to find Lathwi."

The name was like a sponge that sucked all of the air out of the room. For one supremely uncomfortable moment, the only thing the two men could do was stare at each other. Then Jamus broke down and began to gabble.

"I can't do it, Pawl. I just can't. You know how I feel about that—" He tried to restrain himself, but the effort proved to be futile. "That dragon-bitch. She killed Liselle. Jammed a knife right into her skull. Dreamer, I can still feel the weight of her body in my arms—" He clenched his eyes shut as if to blot out the memory, then sniffed loudly and dragged a fist under his nose. "But I can't stand much more of this, Pawlie. I feel like a man on the brink of a very steep cliff. Maybe, if I gave Lathwi to her—" He licked his lips as if savoring the possibility. "Maybe she'd leave me alone afterward."

"So you're asking *me* to go and look for her, is that it?" Pawl asked.

"Yes," Jamus said. "That's it. I know it's a lot to ask, given the way she left you half-dead to find your own way home, but if anyone stands a rat's chance of tracking her down and bringing her back, it's you."

Pawl stiffened ever so slightly, as if the demon-scars on his back had contracted. Those wounds had taken eight months to heal, after coming damn near to killing him. Yet through it all, he never uttered a word against Lathwi. And he did not seem inclined to change his habit now.

"Commander Guzman isn't going to allow me to go kiting off at a time like this," he said instead. "We've got a lot of new recruits—all edgy because of this ghost-plague. They need close supervision."

"I'll take care of the garrison commander," Jamus said, with the confidence of a seasoned string-puller. "Hell, I'll take care of your recruits, too. I know just the man for the job."

"Randall?" Pawl asked. At Jamus' nod, he lapsed into a disapproving frown. "He's a good man, but still green. This new lot needs someone with more experience."

"Then I'll get someone with more experience. Just say you'll do it."

"I'll do it," Pawl said.

Such immediate, unconditional consent surprised and confused Jamus. He had been expecting serious, possibly insurmountable opposition; a reluctance second only to his very own. "Really? Just like that?" He could not help but ask. "But why?"

"Because if Lathwi can get rid of your ghost problem, then maybe she can get rid of everyone's ghost problem, " Pawl said. "Every man, including Commander Guzman, should be willing to do whatever he can, whenever he can, to achieve that goal."

"Yes," Jamus said. "Quite right." This, even though he hadn't been thinking of anyone but himself when he had asked Pawl to find the dragon-bitch. This, even though he would never see her as anything other than the lesser of two monumental evils. "Quite right.

"When can you leave?"

શ્૦ભ

Jamus was reviewing a Nyssian trade proposal over a cup of gish-laced tea when his secretary slung the door to his office open without knocking first. "Your pardon, my lord," the slight, mole-faced man said, "but I think you should see this."

"See what, Arn?" Jamus snapped, not at all happy to have been disturbed. "What is it that can't wait until I've finished my morning tea?"

Arn cast a nervous look over his shoulder, then licked his lips and said, "I think it would be best described as a mob, my lord."

That catapulted Jamus out of his cushy chair. Moments later, he was standing on the catwalk that circled the garrison's upper reaches. On a clear day, he could see a fair chunk of the city from here. Today, however, all he saw was a mass of surly, red-faced people. The leading edge of this crowd came to a stop in front of the garrison's wooden gates. The tail-end was still straggling in from the bazaar, squatter's row, and the tavern district. As Jamus watched, a disembodied grumble funneled into a full-fledged chant.

"Remove the curse! Remove the curse! Remove the curse—now!"

Jamus snorted, a bitter exhalation. As if it were that blasted easy! As if they were the only ones being haunted. *Find Lathwi.* Hell, he didn't even try to sleep anymore. He just drank wine—or better yet, gish—until he passed out. Nothing bothered him then, not even ghosts with heart-shaped faces.

Someone below spotted him. The next thing he knew, the crowd was chanting his name in an ominous way. "D'Arques. D'Arques. D'Arques." He raised his arms, both an acknowledgment and a call for silence. The noise levels fell, albeit grudgingly. Jamus pitched his voice into the lull.

"Citizens of Compara," he said, "you have the governor's profound sympathies. He knows how cruelly you have suffered over the past few weeks, and how heroically you have endured. And while he regrets the necessity of it, the governor asks for your continued patience. For while everything that *can* be done *is* being done, we have not yet found a way to end this plague."

A jeer rose up from the crowd—a gish-laced, "Bullshit! The whole lot of you are sitting around with your thumbs up your arses, waiting for us to go mad so you can attach our properties."

Jamus gave his head an avuncular shake. "No one's going to have their property attached, friend," he said. "Now go home. Try to—" Out of the corner of his eye, he saw something arcing toward him. Before he had a chance to get out of its way, a tomato splashed against the side of his head. The crowd cheered, then started chanting again. Jamus combed the shattered fruit out of his hair with his fingers, then flicked its remains over the wall as if they were diseased.

"Are you hurt, my lord?" Arn asked, as Jamus stormed in from the catwalk. He had a towel in one hand and a mug of tea in the other. "Shall I send for the physician?"

"It was just a tomato, Arn." He draped the towel over his head, then grabbed the mug and took a swig only to nearly spit it out an instant later when he realized that he was drinking unadulterated tea. "What'd you use to brew this stuff—old socks and skivvies?" Before his secretary could reply, Jamus shoved the mug back into his unready hands and said, "Never mind. Just go and get Guzman."

"I can't, my lord," Arn said. "The garrison commander led a company into the countryside this morning to keep the peace."

Jamus scowled. "What about Wynn?"

"The governor is with his wife and newborn son in Bellemares-By-The-Bay, and is not expected back until tomorrow."

"Oh. Yes, of course." He'd forgotten that Wynn had been called away to help his slender-hipped wife through a complicated and almost lethal childbirth. And while daddy was away, Jamus was in charge. Once upon a time, he would've thrilled to the challenge. Now, however, he could hardly bear to be bothered. *Shit.* Why had that silly little cow picked now of all times to drop her load?

"Send for Randall then," he said.

"As you wish, my lord," Arn said, and went hurrying off.

Jamus took a moment to towel the tomato pulp and juice from his hair, then went back outside for another look at the situation. The mob had grown larger and uglier in his absence. As soon as it caught sight of him, fruit and stones began to fly.

"You are hereby ordered—" He sidestepped a chunk of rock. It went whizzing past his head. "—to disband and disperse." An apple splattered against the wall in front of him. "Further encroachment will not be—" A stone caught him in the cheek, drawing blood. He uttered the last word through gritted teeth. "—tolerated."

The mob took up a new chant. "Down with D'Arques! Down with D'Arques!"

He retreated into the building, muttering, "Down with D'Arques, is it? We'll just see about that." Randall was waiting for him just beyond the entryway. The young man was flushed as if from exertion, but there were spangles of excitement in his eyes. Jamus approved of that. It showed heart.

"My lord," he said. "You wished to see me?"

"I did," Jamus said, and then suffered a guilty pang. *A good man, but green.* He hadn't meant to disregard Pawl's advice. He'd simply never gotten around to considering anyone else for the job until Commander Guzman cornered him the morning after Pawl's departure and demanded to know who was going to take the swordmaster's place while he was out running errands for Jamus like some raw recruit. Randall's name had popped out of his mouth before he could stop it. And he wasn't a bad choice, really. Everybody started out green. "You're aware of the situation?"

"I am, my lord."

"And how stand your men?"

"They stand ready, my lord. How do you wish to proceed?"

Jamus dabbed at his cheek with the hem of his sleeve. The sting from the wound revived his irritation. "Arm them with staves, then assemble them in the courtyard. If the rabble will not disperse of its own volition, I may send you out to help it along."

"We'll be ready, my lord," Randall said, in parting.

"Good man," Jamus said, then curled his lip as a tiny voice in his head whispered, *Still green.* Bloody Pawl. He'd been gone for over a week now. If he were any kind of tracker at all, he would've been off and back already. How hard could it possibly to find a woman who lived like a dragon?

No harder than dispersing a mob, he supposed.

He headed back toward the catwalk. As he did so, a movement in the courtyard below caught his eye: men falling into formation. They were a motley-looking lot, mostly young city toughs and immigrants, but Randall had them stepping high and proud. When one recruit complained about being issued a stave instead of a sword, Randall borrowed the lad's weapon and proceeded to show him exactly what a thick wooden club could do to unprotected flesh. Jamus winced at the first *thwack* and then lofted a thought at Pawl: *ha, not so green after all.*

When the troops were all set, Randall gave the nod to Jamus. Jamus took a deep, bracing breath, wishing it were a drink instead, and then showed his face to the mob once again. It started chanting immediately. *"Down with D'Arques. Down with D'Arques."* He had to shout to make himself heard over the din.

"Citizens of Compara," he said, "this is your last chance. Disperse immediately, or you will be arrested."

For one hope-filled moment, the chanting stopped. Then someone yelled, "Down with the whole damned garrison!" and the crowd surged forward with a roar. An axe-head flashed silver in the sunlight, then buried itself in the front gate. An instant later, a hail of torches came arcing toward the wall, along with bladders stuffed with broken glass and nails. One of the recruits chanced to take a piece of glass in the throat. The sight of his blood infuriated Jamus. No one attacked his men with impunity. *No one.*

He signaled Randall, who signaled the gate-keepers. As the gates groaned slowly open, troops rushed in to fill the void.

"Secure the area!" Jamus commanded from the heights. "Drive them back." And then, still enraged, he added, "Teach them a lesson they'll never forget."

Chapter 3

*L*uke threaded his way through the trees—two parts stealth, one part tension. He was trespassing. He knew that. He also knew what the penalty for being caught was apt to be. Nevertheless, he pressed on, down the wooded slope and into a ravine. There, he came upon a trail so unabashedly wide and open, a blind city dweller could have found it. His guts lurched, a spasm of excitement and nerves. He was getting close now. Now all he could do was hope that the rumors he had heard over the past few weeks were true.

The run guided him to an opening in the hillside. At one point in time, it must've been a mere crack, the offspring of some forgotten earthquake. But over the years, rain, wind, and other forces had shaped it into a crude archway. Luke fingered a fresh scratch in the stone, then made a gesture for luck and stepped inside. The air immediately turned cool and dry. Moments later, the way turned dark. But while he could have made a torch for himself, he did not do so. If the rumors were true—and he prayed to all things sacred and sweet that they were—then the end of his quest was somewhere in this passageway. But if they were false, well, he stood a better chance of surviving his mistake in darkness. Uncle Santana called this 'hedging one's bets'. It just seemed like a good idea to Luke.

As he worked his way along the left wall, he grazed a heap of rubble with his toe. Unseen stones clattered across the floor, loud as a passing hail-storm in this hollowed-out space. Luke froze, trying to become a part of the tenderized silence that followed. Katya should've chosen someone else for this task, he thought, as he waited to live or die. Even Mim, his ten-year-old cousin, moved with more cunning and grace. But as inadequate as he felt, he never considered giving up. He had been appointed. The quest was his. And The Little Mother had had her reasons for choosing him. She said fortune favored him.

And that was true.

He tapped the good luck piece that he wore cinched at his waist. From the very moment the Great One had presented it to him, misfortune had forgotten his name. Every time, he looked back on that night, he was overcome with wonder. Had he really dared to steal from her?

The silence continued. The darkness remained unbroken, too. Luke decided to press on. He took more care with his footfalls now. Someone seeing him from behind might have mistaken him for a dancer or a thief. Soon, the faint odor of sulfur appeared in the air. This was a good sign, he told himself. Then, only half-convinced, he tapped the fetish again. It gave him patience and strength—skyfolk qualities. It made him feel connected to those incredible beings.

It did not, however, stop him from bumping into solid rock.

The wall's presence confused him. There was supposed to be, well, he didn't know what exactly, but *something* here, a chamber perhaps or another passageway, anything but a dead-end. He patted the rockface down, searching for hidden openings, then swore gustily when none turned up. The rumor-mongers had played him false after all. This was the wrong place.

"I don't understand," he muttered to himself. He'd been prepared for success or sudden death, but not the prospect of starting his quest all over again. "I would've sworn that a Great One lived here."

An instant after he uttered the words, a triangular head burst forth from the wall across from him. A mouthful of daggers flashed white in the dark. An ominous rumble shook the air. Luke's heart slammed into his ribcage. His mouth went chalky and dry. But even as animal instinct clamored for immediate, headlong retreat, he forced himself to hold fast. For this dragon had blue eyes.

"Great One," he said, trying in vain to keep his voice steady. "Forgive me for the intrusion, but I come bearing news."

The dragon's thin upper lip curled back, exposing more tooth. A moment later, a talon-tipped forearm came slashing toward him from the wall. Luke cringed, anticipating the killing blow that was his just due for guessing wrong, then whuffed his surprise as the forearm wrapped itself around his waist and hauled him toward solid rock. Before he had a chance to wonder or worry or even close his eyes, he passed through a thick gray haze and into a spacious chamber that smelled of heat and a dragon's musk. It was, however, like no dragon's nest that he had ever heard of. Fires flickered in wrought-iron braziers, casting reddish-gold light throughout the room. A bookcase crammed with books and sundries stood against the far wall.

And then there was the resident dragon.

She was small for an adult, but handsomely proportioned. Her wings were folded against her back. The tip of her tail was twitching. Except for the calico markings on her face, she was all black. Torchlight glistened on her scales. Power shone in her eyes. She was staring at him. She looked hungry.

"You know me, Great One," he said. "You gave me a gift."

Her blue eyes flicked from his face to the dragon's claw on his belt. A moment later, the air around her began to thicken and shimmer. Luke watched on in wonder as this mage's haze swallowed her up, but when it started to writhe and warp like a bladder full of squirming maggots, he had to look away or be stomach-sick. By the time he felt steady enough to chance another peek, a woman stood in the dragon's stead. She was much as he remembered her: tall and muscular, with a scruffy head of long, black hair, a scarred face, and a mouth that did not know how to smile. She was staring at him again. She still looked hungry.

"Lathwi," he named her, grinning with relief and boyish pride.

"Why—are you—here?" she asked. Her voice sounded hoarse, as if from disuse, and she did not seem entirely sure of the words that she had just used.

"I am Luke," he told her, "Santana's nephew—"

She cut him off with a scathing hiss. "There is nothing wrong with my—memory, boy. Tell me something I do not know."

A flush blazed its way into his cheeks. It was mostly chagrin for having offended a Great One, but there was also a pinch of resentment in the mix, too, that for being called a boy. He was twenty by Santana's reckoning, old enough to have a boy of his own. So, in spite of his red face, or perhaps because of it, he squared his shoulders and stood a little taller.

"Katya sent me," he said. "The Little Mother is troubled. For on our way to the tribe's midsummer gathering this year, we happened upon two dead dragons."

"Stupid dragons die every day." Lathwi said.

"But these were murdered!" he blurted, mortified by her indifference. "Somebody sliced their bellies open and rooted through their bowels."

Now *that* was news worthy of a dragon's consideration.

Lathwi contemplated her uninvited visitor for a long moment. His familiarity did not make her any happier to see him. She had little use for humans these days. They were too noisy. And too much trouble. After her adventures with Galza and Malcolm Blackheart, the only society she craved was that of dragons. Yet for wise old Katya, she would make an exception. The dowager was dragon-wise. The dowager was a—friend. A measure of respect for her emissary was due.

Having decided that, she leaned back on her heels to shift some of her standing weight onto her tail and thereby make herself more comfortable. Too late, she recalled that she was no longer in possession of such an appendage. An instant later, she landed on her butt with a wholly undignified plop. Stupid human form, she fumed, as she picked herself up from the floor. It was so impractical. And much too soft. She had only taken it so she could talk to the boy. Lucky for him, he showed no signs of having enjoyed her clumsiness. His eyes were still round with wonder. His lower jaw was still slightly slack. When she beckoned him closer with a wave of her hand, he looked as though he might throw himself at her feet.

"Relaxe," she told him, and then pressed her fingertips to his temple. "Think back to the first dragon you found. I wish to see what you saw."

Although the memory made him heart-sick every time he recalled it, he could not refuse a request from a Great One. So he closed his eyes and thought back to the cruel summer day when Mim cried out, "Look, Maman! There's a Great One sleeping in that field."

The caravan creaked to an immediate stop. But even as Luke's father and uncles and cousins scrambled to camouflage the wagons, they heard a sharp whistle—Santana's signal to stop. A moment later, Luke saw him hurrying from one driver to the next.

"We are too close," he told Luke's father in his turn. "We must withdraw before The Great One wakes up and sees us." He turned and pointed to a ridge in the distance. "We'll camp up there for the night."

Disappointment coursed through Luke like a draught of swamp water. He would have liked nothing better than to stay here and watch the dragon rouse from its nap. Such opportunities were few and far between—especially for those like him, who would watch the skyfolk all day long if they could. But he never thought to argue against their leaving. The safety of the caravan *always* came first.

He started to get back onto the wagon only to be pulled immediately down again by an urgent, half-volume command from Santana's wife, Gem. "Mim, no! Come back here!"

Instinct cranked Luke's head toward the big-bellied mound in the field. And sure enough, there was his fearless, ten-year-old cousin, running toward it as if it were a puppy in need of a cuddle. Santana was already chasing after her, but she had a huge head-start on him, and he was not as fleet of foot as he had been in olden days. The next thing Luke knew, he was on the run, too. He caught up with his uncle in a heartbeat, then overtook him.

"She *must* survive," Santana said, in passing.

But she was over halfway to the Great One now. Catching up with her before she threw herself at it would be a feat worthy of song. He ran hard and headlong, wincing all the while at the wild, thrashing sounds he was making. If the dragon woke now, it would have both him and Mim for tea. He projected a thought at her: *come back now!* To his surprise and relief, she slowed to a stop. Moments later, she half-turned to share a frown with him: his reward, he supposed, for trying to spoil her fun. He gestured, motioning for her to join him. She turned her back on him and stayed put. He ground a curse between his molars and went after her.

"Something's wrong," she said, as he scooped her up and into his arms. She was still frowning. Her eyes were all for the dragon. "Look at it, Lukie."

Despite his towering need to get his cousin to safety, Luke could not resist a peek.

The Great One was sprawled on its side less than three wagon-lengths away. Its hide was a ruddy color freckled with tiny black specks. Its head was out of sight. It was much, much smaller than Luke had first imagined. And—it seemed very, very still.

"I cannot hear it breathing," Mim said.

Now that she mentioned it, neither could he. His fear for her survival evaporated, but the taste of dread remained in his mouth. He pivoted toward the caravan, then turned Mim loose like a pet pigeon. "Back to your maman now, little one," he told her. "This is not the place for you."

She took one last look at the dragon, then went scurrying back toward the wagons. He waited until she was in her mother's arms before heading the other way. As he neared the too-still Great One, a sharp, septic tang invaded his nose. At the same time, an angry buzzing rose up in his ears. He made a sign to avert evil, and then cried aloud as he came close enough to see the rest of the dragon. Its underbelly had been slit from breastbone to sexless crotch. Its innards had been scooped out and hacked into pulp. The black spots that he had taken for freckles were actually hundreds of flies. At the sight, he dropped to his knees and started vomiting....

Lathwi withdrew from the memory with a scornful curl of her lip. Human minds were like a Comparan bazaar—crowded and crude, colorful but confusing, a jumble of ever-changing images and superfluous details. She much preferred the organized minds of dragons. Still, she could not quit now. Katya had wanted her to have this knowledge. And—she was curious.

"Think back to the second dragon now," she told Luke. "Try to focus on the discovery rather than the events that surrounded it."

This memory began with Luke hunting in a woods, but it quickly acquired many of the same aspects as the first: a large meadow ringed by trees; a juvenile dragon; and systematic mutilation. But to Lathwi, this murdered dragon looked alarmingly familiar. It was gangly and unsexed, as most five-year-olds were, and its scales were the color of a hunter's moon. Her tanglemate, Eldahzed, from Taziem's last clutch, matched that description. And it had never been very good at getting out of trouble.

As soon as Lathwi withdrew from the human's mind, she Voiced her tanglemate's Name. There was no reply, no spark of contact. The Call simply faded away. She Called again, a different Name this time, and then focused on Luke.

"Katya was right to send you," she said. "Now say where you were when these memories—"

A faint psychic tingle cut her off. This was ward-magic, a silent alarm. Someone was prowling through her outer caves. She probed the darkness with a tendril of her Will, then turned her scowl on Luke.

"Did you come here with others?" she asked.

"No, Great One," he replied. "I am alone."

She hissed, venting annoyance, then summoned her Will and cast a hasty illusion over herself. "It is easier than a true Change," she said to Luke, who was now gaping at the leering dragon's head that she had given herself. "And few linger long enough to see if it is real or not."

With that, she poked her head through a span of illusory rock. A man shouted, a startled whoop of astonishment and alarm. She couldn't see his face in the passageway's all-encompassing gloom, but the timbre of his voice unlatched old memories. A puzzled scowl displaced her dragon's leer.

"Pawl?"

He lowered the sword that had jumped into his hand. Before he could raise it again, she grabbed him by the wrist and hauled him through the warded entryway. He blinked the vestiges of darkness from his eyes, then looked her up and down, and said, "You're one of a very few people who can still surprise me at will." A moment later, he added, "You're looking well."

Lathwi returned his scrutiny with a dragon's unblinking composure. The last time she had seen this man, he had been on a horse, westward bound as she headed east. His back had been torn open by krim. The wounds had been infected. He bore no outward sign of that mauling now. Indeed, he was much as she remembered him: tall and sinewy, with stern features and penetrating eyes. There was a trace of silver in his warrior's braid now, and the lines on his face were deeper, but these minor changes suited him. Had she been predisposed to stating the obvious, she would have said that he looked well, too.

"Why have you come?" she asked instead.

Pawl did not reply. He was too busy entertaining questions of his own: *How have you been? Where have you been? Why didn't you look for me in Compara?* For as soon as that heart-stopping dragon illusion had given way to her oft-scarred face back in the passageway, feelings that he had believed long-dead came surging back up from their graves at him. He felt dizzy and off-balance, fumble-tongued as a schoolboy.

And speaking of which—

He glanced at the cub who was standing to Lathwi's rear. A gypsy lad, he figured, judging by the knives in his belt and the golden rings in his ear. And he was not as young as Pawl wanted him to be. His chin bore stubble instead of down, and there was a manly breadth to his chest and shoulders. Even so, he couldn't be more than twenty years old—twenty-one, at best. What use could wild, solitary Lathwi possibly have for such a youth?

"Why are you here?" she asked again, and this time, her tone was pointed enough to penetrate the soft shell of his thoughts.

"Jamus sent me," he replied.

"Why would he do that?" she wondered aloud. For Jamus *hated* her. He had said so the last time that they had been in a room together.

"He has seen Liselle," Pawl told her.

"Liselle is dead," she pointed out. That was why Jamus hated her. He had it in his mind that Lathwi was responsible for his chosen's death—as if Liselle had not invited herself along on that desperate trek to Taziem's mountain. As if the sorceress had had no mind or Will of her own. If Lathwi had left Liselle behind, Jamus had argued, she'd still be alive and well. His logic failed to take Galza's then-boundless malice into account, but then, he had never been a particularly discriminating thinker.

"Her body may be dead," Pawl said, "but her spirit is not at rest. It has appeared to him three times now. And each time, it has commanded him to find you." He glanced in Luke's direction, unsure of how much more he wanted to say in a stranger's presence, then decided that the gypsy was trustworthy simply by association. "He hasn't been the same since—well, you know, since Liselle's death. He has let everything go to seed: his job, his household, even his appearance. But I tell you truly, Lathwi. He was holding his own until Liselle's ghost showed up. Her visitations are ruining him."

Jamus' plight roused no sympathy in Lathwi. For while she had come to tolerate that garrulous peacock of a man as an occasional companion during her stay in Compara, she had never developed much of a taste for him. So what if he went mad? It was no concern of hers. Unfortunately, she could not dismiss this talk of Liselle's ghost so easily. Liselle TrueHeart had endured much on dragonkind's behalf. That could not be forgotten. Or ignored.

"Liselle's isn't the only ghost in town these days, either," Pawl went on to say. "Compara seems to be infested with them. They've been haunting people in their sleep. The city's turning edgy and mean."

Until then, Luke had been content to wait and listen. But the outsider's talk of a ghostly infestation made the hair on his arms stand straight up. He touched his good luck piece to ward off any specters that might be in the vicinity, then barged headlong into the conversation.

"The younglings in our caravan have been troubled by night frights lately, too," he said. "Katya thought they were being haunted by the memory of murdered dragons, but perhaps ghosts are behind this, too. If so, I would like to know how such a thing is possible."

Both he and Pawl looked to Lathwi for answers. But before she had a chance to admit that she knew absolutely nothing about spirits and their ways, ward-magic tingled through her for the third time that day. A moment later, a thought popped into her head.

"You Called. I have come." The accompanying image contained a pair of sly, hunter's-moon eyes.

"You made remarkable time," Lathwi noted.

"We were already on our way when you Called."

"We?"

"Masque is with me. We had a craving for fresh lore."

"You may indeed learn something new today," Lathwi said, *"but the lesson will not come from me. It appears that strange times are upon us again."*

"How strange?"

"You must decide that for yourself. But before I let you in, send Masque away. Today's lessons require a wise head and sturdy attention-span."

The presence in Lathwi's mind withdrew only to reassert itself a moment later with the draconic equivalent of a chuckle. *"The youngling is not happy, but it goes nonetheless. Now let me pass."*

Lathwi lowered her magical defenses. At the same time, she glanced over her shoulder at Luke and Pawl. "Get out of the way," she told them, "and do not be afraid. She likes people now."

Pawl backed away, posthaste, toward the most out-of-the-way corner in the room. He knew what was on its way in, there wasn't an ounce of doubt in his mind, but even so, he wasn't ready for the dragon's head that came gliding through a seemingly solid span of rock and into the chamber. He wasn't any readier for the long stretch of scaly neck that followed, or for that unbelievably massive body. The gypsy lad dropped to his knees and prostrated himself before the cruel-eyed, saber-taloned creature. But all Pawl could do was stand in its shadow and stare, for his knees and jaw were locked. He had never felt so small, or so trapped.

Taziem glanced from one man to the next, then turned to share a dragon's grin with Lathwi. *"You did not tell me there were humans here. Are they sorcerers?"*

"No," Lathwi replied. *"But neither of them are as ordinary as they seem, either."*

"Ooh, a riddle. I like riddles." The she-dragon focused her attention on the human who had dropped to his knees, eager to find out what was so extraordinary about him. From the little she could see of him, he looked young and scrawny—and there was nothing unusual about that when it came to humans. But then she noticed something else. *"This one carries a claw."*

"I know. I gave it to him. His people revere dragons."

"How sensible of them."

"He has come here bearing news about our kind. That news is the reason I Called you."

Taziem's curiosity flared like a patch of dry scales. But she did not allow herself to scratch it right away—she wanted to solve the mystery of the other human's presence first. He was tall and well-muscled for a man, and stood on his feet instead of his knees. When their eyes met, he did not look away. She liked that. Courage enhanced stature. And stature was a sire's domain. She shaped an image of him dancing among the clouds and lobbed it at Lathwi. *"Is he your Chosen?"*

Lathwi dismissed the guess with a shrug. *"I have no Chosen."*

"Then why is he here?"

"He came to bring me back to Compara. He says Liselle TrueHeart is asking for me."

"The TrueHeart is dead."

Lathwi shrugged again. *"I did say that strange times were upon us."*

"So you did."

Taziem extended her neck, bringing her head closer and then closer to Pawl's. He shuddered as she drew near, but did not look away even though she could see spangles of fear swimming in his stag-brown eyes. The she-dragon rumbled approvingly.

"He is not a dragon," she said. *"But you could do worse."*

Pawl went suddenly boneless. An instant later, he slumped to the floor in a faint.

"Is he ill?" Taziem asked.

"I do not believe so," Lathwi replied, and then stated a totally unrelated thought in lieu of the truth. *"He has been traveling for many days. He must be tired."*

"Let him sleep then. I will hear more of this news that you mentioned earlier."

Lathwi nudged Luke with her toe, urging him to stand up. As he scrambled to his feet, she said, "My mother wants you to tell her why you are here."

"But—"

His agitation amused Lathwi. He was so flustered, he did not even know where to look or what word to say next. But it was quite easy to read his mind. "My mother has a fair understanding of human-speak. All you need do is speak clearly and succinctly. And look at her when you're talking."

Luke could not believe the extent of his good fortune. Only a very privileged few had ever come nose-to-nose with a Great One other than Lathwi and lived to tell the tale. And as far as he knew, no one had ever had a conversation with one. His people would sing of this day for generations to come! He touched his good luck piece, then raised his eyes to the she-dragon. And oh, what a magnificent creature she was: black as night, big as night, with a beautifully shaped head and eyes like liquid amber. His pulse quickened. His mouth went dry. Now that his moment had come, he did not know what to say.

"It is not wise to keep a dragon waiting," Lathwi reminded him.

His heartbeat quickened again—a panicked little flutter that kick-started his brain. "Great One," he blurted, "forgive me for gawking. But the sight of you takes my breath away. You're as beautiful as a moonlit night, and as dread as death itself. Thank you for allowing me to stand before you. If it weren't for the grievous news that brought me here, this would be the most glorious day of my life."

Taziem rumbled, applauding the youngling's attitude. *"If more humans thought as this one did,"* she told Lathwi, *"there would be far less strife in the world."*

But her pleasure crumbled like so much dry dung as the gypsy told his tale. For he was lavish with his details. And Lathwi illustrated some of his words with images that she had plucked from his mind earlier. By the time Luke finally fell quiet again, the tip of Taziem's tail was twitching furiously.

"That was Eldahzed," she told Lathwi, lacing the thought with a mother's surety.

"I know," Lathwi replied. *"Did you recognize the other?"*

"No. But that is irrelevant to this mystery. The important thing is the manner in which both younglings were killed. That does not have the look of a coincidence, or an accident. Nor was it done by dragons. Not even a rogue sire in full rut would kill a youngling so fresh from the nest and root through its bowels afterward."

"I agree," Lathwi said. *"These murders look like human handiwork."*

Taziem challenged that conclusion with a snort. *"A human would have had to subdue those younglings before he killed them. Do you know of any man strong enough to do that?"*

"Not any one man in particular," Lathwi replied. *"But humans often hunt in packs. And they often rely on subterfuge instead of strength."*

"Men? Hunting dragons?" Taziem marveled, projecting a desire to disbelieve it. *"Why would they do such a thing? They did not even take any of the meat."*

"Some men kill the things they fear, Mother. Others kill for the sport of it. And then there are those who kill for no reason at all. They simply like to cause death. Whoever these dragonslayers may be, though, and whatever their motives, I have the feeling that their killing spree has just begun."

Taziem hissed, a sound both scandalized and scornful. She was The Learned One, a self-proclaimed expert on men. She had been pleased to think that she understood their ways. How galling it was to realize that she was as naive as any newborn. Killing simply for the sake of killing was wicked, an abomination. Any sensible creature knew better.

"We cannot allow humans to come to think that they can kill our young out of fear, fun, or any other reason," she told Lathwi. *"These murderers must be stopped."*

Lathwi wholeheartedly agreed with that sentiment, but before she could Voice her opinion, a soft, rustling noise distracted her. She traced the sound back to Pawl, who was just starting to rouse from his faint. As soon as she laid eyes on him, she remembered his reason for being here: Liselle. An eddy of conflicting desires spiraled its way through her then. She shared her torn feelings with Taziem.

"I want nothing more than to hunt down the men who killed Eldahzed and feed them, one by one, to a newborn tangle," she said. *"But Liselle TrueHeart beckons me as well, and although I would have it otherwise, her need feels more compelling."*

"Your path is clear," Taziem replied, radiating certainty. *"The TrueHeart has Called. You must go to Compara."*

"But what about the youngling-slayers?"

At that, Taziem flashed her a dragon's smile full of teeth and guile. *"Leave them to me."*

Chapter 4

*A*re *you sure you want to do this?"* Lathwi asked, as she and Taziem stepped out of Lathwi's sanctuary and into the pitch-black passageway beyond. *"Being soft is not an easy way of life."*

Taziem responded with the mental equivalent of a cocksure shrug. *"If you can do it, so can I."*

"Perhaps," Lathwi said. A moment later, she swung around and boxed Taziem soundly in the nose. *"Softlings are prone to painful little surprises,"* she said, ignoring the warning hiss that added menace to the darkness. *"You would be wise to remember that."*

"Surprises keep life interesting," Taziem said, all hauteur and wounded dignity now. *"And the pain from that punch was as fleeting as a thought."*

Lathwi denounced her mother's sloppy thinking with a snort. *"That punch was the mildest of blows, a lesson given with the best of intentions. But you will learn a different sort of lesson if dragonslayers catch you unawares. Those kind of men are skilled at hurting things; the doing gives them pleasure. What will you do if you find yourself at their mercy?"*

"I will Change back and eat their hearts."

"If they do not kill you first."

The end of the passageway loomed ahead. Its mouth was filled with bright yellow light. Lathwi stopped to let her eyes adjust to the dazzle, then turned to face her mother.

"You are determined to do this?" she asked.

"I am," Taziem replied.

"Then straighten your back and stand upright," she said aloud. "When you walk, let your arms hang free at your sides instead of holding them out in front of you like some frightened frill-neck lizard. And no more mind-speak. Humans talk with their mouths."

The criticism stung Taziem. No one had ever compared her to a frill-neck lizard. Ever. She turned a resentful eye on her fosterling and said, *"You know that this is not the first time that I have taken this form."*

"I know," Lathwi replied. "It is, however, the first time that your life may depend on it. So hold your head up and keep your neck straight. And stop dragging your feet."

They strode out of the passageway and into the ravine. Lathwi had told Luke and Pawl to wait outside so they wouldn't distract Taziem while she was transforming herself. Now neither man was anywhere within sight or smell. As she looked around for signs of their whereabouts, annoyance lumbered through her like a winter-fat fisher-bear. Leave it to humans to complicate a journey before it even started, she thought, and then hissed her vexation aloud as Taziem pointed to an old oak tree that overlooked the ravine. Pawl and Luke were both perched in its upper reaches.

"What are they doing up there?" Taziem wondered.

Lathwi made no reply. She was already on her way to investigate. She took the fast route rather than the easy one. It took her straight up the ravine's rock-and-bramble side. As she neared the tree, it became obvious that the boy was spying on something in the woods to his left, and that the swordmaster was massively annoyed. His jaw muscles were taut. His scowl was as vast as a thundercloud. But she was not impressed.

"You picked a strange time to go honey-hunting," she said, striking a disapproving pose amidst the oak's gnarled roots.

"This was his idea," Pawl grumbled, and turned his scowl on Luke. "He said we would be less noticeable up here."

"Less noticeable to whom?" she asked, intrigued by the answer in spite of herself.

"The little calico!" Luke replied, radiating excitement. "Look—there it is, rolling among the bones of its kill. How beautiful it is. And how happy."

Pawl loosed a bitter snort. "Happy? Hell, it ought to be ecstatic. I paid a month's wages for that horse."

Lathwi went storming off in the direction that Luke was pointing. Her thoughts were peppered with irritation for Masque—not because it had killed Pawl's horse, hungry dragons did that sometimes and who cared about a dumb pack-beast anyway, but because it had been told to go away and it had stayed. Such disobedience could lead to disrespect. And *that* could get a dragon killed. The youngling had to be taught better manners. So she tracked it down, hunting first by sound and then by sight as the thrashing and crashing of dragon sport led to glimpses of black, red, and tan through the trees. She sent it an image of herself: soft and pink and scowling. It quit its playing immediately, and sat up on its hindquarters to greet her.

"Lathwi!" it crooned, as she strode toward it. *"It is good to see you again. Look, I killed a horse. I ate most of it already, but you can have what is left. Or perhaps you would like to play instead. That would be nice. I know many games."*

"Masque," she scolded, before it could prattle on, *"you were told to go away."*

It flashed her a sly grin flecked with gore. *"I did go away. I simply did not go very far."*

Lathwi's annoyance unraveled, pulled loose by pride. Masque was her favorite tanglemate, and not just because it was undersized like her. This little dragon was clever. This little dragon liked to learn. On any other day, she might've rewarded it for its witty reply. Today, however, she had to punish it. For its own good. So she summoned her Will, then cracked it at the youngling. It let out a honk of surprise and pain as the tip of an invisible whip snapped against the softest part of its muzzle.

"Now you are to leave my territory," Lathwi told it. *"You may not return until I invite you back. And the next time you disobey an elder, you will get teeth and claws instead of a flick."*

Masque smacked its lips at her. *"You are no fun."*

"Sad but true. Now be gone."

The youngling unfurled its wings and gave them a saucy rustle. Under Lathwi's watchful eye, it then invoked the secret Name of Wind. A breeze kicked up. Masque welcomed it with a croon. Then, even as it went airborne, it lashed out—a lightning-fast sweep of the neck that brought its jaws to within an inch of her face.

"I am going," it told her, a thoroughly dignified thought lined with a single strand of juvenile glee for having mock-challenged an elder. *"I will see you when I see you."*

"Be wary of humans," Lathwi replied, thinking of Eldahzed. *"If you are in Need, Call."*

By then, Masque was aloft and away.

Lathwi rejoined the rest of her traveling party. Luke was hovering near Taziem, who was busy licking the scratches that she had gotten while climbing up the ravine. Pawl was standing as far away from the both of them as he could manage while still remaining in the oak tree's vicinity. The swordmaster did not look pleased, no doubt because Masque had eaten his horse. She shrugged the small matter of his displeasure aside. Anyone who brought horses into dragon-country should expect to lose one every now and again.

"Well," he said, as she converged on him, "we had best get started. It's a long walk to Compara." He raised his hand to Taziem and Luke—an enthusiastic farewell. "A pleasure to have made your acquaintance," he told them. "Good luck finding those—dragonslayers."

"May luck be with you as well," Luke replied. "But there is no need for farewells just yet. Our paths overlap for a day or two. Now that you are without a horse, we will be able to keep up with you."

Pawl wanted desperately to refuse the suggestion. It was bad enough that he had lost his prized mare to a small dragon. He did not want to think about what else he could lose to a big one—even a big one who now wore the shape of a woman. He glanced at Taziem out of the corner of his eye. She was almost three hands taller than he was, and solid as the earth itself beneath the short, ragged shift that she wore. Her skin was as black as the sky at night; her eyes were a sly shade of gold. A full head of hair might've made her seem less fey, but all she had was a nappy little cap that hugged her skull. She was, Pawl thought, a terrifying sight. And human form or not, he couldn't bring himself to trust her.

But Lathwi embraced the idea of traveling with Taziem. "There is a chance that the dragonslayers are in this vicinity," she said. "If they are, I want to take part in their eradication."

That was just the kind of talk that made Pawl nervous.

Nevertheless, the four of them headed out. Pawl walked point, Lathwi followed. Taziem and Luke brought up the rear. Less than an hour into the hike, Taziem said, "My feet hurt." A half-mile later, she said, "My legs ache."

She plopped down on the back of a rotting log. The log splintered beneath her weight. She rumbled testily, ready to complain again, then made a happy little crooning noise as Luke dashed in and began to rub her calves.

"Ooh," she said. "This is nice."

"Maybe so," Lathwi said, "but it is a thing best reserved for the end of a day. We are still at the beginning of ours. So get up and start walking."

"But I am not accustomed to walking for so long," Taziem said, switching to dragon-speak, *"especially on these two ridiculous paddles."*

"I told you being soft was no easy thing," Lathwi thought back, projecting a complete lack of sympathy. *"You can still change your mind if you want."*

"No."

Lathwi shrugged. *"As you wish. But if you continue to slow me down like this, I will leave you behind."*

Taziem dismissed the ultimatum with a petulant sniff, then stood up in one fluid movement. Luke was right there by her side, ready to help if she needed it, even though he probably would have done himself an injury trying to budge her.

Pawl watched from a safe distance as Lathwi goaded Taziem back to her feet. Despite the differences in their size and skin color, he could see how someone might take them for mother and blood-daughter. They both carried themselves as if there were more to them than met the eye. And both projected an air of independence that mocked human need. What possible use could such a being have for a simple man like him? Lathwi was already complete without him. But even as he thought to surrender his hope, he spied the knife that she was wearing strapped to her calf. He had given it to her at their last parting. It gladdened his heart to know that she had kept it all this time—and to think that she had done so in memory of him.

Taziem heaved to her feet then. Lathwi was already walking his way.

"We go now," she told him. "There will be no further delays."

Whatever you say," he replied.

∞∞

The foursome hiked the afternoon away. It was slow-going through hilly, heavily forested country. Pawl found himself missing his horse on more than one occasion. Still, he was not entirely unhappy. Lathwi's companionship made that impossible, despite the fact she never walked alongside him, or spoke more than one or two words at a time. Her mere proximity was potent enough to satisfy his cravings. Or so it seemed for now.

He looked up from his trail-blazing to gauge the time. The sky was still blue but starting to darken now. The summer evening sun was visible as a dazzling series of glints through the canopy. Time to make camp for the night, he supposed, only to realize that he was smelling the barest suggestion of a cookfire and roasting meat already. He turned to share this discovery with the others, but he was too late. Taziem was sniffing at the air and licking her lips. Lathwi had a feral, death-to-dragonslayers look in her eyes. And as for Luke—well, he had gone missing. Pawl opened his mouth to ask Lathwi when *that* had happened, then clamped it shut again as the gypsy cub came prowling out of the bush toward him.

"There's a camp in the dingle on the other side of this hill," he told Pawl. "Seven men, no women or children. It looks like they've been there for a week, maybe more."

"Thieves?" Pawl asked.

Luke dismissed the possibility with a shake of his head. "I saw no lookouts, and few weapons. They didn't seem the violent type, either—if you know what I mean."

"I do," Pawl said, trusting a gypsy to know what faces violence wore. "But while I appreciate your intention, I want you to tell me before you go and do something like that again."

Luke's mouth flattened into a disapproving line. At the same time, his eyes went cold. Looking Pawl square in the face, he said, "I am the emissary of Katya, Dowager Queen of The Wandering Tribe. I do not need permission from an outsider to come and go."

"You're absolutely right," Pawl said, in his most reasonable tone. "If you want to pop in and out of our company without telling me, you go ahead. But don't blame me if I mistake you for an intruder on your way in or out and cut you up a bit."

"You'd have to catch me first."

"Let us hope that I'm never put to that test."

Although Lathwi appreciated the fencing that was going on behind the two men's words, she had no desire to listen to any more of it. So she grabbed Taziem by the wrist and started on her way again.

"Where are you going?" Pawl was quick to ask.

"I want to look upon these seven men," she replied. "If they are dragonslayers, I will know it and they will die."

Pawl ground his molars against an urge to groan. He did not want to get involved in this hunt for dragonslayers. It was not his fight, or his business. He had come to bring Lathwi back to Compara—nothing more, nothing less. But he knew better than to hope that he could talk her out of descending on that camp. She had that look in her eye again, a look so intensely focused, it excluded all purposes save her own. So he held his tongue and resumed his position as point-scout.

Taziem was aware of the human-named-Pawl's displeasure, for his scowl was very expressive, but she made no effort to puzzle out the reasons for his unhappiness. She was much too busy enjoying the novelties of being human—especially her heightened sense of touch. As she walked, she fingered every new thing that came her way: a crow's feather, tree bark, a snail's discarded shell. Textures were intense, and oddly exciting. She could not get enough of them.

The air was thick with the smells of roasting fat and woodsmoke now. She could see a handsome orange fire dancing among the trees at the bottom of the hill, and a crowd of shadowy figures.

"Kit, you lazy son of a flea-bitten hound," one of those shadows growled. "If you don't take a turn at that spit, you ain't gettin' any when it's done."

"Stuff you, Wal," another shadow growled back. "I went out and killed the damn thing."

"Big deal. It was almost dead anyway."

The human-called-Pawl gestured for a stop. Taziem ignored him. On the trail, he had wanted her to move faster. Now that she was where she wished to be, he wanted her to slow down. Silly creature. He needed lessons in logic. Dragon-bold, she strode down the hill and right into camp.

"Sweet bleeding Dreamer," somebody gurgled. Then all conversation, all activity ceased. For one awestruck moment, the crackle of fire feasting on wood and molten fat was the only sound in the world.

Taziem took that moment to assess the campers. They were not tanglemates, that much was clear, for they were not even close to being the same age. Some were cub-like, others were quite mature. They were of various sizes and shapes as well, and one of them bore burn marks on his soft, pale face. All had fear in their eyes—all but one grizzled old bull of a man. He seemed delighted to see her.

"You all by yourself, darlin'?" he asked, and then swore as Pawl stepped into view.

"There's four of us altogether," the swordmaster said, striving for a nonchalant tone. "We smelled your fire from a distance, and decided to drop in."

The old bull sized Pawl up with a single pop-eyed glance, then thrust a callused hand in his direction. "The name's Wally," he said, "and as far as I'm concerned, you're welcome to stay as long as you like. We don't get to see too many women close-up."

"These two are like no other women you've ever met," Pawl said, tongue firmly in cheek. "And they'll gladly turn any or all of you inside out if you offend them."

"I don't doubt it," the man with the burned face said, nervously eyeing mother and daughter. "Dreamer, they sure do grow 'em big in these parts." A moment later, he stuck out his hand. "My mates call me Kit."

Other introductions ensued, but neither Taziem nor Lathwi paid attention to them. They were busy exchanging impressions.

"These are not the dragonslayers," Taziem said.

"How can you be sure?" Lathwi asked. *"Between the seven of them, they have the strength to hold a youngling down. And the one called Kit could have gotten those burns from a dragon."*

Taziem disparaged such sloppy thinking with a snort. *"Younglings cannot breathe fire. And these men do not smell of dragon's blood."*

Embarrassment blazed through Lathwi like the onset of a fever. In her eagerness to catch the youngling slayers before they could murder again, she had blinded herself to the obvious. But she cordoned off every last shred of chagrin before offering Taziem her next thought.

"Then this visit has served its purpose. Shall we move on?"

"No," Taziem replied. *"I ache all over from so much walking. I will stay here tonight. Perhaps Luke will rub my legs again before I go to sleep."*

Lathwi pictured the gypsy as a fawning lapdog. Taziem dismissed the image with a snort. *"You were the same as a youngling—very respectful and considerate. You would do well to remember those days."*

Just then, Pawl imposed himself on their conversation. In a voice pitched low for privacy, he said, "We have been invited to share their fire and food. What think you?"

Taziem grinned, exposing a mouthful of slightly too-sharp teeth. Aloud, she said, "I think I hunger."

The man called Wally let out a whoop. "Break out the gish, boys," he said. "We got us a party." Then, as one of the men went trotting toward a shabby-looking tent in the background, he turned to Taziem and winked. "Dinner's gonna be an hour or so, darling, so why don't you have a seat right here—" He patted the back of the fallen tree on which he was perched. "—and keep me company for a while?" When she made no immediate move to join him, he added, "I'll take good care of you, I promise I will, and you can tear my eyeballs out if I insult you in any way."

Taziem studied the man for a long moment. He had a long, wiry beard and hairy arms. His belly bulged like a youngling's after a good gorging. He could be fun, she told herself. And if not, well, perhaps she would learn something anyway. So she strode over and sat down beside him. As she did so, his face blossomed with pleasure.

"I never seen a black woman before," he said. "Is your skin as soft as it looks?"

Taziem flashed him a coy smile, encouraging him to see for himself. But he was not quite so brave. "Not much for talking, are you?" he said instead. "Well, that's fine by me." He grabbed the jug from which Kit was drinking and handed it to her. "Here, have some of this gish. It'll put hair on your chest."

The notion intrigued her so she took a sip. The gish warmed her throat as it went down and made a pleasant afterglow in her belly, but no hair appeared on her breastbone. Wondering if perhaps she had not swallowed enough, she took another, bigger swig. The glow in her belly crept into her veins.

"This is very tasty," she told Lathwi, but did not offer to share.

Lathwi would not accepted such an offer anyway. She had quite liked her first taste of gish, too—that, and the tingly sort of warmth that it brought to her innards. But she had in no way enjoyed its aftereffects the next morning. Her head had been so sore, it could have burst like a rotten gourd and she would not have cared. That was why her first experience with gish had also been her last. She made no mention of this to Taziem, though, because as Taziem herself had said on numerous occasions, experience was the surest teacher. Instead, she sat back in the deepening twilight to observe the goings-on. Pawl was discussing the day's weather with a cluster of campers, Luke was hovering in the background, waiting for a chance to wait on Taziem, and Taziem was—well, Taziem was fraternizing with Wally. That stunned Lathwi. She'd expected her rather aristocratic mother to overlook such a flabby, loud, and oh-so-hairy creature. She shook her head, a gesture of amazement and respect. Leave it to the Learned One to defy expectation.

"Cosians brew the best beer," a man called Tap said. He was small and wiry, with the scruffy, half-grown mane of a juvenile lion. "It's blacker than a cold winter night, and bitter enough to quench any thirst."

"Of course it's black," Wally boomed. "They make it out of swamp-water."

Laughter ensued. The gish jug bobbed from hand to hand again. When it came to Pawl, he handed it on to the man with the burns on his face without taking a swallow. As an afterthought, or so it seemed, he said, "I've got a salve in my pack that might help with those scars."

"Thanks," Kit replied, "but they're pretty much healed already."

"What happened?" Pawl asked. "If you don't mind my asking."

"Nah, I don't mind." The man took a pull from the jug, then wiped his mouth on his dirty sleeve and said, "A dragon attacked the gold mine we were working."

Pawl tensed. So did Lathwi.

"It seemed like a sweet deal at first," Wally chimed in. "That mine was so rich, you could almost pull the gold from the rock with your bare hands. And even though the dig was south of the borderlands, we were being paid northern wages, with over-quota bonuses.

"But nobody told us about the dragon.

"It came roaring out of the sky one evening as we were heading for the mess-tent. Fires broke out. Men panicked. Me and the boys bolted for the mine for cover. That's when Kit here got burned: the dragon scorched him in passing. But even he has to admit he was one of the luckier ones. By the time that red bastard flew off, the whole camp was in blazes, and five men were dead."

The image of an enormous, cinnamon-colored dragon popped into Lathwi's head. It was accompanied by a Name: Bij, her mother's Chosen. *"He has been roaring about people trespassing on his territory these past few years,"* Taziem said. *"Apparently, he has decided to try and terrorize them into going away. I told him that such a ploy would not work, but he refuses to listen to me. He hates humans too much to try and understand them."*

"...so while we're getting patched up, this old-timer lets it slip that the dragon has some kind of a grudge against the camp and shows up to level it on a regular basis," Tap was saying now. "Needless to say, we high-tailed it out of there as soon as we got Kit's burns cleaned up. The foreman tried to bribe us into staying, but what good is money in a dead man's pockets? If Veeder wants gold out of that mine, he can get his followers to dig it for him."

"Who's this Veeder?" Pawl asked.

"Ever hear of a southern warrior-cult called the Grangers?" Tap asked. When Pawl shook his head, the wiry young miner said, "Well, Veeder is the head of that cult."

"He's a savage bastard, too," Kit said, as he passed the gish jug back to Wally. "The meanest of the mean. They say he's got most of the south under his thumb already. They say he dreams of conquering the north, too."

Wally snorted. "They say that about every southerner who ever made his mother bleed at birth. The only thing I know for sure about him is that he paid good wages." He scowled in the direction of the fire then and said, "Is that meat done yet?"

It was.

The miners converged on the spit with knives in hand. Scant minutes later, they were back with tin pans heaped with meat. "If you're hungry," Wally said, as he strode past Pawl with a pair of plates, "feel free to help yourself. There's plenty." Then he set a plate on Taziem's lap and said, "Here you go, darlin'. I told you I'd take care of you, didn't I?"

Taziem lobbed a thought at Lathwi. *"I like the way human males treat human females."*

"Not all women would say the same," Lathwi replied.

"Are you not hungered?" Taziem asked, projecting a sense of vast emptiness.

"I do not like the taste of char."

"You always were a fussy eater."

With that, Taziem returned the whole of her attention to the mound of roasted venison on her lap. She fed with typical dragon gusto, but none of the miners seemed to notice or care. They were too busy shoveling meat into their own maws. Uninterested in watching this frenzy, Lathwi got up and meandered into the woods. A few minutes later, Pawl joined her. He had two fresh-cut staves with him. The smell of sap made the night seem sticky.

"I was wondering if you remembered any of your lessons," he said

"I remember everything," she replied, no boast but a simple matter of fact.

"Would you care to prove it?" he asked, offering her one of the staves.

She accepted the challenge with a grin that took a chilling turn as she adopted a fighting stance. "If you even think of whacking me for being out of position," she said, "I will give my mother permission to eat you."

While Pawl's swordmaster facade never wavered, shockwaves rippled through him nonetheless. Distraction through intimidation: it was bold strategy against a superior opponent. And damned if it wasn't working—if only just a bit. His shock dissipated, leaving admiration in its wake. Sweet Dreamer! Now here was a fighter worthy of her sword.

They started with the old exercises: thrust, parry, jab; jab, parry, thrust. Lathwi was rusty at first, but she held true to her claim. The forms, the steps, the strategies—she appeared to remember them all. Pawl stepped up the pace, once and then again. Lathwi responded with glee, smiling as she never smiled at rest. No words passed between them, but he did not care. It was enough to be dancing this dance with her.

The drill session went on for a good long time, and might have lasted even longer if a round of excited shouting had not broken out back at the campsite.

"C'mon, Taz, give 'em a roll!"

"Fox-eyes will get you a luc!"

Lathwi arched a curious eyebrow at Pawl. She was breathing just a little harder than Pawl was. She smelled of good, clean sweat. "Why would somebody want a fox's eyes?" she asked. "Are they good to eat?"

"They're not talking about real fox eyes," Pawl replied, trying not to smile at her mistake. "It's just a term used in dicing games."

That piqued her interest. She liked games. And she was in a mood to play. So she pitched her stave into the night without another word and headed back toward camp. As she did so, she heard Wally roar, "Har! Wagon ruts. Bad luck, darlin'. You lose." A moment later, Kit called out. "My turn, Taz. Lemme see a dozen pearls."

Now that their bellies were full of meat and gish, the miners were a much livelier and louder lot. Indeed, they seemed to Lathwi like a party of juvenile carrion crows at their very first carcass—laughing and cawing and hopping from foot to foot as they tried to steal morsels from each other. And Taziem seemed quite at home in their midst. She had a mug of gish in one hand and a pair of small wooden cubes in the other. Luke was standing watch at her shoulder. Wally was whispering in her ear.

"C'mon, Tazzie," Tappy urged. "Toss 'em."

Taziem cheerfully obliged. The miners let out a raucous cheer as the cubes rolled to a standstill, but Luke made a sour face and handed Wally a small copper coin. Lathwi wondered about that.

"How is this game played?" she asked Taziem.

"My task is to throw these hunks of wood called dice," Taziem replied, a thought fringed with a predator's pleasure. *"Somebody else predicts which combination of faces will turn up. When my throw matches the prediction, Wally and the other men give me things."*

Lathwi made the connection immediately: dicing was another word for gambling. How disappointing. She much preferred contests of skill or strength to those of luck. But while she no longer had any desire to join the game, she was still curious enough about its particulars to stand in the background and watch it being played. Taziem threw the dice, again and again and again. When the throw was true, she gleefully collected the miners's bets and stashed them out of sight. When the throw turned up bad, she simply shrugged and scooped the dice up again, seemingly unaware that Luke was covertly paying off her bets out of his own pocket. Lathwi rumbled to herself. That was *not* the proper way to gain stature in a dragon's eyes. Adult dragons did not respect generosity. Nor did they appreciate being misled. Had Lathwi been so inclined, she would have advised Luke to withhold his coins until Taziem promised him something in return for them. But she was not the type to tender advice, solicited or otherwise. The gypsy would have to learn on his own.

And so would her mother. Lathwi hoped to be there on the day when Taziem went to gamble without Luke by her side.

As Lathwi watched on from the shadows, the miners drank the gish jug dry. One by one, they then scooped up their winnings and went shambling off in search of their bed rolls. Soon, Wally and Taziem were the only ones left in the dicing circle.

"Well, darlin'," he slurred, "what do you say? I have a tent. You wanna join me for a little tupping? I'm prolly not the best-looking man you ever saw, but I know a trick or two that'll make up for that."

Taziem lobbed a query at Lathwi. *"What is tupping?"*

Lathwi responded with a wry image of two dragons in rut.

Taziem snorted, amused by the man's audacity and then arched her neck to show it off. *"How very intriguing. It had not occurred to me to study this aspect of human behavior."* A moment later, she asked, *"What are these tricks he speaks of?"*

"*I do not know,*" Lathwi said.

"Well, Taz?" Wally prompted. "You interested?"

"Yessss," she replied, flashing him a playful dragon's grin. "I wish to know more of these tricks."

He gaped at her for a moment as if dazed by his good luck, then scrabbled to his feet and ushered her to hers. "Anything you want, darlin'," he gabbled, as he led her into the night. "Anything at all."

Lathwi rolled her eyes. Now her mother had two lapdogs in her thrall. Whatever did she see in such unbecoming and such un-dragon-like behavior? Minded of the gypsy, she glanced toward the spot where she had last seen him. But the man who was standing those shadows now was Pawl, not Luke, and he was scowling in the direction that Taziem and Wally had gone.

"Aren't you going to warn him?" he asked, in a low, fierce voice.

"Why would I do that?" she asked.

"She's had enough gish to knock out a horse."

She shrugged, unconcerned. "My mother is not a horse."

"But she's not a woman, either," he argued.

"Would you care to bet on that?"

He glowered at her for a moment, looking outraged and appalled and frustrated. Then he turned his back on her with a muttered curse and disappeared into the night. In his absence, her thoughts turned to her belly. That drill session had left her exceptionally hungry. And charred or not, there was still a lot of meat left from the miners' feast. She unsheathed her knife, then padded over to the spit to help herself. As she did so, a muted play-rumble rippled out of the darkness. An appreciative groan followed, then a series of grunts. She had no desire to listen to more of such noises, so she moved beyond the fire's dying light in search of a quieter place to eat. But as she hunted for an agreeable spot, a large blur with yellow eyes sprang at her from out of the darkness. It hit her in the chest and knocked her to the ground. As she rolled away from its weight, something both furry and sharp grazed the left side of her neck. She hissed, more from insult than injury, then leapt to her feet. The shadow-cat sprang at her again, only to fall dead at her feet.

"Sweet, suffering Dreamer!"

She pivoted toward the voice to see Pawl hurrying her way. He did not take his eyes away from the cat until he had prodded it several times with his sword. "No blood," he murmured, as he examined it. "No marks of any kind." When he finally looked at her, his expression was so puzzled as to be almost comical. "How'd you do it?"

She shrugged. "I stopped its heart with a Word."

His bafflement gave way to self-disgust. "I should have guessed," he said, with a small shake of his head. "But I always forget about that part of you.

"Are you hurt?"

As if in response to the question, her neck began to sting. When she probed the area with her fingers, she found three blood-sticky welts in the flesh below her ear. She hissed at herself for walking right into the cat's ambush, and for wandering around in the woods with her hood down in the first place. Any other fool would have been half-eaten by now. Fortune had favored her again.

Then she realized that her amulet was missing.

She dropped to her knees and began sifting through the dirt and weeds and fallen leaves that constitute a forest floor. That amulet allowed her to work magic any time and any place she so desired without fear of detection by other sorcerers. That amulet was a safeguard beyond compare. If she could not find it, she would have to create a new one, and *that* was not a process she cared to repeat. Ever.

"Lathwi," Pawl said, a naming both urgent and wary. "I think you had better take a look at this."

"Not now, Pawl," she told him, not bothering to look up. "I have lost my amulet. I must find it."

"The amulet can wait," he insisted.

She twisted around to snap at him for distracting her only to be distracted again by a pale, bluish-white glow that was bobbing through the woods and toward them. At first, she supposed it was one of the miners with a lamp, but as it drew nearer, she changed her mind. For there was no body behind this glow; it had a shape all of its own.

"Liselle," she blurted, recognizing the heart-shaped face.

In reply, the apparition moaned Lathwi's name. Someone else might have found the hollow, windswept sound frightening. But Lathwi was too intrigued to be alarmed.

"How is this possible?" Lathwi asked.

"Some evils transcend death. Others find ways to corrupt it."

Lathwi scowled. Dead or not, her ex-mentor had not changed in one respect—she still loved to confuse an issue with too many words. "Your meaning is not clear."

"What is clarity to a ghost?" A bitter half-smile shimmered across her nebulous face, then lapsed contrite. "Forgive me. The Dreamer understands all thoughts, even as they are being formed. One gets so very used to these things."

Tendrils of impatience began to strangle Lathwi's curiosity. Leave it to Liselle to find a way to vex her from the grave! "Just say why you are here."

"One moment, I was sleeping in The Dreamer's embrace," the ghost said. "The next, I was being dragged from Her side along with scores of other souls. We struggled. We wept. But all for naught. The Dreamer slept on, and we were sucked back into this world." She let out a wail then, a hair-raising sound of loss and despair. "Why did You forsake us, Mother? Why did You let us go?"

Although Lathwi was not the least bit surprised to hear that the feckless Dreamer had abandoned Liselle, she did not say so aloud. That would serve no intelligent purpose, and besides, she remembered all too well how she had felt when Taziem evicted her from her nest. The sense of isolation had been so intense, she might have gone rogue from it if she had not been promised an eventual reprieve.

"How was such an ill accomplished?" she asked.

The anguish bled away from Liselle's spectral eyes, leaving them cold and gray as death-wounds. "I believe it was the work of a necromancer—"

"I do not recognize that word."

Liselle scowled just as she had when someone interrupted her back in olden times. And her tone acquired the same impatient edge. "A necromancer is a mage who uses the power of death to work his spells."

"But why would he use that power to disturb the dead?" Lathwi wondered aloud. "What good are ghosts to a sorcerer?"

"He sent us north with a compulsion to haunt the living—"

"Why?" Pawl asked sharply, as if he were grilling some careless recruit.

Quick as a passing thought, the ghost's visage changed. Its woeful eyes became hollow sockets. The semblance of skin shredded into rotting tatters. An instant later, its original facade returned and it went on with what it had been saying as if Pawl had never spoken. "But I do not believe that that is his sole purpose. For even as I was being torn from The Dreamer, I felt a faint, fleeting presence. I think it was looking for someone."

"Who?" Lathwi asked.

"I do not know," the ghost replied.

"So what would you have me do?" Lathwi asked.

"You must find this necromancer and destroy him."

Liselle was a more commanding presence as a ghost than she had ever been as a flesh and blood woman. Even so, Lathwi was not about to go charging blindly off to do her bidding—if she went charging off at all. She had no grudge against this necromancer. True, he did not sound like a pleasant individual. But if she were to go around destroying every person who offended her superior sensibilities, there would be very few people left on the world.

"Why?" she asked.

The apparition flickered as if it were struggling to stay in focus. The look on its face was one of surprise and irritation. "Why? Because he knows things that no mortal should know. That's why. Because he has the power to break into The Dreamer's Keep and steal the dead."

Lathwi shrugged. "That is your Dreamer's problem, not mine."

"Then think of all the misery he's causing," Liselle urged, "to the living as well as to the dead. You must stop him before he drives more ghosts into the north to haunt its people."

Again, Lathwi shrugged. "That is none of my concern, either. The dead do not bother dragons."

The apparition flickered again, and this time, only one side of its face phased back into focus. The other half remained an ethereal blur. In a withering, hollowed-out voice, it said, "I had forgotten how intensely selfish you are, Soft One. And I do not thank you for the reminder. Nevertheless, I appeal to you to do this deed one last time. If you will not do it for any other reason, then do it for me."

"Why?" Lathwi persisted.

"Because I will never be able to return to The Dreamer's embrace otherwise," the ghost admitted, and then loosed another despairing wail. "I will be trapped here, doomed to an eternity of hopeless exile." It extended an ethereal hand. "Please. I beg you by the bonds that we once shared. Do not condemn me to such a fate."

A swirl of wry amusement eddied through Lathwi. It seemed that death had had even less impact on Liselle than she had imagined. For her old mentor had always been quick to accuse others of being selfish even as she tried to pretend that she was otherwise. But now that the truth of the matter was out in plain view, Lathwi's path loomed clear as well. She would not abandon her hunt for dragonslayers on behalf of strangers, be they living or be they dead. But she would do it for The Trueheart—because she had Called, and because she was in Need. As Taziem had said, respect was due.

"Tell me where I may find this necromage," she said.

The ghost sagged as if with relief. A moment later, it began to disintegrate as if suspense had been the only thing keeping it intact. Lathwi summoned her Will, thinking to use her power to sustain its presence, but the phantom forestalled her with a shake of its head.

"It will not help," it whispered. "The compulsion is drawing me away."

"Will you come again?" Lathwi asked.

"I will try. But you are very hard to find when you are wearing your amulet. And you must not take that off again."

"Then look for me instead," Pawl said. "I'll be with her."

The ghost glanced in his direction. There was almost nothing left to it now, just a pair of bereft eyes contained within a wispy ribbon of blue-gray mist. "The necromancer has made his stronghold at Death's Door," it whispered, and then disappeared like a slip of smoke in a wind. Pawl stared after it until Lathwi called his attention to her. She was feeling around for her amulet again, and grumbling furiously at the same time.

"Death's Door? Death's Door? What does that mean? Is the mage dying? Must I kill myself to find him?" She hissed. "What a stupid time for her to take up riddling."

"It's a place," Pawl said.

Her head swiveled toward him. A warning gleamed bright in her eyes. "What did you say?"

"It's to the south and east of here," he elaborated, "somewhere in the hills beyond the border. Wally mentioned it earlier. He said Veeder's men are camped somewhere around there. Apparently, it's not a very nice place."

"That is the way of most sorcerers' strongholds," she said, and then loosed a glad croon as she plucked her amulet up from the ground.

"Want me to scrounge up a tie for that?" he asked.

"No," she replied. "The chain must be made of something that bears my essence."

She sat herself down in the dirt, then pulled a hank of her long, black hair over her shoulder and began to weave it into a tight, thin braid. When she was done, she cut it off with her knife. Acting on an afterthought, she then began hacking at the rest of her locks.

"No!" Pawl yelped. "Don't."

"Why not?" she asked, looking at him askance. "Hair is a nuisance and unsightly, too."

"In the southlands, short hair is considered indecent," he said. "The most tolerant Southerners will only shun you for that. The least tolerant will try to kill you."

She hissed. "Fools. Someone should teach them the true meaning of indecency."

But to Pawl's relief, she returned the knife to its sheath and resumed her repairs. As she threaded the braid through the stone's tiny eye, she asked, "Did Wally happen to mention how many days it will take to reach this place?"

"He said it took him and his mates a month to get here from Veeder's gold mine on foot," Pawl replied. "If we scrounge ourselves a couple of horses, we can cover the same distance in less than a fortnight. And unless I miss my guess, that will put us in the same vicinity as Veeder's camp. He's not going to let something that rich go unguarded."

"We?" Lathwi asked, in a tone as arched as her eyebrow. "Us? I thought you were bound for Compara."

"Jamus sent me to find you in the hope of appeasing Liselle's ghost. It now seems that I can best do that by going south with you. Besides," he added, without prompting, "I'm curious about General Veeder. I want a look at this army of his."

She wrapped the braid around her neck, then Willed its ends to form a seamless bond. Afterward, as she tugged on the chain to test its tensile strength, she looked Pawl in the eye and said, "This Veeder is no concern of mine. I will not go the least bit out of my way for him."

"I didn't figure you would," he replied. "But since he and your mage seem to be keeping the same company these days, I don't think that will be a problem."

Her eyes narrowed as if she were trying to see past him and all the way to Death's Door. "You think the two are allied?"

"At this point, they're connected only by circumstance," he said. "But their being in the same vicinity at the same time seems like more than a mere coincidence. Wouldn't you say?"

Now that she thought about it, their proximity did seem suspicious. But that did not make a whit of difference to her game-plan. She was hunting for the mage, and only the mage. His allies were free to do as they pleased as long as they stayed out of her way. She said as much to Pawl, too, but he did not seem to hear. He was rubbing his knuckles across his stubbled chin and staring into the night.

"Maybe the garrison commander at New Uxla will be able to tell me more," he said at last. We have to stop there anyway."

"Why?" Lathwi asked, instantly wary. One stop here, another there, and the next thing she knew, she'd be a year older and still no closer to finding the mage. Humans had a terrible tendency to dawdle.

"Well, for one thing," Pawl said, "an old shield-mate of mine owns a stable there. We'll be able to buy horses from him. And for another, that's the closest messenger relay station in this area. I need to get a message to Compara."

Those last five words triggered a memory in Lathwi: her standing in the middle of a Comparan bazaar with Pawl. She had a message for Jamus tucked into her belt and no idea as to where to deliver it. *"Is it important?"* Pawl had asked her. She repeated the question now.

"I would say so, yes," he said. "The sooner Jamie knows that there's a sorcerer behind Compara's plague of ghosts, the sooner he can take appropriate countermeasures. And from what I saw in the hours before I left the city, sooner isn't soon enough. If there were a quicker way of getting word to him, I'd do it."

The memory continued. In it, Pawl took the message from her and ordered one of his underlings to deliver it. Now seemed like an appropriate time to do the same—not for Jamus' sake, but for the swordmaster's. For some reason, his peace of mind mattered to her. And if helping him out now meant that they would not have to stop in this New Uxla later, well, who could find fault with that?

"Write your message down on something," she told him. "I will see that Jamus receives it. Ask me no questions," she warned, as he opened his mouth to do just that, "for you will not like the answers."

"I'll be back," he replied, and then hurried back to the campsite. Curiosity dogged him every step of the way. *What was she up to? What could she do? And why was he so thrilled?* He scavenged a scrap of deer-hide from the midden heap, then carved a note into its hairless underside with the tip of his knife. When he was done, he sprinkled ashes over the writing, then rolled the scrap into a tight scroll and headed back toward the spot where he had left Lathwi. On his way, he wondered once again what she had in mind. It would have to involve magic, he supposed. Elsewise, she would not be so secretive. But she was wrong in thinking that he would be opposed to her using sorcery to get his report to Jamus. Indeed, he rather liked the idea—and not just because it was expedient. When that scroll popped into his lap from out of nowhere, Milord Jamie was apt to piss himself and anyone else who happened to be in the vicinity.

Pawl chuckled at the image that came to his mind. He was still chuckling when he rejoined Lathwi. She did not ask what he found so funny. She simply took the scroll and bade him to go away. "Give my old friend an extra scare for me," he said, and then cheerfully went in search of his bed-roll.

As soon as Pawl was gone, Lathwi Voiced a Name. When she received no reply, she Called again. *"I know you are here, little one,"* she said. *"Be not afraid. I am not angry with you for following us."*

Again, silence followed her Call. Moments later, however, a soft, steady rustling stirred up the darkness. Moments after that, a calico shadow appeared among the trees. As it strode toward her, it broadcast a grumpy thought.

"I was not afraid. I was sleeping."

"If you wish to go back to sleep, do so," Lathwi said, radiating nonchalance. *"I will let the scavengers have this shadow-cat carcass."*

Interest flared in her young tanglemate's mind along with an impression of a vast, unfillable void. *"Cat? I like cat. And I am not* that *tired."*

"Then the meat is yours."

Masque rushed the carrion and began to gobble it down in typical eat-it-or-lose-it style. In almost no time at all, only a few tufts of fur remained. The youngling gave these a hopeful sniff, then smacked its lips and flopped onto its back. Lathwi strode over and began to scratch its belly.

"Mmm, that feels good," it crooned. *"Get the armpits, too."*

Lathwi scratched until Masque's thoughts turned into a contented hum. Then she extended a thought. *"I would have you do something for me, little one."*

The hum acquired a wary edge. *"What would that something be?"*

She answered with a series of images: the scroll; white-walled Compara; Masque flying the distance between here and there. The youngling rolled onto its belly and stared at her. Its thoughts were abuzz now. A sly gleam danced in its amber eyes.

"I will do this for you," it said, *"but only if you promise to let me come and see you whenever I want."*

"I cannot do that," Lathwi replied.

"Then promise to give me a diamond every time you send me away." When Lathwi refused this, too, it loosed a scornful sniff and then curled itself into a ball. *"Then go away. I am very tired."*

"Then go to sleep, little one," she urged it, projecting unconcern. *"I will Call Pinch and ask it to do this thing. Pinch is bigger than you. Perhaps it will not be so tired."*

The youngling let out a disapproving hiss, and then hooked necks with her before she could walk away. *"Do not Call Pinch, Soft One,"* it said. *"That dragon will lose your scroll, eat your human, and then tell everyone how it tricked you afterward. I will do this thing for you, if only to spoil its fun."*

In reply, Lathwi freed herself from Masque's neck-hold and touched noses with it—a gesture of affinity and affection. She was not angry with her tanglemate for trying to coerce a promise out of her. That was the way of dragons—young and old. The old simply knew how to play the game better.

"I will not Call Pinch," she told it. *"I want you to go to Compara for me."*

The little dragon nuzzled Lathwi, commending for her good sense, and then went suddenly forlorn. *"Must I go now, though?"* it asked, filling the thought with entreaty. *"I truly am quite tired."*

Lathwi's affection crested to new heights. She cradled Masque's triangular head in her hands and smiled into its eyes. *"No, little one,"* she replied, *"you do not have to go just yet. Let us curl up right here and sleep until morning."*

And that was exactly what they did.

Chapter 5

ragon!"

Lathwi was on her way back to the camp with a belly full of rabbit when she heard the shout. Her immediate reaction was to wonder why someone would be shouting at her on such a fine morning.

"Run for it, boys!"

With that, the truth of the matter dawned on her—a slow, rosy bloom of sardonic amusement and scorn. The shouter was not talking to her. Nor was he talking about her. She was becoming as self-centered as Taziem, she told herself, and then snorted. Taziem would no doubt consider that great progress. She wondered if her mother had caused the current uproar. It would not be unlike her to Change back into dragonform so she could hunt for breakfast.

"C'mon! Run! It's probably right behind me."

Lathwi snorted. He was sorely mistaken if he thought he could outrun a dragon. Even leisurely Taziem could cover a lot of ground in a hurry when she was hungry. Like as not, though, the shouter would never find that out—leastwise not today, she thought, as she strode into the camp. No dragon in these woods could possibly be *that* hungry.

The miners were standing in a clump around the stone-cold fire-pit. They looked disheveled, disarrayed, and thoroughly hungover—all save the one called Kit. He was as agitated as a hungry shrew.

"Don't tell me what I did or didn't see," he was hollering now. "The damned thing nearly walked right over me while I was popping a squat in the bushes. You gotta believe me, fellas—there's a dragon out there. A big black and red one."

"Just like there was a giant albino spider in the mine that time, right?" Tap jeered. "C'mon, Kit. You always get like this when you drink too much the night before. And you know as well as I do that dragons don't go aground in the woods. The trees bother them."

Lathwi wondered where they had gotten that idea. Back in the days of Ever-Light, dragons had actually made their nests in the tops of sky-scraping dragon-trees. And while Galza's minions had since burned all of those marvelous trees from the face of the world, the skyfolk still had a tender spot in their hearts for living wood. She rumbled to herself. Dragons bothered by trees? Some humans would believe anything.

Meanwhile, the human called Kit refused to be pacified. He glanced to the left and to the right, sputtering all the while, and then demanded to know where Wally was.

"He hasn't shown his face yet this morning," Tappy said, smirking as he glanced toward the old man's tent. "The poor devil must be exhausted."

"Well, as soon as he comes out," Kit said, "he's gonna hear about this. It's time we moved on to Timberton. It'll be safer there."

"At least until the next time you get drunk," somebody cracked.

"Shut up," he snarled back, and then started like a spooked jackrabbit as a rustling sound broke out in the woods to his rear. "Oh," he said, as Pawl and Luke came strolling into camp. "It's just you."

"'Morning to you, too," Pawl said in passing. He looked spry and well-rested—happy, Lathwi would have said. But as he and the gypsy converged on her, he kept the miners in surreptitious view. "What was all the shouting about?" he asked, when he was close enough to pitch his voice low.

"One of them thought he saw a dragon in the woods," she replied with a shrug.

Pawl gave the woods a wary sweep with his eyes. "Did he?"

"I do not know," she said. Which was the truth, dragon-style. Kit had claimed to see a red and black dragon. That could have been Masque. She had sent the youngling off with Pawl's message, an image of Jamus, and a True-Finding spell early this morning, but it could have decided to double back for one last fortifying snack. Since she had not been with the miner or the youngling at the time of the sighting, she could only speculate. And that was not the same as knowing for sure.

Her ignorance seemed to relieve him. He lowered his guard, then dug three shiny red apples from the rucksack that he was carrying. Lathwi refused the one that he offered to her, but Luke snapped his share up without a moment's hesitation. As the two men ate, Pawl briefed Lathwi.

"I told Luke about our change of plans," he said between bites. "He wants to know if Taziem is coming with us. Frankly, I'm curious about that, too."

"Taziem has sworn to find the dragonslayers," Lathwi said, both a reminder and a rebuke. "Dragons do not forsake their vows."

Pawl smiled around a last mouthful of fruit. "Then what are we waiting for?" he asked. "Let's be on our way while the day's still cool."

Before she could say yea or nay to that proposal, the flap to Wally's tent opened with a leathery snap. A moment later, Taziem strode forth, nostrils flared to test the air. The thought she pulsed at Lathwi was surprisingly lively.

"*Tell Luke to bring me something tasty to eat,*" she said. "*I am very hungry this morning.*"

Lathwi snorted. "*You can talk. Tell him yourself.*"

Taziem offered her an image of a dragon's snarl, then started across the campsite. There was an unselfconscious bounce in her step. Her eyes gleamed clear and pain-free. Lathwi would never have guessed that she had spent the whole of last night drinking gish.

"How do you feel?" she asked, as Taziem approached.

"I am very hungry," Taziem complained.

An instant later, Luke was gone. He left so quietly, and so quickly, Lathwi did not even catch him in the act, and she was very good at noticing such things.

"I'm off to the creek to fill our canteens," Pawl said to Lathwi. "Let me know when you're ready to leave."

As he hurried off, Taziem gave his backside a long, speculative look. "*That one is very well-made,*" she noted. "*How is his endurance?*"

"*He survived a mauling by krim,*" Lathwi replied, which was the ultimate in endurance as far as she was concerned. "*Why do you ask?*"

Her mother glanced back toward Wally's tent. "*That one proved to be a disappointment.*"

"*How so?*"

"*He showed me a few of his so-called tricks,*" she said, projecting a daisy-chain of erotic images that were both unabashed and explicit. "*But just when things were starting to get truly interesting, he let out a groan and went cold.*" As she replayed that thought, she looked for Pawl. But he was no longer in sight. "*Why is he in such a hurry? Can he not see that I am not ready to resume our journey yet?*"

"Our paths no longer coincide, Mother. Liselle TrueHeart came to me last night."

She passed on the memory of that midnight visitation, and then chased it with her decision to go south after the necromage. Afterward, Taziem rumbled approvingly. "*The TrueHeart sacrificed herself for dragons,*" she said. "*Her Need cannot be ignored.*" Then an impression of danger crept into her thoughts. "*You will have to take care when you cross into that country. For you will also be crossing into Bij's territory, and he does not like trespassers, be they men or dragons.*"

Lathwi wondered if she should mention that to Pawl. If he knew about Bij, he might change his mind about going with her. She was not completely sure that that was a good thing at this point. And before she could make a decision one way or the other, a shout distracted her.

"Hey, fellas! C'mere."

Once again, the man doing the barking turned out to be Kit. Lathwi spotted him in front of Wally's tent. He was waving his mates toward the opening. They scorned him with hoots and jeers. One of them made a joke about him finding the dragon's lair.

"You got it all wrong," Kit said. "It's Wal. He's dead."

"Dead?" Lathwi echoed, chasing the thought with a pulse of mild surprise.

Taziem shrugged her wonder aside. *"I told you he went cold."*

Pawl returned from the creek just in time to hear that Wally was dead. Horror sprouted within him, a trellis for his guilt. He *knew* he should not have let Taziem mingle with these miners. Or, barring that, he should have exposed her for what she really was. Poor old Wally would've stood a chance then—or at least a running start. But no, Pawl had held his tongue and now Wal was dead. He could just imagine what lay beyond that tent-flap: blood-splattered canvas and body parts everywhere. As soon as Kit and his mates got over the shock of that, they'd be out for blood themselves. Then Taziem—with Lathwi's help, no doubt—would make stew-meat out of the whole lot. Pawl did not want that to happen. So he made a bee-line for the tent, meaning to issue an emphatic warning and be off. The miners were inside already. He could hear murmuring: "Sweet, suffering Dreamer," and "Can you imagine it?" He could. Nevertheless, he ground his trepidation into a sour paste between his molars, and then pushed the flap out of his way. There was no blood in sight, and no gore. There was only old Wally, sprawled on his back on a pile of rancid furs, stark naked and still stiff where it counted. His eyes were wide-open. His mouth was a surprised little 'O'.

"That's the way I wanna go," Kit said.

"Likewise," Tap murmured.

The miners took one last look at their erstwhile companion and then started filing back out of the tent. No one said anything about revenge or retribution. Nor did anyone mention Taziem. Kit gave Pawl a brotherly clap on the back in passing. Tap shook his hand as if in thanks. Pawl was astounded; amazed; abashed. How could he have been so wrong about these men? And how could he have been so wrong about *Taziem?*

He turned to leave only to find Luke standing behind him. The young gypsy had a brace of rabbits in his hand.

"Do you think The Great One will like these?" he asked.

"It would appear that I have no talent for predicting the predilections of dragons," he said, glancing back at Wally's body. "Still, if I were you, I wouldn't be in such a rush to please her. Otherwise, you could wind up like this fellow."

"Do you truly think so?" Luke gazed at the corpse for a long moment. As he did so, he gnawed on his lower lip like a man tempted. "I have been told that I am lucky," he said at last. "But that—" He gestured at Wal's hard-on as if it were a battle-standard to be saluted. "—that would be the ultimate honor."

Pawl rolled his eyes, then took his leave of the tent. He would never understand some people, no matter how hard he tried.

"Come on, Lathwi," he said. "Let's get going."

Minutes later, they were on their way.

Chapter 6

*Y*ou*'re a damned disgrace, D'Arques!"*

The words echoed through Jamus' head, bitter counterpoint to the pounding of his horse's hooves on the dusty, hard-packed road. That rhythm sounded like *his fault, his fault, his fault.* He wanted to deny it, but could not. Twenty-six people were dead. Scores more were injured. And the renowned Comparan bazaar had been trampled into the cobblestones.

His fault, his fault, his fault.

In his mind's eye, he could still see Randall marching his troops through that gap in the garrison gates. The rioters drew back a few steps, a viscerally satisfying sight, and then surged forward again like some great, flesh-and-blood tide. From his vantage point on the catwalk, Jamus heard Randall order his men to disperse the mob. Then someone fell to a soldier's stave, and the world beyond the gate erupted into a battle zone. Rocks and bottles whizzed through the air. Staves flew fast and furious. One rioter went down, then another. Randall ordered his recruits to give quarter when possible, but they had the taste of blood in their mouths and discipline's bit between their teeth, and so continued to dish out punishment. Three more rioters dropped. The mob began to pull back then, no orderly retreat, but a human stampede that trampled everything in its way. The surgeon said at least ten people died that way.

His fault. His fault. His fault.

All he had wanted to do was scare the rats back into their holes!

And teach them a lesson they would never forget.

Twenty-six people. Twenty-six fools. Their blood now stained the paving stones in front of the garrison gates. Their friends and relatives now clamored for Jamus' head.

And Wynn Rame seemed ready to give it to them.

"What were you thinking?" the governor had bellowed, upon his return to the city that night. "Didn't it occur to you that the troops might be just as unstable as the mob?"

"No, Milord," Jamus said, trying hard not to remember the look on Randall's face as one of the recruits—the city tough who had wanted the sword—bashed his skull in like a pecan shell. "It did not."

"You were drunk, weren't you?"

"I was not," he said, righteously, because there was a difference between drinking and being drunk. Then, because he had had a few drinks since then, he gave Wynn some of his own cheek back. "If you don't mind my asking, Milord, what would you have done in my stead? What would you have done if you hadn't been in Bellemares-By-The-Bay, coddling a wife who's young enough to be your granddaughter?"

Wynn turned a lavish shade of red, and then exploded when Jamus mocked him with a snicker. "You're a damned disgrace, D'Arques. Do you hear me? *A disgrace.* There was a time when you cared—not just about yourself, but about the people you're supposed to serve. Now you're just a blowfly looking for its next feast."

"A blowfly?" He knew then that Wynn meant to sack and maybe even scapegoat him, for he was never insulting to those in his service. Resentment burned through Jamus like a shot of gish—*Didn't eighteen years of loyal service count for anything?*—then fizzled into resignation. The job no longer appealed to him anyway. "Bizz-bizz then," he said. "Would you like my resignation in ink or blood?"

"In ink, if you please," the governor said, . "We've seen enough blood around here as it is."

Jamus grabbed the nearest piece of paper, quilled a hasty *I quit!* on its face and then slung it at his former boss. Wynn gave it a cursory glance, then shrugged. His flush was gone now, faded back to a colder shade of fury, but there was a hint of regret in his steel-eyed gaze.

"The politically astute thing to do would be to put you on trial for those twenty-six deaths," he said. "But out of respect for the decent man you once were, I'm only going to exile you. Be gone from Compara by sunrise. If you know what's good for you—and it certainly doesn't appear so anymore—you'll stay away for however long it takes for people to forget you."

Jamus popped up from his chair and sketched the governor a jack-in-the-box bow. "Many thanks for your consideration, Milord. Now, if you'll excuse me, I must go home and pack. I'm going on a trip, you know."

And so here he was, southbound to Hillshire. He had a house in the country there, a little homestead where he could play the gentleman farmer for a few years—*or however long it took the people of Compara to forget him.* He had no doubt that they'd do just that eventually. But there would be no forgetting for him. Twenty-six people were going to follow him for the rest of his life. He could almost feel Randall's surprised eyes boring into his back now.

A good man, but still green.

He pulled a flask from his breast pocket and took a swallow, hoping to medicate himself into a better mood. Bad enough that he'd been exiled, he thought. There was no need to make it worse by being morbid. He took another swig, simply because one was never enough anymore, and then urged his horse to a faster walk.

"Come on, old nag," he said, feeling better already. "If we hurry, we can make the manor by midnight."

Images of his new home came to mind: a cold, cobwebbed hearth, fallen ceilings in the back rooms, an *outdoor* privy. It would take months of hard work to restore the place to a semblance of its former coziness. And even with years of work, it would never be as comfortable as the home that he had left behind. He sighed. Ah, well. The change would do him goo—

The thought fell short, tripped up by the sound of something moving in the woods to his right. He twisted around in his saddle and squinted at the brush, but all he saw was leaves and shadows. Just nerves then, he supposed. But all of a sudden, heading straight to Hillshire didn't seem like a smart idea. As Wynn had so kindly pointed out, he was not very popular in these parts at the moment. Someone could have seen him leaving the city this morning and decided to follow in the hope of leading a mob back to his bolt-hole at a later date. And while Jamus was not particularly keen on life these days, he had not come to the point where he wanted to be murdered in his sleep. He really ought to take a more circuitous route, he thought, and camp in some farmer's haystack tonight. And to be safe, he ought to forego the charms of that farmer's wife or daughter, too—which was the only pleasant thing about sleeping in a haystack.

"Damn you, Wynn," he grumbled. "You should've just hanged me."

Just then, the bushes to his left flank rattled. He did not have to turn around to see if there was anybody there this time. His horse was prancing in place now, telegraphing a nervous warning. He gave it a nudge, urging it forward. It gladly began to run.

ဢ ၷ

The tip of Masque's tail quivered with excitement as the man's beast broke into a run. A chase, a chase! Oh, how it loved a chase!

It took to the air with a gleeful bound and then danced its joy to the sky. It did not have to worry about losing the man. Even if he decided to abandon the road for the cover of the forest, he could not escape Lathwi's true-finding spell. Masque would catch him, yes, yes, it would. So it romped above the treetops, playing tag with a cloud and then its shadow until those games grew boring. Then it went racing after its quarry again. To the youngling's vast delight, the man and his horse were still galloping down the road when it finally caught up with them.

How convenient! How fun! That human was going to be *so* surprised.

Masque flew ahead to a patch of open road. There, it went aground and hid itself behind an illusion of rocks and trees. It was not a very good illusion, for Masque had just begun to practice this variety of magic, but The Soft One had said that almost any illusion would serve as a blind so long as no one suspected that the blind was there. And Masque was almost certain that a roadside illusion was the last thing on this particular man's mind at the moment.

As it waited for him to come into view, Masque crooned to itself. It liked magic. And The Soft One said it had a real talent for it. Masque liked The Soft One, too. That was why it had agreed to carry this nasty-tasting piece of hide for her. It had no interest in why Lathwi wanted the man to have the hide. The Soft One was wise beyond its ken, almost as wise as their mother, Taziem. Her reasons for doing things were often difficult to comprehend. Some days, Masque was willing to try and overcome those difficulties, just for the pleasure of being able to say that it had done so afterward. Other days, like today, it was content to remain ignorant and have fun.

An impatient spasm rippled through the youngling. The human should have been here by now. What was taking him so long? But before it could invoke the true-finding spell to locate him, Masque heard the uninspired clip-clopping of a tired horse's hooves. A moment later, the beast and its rider came poking into view. They both looked grouchy and played-out and winded.

Masque grinned to itself, then sank into a crouch. Its tail quivered in anticipation. This was going to be such fun!

ℰℭ

Jamus rode hard and fast until he was sure that he had put his unseen followers well behind him. Then, mindful that he no longer had the governor's entire stable at his disposal, he slowed his horse to a walk to let it catch its breath. He'd given up all hope and desire of reaching Hillshire by midnight. Indeed, he was now debating whether he should go there at all. For even if he *had* outrun today's shadow—and he was not laying any odds on *that*—he'd been sighted on the road to Hillshire. That would tell anyone who knew him where he was going. And that kind of information was always for sale for the right price. He knew, because he'd bought plenty of it during his tenure as Wynn Rame's lieutenant. A careful man would flip a coin at the next cross-roads and then ride like hell into nowhere.

As he made up his mind to do just that, an outcropping of rock on the side of the road snagged his attention. Its outlines bore a strong resemblance to those of a big lizard basking in the sun. Which was amusing, but odd, too, because he had never noticed this particular formation the score or so other times that he had traveled this road. And he liked to think that he would have noticed something that remarkable in his younger days. So he reined his horse toward the outcrop, meaning to have a quick look at it in passing. The next thing he knew, he was sailing through the air, and his horse was barreling down the road without him.

He landed hard on his back. The ground knocked the wind from his lungs. Tiny white spangles swarmed across the field of his vision. He struggled to his knees, gasping for breath, only to be slammed onto his back again. This time, something heavy pinned his torso to the ground. He shook his head, trying to clear his vision. A face hazed into view. It was triangular and lean, with cruel, golden eyes and a mouthful of daggers.

"Sweet, suffering Dreamer," he croaked. Instinct urged his hand toward the sword at his side, but he was pinned, and could not move, not even to save his life. He croaked again. "All right, you big bonehead. If you're going to eat me, make it quick."

Masque recognized the sharp tang of red-blooded fear that was radiating from the man in thick waves. That excited the youngling. So did the sound of his voice. This was the first time that anyone other than The Soft One had addressed it in man-speak. And it had understood all of the words of the words except 'bonehead'.

"I am Masque," it told him, infusing the thought with pride. *"I am clever. I am quick. I do not need to eat you."* It was only when he continued to stare in wild-eyed anticipation that the youngling remembered that most men could not hear dragon-speech. Silly Masque, it scolded itself. That was not very clever at all. But there were other ways of telling this man that it meant no harm. It craned its neck toward him, meaning to touch noses. Surely he would understand that!

Jamus' heart skipped a dozen beats as the dragon's muzzle closed in on him, and then began pulsing double-time. At the same time, details from his short, often sordid life passed before his eyes. The only highlight was Liselle. He called out to her as the smells of sulfur and carrion folded over him. A moment later, the dragon made contact, and the world went black.

Masque let out a surprised chirrup as the man went limp. Lathwi had never done such a thing after touching noses! Perhaps he was the one playing a game now. Perhaps he wanted it to try and rouse him from his feigned slumber. It chirruped again. How fun! It had not expected the man to be this sporting! So Masque nudged him with a forearm, once and then again. Then it rolled him into the ditch that ran alongside the road. When he did not respond in any way, Masque decided that the man had changed his mind about playing. That didn't bother Masque. For Masque was hungry now. Masque wanted to eat. And, it happened to know that there was a tasty-looking horse running loose on this very road. So it dropped Lathwi's scroll on the man's chest and went merrily on its way.

ℬℭ

Jamus came to with a drowning man's last gasp. An instant later, he was on his feet, sword in hand, ready to fight off snapping jaws, slashing talons, and whatever else he found in his way. Several moments passed before he realized that there was nothing for him to fend off. The dragon was gone.

And he was still alive!

He patted himself down, searching for wounds that were not there. Except for a few bruises on his chest and some track-marks on the road, there was absolutely no proof that he had just been attacked by a dragon. Blessed Dreamer! What had happened here?

Rendered weak-kneed by his extremely good fortune, he plopped backward and onto his butt. A moment later, he decided to steady his still-quaking nerves with a drink. As he reached for his flask, he spotted a long tube of rolled-up deer hide among the rocks and weeds. It was such an odd sight, in such an odd place, he could not stop himself from picking it up. It had a greasy feel to it, and reeked of rancid deer fat—not an encouraging combination. Compelled by curiosity and old habit, he unfurled it anyway. As he did so, a smattering of ashes flurried onto his lap. That brought the faintest suggestion of a smile to his face. Those ashes could not have gotten rolled up like that by any accident that he could imagine. Therefore, this had to be some sort of communiqué.

So he was not surprised to find the half-engraved, half-smudged note on the hide's soft underside. But when he saw that it was addressed to JDD'A, his jaw dropped like a frigate's anchor. For those were *his* initials. And that was Pawl's mark at the bottom.

What was going on here?

'I found Lathwi,' the message read. 'We're heading south after a mage who's disturbing the dead. A southern warlord by the name of Veeder might also be involved. Am investigating. Will write again from New Uxla.'

Jamus read the message a half-dozen times. By the third reading, he had his flask in hand. By the sixth, the flask was empty. He went over the message again anyway, just because he couldn't stop himself. *I found Lathwi.* That sent resentment coursing through him like a draught of bad wine. Now he knew who to blame for the dragon—The Dragon Bitch herself. He should have known. Should have. Knowing her, she had probably told the damned thing to eat his horse, too. And now she was leading his best and only friend *south* on another curra-brained adventure.

He cursed Pawl for a fool. The last time he'd gone *investigating* with that changeling, he had come home with one foot and most of his back in the grave. Did he think that such a thing could not happen again? Hell, they were chasing after the same sort of bastard who had killed Liselle. Pawl would be lucky to get home at all this time.

That was unacceptable. Un-accept-able. A man had to draw a line somewhere, and for Jamus, this was it. He had lost everything else that he had ever owned or loved to Lathwi. He could not—would not—stand idly by while she sucked Pawl away, too. He had to catch up with him. He had to—stop her.

He staggered to his feet, then set off down the road. He was heading south, but not to Hillshire. He was on his way to New Uxla.

Chapter 7

*P*awl inhaled deeply through his nose, savoring the humid tang of vegetal growth. The smell reminded him of his grandparents, who had raised forty-four seasons worth of potatoes and tobacco on a river-valley farm north of Compara. He could still see the old man, his eyes all shiny with hope and pride, as he formally offered the holding to Pawl on the day he came of age. And he could still hear his gramma's gasp of disappointment and grief when he declined the gift. "The work is too hard for me," he'd joked. This, instead of telling them that he couldn't bear the thought of treading the same old patch of ground, year after year after year. This, instead of admitting that he dreamed of adventure, and a chance to see the world.

And now here he was, on the road to an uncertain end with a scar-faced sorceress who lived in a cave and communed with dragons. Ol' Da and Gramma had to be howling with laughter in their graves.

He and Lathwi had cleared the last of Tryssa province's rolling, hard-wooded hills yesterday. Today, they were almost halfway across the vast, fertile valley that defined the borderlands. Seemingly endless fields of ripening corn, sugar beets, and barley bracketed the rutted roads here. The horizon was aggressively flat and green. Lathwi stared straight ahead as she walked, as if she already had the necromage in her sights.

And who knew? Perhaps she did.

He studied her out of the corner of his eye. Since they'd started traveling together again, they had regained a measure of their old rapport. But he could not get over her five-year hiatus. Questions skirled though him like autumn leaves in a breeze. *Where she had been? What had she done? Had she taken up with somebody—somebody like Luke?* She had not seemed overly fond of the gypsy cub, but then, it was so hard to tell what was important to her. And the lad had seemed quite at home in her cave.

Finally, he could not stop himself from asking.

"So," he said, "whatever befell you after The Rogue's downfall? I looked for you in the days following my return to Compara, but you never turned up."

If she was surprised by the abruptness of the question, she did not show it in any way. "I returned before you did," she said, "and I left again as soon as I brought Liselle's body to Jamus. He threatened to have me killed otherwise."

"Oh," he said, smothering a flash of resentment toward his old friend. "I suppose I should have guessed that." Then, because she had answered one question, he felt free to ask another. "Where did you go after that?"

"I went looking for Shoq's cave. When I found it, I claimed his territory for my own."

"Ah. And what did you do there?"

She shrugged. "I ate. I slept. I played."

"Is that all?"

Pawl's persistent interest in her day-to-day doings roused Lathwi's curiosity. It was not like him to ask so many pointless questions, she thought. Perhaps he was testing her memory, or playing some kind of a game. She liked games, so she decided to indulge him.

"I also read many books about magic and sorcery," she said, "for I had much to learn and no one to teach me. Later, I began sharing my knowledge with Taziem and—"

He made a strangled sound that could've been a curse. "You're teaching sorcery to dragons?"

She shrugged again. "Only those who have an interest in it. I thought you would have guessed that when my mother transformed herself into a woman."

"I thought *you* did that," he said, and then wrung his surprise into a disapproving scowl. "Did it ever occur to you that it might be dangerous to teach dragons magic?"

She mocked his fears with a sly half-smile. "Everything is dangerous in its own way, Pawl."

"Yes, but—"

"All dragons possess the potential to work magic," she told him, "but most cannot be bothered to learn more than the Names of Wind and Water and Fire. Only a few, like Taziem, have the strength of mind necessary to become sorcerers. And of those few, not one has ever used its talents to summon krim to this world or commit murder or drive the dead from their rest. It is human sorcerers who are dangerous in the way that you mean it."

Heat blazed its way up Pawl's neck like a fast-moving rash. Leave it to Lathwi, he thought, to turn his prejudices inside-out like an old pocket. Leave it to her to dismiss his suspicions as so much lint. And the galling thing was—she was right. Dragons might well be cold-blooded, but at least they had reasonable ambitions. Men always seemed to want *more*, no matter how much they had already. And some men were willing to stoop to anything to satisfy their desires. The fact that this often made them champions in other men's eyes left Pawl ashamed of his own kind.

Lathwi could tell by the color of Pawl's silence that he was reshaping his opinions about dragons. That pleased her, for he was much too smart—and courageous—to hold such an outsized and malformed fear. She did not begrudge him a healthy respect for the skyfolk. As Taziem liked to say, only younglings and the addle-witted were fearless. But his habitual willingness to believe that the best of dragons could never behave any better than the worst of humans rankled sometimes. He knew her. Therefore, he should know better.

The thought of Taziem turned her eyes toward the sky. But she saw no dragons flying overhead, just a delegation of vultures circling in and out of a thick, gray cloud. As she watched them, a passing breeze filled her nose with the smell of scorched earth. She sneezed at the stink.

"I wonder what caught their attention," Pawl said. He, too, was peering up at the buzzards.

"Vultures circle over dead or dying meat," she told him, matter-of-factly.

"I know," he said. "That's what worries me."

"Why?"

He cranked his head in her direction. A vague scowl ridged his brow. "Because this is farm country, not wilderness. And farmers usually don't let carrion sit around long enough to attract buzzards. They think scavengers spread disease."

Lathwi despised the theory with a hiss. Silly farmers. Scavengers kept the world healthy by eating dead meat before it could rot and give rise to flies.

"And then there's that big cloud of smoke," he went on. "It's not the right time of year for burning off the fields. And—" He scuffed at the cracked, hard-packed road with his boot. "It hasn't rained here for at least two weeks, so it wasn't a lightning strike."

"Why does this matter to you?" she asked.

"I don't know," he said, still scowling. "It just doesn't feel right." He transferred his scabbard from his back to his hip with one easy, time-perfected move. "Be ready for anything."

She snorted. As if there were any other way to be.

As they continued down the road, the smell of roasted dirt grew so strong, it began to make Lathwi's head throb. She sneezed. She snorted. She considered Changing into a creature without a nose. But before she had a chance to do so, the rows of head-high corn that fletched the road abruptly flattened into a blackened wasteland. Field after field after field stood burned, a sight to equal the stink. Fire was Lathwi's friend, and she knew how hungry it could get, but even so, she was impressed by how much it had eaten here.

"These must have been very tasty crops indeed," she said.

Pawl made no reply. He was scowling at the thick, gray cloud again. Now that the corn no longer impeded their view, he had no trouble tracking the smoke back to the source. It was coming from the ruins of a nearby farmstead. The house was burned and half-collapsed. The barn to its rear had also been torched. He could not yet see what was burning, but he meant to find out.

"Do you mind if I take a closer look?" he asked, even as he started down the road again. "I need to know what happened here."

She shrugged, then tagged along simply because she was headed in that direction anyway.

As they closed in on the ruined farmstead, details emerged from the blackened gloom. Several horses were picketed to a post in front of the house. Two others were hitched to a rugged buckboard wagon. So while there were no people in sight, Lathwi knew that they had to be somewhere nearby. She could not help but wonder why they were here. There was certainly nothing attractive about so much char. The smell fouled her nose. And the lingering wisps of smoke in the air made her eyes itch.

They followed the road into a large fore-yard. The ground here was trampled, a confusion of hoofprints, boot-marks, and other scuffs. Pawl sank into a crouch to study these tracks, then motioned for Lathwi to join him.

"Look," he said, pointing at a pair of deep grooves in the dust. "Someone dragged a body that way." He gestured toward the barn. "In fact, someone dragged several bodies that way."

She glanced in that direction, but saw no bodies, only a plume of smoke rising up from behind the barn. From this distance, the smoke had an oily, roasted-meat smell that turned her stomach.

"I think this someone is still here," she said. "I think he is burning the bodies you speak of."

"I think so, too," Pawl said.

"Why would someone do such a thing?"

"I don't know," he said. "To stop a disease from spreading, maybe. Or maybe to hide a crime."

She hissed at such a despicable possibility, then loosened her knife in its sheath. "Maybe we will not have to go into New Uxla for horses after all."

"Maybe," he replied. "Just don't do anything hasty."

They prowled their way across the yard, quiet as a pair of natural-born predators. As they circled around the ruined barn, an odd, rhythmic thunking snagged their attention. It was soon joined by low-throated chanting. Pawl raised a hand, signaling Lathwi to stay put for a moment. Then he rounded the far corner.

To his surprise, he found himself looking at a group of men dressed in homespun cover-alls and broad-rimmed hats. Most of them were on their knees: praying, it seemed. The youngest was filling in the last of four graves—thunk, sling, thunk, sling—this, as an enormous bonfire raged in the background. Although Pawl could not be sure, he thought he saw two skeletons encased within those orange flames.

"What goes on here?" Pawl asked.

The men on their knees returned to the here-and-now with a chorus of startled gasps. At the same time, the young grave-digger shouted, "Raiders!" Then he menaced Pawl with his upraised shovel and said, "Get back, you! I'll brain the life out of you if you come any closer."

"Put the shovel down, lad," Pawl told him, in a firm but friendly tone. "My friend and I mean you no harm."

The boy jabbed the spade in Pawl's direction and snarled, "Says you, north-man. But I don't see no friend. If he's here, tell him to show himself—now."

Pawl twitched him an amused smile, then called out. "Lathwi? Will you join us? These people wish to see you."

Oh so casually, Lathwi rounded the corner. As she did so, the lad turned a violent shade of pale and swore. "Random save us! He's got a demon with him. Run, Da, run! I'll hold it off as long as I can!"

"My friend is no demon," Pawl assured him.

"Says you. But everyone knows that North-men are liars and demon-lovers. My Uncle Rosco says so." The spade was trembling in his hands now, but he barred Lathwi's with it nonetheless. "Run, Da!"

"I will do no such thing, Eldon," one of the older men growled, as he struggled to his feet. "Now quit your yammering before you embarrass us all."

"But Da, can't you see? That one's a de—."

Lathwi cut him off with an offended hiss. "You speak nonsense, youngling. I am no demon."

"Prove it," he challenged. "Cut your palm with a knife. If you bleed, we'll know you're telling the truth. Otherwise, we'll throw salt on you and watch as it eats your flesh away."

She scorned the suggestion with a snort. "I am not going to do myself an injury to put your feeble mind at ease. And you know nothing at all about demons if you think that salt will destroy one."

"How would you know?"

She did not deign to answer him. Instead, she turned to Pawl and said, "Let us be off. I have no patience for fools today."

"Wait," Eldon's father said. He was standing next to his son now. Both of them were burly, farmer-brown men, with dark, deep-set eyes and broad, fleshy mouths that tended to curved downward. But where Eldon's expression was belligerent, his father's was more careworn. "I am called Markham, son of Tuck. May I ask what brought you here?"

"We saw the burnt fields, and then your smoke," Pawl replied, glancing toward the pyre. "I wanted to find out who was setting fires."

"And who are you that you should care?" a squat, white-bearded man wanted to know.

"I am Pawl, swordmaster of Compara." He set a hand on the hilt of his sword, then arched a wry eyebrow at the old man and added, "Would you care to examine my credentials?"

Markham raised his hands as if to ward off a blow. "Pardon our rudeness, Pawl of Compara. We're tired, and our hearts are sore. These people—" He nodded toward the graves. "—were friends. And they're not the first we've lost, either. Those damn raiders have struck four times in the past six months."

"Who are they?" Pawl asked. "Do you know?"

"Oh, we know all right," the old man said, and then spit like someone who could not bear the taste in his mouth. "Southern warrior-scum."

"How do you know?"

One of the other farmers doffed his hat to reveal the mangled remains of his right ear. "See this?" he asked. "That's how I know. I was pitching hay for the Sterling twins when raiders hit their farm. They all had twisted beards and tattoos—that's warrior class all the way. It was worth the price of an ear to see the look on that one fellow's ugly face when my pitchfork took him in the brisket."

"Does the garrison commander know about this?"

The one-eared farmer sneered. "Of course he knows. We've complained to him at least a dozen times already. A fat lot of good it does, though. Trevor Stone *says* he's assigned extra patrols to the border. Trevor Stone *says* those patrols are doing the best they can. But if you ask me, I think Trevor Stone is blowing smoke out his fat arse."

"That's not true!" Eldon brayed, red-faced with fury. "Commander Stone is doing the best he can with the few men he has at his disposal. If you want him to do better, you and Da and the others should give your first-borns permission to join his troop instead of keeping us chained to your yokes like slav—"

Markham backhanded him across the face, a powerful slap that left his son's eyes shimmering with watery resentment. "There's more where that came from, boy," he said. "Just keep flapping your jaws." When Eldon remained silent, he loosed a satisfied grunt, and then turned to Pawl as if nothing untoward had transpired. "It will be dark soon," he said. "I would be honored to shelter you and your...*friend*...on my farm for the night."

Pawl looked to Lathwi, who bounced the decision back to him with a shrug. Her indifference suited him. She might not care where they spent the evening, but he did. He was tired of sleeping on hard ground, with mosquitoes buzzing in his ears. He was tired of venison jerky and fruit, too. A decent meal and a bed would be a welcome change. So he gave Markham a respectful nod and said, "Thanks. We'd appreciate it."

"Good," the farmer replied. "But before I can return to my stead, my friends and I must finish our prayers for the dead. You may stay if you so desire, but *she*—" He cast a quick, sideways glance at Lathwi. "—must wait elsewhere. Women are not permitted at sacred ceremonies."

"I have no wish to intrude," Pawl said. "We'll both abide in the fore-yard."

"So be it," Markham said. Prompted by an afterthought about opportunistic horse thievery perhaps, or perhaps just a desire to have the boy out of his hair, he added, "Eldon will keep you company."

"Da!" his son bleated, but no avail. Markham and the other elders turned their backs on him, then returned to their prayers.

"I do not understand," Lathwi said, as she and Pawl headed back around the barn. "Why do these people bury some of their dead and burn others?"

From two paces back, Eldon jeered. "Do you know nothing? Women bear life, as the earth bears life, so they are given to the ground. Men rule women, as the sky rules the earth, so we are given to the heavens."

Lathwi could see the connection between women and the earth, but the rest of it was nonsense. The sky did not rule the earth; it existed in and of itself. And men did not rule women—leastwise, no women that she knew. As far as she could tell, the only thing that men and the sky had in common was a prevalence of wind. She didn't bother saying so to Eldon, though, for she deemed him beneath her notice.

Back in the fore-yard, Pawl found an unoccupied hitching post to lean against and then pulled a whetstone out of his pack. An instant after he unsheathed his sword, Eldon appeared at his elbow. The boy's eyes sparkled with adolescent awe and relish now. His fingers twitched with desire.

"Can I hold it?" he asked.

Pawl remembered what it had been like to be stuck in a place that did not fit his ambitions. So, moved by pity, he offered Eldon the hilt. A smile like a new day dawning lit up the lad's face.

"Ah," he crooned, as he hefted the weapon, "now this is how a man should feel." He swiped inexpertly at the air, then looked to Pawl again. "Have you been reassigned to New Uxla? If so, will you give me lessons?"

"Sorry," Pawl said. "We're just passing through."

"On your way to where?" the lad asked. "To the coast of Cos, to battle pirates?" He hacked at an imaginary cut-throat. "Or maybe the Quylan plains, to drive the nomads back into the desert?" He gutted a sand-man that only he could see. "Or could it be that you're heading south—" He stopped in mid-thrust to grin at Pawl. "—to bring the chief of the raiders to his knees?"

Pawl twitched him a dry little smile. "Like I said, we're just passing through."

"Can you take me with you?"

"Sorry."

At that, the boy began stabbing and slashing at the lengthening shadows as if they were the stuff of thwarted dreams. Sweat beaded on his dirt-streaked face. Frothy gobs of spittle built up at the corners of his froggy mouth. Concerned that he might do himself an injury, Pawl called for the return of the sword. Eldon lowered the weapon, but made no move to give it back. Instead, he turned to Lathwi, who was happily lounging in a last, lingering puddle of sunlight.

"Digging graves is thirsty work," he said. "Fetch me some water from the well."

"Fetch it yourself," she replied. "Or stay thirsty."

His eyes narrowed. His face went cherry-red. He closed the gap between them in an instant, then pointed Pawl's sword at her breastbone.

"If you are indeed a woman," he said, "you will do as you are told."

Lathwi curled her lip at him—a display of profound annoyance. He did not heed the warning. Indeed, like a purebred fool, he pinched his mouth into a triumphant smirk. She made a move as if to get up, but then kicked his feet out from under him. The sword went flying. So did he. A heartbeat after he came to ground on his back, she was on him like a shadow-cat. The edge of her knife was against his throat.

"I was taught never to raise a sword to a person unless I was prepared to die," she said. "Did you learn this lesson, too?"

He shook his head ever so slightly. His eyes were wide with fear. "Too bad."

"Please don't kill him, Lathwi," Pawl said, as he plucked his sword up from the yard's dust. "Otherwise, Markham will retract his offer of hospitality. And I really don't feel like sleeping on the ground tonight."

She peeled the knife away from Eldon's throat, leaving a thin necklace of blood behind. As he gasped with relief and pain, she thrust her face into his breathing space and showed him her teeth. "The swordmaster has saved you this time," she said. "But if you ever challenge me again, I will not be merciful."

With that, she got up and strode over to the well for a drink of water. A moment later, Eldon scrabbled to his feet. Streaming dust and ill-will, then he went storming over to the hitching post where Pawl was once again perched. The swordmaster was whetting his sword now, and did not look up as the boy approached.

"Why didn't you help me?" Eldon demanded.

"You're alive, aren't you?" Pawl asked.

The boy tried a different angle of attack. "You should punish her for drawing a knife on me."

"Why would I want to do a crazy thing like that?"

"Because you're a man. And men govern women. It is the natural order of life."

"Maybe that's the way it is in this part of the world," Pawl replied. "But where I come from, men don't yank on a dragon's tail and then cry foul when it swivels around to bite them." He looked up from his work to scorn Eldon with a look. "You got everything you asked for, boy, and less than you deserved. Now be a real man and learn something from the experience."

Eldon opened his mouth to say something more, but before he could get a word out, the funeral party came trudging into the yard. Although Markham's shoulders were stooped with fatigue, he noticed the welt that now ringed his son's throat immediately.

"What happened?" he asked.

"I let him play with my sword, and he got cut," Pawl said. "He's lucky it wasn't worse."

Markham shot the boy a disgusted look, then sent him to give the other elders a leg up onto their horses. "And he thinks he'd make a good soldier," the farmer sneered, as Eldon went skulking off. "Damned fool."

Pawl was inclined to agree with the man, but he did not say so aloud. For when it came to their sons, fathers often said one thing when they meant something else.

They traveled to Markham's farmstead by wagon. Pawl sat up front with the old man while Lathwi and Eldon rode in back with the shovel, an old blanket and a few sacks of feed. Although Lathwi had good reason to be unhappy about being stuck with Eldon's company, she made no complaint. Instead, she curled up with her back to him and went to sleep. Eldon scowled at her for the length of the ride.

Although it was dark by the time they reached the end of their road, Pawl could tell that Markham was prosperous. His house stood two stories tall, with glass windows protected by fancy, wrought-iron grills. The tall, white barn in the distance seemed to be bulging with hay.

"Wife!" Markham shouted, as he stopped the wagon alongside a well-used sitting porch. "Send Cheron out to tend to these horses. And tell Josephine to set another place at the table. We have guests." In a normal tone, he added, "Eldon, go and wash yourself. Be sure to say prayers of purification, too, or the dead will coming looking for you."

Eldon bounded from the wagon with an enthusiastic, "Yes, Da!" An instant after he disappeared into the house, a stout woman in a plain homespun gown appeared in the front door. Her rosy cheeks belied the worry in her eyes. She gave her crown of braids a nervous pat, then nodded at Pawl without ever quite looking at him.

"Be welcome in our home, good sir," she said, and then turned those worried eyes on Markham. "Husband, how went it? Did anyone sur—"

He cut her off with a somber shake of her head. "None of that now, wife. We are all hungry and heart-sore. You will take this woman—" He gestured at Lathwi, who had just sat up from her nap. "—and make her a place at your table."

The bloom in her cheeks paled to ash as Lathwi hopped out of the wagon, but she extended a pudgy hand just the same. "This way, friend," she said. "You'll be wanting a wash before you eat."

Actually, Lathwi wanted no such thing. Too much washing left her skin itchy and dry. But that nap had made her hungry—hungry enough to endure an inane ritual or two. So with a smack of her lips, she followed the woman into the house. Markham and Pawl trailed after them, but only as far as the sitting room. There, the farmer gestured for Pawl sit down in a well-padded rocking chair by the half-open window.

"I must go and purify myself before supper," he said. "My sons will see to your comfort."

"Thank you," Pawl said.

A moment after Markham disappeared, he was visited by a procession of young boys. One bore a basin of warm water; another, a clean hand-towel; and the last, a glass of sweet wine. Pawl gladly availed himself of all three, and then rocked back in his chair. The room smelled of lamp oil, fresh air, and baking apples. In the background, he could hear cows lowing. A sense of well-being stole over him. He might've dozed off if a loud clang hadn't startled him back to wide-eyed wakefulness. A moment later, a clean-faced but still sullen Eldon poked his head into the room.

"Da says you're to come to board now," he said. "This way."

The boy led him into a room that was almost all table. And the table was heaped with food: roasted mutton and sugar corn; barley bread and pole-beans, and a big pitcher of fresh buttermilk. Markham sat at the head of the board. Two sons sat to his left. One sat to the right. Pawl went to take the seat next to him, but Markham motioned him to the chair opposite from his own—a seat usually reserved for the eldest son. Eldon took the spot beside his brother without a word.

"Let us pray," Markham said. "All praise to The Dreamer for making our lands fertile. All praise to Her consort for sending life-giving rains—and for leading the raiders away from our stead."

"Thanks be to He and She," his sons echoed in unison.

"Well said, sons," Markham said. "Now dig in."

"But what about your womenfolk?" Pawl asked, as platters started bobbing from hand to hand. "Where are they?"

"In the kitchen," Markham replied gruffly. "Where they belong."

The thought of fierce, scar-faced Lathwi cooped up in a kitchen with a gaggle of prairie hens both amused and dismayed Pawl. But he had no doubt that she was in good hands, so he kept quiet and concentrated on his supper. No one tried to coax him out of his silence. Indeed, aside from the occasional "Pass me some of that," no one talked at all until Markham's plate was finally empty.

"Would you care for another helping of anything, Pawl of Compara?" the master of the house asked then.

"No, thank you," Pawl replied, struggling to remember the last time he had felt so full. "You're a most generous host."

"In that case—" The farmer leaned forward like a big cat getting ready to strike. His sons all sat back as if to get out of his way. "Perhaps you could do something for me in return."

Pawl leaned back in his chair and laced his fingers over his belly. "What did you have in mind?"

"Talk to Trevor Stone," Markham said. "Tell him about this latest attack. Make him understand how desperate things are out here. You're a warrior, he'll listen to you."

The request did not seem unreasonable to Pawl—especially since he meant to stop in New Uxla for horses anyway. And he was curious as to what Commander Stone might have to say about these raiders. The fact that their forays coincided with rumors about a southern warlord on the rise made him very, very uneasy. Yes, he decided, a trip to the garrison definitely was in order.

"I'll do it," he said.

"Splendid," Markham said, and smiled. Everyone at the table relaxed. "If you wish, Eldon will give you and your friend a ride into town in the morning."

"That would be nice," Pawl replied, and then tried to fight off a yawn to no avail. "Pardon me," he said afterward. "I'm not used to eating so well at the end of a long day. I'm going to have to turn in soon or nod off where I sit."

"My wife has prepared a bed in the barn for your friend, but you are welcome to sleep here in the house," Markham said. "Eldon would be quite happy to give up his cot for you."

That's not how it looked to Pawl. Eldon was hunkered down in his chair like a turtle in its shell, and he wore a look of tight-lipped resentment. Although Pawl didn't particularly care for the lad, he had seen enough to know that at least some of his rancor was justified. Markham treated his first-born more like a servant or a dog. Or a woman. Pawl thought he'd be more than a little sullen, too, if he were in the young farmer's boots. So he decided to be gracious.

"I thank you for the offer," he said, "but I've imposed on your family too much as it is. By your leave, I'll sleep in the barn, too. In fact," he added, talking around another yawn, "I think I'll head that way now."

Markham shrugged. "However you please, Pawl of Compara. I'll be off working in the back fields by the time you leave tomorrow, so I'll bid you a swift and safe journey now. Give Trevor Stone my regards."

"That and more," Pawl promised, then took his leave of Markham and his sons.

What strange people, he marveled, as he strolled out of the house and toward the barn. Although their allegiance was to the north, they were very southern in many of their attitudes—especially when it came to women. Gramma had always presided at Ol' Da's side: in the fields, at the supper table, on the porch. And she would've boxed her beloved husband's ears for a month for consigning a female guest to the kitchen.

As it turned out, though, Lathwi saw nothing wrong with such treatment.

"The women gave me a cut of meat and a cozy seat by the hearth-fire," she said, as she lounged in the hayloft's thatched shadows. "It is more than I would have done in their stead."

"Did they talk to you?" he asked.

She snorted. "I am a dragon. They are tit-mice. What would they say?"

"I thought they might talk about the raids."

"They did that," she replied, "but only amongst themselves." Then, because she knew he would ask and because she had indeed eavesdropped out of long-standing habit, she added, "They are afraid that the raiders will attack this place next. They are afraid of being violated and killed. They are afraid of everything, or so it seemed."

"Not everyone is as fearless as you, Lathwi," he reminded her, with just a hint of a reproach in his voice. "And their concerns are legitimate." Almost as an afterthought, he added, "That's why I promised Markham that I would speak to the garrison commander at New Uxla on their behalf."

She rumbled, a sound of surprise and dismay. Dragons avoided making promises whenever possible, because once a promise was given, it had to be honored regardless of the time or trouble involved. And while Pawl was no dragon, she had always thought that he believed the same way.

"I do not understand your interest in this matter," she said. "These people are being challenged for their territory. They must either repel the challengers or move on. That is the natural way of the world, and no amount of talking is going to change it."

"That might be the way of things among dragons," he countered, "but it gets a bit more complicated among humans. You see, most of the crops grown here are carted off to Compara and the other northern cities for consumption. If the raiders keep on burning fields, these farmers won't be the only ones staring a lean winter in the eye."

She shrugged. People who chose to depend on others for food should expect to go hungry from time to time.

"Not only that," he went on, "but dragons don't kill more than they can eat at any given time. These southern bastards are trying to destroy the whole herd so absolutely no one can eat."

"That is wrong," Lathwi said, and then fingered the facial scars that one long-dead southerner had given her.

"So do you want to tag along when I go to see the garrison commander?"

She snorted. "It is your promise to keep, not mine, Pawl. I will do as I see fit when the moment comes."

With that, she curled up in the hay like a hole in the darkness. A moment later, her breathing became slower and deeper. He shucked his leather jerkin, then closed his eyes, too, but while he was weary, he could not seem to fall asleep. At first, thoughts of General Veeder and Trevor Stone kept him awake. He wondered how much one knew about the other, and if Jamie knew anything at all about either of them yet. And even as he set such questions aside for the night, he began to overheat in the loft's stuffy confines. He clawed his way out of his undershirt, then dragged himself closer to the window. That made him feel better—until the straw made his skin burn and itch. He began tossing and turning in earnest then, as desperate as a dog with a bad case of fleas.

The next thing he knew, he was nose to nose with Lathwi. Even in the dark, he could see that she was not pleased.

"What ails you?" she asked.

"It's my back," he groaned in reply. "It feels like it's covered with fire ants."

"Roll over and I will scratch it for you," she said. "Otherwise, we will both be up all night."

Eager to end his torment, he did as he was told. The feel of her fingernails on his back nearly made him shout with pleasure. "Don't stop," he begged instead. "Please don't stop."

She made a rumbling noise deep in her throat. It could have been amusement. It could have been contempt. He didn't care either way.

"I used to do this for Taziem," she said. "She particularly liked it here—" She jabbed her fingers into his armpits. He yelped with pain and surprise. "—and—" Her hands slid down his sides, then over the rounds of his hipbone. "—here." He bit his lip, and went very still. A moment later, she went back to scratching his shoulder-blades.

"These have healed nicely," she said, referring to the terrible scars that striped his back. They were the mark of krim; and of a battle fought and won. "Any dragon would be proud to bear them." She traced a finger over the worst of the old wounds. The flesh quivered. That amused her, so she did it again.

He growled. "That tickles."

She was delighted to hear it. Tickling her old tanglemate, Shoq, had been one of her favorite games. How fun of Pawl to let her play it with him! She began searching for his softest spots in earnest: armpits, ribcage, belly. When he pinched the flesh around his hips, he growled again, then grabbed her by the wrist and flipped her. The next thing she knew, he had her pinned to the floor. He was breathing hard now, as if he had just run a footrace, and there was a curious light in his eyes. He stared down at her for a moment, then brought his face closer. She struggled—partly because it went with the game, and partly because it seemed like he meant to bite her. But while his mouth did indeed graze her lips, she felt no pain, only a light, lingering pressure. This so surprised her, she forgot to resist.

"Why did you do that?" she asked afterward.

He arched an eyebrow at her. "Haven't you ever been kissed?"

"Is that what that was?"

"Yes."

"What purpose does it serve?"

The excited tingle that had been coursing through Pawl's veins became a sudden numbness in his brain. It had seemed to him that she'd been trying to arouse him with her horseplay. It had seemed to him that she had finally come to desire him as he desired her. The magnitude of his error—and her innocence—was as stunning as a sharp blow to the head. He felt foolish; dazed; betrayed. It took every ounce of control in his possession to keep his voice steady.

"Kissing can serve many purposes," he replied. "Between friends, it can be a greeting or a gesture of thanks or just a bit of fun. Between people who are more than friends, it's often a prelude to pleasure."

"What kind of pleasure?"

An offer to give her a sample crowded into his mouth, but he ground it to a sour powder between his molars. He had his pride. And his self-respect. He would not take advantage of her like that. Would not, would not, would not.

"Pleasures of the flesh," he told her. "Like those that Taziem and her miner friend shared the other night."

She rumbled, recalling the erotic images that her mother had shared with her. "So kissing can be a prelude to coupling."

"Sometimes." And now that his feathers were in thorough disarray, he felt free to try and ruffle hers. "You're fully grown. How is that you don't know these things?"

She shrugged. "Taziem is the one who is fascinated with such behavior, not me."

"Don't dragons couple?"

"Yes, but it is not the same. When a female comes into season, she invites the sire of her choice to sky-dance for her. If his performance arouses her, they mate. No kissing is involved."

"I see," he said. "And have you never invited someone to dance for you?"

She dismissed the idea with a scowl. "Mating results in pregnancy. I have no wish to bear young."

"There are ways of getting around that," he told her.

Surprise reeled through her. Curiosity rose up in its wake. She flashed Pawl a grin laced with the memory of Taziem's erotic images and said, "Show me."

Chapter 8

Dawn found Pawl and Lathwi on the road to New Uxla. She was nestled in the back of the wagon, fast asleep. He was riding up front with Eldon. The lad was all eyes and no mouth for a change, perhaps because Pawl had happened to mention that this was a perfect morning for an ambush. The tule fog was so thick, they could not see more than a few feet beyond the horses's ears. And if there *were* any raiders left in the area, they'd be able to hear Markham's squeaky old buckboard coming from a mile away. But while Pawl rode with his scabbard between his knees, he wasn't expecting any trouble. Indeed, trouble was the furthest thing from his mind.

He glanced over his shoulder to peek at Lathwi. Her face was half-hidden in the crook of one arm, but he could still see her expression. It was somewhat fierce, even in sleep, and gave no secrets away. This came as no great surprise to Pawl. He wasn't so foolish as to think that last night's romp would change her in any way. She would always and ever be true to her own nature.

But sweet, suffering Dreamer! What a night it had been.

His back stung from a farrago of scratches, and the bones of his hips were bruised. Every time one of the horses flicked its tail or tossed its mane, he remembered the feel of her thick, black hair knotted in his hands. Every time the wagon struck a rut and bucked, he remembered her beneath him. And every time he looked upon her, he remembered the wonder in her eyes after that first do-or-die kiss. Even now, he couldn't quite believe that he had finally dared to declare himself.

"Does she follow you to atone for a crime?" Eldon asked. "Or do you pay her?"

The question caught Pawl in the middle of a heart-shaped thought, so it took him a moment to process it. As soon as he had done so, he wished that he had not bothered. "She's a shieldmate," he replied coldly, "not a camp-follower."

"I only asked because she bears the marks of a thief and a whore," Eldon said, pressing two fingers to his cheek to imitate her scars. "And—" His expression shifted, becoming both roguish and sly. "I know what you were doing last night. I heard you on my way to the privy."

"Your ears must be sharper than my eyes," Pawl said. "The only privy I saw on your father's farm was closer to the house than the barn."

Eldon shrugged. "It's easy to lose your way in the fog."

"It's also easy to get your nose broken. All you have to do is poke it in the wrong person's business."

The boy's smug facade collapsed into something resembling remorse. "I meant no harm, swordmaster. Truly. It's just that I've never met a woman like your friend, and I don't know what to think. Are all women from the north like her?"

"No," Pawl said, still radiating displeasure. "There is no one like her—anywhere. She's unique."

"I'd like to visit the north someday," Eldon said. "My Uncle Rosco says you can ride for days there, and see nothing but green trees and water. He's invited me to come with him when he carts this year's harvest off to market, but my slave-driver of a father won't permit it. He's afraid that if I leave the farmstead, I'll never return to it. And you know what? He's right, damn him. I was *born* to be a soldier."

If this had been some other farmer-boy, Pawl might've encouraged him to pursue that dream when he came of age. But he'd already seen Eldon in action and knew him to be wrong-headed—a bully in the rough whose philosophies were peppered with savagery. Such men typically became the sort of soldiers who preyed on the defenseless and weak. Wars were ugly enough without that kind. So Pawl made a point of staying quiet.

As the sun inched its way into the sky, it burned the ground-fog into a milky haze. A bump on the otherwise smooth horizon appeared: New Uxla. It was farther away than it looked. Flat land played tricks with the eyes. Even so, Pawl was glad to know that this ride was coming to an end—and not just because he wanted to be done with Eldon. His backside was numb to the bone from bouncing up and down on a hard wooden plank all morning, and his back felt like an old, knotted rope. Put him in a saddle, and put him in it soon!

The wish brought his old shieldmate, Gordyn, to mind. It had been several years since he had last stood face to face with the great, gruff redhead, but shieldmates did not forget each other—not even when forgetting seemed the wiser choice. And Gord was a memorable fellow. He drank and brawled like a Southerner. He refused to eat red meat. Sober, he was profane. Drunk, he could sweet-talk the britches off of a dockside whore. He had been a bit of everything in his day: soldier, farrier, card-sharp; mercenary, outlaw, sot. All of which left him in good stead as a horse trader working the borderlands. Pawl was looking forward to seeing him again as well as to introducing him to Lathwi. He had absolutely no doubt that those two were going to hit it off.

As if in response to him thinking about her, Lathwi came awake with an affronted sneeze. Afterward, she sat up and rubbed at her still-itchy nose with the back of her hand.

"Someone is burning horse dung," she said.

"Wood is scarce here in the borderlands," Eldon said, oozing contempt for her ignorance. "We do not feed it to our ovens."

"No wonder that Fire eats so much when it gets loose in the fields," Lathwi said to Pawl. "After a steady diet of dung, even grass must taste wonderful."

She shifted, trying to get comfortable. As she did so, she caught her first glimpse of New Uxla. It was as she had expected it to be: a prairie-mushroom-like ring of squat, sod-and stone buildings huddled around a hulking, slouch-shouldered garrison. The main road was a rutted strip. A thin, gray haze hung over the place like bad breath. She shook her head. She would never understand humankind's penchant for living in crowded, ugly nests.

"Isn't that a sight to gladden the heart?" Eldon asked, as they neared the town's first buildings. He squared his shoulders, then flicked the team's reins with sudden vigor. "Yah! Giddup there." He drove the wagon up to the garrison's broad gate, and then set the brake. "There," he said. "From our door to the commander's."

Lathwi hopped out of the wagon without a word, but Pawl lingered a moment to offer the lad his hand in feeble thanks. That proved to be a mistake, for Eldon latched on to him like a drowning man.

"Swordmaster," he said, in a strained voice, "I have done well by you in bringing you here, have I not?"

"I suppose," Pawl replied.

"Then perhaps you will return the favor and recommend me to Commander Stone. All you need say is that I'm your nephew, and that I'm old enough to enlist with him."

Pawl denied the request with a shake of his head. "I cannot lie to a superior."

"Then take me with you," Eldon begged, tightening his grip on Pawl's arm. "I'm good with my hands. I'm good with horses, too. I could be your groom. Please. Take me with you when you go."

"I'm sorry," Pawl replied, as he extricated himself from the boy's grasp, "but I cannot do that, either."

Eldon's face turned a thwarted shade of red. The tension that had been building within him spewed forth from his mouth as a spray of furious words.

"Cannot, swordmaster? Or will not? You pretend to be an honorable man, but you're a fake, just like my father. He hides behind his farm. You hide behind a woman." He pointed at Lathwi, who was waiting for him with unabashed impatience. "Your bitch doesn't like me, so you spite me to please her. You're no true man to be ruled in such a way. You're weak, an abomination. You deserve a coward's death."

"There's only one coward here," Pawl said, as he got out of the wagon, "and it's not me, boy. You had best change your ways before someone decides to kill you just to shut you up."

"You'll be sorry you spited me," Eldon shouted, as Pawl and Lathwi started down the street together. "I spit on you. I piss on you. You're dirt beneath my heel." When he got no response, he turned on his heel and went marching over to the sentry post. "I need to see Commander Stone," he told the sentries. "It's a matter of life and death."

৳০ ০৪

As Lathwi and Pawl strode down the street, the people of New Uxla scrambled to get out of their way. Most of these were farmers and their sons, come to town to stock up on dry goods. Pawl didn't have to ask to know what they were thinking. It radiated from their scowls, a worry trimmed with fear and more than a little hate: *Marauders!* He could not quite blame them for being so hostile, but it seemed rather unproductive. It was times like this that a man needed all the friends he could scrape together.

"Sheep in a pen," Lathwi said. Just for fun, she bared her teeth at a plump young woman who was peeking at them through a shop's dusty window dressings.

Pawl shrugged. "I'm sure we look like wolves."

"*I* look like a dragon," she told him, and then lapsed into a frown. "Where are we going? I thought you wanted to talk to someone at the garrison."

"I do," he replied. "But first things first. I need a horse. A big, fast horse with a nice, easy seat. I've had it up to my saddle-sores with wagons."

"You're getting soft," she said smugly.

He pretended not to hear.

Gordyn's Horse Emporium sat on an oversized lot at the far edge of town. Pawl spotted the barn first. It looked much like the one he had slept in last night except for the sloppy ochre paint-job and the larger-than-life likeness of a rearing stallion on its roof. A moment later, the air acquired the distinctive, dusty-sweet tang of horses, manure, and hay. Then the front paddock came into view. It contained at least a half-dozen animals.

"Looks like we're in luck," Pawl said, and poked his head into the barn's double doorway. "Hey, Gord-o!" he shouted. "Where the hell are y—!"

Lathwi did not see what happened next; she had been eyeing the horses instead of Pawl. But she heard him go quiet in mid-shout. And a moment later, she heard a muffled thud and a string of curses—the sounds of a struggle. She pivoted toward the barn door. He was nowhere in sight. Therefore, it was reasonable to assume that he was making at least some of the scuffling sounds that were now spilling into the courtyard. Immediately curious, she went to investigate.

A blizzard of flying hay met her at the barn-door. It was coming from a tangle of flailing limbs: Pawl grappling with a massive red bear of a man. She looked for weapons. Seeing none, she gleefully hurled herself at the stranger's back. "What the hell?" he grunted. An instant later, he grabbed her by the scruff of the neck and flung her over his head. She landed on her tailbone halfway across the barn. He charged after her only to pull up short and gape.

"By The Dreamer's bleeding tits!" he said. "You're a woman."

She grinned at his mistake, then launched herself at him again. As she drove her head into the ample cushion of his belly, she heard Pawl say, "Lathwi, meet Gord. Gord, this is Lathwi."

"Pleased—to meet you—Lathwi," Gord said, straining the words through gritted teeth. He had her in a bear-hug; she was on the verge of breaking free. "You're—a little different—from the women I usually—see—around here. Any chance—I could talk you into—staying—for a while? I'm—rich."

"Your barn isn't the only thing around here that's full of shit, Gord," Pawl jeered. "Now let her go before she does you an injury. I don't have the time to nurse you back to health."

Gord laughed—the booming har-har of a man who knows he's perfectly safe. Then he released Lathwi only to spin her around and plant a resounding kiss on her lips. "I'll wrestle with you any day, wench," he said. "Would you happen to like warm mud?"

Lathwi made no reply. She was too busy evaluating Gordyn's kiss. It was neither as intriguing nor as pleasant as Pawl's had been—mostly because of that coarse, scratchy beard of his. What was the point to cultivating body hair, she wondered, especially about the mouth? But as unappealing as she deemed that kiss, she *had* learned something from it: not all kisses felt the same. That was good to know. She would never have guessed it.

Meanwhile, the two old shieldmates resumed their greeting ritual. They shook hands, then embraced and clapped each other on the back. "Been a long time, boy-o," Gord said. "You look well."

"As do you, old dog," Pawl replied.

"Shall we drink to that?" Gord asked

"Gladly," Pawl said, and then caught the crook of his old friend's arm before he could pull a jug from its hiding place. "But I've got to take care of some business first."

"Then get a move on, mate. You're wasting good drinking time."

"Actually," Pawl said, casually tracing patterns in the hay-dust with his toe, "this is my first stop. Lathwi and I both need a horse."

Delighted spread across Gordyn's face like a pool of spilled cream. "Well, why didn't you say so? Business is business. Step this way. By the by," he added, as he led them out to the front paddock. "How much money were you planning to spend?"

Neither Pawl nor Lathwi found any prospects in this corral. "Dumb farm beasts," she said to Pawl. And he was forced to agree with the assessment. "Well, what did you expect?" Gord said. "Most of my return business comes from farmers." But he led them to another corral at the back of the stables There, Lathwi singled out a feisty red stallion. As she watched it, it kicked at a leggy yearling that had drifted too close. That convinced her.

"I will take that one," she said.

"Are you sure?" Gordyn asked. "He's not the gentlest thing on four legs."

"That is good."

He shrugged. "It's your money. And your funeral."

Meanwhile, Pawl got up on a big gray gelding's back and put it through its paces without a saddle. It had a good, easy stride and plenty of power. The roan that Lathwi fancied did not seem to mind its presence, either. "We'll need tack, too," he told Gordy, as he dismounted, "and a half-sack of grain. I'll give you fourteen lucs for the whole lot."

Gord snorted. "Like hell. You'll give me twenty, and say thanks for the discount. Those are my best animals."

"I'll go as high as sixteen," Pawl replied, "but only if you throw new shoes for the beasts into the pot."

"Done."

They shook hands. As they did so, Gord broke into a triumphant grin. "Gotcha, boy-o. I would've settled for fifteen, shoes included."

"And I would've gone to seventeen if pressed," Pawl said.

"Bastard."

"Piss-pot."

Gord laughed. "Just like the old days. Now go and do whatever it is that you've come to do. I'll shoe your nags while you're gone. When you get back, we'll get drunk."

"Feel free to start without me," Pawl said, and then turned to Lathwi. "Do you want to come to the garrison with me?"

"No."

"Well, if you're gonna stay here," Gordy said, "you're gonna have to stay out of sight. If the high-and-mighty-minded people of this pathetic piss-hole of a town see you hanging around here unescorted, they'll blacklist me for encouraging indecency. And I'm still recovering from the last time I offended their superior moral code."

"No one will see me in your loft," she said, and then cast Pawl a sly look. "Unless they come looking for me."

Pawl let out a little cough. At the same time, a pair of small pink shoals appeared on his cheeks. "Well, the sooner I'm off, the sooner I'm back," he said, and then hurried off with no further ado.

Gordyn arched an eyebrow at his friend's retreating back, then looked to Lathwi and asked, "Where's he off to, anyway?"

"He is going to the garrison to talk to Trevor Stone," she said.

He made a sour face, as if a bad smell had just gone wafting past him. "Trevor Stone? Feh. What's he want with that useless sonuvabitch?"

"He wants to talk to the commander about the raiders who have been attacking the farmers."

He shook his head and tsked. "Poor Pawlie, he's wasting his time. Trevor Stone won't want to stop eating long enough to talk about a few raiders." He handed the roan's lead to Lathwi, then gestured toward the tin-roofed smithy's shed that abutted the rear of the barn. She headed that way. He followed with the gray in tow, complaining about the garrison commander all the while.

"He was a decent enough sort when I first came to town. But he's changed some since then. These days, he'd rather dress up like a foreign prince and parade through New Uxla than go afield with his troops. And when he does go out, he usually comes back the very same day. I'll give him one thing, though—he sure as hell knows how to handle the folks around here. Every time they're ready to hand him his balls, he finds a way to calm them down."

He tied the gray to a hitch in front of the smithy, then sat down in front of his anvil. But instead of getting to work, he scrubbed his mouth with the back of his hairy hand. "Feh!" he said. "Talking about that turd has left a bad taste in my mouth. Pass me that jug over there, would you, sweetling?"

She obliged him, but only because the jug was within her reach.

"Want some?" he asked, after taking a long pull. When she declined with a shake of her head, he snarled and said, "Then what good are you? G'won, get out of here. I've got horses to shoe."

She shrugged, then headed back into the barn. But even as she searched for the ladder to the loft, a wizened old man in a tattered, dirt-brown robe snagged her attention. He had merry eyes and a crooked, gap-toothed smile. He was capering in the doorway like a carnival monkey.

"Oyez, Daughter of Dragons," he said, as their eyes met. "Come with me. I have something for you."

Instantly intrigued, she started after the old man. He scampered out of view only to reappear at the far end of the front paddock. "Come this way, daughter," he urged her, and then scampered off again. She followed him to a trash-strewn alley, but balked when he beckoned her into it.

"I have no wish to tramp through New Uxla's garbage," she said.

"No more tramping," he said, with a half-wit's grin, and then beckoned her again. "Come. Choose. We will decide the future with my bones."

That rekindled her curiosity like a lightning strike. *Anything* involving the future demanded her immediate and complete attention. So she closed ranks with the old man, then sank into a crouch next to him. He smelled of dirt, but did not stink. His face was a weathered treasure map of creases, folds, and wrinkles. He studied Lathwi for a moment with his merry, diamond-bright eyes, then shrugged off the homespun satchel that he had been carrying on his shoulder and opened it to her.

"Pick one," he said. "After you look at it, show it to me."

She thrust her hand into the sack without a second thought. Her fingers registered a myriad of sensations: brittle, coarse, spongy, hard. She chose a small, cylindrical object that felt smooth and cool like a river-washed stone, simply because it pleased her to touch it. When she drew it forth from the sack, she saw that it was not a rock at all, but a piece of bone. The old man chuckled at the sight..

"A dragon knuckle-bone," he said. "That is good, yes, very, very good, you know who you are. You keep that, it will keep you well. And ere you reach your quest's end, it will aid you in another way."

She arched a wary eyebrow at him. "What do you know of my quest?"

He chuckled again, then thrust the sack at her. "Grab as many bones as you can in a single handful and cast them on the ground all at once."

Compelled by a now-raging case of curiosity, she did as she was told. Afterward, as she scowled at the sprawl of bones, the old man clapped his hands and gloated. "Look, there it is," he said. "The future for all to see."

"All may see it," Lathwi said, "but only a few perceive its meaning. Tell me what this casting says, Bone-Man."

He pointed to the bone closest to her foot. It was part of a small predator's lower jaw. A dog, she thought. Or perhaps a stoat. "You are being hunted," he told her. "You will be found. The hunter has bitten once already. If he bites again, your quest will fail."

The prediction concerned Lathwi, but only a little. She was no youngling, foolish and fun-loving and easy to deceive. Even the most accomplished of dragon-slayers was going to have a hard time bringing her aground. And she had turned the hunter into the hunted on more than one occasion.

"What else?" she asked.

His gnarled finger moved on to the next piece: an ivory caplet that looked like the top of a human skull. "Look here," he said, "the bones of dreaming. Something of great power will be given to you in a vision. It will not be yours to keep as it is, yet you will be its keeper."

"I do not understand," she said.

"Neither do I," he said, although the lights in his eyes suggested otherwise. "But look, the next bone came from a fish. You will come to your vision through water."

"This forecast is most obscure," Lathwi said. "Can you not simply tell me where I need to go?"

"It is you who cast the bones, not me," he said. "And I cannot tell you where to put your feet, for then you would be treading a path of my making. Go where you must, whether you want to or not. If you hesitate, your quest will fail, and a darkness will move back into the world."

That surprised her, for she had only accepted this quest to appease Liselle's ghost. The necromancer that her ex-mentor wanted her to slay must be even more unpleasant—and powerful—than she had imagined. She squeezed the knuckle-bone in her hand as if it were the mage's neck. She would not fail this quest. She had promised. And there was enough darkness on this world already.

"Look," the Bone-Man said, calling her attention to a last jumble of bones. "These are lives that are entwined with your own." There were, she noted, more than she would have expected. "These three—" He pointed to a daisy-chain of U-shaped chicken bones. "—will each make a wish in the days to come." He tapped the first bone with a finger. It shuddered, but did not move otherwise. "This one's wish will come true." He tapped the third bone, then nodded approvingly as it flipped free of the others. "This one's wish will lead to hidden desires. And this one's wish—oh, how sad." The middle bone snapped at his touch, and fell into two pieces. "This one's wish will kill him."

"What is that one's name?" she asked. "Do you know?"

The old man made no reply, perhaps because he was preoccupied with picking up the bones that she had cast. His eyes did not seem quite so merry now. His idiot grin had gone flat. She reached for his arm, meaning to press him for the answers to her questions. As she did so, a voice rang out.

"There she is!"

In one fluid movement, she swiveled out of her crouch and toward the mouth of the alleyway. She saw the two soldiers first—their drawn swords glinted in the sunlight. Then she spotted the thick-witted farmer's boy who had carted her and Pawl into town. He was standing behind the soldiers with his hands on his hips, unconsciously mimicking his sire. His triumphant, frog-mouthed smirk was all for her. She bared her teeth at him, then half-turned to share her irritation with the old man. But in the moment or so that she had been looking the other way, he and his bag of bones had vanished. She had no time to wonder about that, though, for Eldon's soldiers were now closing in on her.

"Put your hands in the air where we can see them," the taller of the two told her. "You're under arrest."

"Why?" she asked.

"You've been accused of murder and mayhem," he replied. "We have a witness who swears that you were among the raiders who attacked the Voss farm yesterday."

"Your witness is mistaken," she said.

"I am not," Eldon claimed, pushing past the soldiers so he could taunt her at close range. "I was running errands for my da when I saw you and the others thundering down the road. I hid in a field as you rode by and then followed you to Bo Voss's place. I saw you stab Bo again and again and again. I saw your murdering friends do worse. I didn't tell anyone at first, because I was ashamed of myself for not trying to help Bo. But when you and that other fellow showed up at our farm, pretending to be travelers so you could size up our defenses, I told Da who you really were. He bade me to drive you into town and turn you over to Commander Stone. And that's exactly what I did."

Lathwi locked eyes with the soldier who had spoken to her, and very calmly said, "This youngling is a liar."

"The commander doesn't think so," he replied.

"That's right," Eldon gloated. "And tomorrow, he's going to hang you and your chicken-shit friend in the town square as a lesson to other marauders."

"I have a different lesson in mind," she said, and wrung her mouth into a chilling half-smile. "It is for a certain young fool who does not know when to leave well enough alone." The soldiers shifted, meaning to set themselves between her and the boy. With her Will and a brusque Word, she rendered them unable to move. As they stared at her, wide-eyed with surprise and the beginnings of fear, she said, "Have no fear. I bear you no grudge. But this little dog—" She turned her dragon's smile on Eldon. "—has dared too much, too often."

The boy paled. A moment later, he turned on his heel and bolted. Lathwi let him get to the top of the alleyway, then reached out with her Will and hauled him back like a big, ugly fish. As she forced him to kneel before her, the sharp, yellow tang of urine crept into the air.

"I knew you weren't a woman," he said.

"I never said I was," she replied. "I only said I was no demon. I also said that if you ever challenged me again, I would not be merciful. Do you remember that?"

"I only did it so Trevor Stone would think well of me!" the boy gabbled. "It was the only way to get into his service. Please! I don't hurt me. I meant no—"

She cut him off with a hiss. "You are a coward as well as a liar. You will not be missed."

"Please," he begged. "Don't kill me!"

"As you wish," she said, smiling as the Bone-Man's prophecy came to mind.

Then she summoned her power.

The air around the farmer's boy began to shimmer. A moment later, it thickened into an opaque sphere that engulfed him. The sides of this cocoon bulged and rippled as the boy tried to break free of it, but the only thing that escaped were his muffled pleas for help. She spoke a Word. He doubled over, then dropped to his hands and knees. His nose grew longer. His chin disappeared. She began focusing on details: tongue, fur, tail, even a certain scent. When the Change was complete, she stamped it into place with her Name and then collapsed the sphere.

A medium-sized bulldog with worried, close-set eyes stood before Lathwi now. As soon as it realized that the sphere was gone, it menaced her with a snarl and then ran for its life. Although Eldon-dog was still technically male, she had Willed it so he would always smell like a bitch in heat. That, instead of killing him outright. That, to satisfy a bone-man's prophecy—the one about a wish leading to hidden desires. Alas that she could only hope and not guarantee that Eldon-dog would retain a portion of his human awareness long enough to appreciate the ironies of his new life.

"You heard the youngling recant," she said to the soldiers—not a question, but a statement of fact. One of them managed a small nod. "Now you will go to Trevor Stone, and tell him that he was deceived."

The same soldier shook his head, a surprising refusal. With a Word and a scowl, she restored his ability to speak and demanded, "What are your names?"

"I am called Thomas," he replied. "My partner is named Ross."

"And why will you not bring the truth to Trevor Stone's attention?"

"Because we would be killed for doing so," Thomas said. "He is determined to hang you and your friend."

"Why?"

"To show the townspeople that he is working to rid the borderlands of raiders."

"So he is a liar, too."

"I cannot deny it."

Lathwi hissed. Humans were such a deceitful lot—always plotting and telling lies and trying to hide their true natures. If it were not for Pawl, she would leave New Uxla this very moment and never look back. But she could not continue on her way while the swordmaster's life was in jeopardy. Although he was only human, she had Chosen him, and felt compelled to preserve his well-being.

"I must get my friend out of the garrison," she said. "Can you help me accomplish this? Or does your integrity forbid it?"

The soldiers exchanged a look. The one who had his voice back asked, "What do you want us to do?"

"I do not know," she said. "I cannot think with the stench of garbage in my nose. If I release you from my spell, will you come to Gordyn's Horse Emporium with me?"

The color drained from both of their faces. Their gazes turned elusive. She knew enough about people to know that this was not a good sign. "What is wrong?" she asked. When they continued to avert their eyes, she added, "I can compel you to speak if I must."

"We already paid the horsetrader a visit," Thomas admitted. "When he wouldn't tell us where you were, we beat him up a little."

"Is he dead?" she asked. He shook his head. "Near to death?" Again, a denial. "Then he will no doubt be happy to see you again, if only so he can return what you gave him. Now, will you come or not?" At his reluctant nod, she added a warning. "If you try to arrest me or flee, I will Change you into dogs, too. And that spell lasts a lifetime."

"We're with you," Thom said.

So she returned their limbs to them. And true to the man's word, they followed her back to the stables without incident.

"Gordyn?" she called, as she strode into the barn. "Where are you?"

A feeble rustling in one of the back stalls snared her attention. When she went to investigate, she found Gord sprawled in a mound of hay. His face was bruised about the eyes and mouth. The front of his shirt was splattered with drying blood. A jug lay empty by his side.

"Lath?" he mumbled, trying to see past the swelling around his eyes. "Izzat you?"

"Yes."

He sat up in the hay like a man who has just heard his lover's husband calling for her and said, "Trevor Stone's got soldiers out lookin' for you. He's got Pawl already."

"I know," she said, but he was too excited and drunk to hear.

"You gotta get the hell outa here before they find you. Take the roan and ride, don't worry, it's shod, and—" His urgent expression fell flat and then hardened that way. "Shit. You again." He staggered to his feet. At the same time, he beckoned to her. "Get behind me, Lath. The soldiers are back."

"I know," she replied, dragon-patient. "I brought them with me. They are going to help me free Pawl."

His swollen, bleary-eyed gaze darted from her to the two soldiers and then back again. As he did so, a drunken smile spread across his mouth like a crack in thin ice.

"Well, I'll be damned," he burbled. "Count me in."

Then he flopped back down in the hay and passed out.

Chapter 9

*P*awl paced back and forth across the cold stone floor, angry as a bee in a bottle. He should've known, he told himself. He should've guessed. In retrospect, it was all so terribly obvious. He gritted his teeth, trying to stop himself from reliving the memory yet again, but to no avail.

"Well-met, Pawl of Compara," Trevor Stone had said, and clasped his hand like a long lost brother. "What a pleasure it is to see somebody from my homeland. Please, sit down and tell me what's news in my favorite city."

Pawl studied the commander for a moment. He was a stocky man who had gone to fat like some fields go to seed. His cheeks were rosy, and bulged like a squirrel's. His stomach quivered when he walked. He had two chins, pudgy fingers, and a well-padded backside, but even so, he still managed to generate a compelling presence. His dark eyes could pierce a leather jerkin from fifty paces. His frilly shirt camouflaged his belly. And his tan, light-weight trousers and black, knee-high boots made him appear taller than he really was.

"Compara endures as always, sir," Pawl said, as he accepted the proffered chair. "But she's not had an easy time of late."

"How so?" Stone asked, as he settled himself down behind a handsome ironwood desk. "Has there been another outbreak of pox?"

"No, sir. Not pox. Ghosts." At the commander's querulous look, he added, "It seems that a mage is forcing the dead to haunt the citizens of the north."

Stone gave his silvering warrior's braid an incredulous toss. "Now why on earth would he want to do that?"

"I don't know, sir. That's why I've come—"

"Please, call me Stone," the commander said. "We're not quite so formal here on the border." Before Pawl could respond in any way, the man raised his voice and shouted as if the building were on fire. "Nigel!"

The door to the office swung immediately open, and a young man poked his head into the room. Although he wore a soldier's uniform, his red hair was short like a clerk's. He had a narrow chest and a cocky mouth.

"Yes, Stone?" he asked.

"Bring us a bottle of port and a snack to go with it," Stone replied. "A wedge of cheese, perhaps, and perhaps some of that chicken from lunch, too."

"At once," Nigel said, and withdrew again.

"So go on with what you were saying, Pawl," Stone urged then. "What brings the swordmaster of Compara to my doorstep?"

"I'm looking for the mage I was telling you about," Pawl said. "I have it on good authority that he's working out of Death's Door in the south."

At that, the commander planted his elbows on his desktop and made his fingers into a steeple which he then tapped against his nose. "Death's Door, you say. Hmm, that sounds like Seth. The sneak. I didn't think he was that powerful. I wonder what he's up to."

"You know him?"

"Not personally." As he said this, Nigel came breezing back into the office with a tray heaped with glasses, plates, and food. Stone acknowledged him with a glance, then went on with what he'd been saying. "I know of him, though. He's Veeder's mage."

"Would that be *General* Veeder?" Pawl asked, raising his voice so he could be heard over the clamor that Nigel was making. "The leader of the Grange-cult?"

"The one and only," Stone replied. The top of his desk was covered with victuals now: a decanter of port, a pitcher of lemonade, a loaf of bread, a wedge of fragrant goat's cheese, fried chicken legs, and fresh apples. He gestured broadly at the spread and said, "Help yourself."

"Nothing for me, thanks," Pawl said, secretly amazed and not wholly approving of the extent of this 'snack'. He could have lived for a week or more on so much. He made a mental note to take Nigel aside after this interview and suggest that he scale down these between-meal buffets. His commander certainly didn't need them.

"Nonsense," Stone said, as if he had been reading Pawl's thoughts. "Good food stimulates the mind and heart. And soldiers like us need every advantage we can get out here on the border. Now come, what will it be? A glass of port? It's quite lovely. And how about a piece of chicken to go with it?"

Since he seemed destined to lose this fight, Pawl decided to concede graciously. "Now that I think of it, I *am* a bit parched. I believe I'll try some of that lemonade after all." Then, as Nigel poured him a glass, he returned to the troublesome topic of Veeder. "I have no proof as of yet," he said, "but I suspect that there's a connection between this general and the recent spate of borderland raids."

"Oh, you do, do you?" The commander popped a hunk of cheese into his mouth, then washed it down with a swallow of port. His expression was indulgent, half-amused, like that of a father who has been listening to his infant son's babble. "Nigel here—" He gestured at his aide with a chicken bone. "—would have me believe that the raiders are nothing more than a gang of drunken southern youths out to prove their manhood."

Pawl glanced at the redhead, who had assumed a watchful stance behind Stone's chair. He, too, seemed mildly amused—as if this talk of raiders were some sort of a joke. That irked Pawl. He took a drink of lemonade to rinse the disapproval from his voice and then said, "If we were looking at one half-assed, mid-summer's night barn-burning here, I might be inclined to agree with your man. But there have been *four* attacks in the past six months, not one, and all of the available evidence, including eye-witness accounts, points to a band of seasoned warriors, *not* drunken boys. Now, I've heard tell that Veeder has an army somewhere near the border. My guess is that he's using local farms to supply it with food and horses. What he doesn't need, he burns to keep it from the north. And so with one stroke, he strengthens his position in two ways."

A moment's silence ensued. Then Stone began to clap—slow, rhythmic applause. "Well done, swordmaster," he cheered. "Excellent analysis." He held up his empty port glass. As Nigel refilled it, he went on to say, "And as it happens, you're right. Veeder *is* behind the recent spate of raids. He's also preparing to invade the north."

The lemonade that Pawl had been just about to swallow acquired a coppery tang: the taste of confirmed suspicions. "Does Wynn Rame know this?"

"Not yet," Stone replied, and then twitched Pawl a mocking smile over the rim of his port glass. "Relaxe, swordmaster. Veeder's not going to launch his invasion today. I have it on good authority that he's waiting for a sign of some kind. Who knows? It may never come to him."

"Or maybe it will come tonight," Pawl countered. "Isn't it wiser to be prepared for the worst?"

"Don't be naive," Stone said. "If I pestered Compara every time some warlord threatened to go rogue, Wynn would've sacked me a dozen times already. For the time being, my men and I are adequate to the task."

"That's not what the farmers are saying."

The commander loosed a derisive snort. "Ploughbound fools. They think that a build-up of troops in the area will make them safe. But the fact is, it would only drain my resources and tip Veeder off. So long as that ambitious son of the south believes that I don't know what he's up to, *I* have the advantage."

That made sense to Pawl. Or so it seemed. He wasn't thinking too clearly at the moment. The room was too hot all of a sudden, and his stomach was quivering. Hoping to steady himself, he gulped down the last of his lemonade. It still had that odd, coppery taste. He felt himself break into a sweat. At the same time, his mouth began to water.

But what about the farmers and their farms?

He wanted to ask the question, indeed, he thought he had, but neither Stone nor his aide seemed to hear him. They were both smiling now. Nigel seemed slightly out of focus.

"So tell me," Stone said. "What brought you and your friend to New Uxla?"

"Need—horses," he stammered, even as he tried to recall when it was exactly that he had mentioned Lathwi.

"Ah, I see. And what happened to your last mount?"

Pawl slurped back a mouthful of saliva, then said, "Dragon—ate."

The commander laughed. "Good answer, swordmaster. It would be hard to prove otherwise, wouldn't it?"

Confusion gusted through Pawl like a desert wind. Now why would anyone other than his own self care what happened to his horse? Something wasn't right here—no, not right at all. He just couldn't put his finger on it. Yet. Everything seemed to be coming at him through a viscous haze.

"Lucky for me I have a witness who says he saw you lose your horse during the raid on the Voss farm," Stone said, and then gestured Nigel toward the door. "Let him in, would you please?"

Now Pawl's thoughts were in a full-on tailspin. *Raid? Witness?* What nonsense was this? He wanted to stand up and protest these goings-on, but he could not muster the strength to move. All he could do was sit and stare and drool. Then Eldon strode into the room. He shot Pawl a look of pure spite, then came to rigid attention in front of Stone.

"Is this the man you saw?" the commander asked him.

"Yessir," Eldon said. "He killed Bo Voss with his sword after Bo killed his horse."

"You're sure?"

"Yessir."

"All right then, you're dismissed for now. We'll discuss your reward as soon as his accomplice is in custody."

"As you wish, sir," Eldon said, and then marched out of the room like a soldier on parade. As he departed, Pawl struggled to express his undulating thoughts.

"Boy," he said. "Lie," he said.

A distant, almost bemused smile curved across the commander's round, well-fed face. The gleam in his eyes turned remote as well. "Yes. Yes, he did," he said, in a mild, contemplative tone, as if they were talking about the weather. "And the beauty of it is—I didn't even put him up to it. I'm afraid he and fortune conspired against you, friend. And tomorrow, they will see you dead. Care for more lemonade?"

Pawl's gaze darted toward his empty glass. The coppery taste in his mouth took on a harsh new meaning. He'd been—set up. From start to finish. He tried to ask why, but couldn't seem to get his lips around the word. In the meantime, Trevor Stone poured himself another glass of port and leaned back in his oversized chair.

"Shall I slit his throat and dump him in an alley?" Nigel asked. "Or is a shallow grave in the desert to be his final resting place?"

"Under normal circumstances, I'd say the desert," Stone replied. "But it would seem that those stiff-necked farmfolk need to be placated again. What better way to do that than to hang a pair of marauders so soon after the latest raid?"

Nigel cocked a dubious eyebrow at Pawl. "He doesn't look like a Southerner."

Stone shrugged. "It's hard to tell what land a man hails from when he's hooded for execution. But even if we left his face uncovered, few if any of the townsfolk would clamor for his pardon. He's a stranger to these parts, and his death will make them feel safer."

"Until the next raid," Nigel remarked.

"Yes," Stone agreed mildly. "Until then." He reached for a hunk of cheese only to stop in mid-grab and scowl at Pawl. "Get him out of here already, would you? All of that drool is spoiling my appetite."

"At once," Nigel said, and yanked Pawl out of his seat by his warrior's braid.

Pawl remembered lurching to his feet, then a slipping sensation, and then the floor came rushing up to greet him. A moment later, darkness enveloped him.

When at last he returned to his senses, he had found himself in this tiny, windowless cell. It reeked of moldy straw and an ancient slops-pot. The only light came from the crack between the door and the ground. He did not mind that, for his eyeballs were throbbing like two war-drums in their sockets. And his head hurt so bad, it felt as if it were coming apart at the seams. Ugh! He'd had gentler hangovers after leave-long benders with that reprobate, Gord.

The thought of his old shieldmate brought him back to the present—a few hours past the worst of the pain. As he paced forth and back and forth again, things *crunched* beneath his boots: live roaches and tiny bones and the Dreamer only knew what else. He guessed that night had fallen by now, but had no way of knowing for sure. The light from the crack beneath the door remained a dim constant. And time passed in odd waves and folds on death row.

Not that he gave much thought to his pending execution. He had too many other things on his mind. Like Trevor Stone's treachery. Now that the blinders had been torn from his eyes, it was obvious that Veeder was paying the man to keep the border soft. That was how he could afford all of that fine food and those lordly luxuries. Damn the greedy bastard! Veeder could invade any moment now. And when he did, Wynn Rame wouldn't know the first thing about it until the southerner was practically in his lap. Pawl kicked at his cell door, venting frustration and fury. Damndamndamn. He had to get out of here. Jamie needed to know about this. So did Gord. And so did—

Lathwi.

For all he knew, she was in a cell right next to him, cursing and pacing just like he was. He had called out her name several times and gotten no reply, but that did not mean that she wasn't here, only that she hadn't heard him. And while he wanted desperately to believe that she had eluded capture and was now running that new stallion of hers into the ground, he knew better than to put his trust in hope. He had to assume that she was in as much trouble as he was. He had to assume that she needed help.

And that meant helping himself first.

He drove his shoulder into the door again and again, hoping to spring a board or a hinge loose. As he did so, a tendril of ice-cold air raised the hairs on the back of his neck and then his hopes. Where there was a draft, there might be a fingerhold—a chink or hole that he could dig out, expand, exploit in some way. But even as the thought crossed his mind, he forgot it again. For there was a patch of shiny gray fog in the cell with him now. As he watched, it took on a familiar shape.

"Liselle!" he said. "Dreamer be praised! I need your help."

The ghost flinched as if in pain and then said, "Please, do not use Her name in my presence. It only reminds me of my loss."

"Sorry," he said, and then blurted the very next thing that came to mind. "I need you to take a message to Jamus."

"I cannot," Liselle replied, in a voice as chilled as the draft that had heralded her arrival. "Someone else commands me." She glanced about the cell then. As she did so, a scowl ridged her spectral brow. "Where is Lathwi?"

"I don't know."

The ghost flinched again. This time, her distress was almost palpable. "You must find her."

"I'd like to accommodate you," he said, managing a wry tone. "The only problem is, I'm slated to be executed at dawn."

Liselle's scowl deepened. "That must not happen. You are my only link to her."

With that, she disappeared. A long moment later, he heard a melting scream and the muffled scuffling of leather-shod feet on the run. As he listened, somebody scrabbled to a stop in front of his cell and threw off the heavy wooden beam that held the door shut. The door creaked slightly open. Pawl opened it the rest of the way with an emphatic kick and then burst into the hallway ready for a fight. But the guard who had set him free was already racing toward a distant stairway. A thin, gray mist swarmed all around him. The man screamed as if he were being chased by a pack of rabid bears and then disappeared from sight. The mist reversed course and started drifting toward Pawl. As it drew near, he saw Liselle's grievous, heart-shaped face in its midst.

"I have done all that I can do," she told him. "You must do the rest on your own."

"I will," he replied. "Thank you."

She dismissed his gratitude with a frown. At the same time, she started to fade. "Find Lathwi," she urged, in a voice no louder than a whisper.

"I will," he promised, as she disintegrated.

But first, he was going to find Trevor Stone.

෨ ෬

"Something's wrong," Thom whispered, as he and his shieldmate escorted Lathwi into the garrison's lower reaches. "There should be a guard at the foot of these stairs, and another three patrolling the cell-block. Where'd everybody go?"

Ross swallowed hard and said, "Could be a trap. Come tomorrow, we could all be swinging by our necks."

Lathwi hissed at them. "Be calm. If you act like a spooked cat, you will spoil the trick."

And what a remarkably simple trick it was: her walking unarmed into the garrison in the company of her two new soldier-companions. The ruse had been Thom's idea. He said people would assume that she was their prisoner, and that they were taking her to the dungeon. No one would bother her, he said. No one would think her out of place. And so far, he was right—if only because the garrison's lower reaches seemed to be deserted. She did not know why that was so. Nor did she care. Her one thought was to find Pawl and get out—the faster, the better.

As she and her phony captors cleared the stairway, a guard came staggering out of a nearby cell. His uniform was disheveled. His warrior's braid was frayed. He stumbled a few steps, then sank to his knees and covered his head with his arms. A moment later, he began to sob. Ross heaved a private sigh of relief. Thom stifled a groan and called out to the man.

"You there!" he said. "Come here and give me your name so I can report you for being drunk on duty."

The guard half-lurched, half-crawled his way over to them. As he drew nearer, it became obvious to Lathwi that he was distraught rather than drunk. He worked his jaws like a cud-chewing cow. His red-rimmed eyes kept rolling back in their sockets. When he came within a foot of her, he dropped back onto his knees and began weeping again. He smelled of fear, not gish.

"What ails you, soldier?" Thom demanded.

"She—she came to me," the man stammered in reply.

"Who came to you?"

"The lady in the mists," he said. "She was beautiful—a vision, I thought. Then I looked into her eyes and saw my grave. It was dark—and so very cold. My body was full of worms. I could—*feel* them writhing and eating and burrowing through my flesh. I can feel them still." He clawed at his face, then let out a hair-raising wail. "Please! I beg you. Make the worms go away."

Thom retreated a step. Pity and loathing shone in his eyes. "I can't help you, man. I'm just a soldier. Go home and get drunk. Maybe that will help."

"Maybe," the guard echoed, and lurched to his feet. As he went stumbling toward the stairway, Thom made a sign to avert evil.

"Do you know anything about this mist-lady?" he asked Lathwi.

She shrugged, refusing to speculate. "Whoever she is," she said, "she is not here now. Let us find Pawl and be gone from here before she comes back."

Neither of her companions objected to the suggestion. So they split up and went prowling through the cell-block in search of a door that bore the executioner's charcoaled X on its wood-and-iron face. Lathwi held her breath as she moved from cell to cell—not in anticipation of finding Pawl, but because of the massive stench. She could not imagine a crime terrible enough to warrant confinement in such a foul place. She would rather die in the open air.

Ross's shout disrupted her thoughts. "Here! I've found it."

She tracked the man down in a hurry. But even as she closed in on him, she knew that something was wrong. A door with the executioner's mark was standing wide open, but Pawl was nowhere in sight. A dragon's scowl gathered on her brow. Ross was quick to try and placate it.

"It was like this when I got here," he said. "I checked inside for clues, but if there *are* any, I didn't see them."

"A resourceful man, your swordmaster," Thom mused, as he joined her and Ross. "How do you suppose he managed to get out?"

"Perhaps he made a wish," Lathwi said, remembering the Bone-Man's prediction. Then she went on to consider likelier prospects. "Or perhaps he is in another cell."

Thom rejected that possibility with a shake of his head. "I checked the rest of the block. This is the only door that bears the death-X. And Stone wouldn't have put him in an unmarked cell. He doesn't like mix-ups."

"So how now?" Ross asked. "Shall we go in search of him?"

"No," she replied. "I came to free him. That has been done. And now that he is loose, I must be on my way."

"What about us?" Thom asked.

"You are soldiers," she said. "Your place is here. Or, if you can no longer honor a commander who would kill you for speaking the truth, go north to Compara and ask for a man named Jamus D'Arques. It may be that he will be interested in the goings-on here. Tell him that Pawl sent you."

The shieldmates exchanged a troubled look that had a hard knot of temptation at its core. As they weighed the sin of desertion against their duty to a corrupt commanding officer, Lathwi raised an illusion of empty space around herself and headed for the stairs. A moment later, she heard Ross loose a startled cry.

"Hey! Where'd she go?"

"We're probably better off not knowing," Thom told him.

She acknowledged his wisdom with a fleeting smile, then continued on her way: up the stairway, through the garrison, past the guard at the gate. As she stepped into the public domain, she saw Gordyn shambling down the main thoroughfare. He had a jug in one hand and a length of rope in the other.

"Here, doggie," he bawled between swigs. "Come to Gord. Anybody seen my little bitch?"

But he was not as drunk as he appeared to be. Leastwise, he was not supposed to be. Thom and Ross had sobered the horse-trader up over the course of the afternoon, and Lathwi had filled that jug up with water. His rubbery-legged search for a nonexistent dog was another piece of the plan, a pretense that allowed him to be close at hand in the event that she needed help with Pawl or the guards. As he staggered about, drawing all eyes to himself, she crossed the street and joined him. Her illusion was still intact, but she would have bet her wings that no one would have noticed her anyway.

"Have you seen Pawl?" she asked, in voice pitched for his ears alone.

He started. His head wobbled on his neck. "No-sir-ee," he bawled. "Ain't seen hide nor hair of my poor little friend. And I'm running out of places to look."

"Return to the stable," she said.

He drank the jug dry and then stared at it like a man betrayed. "Gone already? Damn that dog! Lucky for her, I got more."

With that, he went staggering toward the far end of town.

Lathwi raced ahead of him, rearranging her plans as she went. Now that she had had a chance to think on it, she was glad that Pawl had gotten away without her. Because now she could set off for Death's Door without him—and without an argument. She was not particularly happy about leaving him behind. Over the past few weeks, her interest in him had taken on a curious new intensity. New appetites had been roused. But she had not forgotten the Bone-Man's prophecies. Someone in her life was going to die of a wish. She most definitely did not want that someone to be the swordmaster of Compara. Therefore she had to cut him out of her life like a wayward thread.

Besides, what use would he be on a hunt for a rogue sorcerer?

"You never told me you were a witch," Gordyn said, as he strode into the barn. His tone was accusing; his gaze, annoyed. But there was no trace of a stagger left in his strides.

"You never asked," she replied, and slung a saddle onto her horse's back.

"No, I guess I didn't." He rubbed his knuckles over his bruised cheek, a pensive gesture, then glanced around the barn. "So where's Pawlie?"

"I do not know," she said, as she cinched the girth. "His cell was empty when we got there. We saw no sign of him."

"So now what?"

"He is bound to turn up here sooner or later. When he does, tell him to go north. Do not allow him to follow me."

The horse-trader snorted. "Have you ever tried to stop that crazy bastard when he's made up his mind to do a thing?"

"Yes," she replied, after a moment's thought. "Yes, I have. He can be difficult."

Difficult?" He snorted again. "Hell, he's downright—"

On impulse, she reached out and touched a finger to the gap between his iron-wire eyebrows. At the same time, she tamped a command into his mind and gave it a trigger.

"—impossible." He blinked back surprise and a little something more. "What'd you do that for?"

"It is merely a precaution," she told him, and then hoisted herself into the saddle. It felt good to sit down, even if the seat was naught but a scrap of leather strapped to a horse's back. She had used magic three times today, and that sapped the strength right out of a body as soft and inefficient as hers. "Now step aside. I must be gone."

He did as he was told. As she urged the stallion past him, he raised a hand to her in farewell. She did not return the gesture. In her mind, she had already left him and the rest of New Uxla far, far behind.

₧ʢ

Gordyn was drowsing in a pile of hay when something solid jammed itself into his sore ribs. He came awake with a pained snark and then bolted upright with his fists out in front of him. A figure loomed out of the darkness. It was tall and lean, and held a length of tapered steel in one hand. The horse-trader grunted, then climbed to his feet.

"I damn near drank myself out of gish waiting for you, boy-o," he said. "Where in hell have you been?"

"Detained," Pawl said. "Where's Lathwi?"

"Gone," Gord said, and then went hobbling off toward his smithy. Pawl followed on his heels.

"How long?"

"An hour or so, two at the most." He stuck a twist of straw into the smoldering fire-pit, then used the resulting flame to light a small oil-lamp. "She went to the garrison to get you out, but you'd already flown the coop, so she figured she was free to take off. Independent wench, ain't she?"

He turned to grin at Pawl only to gape instead. For now that the lamp was lit, he could see his old shieldmate quite well, and he was covered with drying blood. It flecked his face and freckled his chest and left his warrior's braid stiff. Only his hands appeared clean. "Great pustulate mother! How much of that is yours?"

Pawl glanced down at his spattered front, then shrugged. "None of it, as far as I know. Although I suppose that little rat, Nigel, might've scratched me once or twice in his efforts to get away."

Gordyn sucked in a scandalized breath. "You killed the commander's aide?"

"I did," Pawl replied, in a tone as grim as his expression. "Stone is dead as well. It was my duty," he added, as the redhead's jaw came unhinged. "Both of them were on General Veeder's payroll."

The disbelief that had Gordyn's face in its grip hardened into an honest soldier's contempt. Almost reflexively, he clenched his fists. "And here I was, thinking that Stone was just a lazy sack of shit. I hope you served him a traitor's death."

"His men will find him in his nightgown, between soiled sheets. I offered him the chance to fight for a more dignified death, but he squealed for Nigel instead, so I spitted him then and there. And believe me, Nigel fared no better. Afterward, I wrote out their crimes on the walls in blood. That should give any other traitors in the ranks a moment's pause."

"How many more do you think there are?"

"I have no idea. And I'm not going to stick around long enough to find out."

He strode over to the cooling trough and began to wash up. In between splashes, he said, "The north's in serious trouble, Gord. The border is so soft, it couldn't turn back an army of ants. And it looks like Veeder is getting ready to invade. Wynn Rame needs to know these things—as soon as possible. That's why I want you to head for Compara. You're the only one I can trust to deliver a message. You are well enough to ride, aren't you?" he added, taking a break from his laving to give his friend a speculative once-over. "I didn't say so before, but you look like a hairy slab of bad meat. What happened?"

"It was nothing," Gordyn replied, with the bald-faced insouciance of a seasoned brawler, "a misunderstanding among friends. If I needed to, I could ride to the moon and back. But you're the one who should deliver that message, Pawlie. Nobody's going to believe an old piss-pot like me."

"Jamus D'Arques will. Just tell him that I sent you," Pawl said. Then he dunked his head into the trough. A moment later, he pulled it back out. "Besides," he said, as he shook himself off, "I can't go. I have to catch up with Lathwi."

Almost in spite of himself, Gordyn winced. "She told me to tell you not to follow her."

"She always says that." He wrung out his braid. The water that cascaded to the floor was pink. "But whether she likes to admit it or not, she does need help from time to time. I'm going to be there to make sure she gets it."

"I dunno," the horse-trader argued. "She looked pretty damned capable to me. And since when is some woman more important to you than your duty to Compara?"

"Since I met Lathwi," Pawl said, perfectly deadpan. He knew that his old friend was right, that gallivanting after Lathwi when an invasion appeared not only probable but imminent was tantamount to desertion. But he did not care. Not one bit. Something was *pulling* him after her—something stronger than love or sex, something that felt more like compulsion. He could not have turned his back on her now even if he wanted to. And he definitely did not want to. "So are you going to carry the message for me or not?"

"Like you've given me any bloody choice," Gord grumbled, and then disappeared into the barn. When he returned a moment later, he had a shirt in hand. "Here," he said, tossing the garment at Pawl, "put this on. You won't get anywhere looking like you just rode out of a slaughterhouse."

"Thanks," Pawl said. He shucked his leather jerkin, then pulled the blood-stained undershirt over his head. As he did so, he said, "Do me another favor and saddle up that gelding for me, would you? If I ride hard, I can catch up with her before dawn."

"She said not to follow her. In fact, she insisted."

Gordyn's voice sounded strained now, as if he were talking through gritted teeth. His vehemence in taking Lathwi's side amused Pawl. He started to say so as he stripped the undershirt past his eyes, but the sight of a blackjack arcing his way instantly distracted him. He half-turned to avoid the blow. The lead-filled pouch caught him behind the right ear. He thought to voice a protest, but groaned instead. As he slumped to the ground, he heard someone say, "Like it or not, you are going north."

It sounded like Lathwi.

❧ ☙

A sense of being pitched back and forth and back again crept into Pawl's murky dreams. Sometime later, his head began to throb—a slow, dry pounding that would not let him rest. His eyelids rolled back. A horse's belly hazed into view. What little else he could see appeared to be upside down. He let out a groan. The horse plodded to a stop. A moment later, a man sank into a crouch in front of him. He had red hair and a nose full of busted capillaries. His breath smelled of stale gish.

"'Bout time you came to," his ex-shieldmate said. "How do you feel?"

"Bad," Pawl grumbled in reply. "Like one of your damned nags kicked me in the brainpan."

Gord nodded as if in agreement. "I thought I might've hit you a little bit too hard. But I wasn't sure if you'd go down otherwise."

"I'm flattered," Pawl drawled. "But why cold-cock me at all?" His horse flicked its tail into his face. He sputtered a curse, and then said, "Let me down from here already, would you?"

"I had to do it," Gordyn replied. "It was for your own friggin' good. New Uxla was crawling with soldiers looking to harvest your head, and you were being your usual stubborn self."

"You're the stubborn one, not me," Pawl said. But the rest sounded familiar. He remembered killing Stone. And Nigel. And then going back to the Emporium to look for Lathwi. She'd been gone, though. Gone, gone, gone. That's when things started getting fuzzy. "So where is she?"

"Where is who?"

"You know who—Lathwi."

Gord's face took a reproachful slant. "There you go again—Lathwi this, Lathwi that. She's gone, my friend. You gotta accept that. And until you do, you're gonna stay right where you are."

Pawl snarled, venting his frustration, and then strained with all his might against the leather bindings that held him hog-tied to his saddle. The ties did not give, though, not even a bit. All he got for his efforts was a bigger headache and another flick in the face. He cursed under his breath. Gord had always had a way with knots.

"So what did she promise you?" he asked. "Gold? A year's worth of gish? Tell me. I'll double her price."

The reproach in his expression turned into hurt. "You know I'm not so easily bought, mate. Hell, if I had a choice, I wouldn't be doing this. But every time you even think about turning south, I get this overwhelming urge to knock you in the head. That woman wants you in Compara."

Pawl's irritation soared to new heights. He did not want to go to Compara. He could not go. Something was pulling him south. Maybe it was love. Maybe it was duty, or even destiny. Whatever it was, though, it was going to drive him mad unless he could find a way around Lathwi's sorcery.

But how in hell was he supposed to counter dragon magic?

An answer came to him over the drumming of his headache: *by thinking like a dragon.* A smile unfolded within him, but he did not let Gordyn see it.

"All right then," he said. "If that's what Lathwi wants, then that's what she'll get. Now cut me loose before the blood clots in my brain."

Gord wagged a reproving finger at him. "Not so fast, boy-o. I'll need an oath from you first."

Pawl borrowed one of his friend's horse-trading facades—the one that radiated intimate pain and grudging resignation even though he knew he was getting the better of his mark. "I, Pawl of Compara, do hereby swear on my honor to return to Compara."

Relief washed over the redhead in a great, crashing wave. He immediately pulled a knife from his belt and began cutting Pawl's bindings as if they were last year's regrets. As he worked, he said, "I know you're not happy about this, but it'll work out. I'm sure of it."

As soon as the last tie gave way, Pawl slid to the ground like some boneless slug. Gord retreated a few steps, as if he half-expected Pawl to come up swinging for him, but Pawl had no such intentions. His head ached. So did his back. The last thing he wanted to do at the moment was start a brawl. He stretched to pop the kinks from his spine. At the same time, he tried to get his bearings. The hilly, lightly wooded terrain told him that they had crossed into Tryssa province—but just recently. If he rode hard throughout the day, he should be able to recover most of the ground that he'd lost. Lathwi would still be at least a whole day's ride ahead of him, but her trail should still be relatively fresh.

"Do you want to sack out for a while?" Gord asked. "Or did you want something to eat first?"

"I want you to get back on your horse and start riding," he replied, in a level tone. "Head for Compara. Don't look back. I'll catch up with you later."

"Pawlie," the big man said, voicing his name as both a warning and a complaint. "You swore—"

"I swore to return to Compara," Pawl calmly reminded him. "I didn't say when. Or with whom." He'd learned that sleight of tongue from Lathwi herself. "So get going, mate. When you get to the city, remember to ask for Jamus D'Arques." He pronounced the name slowly, with exaggerated care. "He'll know what to do with the news of Trevor Stone's treachery."

"I'm not sure I can do this," Gord said, looking wet-dog miserable.

Pawl gave him a friendly slap on the back and then ushered him toward his horse. "Of course you can," he said. "If that compulsion starts bothering you, just tell yourself that I'm somewhere behind you and then think about a jug of gish. That ought to do the trick."

"And if it don't?"

"Then I suppose this won't be the last time that I wake up to find myself tied to my horse," Pawl replied dryly. "But don't worry, man, it'll work. Just don't think about it too hard."

Gordyn struggled with the idea for a moment longer, then purged himself of his doubts with a sigh. "What the hell," he said. "I'll give it a shot. Thinking's never been my strong point anywise." He slung himself into his saddle. "The last one to Compara buys a week's worth of rounds."

"I'm right behind you," Pawl said. At the same time, he gave his friend's mount a resounding swat on the rump. The horse startled, then broke into a run at Gord's urging. Pawl waited until they were well out of sight, and then headed south.

Chapter 10

Taziem rumbled, a sound of vast irritation and complaint. She had been walking for more days—and nights!—than a dragon cared to count already. Her feet were sore, her throat was desert-dry, and her belly was woefully empty. All this for no good reason! She had not killed, or even seen, any dragonslayers yet. She had not caught so much as a glimpse of another gypsy yet, either, when there was supposed to be a whole flock of them in the area.

"Just a bit further now, Great One," the gypsy cub called Luke kept on telling her, as he blazed their nighttime trail. "We're almost there."

Almost there. She hissed at the hateful words. The next time Luke said them, she was going to bite his head off and eat the rest—even if he only amounted to a mouthful or so. Her stomach growled as if in encouragement. An instant later, a tree root cropped up in front of her big toe. She let out a roar of pain, then flopped down on her backside and keened to herself. Sometimes, being human was not nearly as fun as it looked.

As she sat there, sulking in the dark, Luke came padding out of the shadows. His steps had a lively spring to them now. She thought that boded well for her hunger cramps until she saw his face. The worried ridges on his brow were not a good sign. Ugh. Why did every little thing about people have to be so complicated?

"I have found the gathering, Great One," he said, as he approached. "But no one is dancing or singing as they should be. Indeed, the entire tribe seems *angry*. I heard my father's cousin, Vladimir, speak out against the Little Mother." He swallowed hard. His scowl avalanched, exposing a rich underlayer of puzzlement. "He called her a fraud, and none of his listeners punished him for it.

"That is not like my people."

She craned her neck in the direction from which Luke had come, but the useless thing pulled up short like it always did. She hissed—a sound of annoyance and disgust. Getting used to this body's limitations was much taking longer than she thought it would. She wanted nothing more than to Change back into her dragon shape and fly back to her caves right now. But she did not because she could still hear Lathwi's voice in her head.

"Are you sure you want to do this, Mother? Being soft is not an easy way of life."

"If you can do it, so can I," she had replied. And she was not about to prove herself less able than her fosterling now. That would be the same as

admitting weakness, and *that* would encourage all sorts of disrespect. Young dragons would try to steal from her nest of diamonds; the greediest of them would probably challenge her for her territory as well. Reasserting her dominance would keep her from more interesting pursuits—like learning sorcery. And that was unacceptable. Better to suffer a little now than a lot later.

If she had to suffer at all, that is.

"Is there food to be had at this gathering?" she asked Luke.

"Without a doubt, Great One," he replied.

"Is there gish?"

"Almost certainly, Great One."

She heaved to her feet: a graceless unfurling of her wingless, mostly tailless body. "Then let us go and investigate."

"As you wish, Great One," the cub said, looking surprised and grateful at the same time. A moment later, though, his scowl reappeared, and he waved her back onto the trail with a somber, "This way."

As they wove their way through the trees, the delectable aroma of roasting pig fat invaded the warm night air. A moment later, the smell was joined by the sound of people talking in a hard, loud way.

"We know you have the power, Katya," a bullfroggish voice said. "If you don't use it to shut those brats up, I'll stuff each and every one of them into a sack and drop it in the nearest river."

"If you put your meat-hooks anywhere near my boy," a woman snarled, "I'll pin your balls to the ground with this."

"Enough!" a third voice snapped. "The next one who draws a knife for no good reason will be banished from the tribe for a year."

The talking immediately simmered down to a localized buzz. Even Luke recoiled at the threat. When Taziem arched a curious eyebrow at him, he said, "A gypsy's family is his soul. Separations are—difficult."

She could see a smattering of tame little fires in the near distance now. One of them had drawn a large group of people. Their shadowed faces were set in furious ways. The most wizened human being that Taziem had ever seen stood on the opposite side of the fire. Her back was bowed; her limbs, thin and frail. She used a stout length of wood to prop herself up. And yet, by Fire's shimmering, red-hued light, she looked surprisingly powerful.

"And for those of you who do not know this yet," the old woman said then, "my magic has its limits. I cannot cure that which I cannot understand."

Somewhere in the background, a child squalled. Taziem barely noticed. For as soon as the Old One mentioned magic, her curiosity had swelled like water-logged leather and taken over her thoughts. She *had* to meet this oh-so-intriguing creature! With that in mind, she went barging across the campgrounds and into the crowd, nudging and pushing and otherwise strong-arming anything that got in her way. Angry voices welled up in her wake.

"Who dares? Who goes there?"

Heads turned. Brows furrowed. Then a woman exclaimed, "Look! It's Luke!" Others took up the cry. "Luke's returned. And he's brought someone with him."

As if in response to that revelation, something tapped into Taziem's awareness: a probe both clumsy and suspicious. Although she could have repelled the intrusion with a pulse of her Will, out of curiosity, she did not. As a reward for her forbearance, she got to feel the link go suddenly limp with surprise.

"This is an honor beyond compare, Great One," the presence told her, in an equally clumsy Voice.

"Do I know you?" Taziem asked.

"I do not believe so, but I know you." The revelation was accompanied by an image of Lathwi in her human form. *"She thought of you often while she was with us."*

By now, Taziem and Luke had made their way to the front of the crowd. The old woman on the other side of the fire waved them closer. As she did so, her aura flared red and gold—a short-lived and much faded display of righteousness and power. The crowd retreated a few steps without knowing why. Moments later, Luke dropped to one knee in front of her. His expression wavered between respect and youthful pride.

"Little Mother," he said. "I beg your leave to rejoin the Tribe. I have done all that you asked of me."

"That and more, it would seem," the old woman said under her breath, this while studying Taziem out of the corner of her eye. "But everything in its own time, *babchi.*" In a louder, firmer voice, she said, "So tell me, braveheart: did you find Lathwi?"

"I did," Luke replied, solemn as a bridegroom.

"Did you give her the news?"

"I did, Little Mother. And she wanted very much to return with me to hunt down the culprits. But her presence was required elsewhere, so her mother came in her stead."

A collective gasp rose up from the crowd. Moments later, Taziem found herself surrounded by wide-eyed people. One caressed her forearm. Another patted her thigh. Before she knew what was happening, there were hands all over her—touching, rubbing, stroking. She pulsed an astonished thought at the old woman.

"What is this?"

"Your pardon, Great One," Katya replied, *"but no one here has ever been this close to a living, true-born dragon. Apparently, the temptation to touch is too much for some to bear. I will tell them to desist."*

"That will not be necessary," Taziem said.

"Are you sure?" the Old One wondered. *"As I recall, Lathwi did not like to be touched."*

"I am not Lathwi," she said. And she was liking this experience—a lot. Indeed, she might have indulged the gathering's curiosity well into the next day if a ragged chorus of high-pitched yowls had not shattered the hush that had settled over the campsite. She tensed at the sounds—a predator's reflex. The gypsies jerked their hands back and then retreated like prey. That spoiled Taziem's reverie. She directed her displeasure at the old woman.

"Your younglings need feeding."

"They have been fed, Great One," Katya replied.

"Then why do they yowl so? It is a most disagreeable noise."

Katya heaved a weary sigh. Her shoulders sagged as if deflated. "Our children are suffering from a chronic bout of night frights, Great One," she said aloud. "I cannot seem to cure them of it. That is why everybody here is so unhappy with me."

Luke was quick to exonerate her. "You could not cure them, Little Mother," he said, "because you did not know what you were up against. While I was still in Lathwi's company, a friend of hers told her that a sorcerer has been sending ghosts north to haunt people. So my guess is that you've been driving one fright away only to make room for another."

A thoughtful murmur rose up from the crowd. For a rare change, Katya added her raspy whisper to the buzz. "A plague of ghosts? How terribly, terribly sad. What sort of man would inflict such a curse on people he doesn't even know?"

"The sort of man who should have been killed at birth," Taziem replied.

"Maybe so," Katya said, wringing the words from another sigh. "But I suppose it is of no consequence at the moment. Now that I know what goes on here, there are things that I can do." She thumped her cane against a half-buried stone, summoning the crowd's attention. In the ensuing silence, she said, "Go and fetch your young ones. Bring them to my wagon. Then we shall see what we shall see."

The crowd broke up, buzzing as it went. Katya leaned heavily on her cane for a moment, as if she were using it to siphon strength from the earth itself. Then, resolved or perhaps just resigned to her purpose, she turned toward the covered wagon that stood to her rear. Luke offered her a supporting arm, but she refused it with a brusque wave.

"I have no need," she said. "See to the Great One's comfort."

The cub bowed—once to his queen and then to Taziem. "This way, Great One."

But Taziem's curiosity burned brighter than her hunger now. She wanted to see what old Katya had in mind. She wanted to see what one so withered could do. So she waved the cub aside, too, saying, "I will eat later."

He glanced at his grandmother. She shrugged. "She is a Great One, and will do as she pleases."

Taziem rumbled, accepting the respect as nothing more or less her due. As she did so, a gold-toothed gypsy stepped out of the evening shadows with a youngling in his arms. "Santana," the old woman said, with a tenderness that came of kinship. "Put her inside and then leave us. I will do what I can."

"I know you will, Mother." He carried the child into the wagon, and then helped Katya over the threshold as well. In parting, he planted a kiss on the old woman's brow. As he passed Taziem, he nodded. "It is an honor, Great One."

She flashed him a smile. She liked his golden tooth. Wondering if such a marvel was passed on from generation to generation, she went inside to look upon his youngling.

The first thing she did upon entering the Old One's nest was sneeze. The place smelled of dust and pollen and dead skin. And it looked like a pack-rat's hole. A scruffy mound of furs took up most of the room. A clothes- and card-strewn table occupied the rest. The wooden floor was littered with dented pots and pans; beads, bangles, baskets, and a dragon only knew what else. Even the ceiling was cluttered with bunches of dried plants and flowers. Taziem was amazed. She had had no idea that people lived like this.

Santana had left his daughter on the furs. She was rigid from head to toe. Her eyes were racing back and forth beneath their lids. Taziem squinted. Her focus shifted. A heartbeat later, a vapor hazed into view. It was hovering over the youngling's head, slipping in and out of her dreams. Her dream-self was struggling to repel it.

"This one is fierce," she said, fringing the thought with approval. *"She uses her power to resist the fright."*

A flash of pride gave life to the seams in Katya's face. "Yes," she said, and lit a candle that cast rolling shadows onto the wall. "That is Mim, my granddaughter and heir, queen-to-be of the Wandering Tribe."

"She reminds me of Lathwi when Lathwi was that size."

The old woman's mouth quirked upward at one corner, as if she were a fish that had just been hooked. But before Taziem had a chance to peek at the thought that had so obviously crossed her mind, two more gypsies appeared at the door with children in hand. Taziem curled her lip at the squalling creatures, and then retreated to a fur in the corner to watch the goings-on.

"Put them on the bed," Katya said. "Then leave us."

As the parents did her bidding, she plucked a handful of leaves from one of the plants that was hanging from the ceiling and then crumbled them into a cup of cold water. This she stirred with a forefinger while muttering gypsy words. Taziem could not contain her curiosity.

"What is that?" she asked aloud.

The old woman started as if she had forgotten that Taziem was there. "Hm? Oh, this?" She glanced down at her cup. A bittersweet smile curved across her face. "This is an infusion for strength. I'm afraid my stamina isn't what it used to be."

"What are you going to do?"

"I mean to ward this wagon against ghosts," she said. "But first, I have to get rid of the ones that are already here." She took a sip from the cup, made a sour face and then added, "You may want to go elsewhere. There may be some danger."

"I will stay," Taziem told her. "I am not afraid."

In the innermost chambers of her mind, a place where she alone had ears, Katya wished that she could say the same. She did not work big magic very often anymore, for it sucked the life-force from her like a weasel sucked the yolk from a chicken's egg. But tonight, she meant to do whatever needed doing regardless. Because the tribe came first. And children were the tribe's future.

Another anxious parent appeared in the doorway. Katya gestured him toward the bed-turned-creche, and then went rummaging through a nearby basket. "There you are," she muttered, to a chunk of yellow chalk. "I knew you were around here somewhere."

One of the younglings cried out. "There, there," she crooned, "it will be all better soon." She turned toward the bed and took a quick count. There were twelve heads—thirteen counting the Great One's. It was an auspicious number. "Good," she said. Her heart leapt: a flutter of excitement and dread. "Nothing to do now but get on with it."

So she lowered herself to her knees. An instant after she hit the floor, a pain like knives in the dark shot through her—the malicious bite of arthritis. Ignore it, carry on, draw the star, she commanded herself. Think only of the children. She swept a space clear of clutter with her forearm, then chalked a pentagram onto the floor. When she was done, she pulled a handful of dirt from her skirt pocket and sprinkled it over the diagram.

"Mother Earth," she said, "a daughter seeks your blessing. Lend me your strength to succor those who depend on me."

She stood up. Her knees did not hurt anymore. And weariness had given way to an insular sense of warmth and well-being: the infusion taking effect. *Oh, to feel like this all the time.* She turned to the east and opened her arms as if to embrace a sun that was still many hours away from rising. "Sky Fire, a daughter begs your blessing. Give me the power to restore balance."

The star beneath her feet began to glow—a golden, preternatural gleam that shot up to enclose her as she invoked Air and then Wind for their blessings. Now everything that came within the pentagram's confines would be trapped there.

With her.

But no matter, that. The tribe came first.

She extended a tendril of her Will toward the bed. Almost immediately, it struck a pocket of crypt-cold air. She bared her tobacco-stained teeth in a triumphant grin. *Got one!* The fright scrabbled to free itself as Katya reeled it in, but the earth's blessings were upon her now and she pulled it into the pentagram. It ricocheted throughout its prison as a ball of white mist, then abruptly formed a face that was both horrible and sad.

"Help me!" it cried, chilling Katya with its frigid breath. "I have been unhomed."

"I'm sorry," she said. "But you can't stay here."

One by one, she snared the frights. One by one, she imprisoned them within the star. As she did so, the specters that she had already contained howled like the forsaken souls they were and inflicted images of the grave upon her. She cried—because she was old and mortal and thoroughly unready to quit this world. But she did not give up. Could not. This was for the children.

The children needed her.

Help me. Save me. Set me free.

She did not remember catching the last fright. One moment, she'd been hunting for it; the next, it was zinging around the star like a bee in a jar. Such forgetfulness meant she was getting tired. And that meant that her blessings were starting to fade. Soon, she would be too tired to think straight. She had to ward the wagon before then. Fortunately, raising wards was easy magic. Any novice could do it. *Help me.* All she had to do was draw the earth's power into a protective dome and stamp it into place with her Will. *Save me.* She turned to the west, an auspicious direction, and concentrated on a single thought. In response, a wall of psychic force rose up from the ground. *Release me.* Although she could not see it, she knew it was there: she could feel the connection between them. She extended it to the north. As she did so, the tip of her nose went numb. She extended it to the south. The tracks that her tears had left on her cheeks hardened into tiny slicks. *We have been unhomed.* An overwhelming need for sleep came over her then. The part of her that was not yet frozen wanted to resist the urge, but the rest had already been seduced. Just for a moment, she thought, as she dropped to her knees. The howling in her ears receded into a distant lullaby.

"This is not the way Lathwi sets wards."

She waved the voice off like a pesky mosquito, then lapsed back into a drowse. She was too old to be this cold. It was toasty-warm in her dreams. But the voice was persistent.

"You must close the spell and seal it. Now. Otherwise, there will be nothing to keep the frights from coming back and all of your work will have been for naught."

Irritation flickered within her, but it was a feeble thing, unable to warm more than a single thought. *"If you're so smart, then you do it."*

An impression of alien eagerness welled within her. A moment later, the sound of someone else's magic filled her ears. It was proud music—bold and brash as a dragon's roar. As Katya listened to it, a power not her own flowed into and then through her. The transfusion shocked her weakened system. She bolted awake, burning with sudden pain, and then fainted dead away.

₨⃣

Taziem stood at the top of the gaming circle with a pair of dice in one hand and a mug of gish in the other. Gypsies stood all around her, laughing and drinking and making bets.

"Two lucs says she rolls a wagon track," a fat, bearded man by the name of Kazit shouted.

"I'll wager a gold earring on dragon's eyes!" his smaller tanglemate, Viktor, said.

Taziem bared her teeth at the men—a smile both feral and coy. She had coupled with the hairy one last night. He had started off enthusiastically enough, but quickly grew tired—this despite his commendable girth. Yet this seemed to be typical of human males. They were more imaginative than the average drake when it came to sex, but surprisingly short of stamina. She had yet to find a man whose appetites matched her own. But that did not stop her from looking. And tonight, she had her eye on Viktor. He was not as big as his brother, or as attractively hirsute, but he looked healthy and strong and eager to test his mettle.

"More gish, Great One?"

She snapped out of her thoughts to find Luke at her elbow. He bore a pitcher of gish in his hand. She was not surprised to see him. He was almost always nearby, ready with food or drink or a pleasant back-scratch. She drained her mug in one swallow, then held it out for a refill. As Luke obliged, she returned her attention to the game.

"I will roll dragon's eyes," she announced. With a flourish and the tiniest puff of Will, she then cast the dice. Both landed on the hard-packed ground with their one-spots up. Kaz groaned. Viktor cheered and then blushed—as if he had just grasped the true extent of his good luck.

The dice returned to Taziem. She called for dragon's eyes again. But just as she was about to make the throw, a youngling came galloping out of the night and toward her. She recognized Mim by her aura immediately, and so changed her mind about tampering with the outcome of this cast. A good cheater knew when play a game straight.

The roll came up stag horns. Everyone seemed surprised.

Taziem glanced down, hoping to find Mim gone. But the youngling was standing right there at her side, and the sense that she was projecting was one of abiding patience. Taziem rumbled, a thwarted sound, then shoved the dice into a spectator's hand.

"Why are you here?" she asked.

Mim tipped her head all the way back so she could meet Taziem's gaze. A set of small, gold loops dangled from her earlobes: a girl-child's first. Taziem had observed the piercing ceremony this morning. *"Great One,"* the youngling replied, a thought steeped in reverence, *"The Little Mother has asked me to escort you to her wagon when you have a moment to spare."*

Had anyone else come bearing those tidings, they would have been in for a very long wait. For Taziem was in the mood to drink and gamble and have fun, not visit with an old woman. But part of her fun was playing little magical tricks every now and again, and she could not do that as long as this youngling stood in her shadow. Which was why Katya-Queen had sent her, she suspected. Katya-Queen would have made an excellent dragon.

"Let us go then," she said, masking her resignation with a dragon's hauteur. For she did not want the youngling to know that she could be outmaneuvered.

"This way," Mim said, lacing the thought with joy.

As they moved away from the circle, the shouts and huzzahs of the gamblers gave way to singing, clapping, and laughter in all of its forms. Taziem absorbed the sounds—not because they were all pleasant to her ears, but because they were human and therefore fascinating. She was learning so much! She had had no idea that people were such social creatures. But these gypsies did *everything* together. And—they did not challenge each other over territory or mates or even the choicest parts of a carcass. They *shared*. It was an intriguing concept, easy to perceive but hard to do. Dragon instinct dictated that one's own survival always came first.

An evening breeze brushed across her cheek like a caress. She smiled to herself, amazed anew at how exquisitely sensitive this fragile new hide of hers was. What dragon could have guessed that wind could feel soft; or rain, sharp? Or that there were so many different types of pain? People led such stimulating lives.

A small campfire loomed out of the darkness. By its tame little light, she could see the likeness of a bright blue dragon dancing across a wagon's side. A moment later, she spotted a hunchbacked shadow huddled beneath its outstretched claws. Mim ran up to this lonely heap and embraced it.

"Grandmother," she said, "I have done as you asked. The Great One has come."

"Well done, child," Katya replied. "Now run and fetch me a glass of mead. Will you have one with me, Great One?"

"I have gish," Taziem said, human-style. Then, as Mim went speeding off, she sat down on the ground across from the dowager queen and studied her for a moment. The old woman seemed particularly tired tonight. Her face was haggard, and her dark eyes had retreated deep into their sockets. "Why did you send for me, Old One?" she asked. "Are you ill?"

Katya loosed a snort—a sound of mostly benign envy. "You reckon your age in centuries, but still seem to be in your prime. I sometimes wish that people aged like that: no aching bones or drooping flesh, just a body on a journey through time. Death would come as a moment's surprise instead of a vast relief."

"I do not like surprises," Taziem said.

A look like wonder spread across the dowager's face, then settled into a sardonic half-smile. "Come to think of it, neither do I."

The patter of many little feet on the run came racing toward the campsite: Mim returning with a bottle of mead plus a comet's tail of other younglings who proceeded to gather around Taziem. At first, they did no more than stare at her. Then one brave child dared to pat her thigh, and the dam broke. The next thing she knew, she had children all over her. Out of scientific curiosity, she endured this onslaught for a few moments. But they were noisy creatures with sticky fingers and peculiar, sour-milk scents. Her interest quickly turned to annoyance. She was just about to tell them to go away when Katya did the deed for her.

"Children," she said, "that is no way to treat a Great One. Make your apologies to her and be gone." As the younglings offered their regrets, she looked to her granddaughter and added, "You may go, too, little one. Enjoy the gathering's last hours."

"Thank you, grandmother," Mim said, with a gravity more common to someone five or six times her age. Then she flashed a thought filled with respect, joy, and a single note of sly playfulness at Taziem and headed back toward the main campgrounds. Her entourage followed. In their absence, Katya shook her head and heaved a sigh.

"My apologies for their behavior, Great One," she said. "They meant no offense."

"I understand," Taziem said. "And I would rather see them as they are now than as they were when I first arrived."

The old woman's face darkened with the memory. "Yes, that was a near thing. I was on the verge of declaring an early end to the gathering to prevent a war between clans when you showed up." She took a sip of mead from a delicate little glass and then added, "Not that that would have solved the problem.

"Have I thanked you yet for your assistance with the warding ritual?"

Taziem shrugged. Gratitude was another concept that she was having difficulty in grasping. It seemed so random and after the fact. "You attempted more than you should have that night," she said. There was no reproach in her tone and no scorn, only detached fact. "You would have died if I had not helped."

Another memory flitted across Katya's face. This time, Taziem tapped into it. A sense of waking from a long, cold sleep came over her. The weariness that accompanied it was so profound, it spooked Taziem back into her own thoughts. She *never* wanted to taste weakness to that degree, not even when it came from someone else's memory.

"I did what needed to be done," Katya said, half-smiling as if amused by Taziem's hasty retreat. "And the results were well worth the risk. The children are protected now. Peace and order have returned to the tribe—thanks to you.

"My people are in your debt, Great One."

Taziem saw how Katya had come to that conclusion. Her mistake was in thinking that Taziem had rushed to her rescue out of kindness or concern, when in fact, all she had wanted to do was try her hand at raising wards. But she made no attempt to point out the old woman's error. A debt was like a promise—it conferred power. And a wise dragon snatched up all the power it could get.

"How will you pay this debt?" she asked instead.

Katya held out her gnarled hands, palms up as if to show how empty they were. "What does the Wandering Tribe have that you might want, Great One—gold? Gish? Hospitality?"

"I will think on the matter," she said, refusing to commit herself to an answer too soon. "When I have decided, I will tell you."

"As you wish," the dowager said. "But bear in mind that this is Wayfarer's Eve, the gathering's last night. Tomorrow, the clans will go their separate ways for the year; and barring fortune's whims, none of us will meet again until the next reunion. Collecting a debt from one or all of us in the meantime will not be so easy."

How disappointing! She liked to take her time with these sorts of decisions, savor all of the possible options until one particular taste stood out. As it happened, though, she already knew what she wanted from the gypsies.

"Which clan discovered the dragon carcasses?" she asked.

"Mine did," Katya said, wincing at the memory. "My clan found them both."

"Then I will leave with you when you depart tomorrow. You will return to those ill-starred places so I can see what there is to be seen. Do this, and there will be no more debt between us."

"That is fair," Katya said, and took another sip of mead. As she swallowed, a sly smile curved across her face. "But we would have taken you anywhere you wanted to go, debt or no, if you had but asked."

A rumble boiled up Taziem's gullet, then burst out of her as a full-throated roar of delight. Clever Katya-Queen! She was *very* good at dragon games! They would have to play again sometime.

But not tonight. Tonight, she had other games, and other playmates, in mind. She drained her gish-mug in one last, cheerful gulp, then went in search of Viktor. Katya did not see her go; she had already nodded off. Yet even in her sleep, she continued to smile like the crafty old competitor that she was.

℘ℂ

Taziem tramped through the woods in a self-absorbed trance. Fallen leaves and fir needles poked at the soft spots of her feet. A melange of tree pollens tickled her nose. She was not particularly fond of walking as a means of getting from one place to the next, but it was, she had discovered, better than traveling by caravan. The incessant bumping and lurching of a wagon in motion made her backside sore. The wheels stirred up chaff and dust that burned her eyes. And oh, the tedium! There was nothing to do while riding topside. The wagons were so bouncy and squeaky, she could not even generate a decent thought. Better to walk by herself than endure such unpleasantness.

Her thoughts drifted back to the gathering's break-up two mornings ago. It had been a quiet, oddly unceremonious affair, with each clan leaving at its own time and pace. The order of departure had apparently been determined by the volume of gish consumed by the various wagon-masters on Wayfarer's Eve. Santana had retired sooner than most, so his caravan set out early, well before the sun reached its zenith. And that had been fine with Taziem. Her Wayfarer's Eve lover had not inspired any desire to dally.

Males. They could be so disappointing.

Behind her, leaves rustled: a small, two-legged sound. She half-turned to see Mim racing after her. Although the girl-child was as old as Lathwi had been when her path had converged with Taziem's, Taziem could not recall a time when her fosterling had been so puny—a single mouthful at most, and not even that on a particularly ravenous day. Katya needed to feed her granddaughter more often.

"Great One," she said, as she closed the gap between them, *"may I walk with you?"*

The impression that accompanied the thought was one of juvenile excitement and awe. Despite its clumsiness, Taziem approved of the effort and so shrugged. *"If you can keep up."*

"That will be easy," Mim bragged, brimming with pride. *"I am very fast. Do you want to see me run?"*

"No," Taziem said. Then, because she was on the verge of being bored and this was Katya-Queen's heir, she decided to give the child a lesson. *"Slow down and open yourself to the world all around you. Knowledge comes first to those who use their heads instead of their feet."*

The youngling immediately did as she was told. That pleased Taziem, as did the impressions that she proceeded to scry from the girl-child's mind. She found curiosity in abundance, and a deep well of hope, and the self-confidence of a dragon. She saw joy, enthusiasm, and intelligence—all of this was wrapped around a substantial core of power and potential. Once again, Taziem was reminded of her fosterling. She wondered where Lathwi was at the moment, and if she had found the rogue sorcerer yet. After having seen his frights at work, she had no doubt that he was a man in need of killing.

As if in response to the thought, a magpie in the bowers overhead burst into song. A moment later, Mim began to warble, too—sounds of wonder and surprise.

"Great One!" she cried. "That bird is singing about grubs and worms."

"Listen closer," Taziem replied, *"Perhaps he will tell you his secret Name. If he does, his kind will be your friends for life."*

But there was to be no exchange of Names today. As soon as the bird finished his song, he flew away—presumably in search of lunch. This in no way dampened Mim's excitement. She tracked the magpie's flight for a moment, then turned back to Taziem with a delighted, gap-toothed grin.

"Do all things have a secret Name, Great One?"

"*I believe so,*" Taziem said. "*But some of them will only say it once, so you must pay attention to what you are hearing at all times.*"

Mim hugged Taziem's legs. Then, before Taziem could react in any way, she let out a shout and went racing toward a massive ironwood tree in the near distance. It bore a fluttery red ribbon on a prominent lower branch. As Taziem watched, Mim plucked the strip off and looped it around her wrist. That triggered Taziem's curiosity.

"Why did the tree wear a ribbon?" she asked, as the child came running back to her.

"Because it's big and tall and perfectly straight," Mim replied, "and some fat fool of an outsider decided that it ought to be a ship's mast instead of a tree. An axeman would have chopped it down if he had seen that ribbon on it. Now he'll pass it by." She flashed Taziem another gap-toothed grin. "Da gives me a sweet for every marker I bring home. But I don't do it for the candy. I just like trees."

Taziem looked up at the ironwood's shaggy upper reaches. It was so tall, she could not see its crown. The sight prompted a bittersweet memory that then shaped itself into a thought. "*I like trees, too.*"

"*Truly?*"

"*Dragons do not lie, youngling,*" she said, a haughty reproach. Then she started on her way again as if she were alone. Mim had to scramble to catch up.

"*I meant no offense, Great One,*" she said. "*I was surprised, is all. Outsiders believe that a dragon will not enter a forest of its own accord.*"

Taziem dismissed the absurdity with a snort. "*I am here, am I not?*" At Mim's emphatic nod, she slowed her pace and waxed nostalgic. "*And there was a time, back in the days of Ever-Light, that dragons made their nests in trees.*"

Mim gasped. "*I have never seen a tree big enough to hold a Great One.*"

"*Nor will you. They were all destroyed by Galza and Her hordes of krim.*"

A moment's silence ensued. Then the youngling slipped her fingers into Taziem's unready hand and said, "*Please, Great One, tell me more. I've never heard this story.*"

Mim's ignorance shocked Taziem. Every intelligent creature ought to know about the last days of Ever-Light. It was a part of their mutual past, and the reason why the world was as it was. The next time she visited with Katya-Queen, she would have to take her to task for neglecting her duties to the young. In the meantime, she would do the Old One's work for her.

The memory began with an image of broad-barreled, cloud-scraping, dragon-trees, and then went on to portray the world as it was in the Ever-Light. "*Men and beasts live in harmony. Dragons rule the skies...*" The telling was awkward at first, for Mim was not used to speaking mind-to-mind at length and Taziem refused to entrust such an important memory to slippery human words. Eventually, though, they fell into a workable, walking rapport. *"One day, everything changes—"*

The muted drumming of a horse's hooves jarred Taziem out of the memory. She glanced toward the sound to see Luke riding toward them. His green eyes were narrowed. The corners of his mouth were crimped.

"Mim!" he said, as he approached. "You were supposed to ask the Great One to please return to the caravan."

"I'm sorry, Lukie," the youngling replied. "I meant to, but I forgot. Look, I found a ribbon."

His expression softened as he eyed his cousin's prize only to go hard again as his gaze strayed past her and toward a scabrous patchwork of tree stumps. "Well done," he said. "I only wish that you had collected more on our last pass through these parts."

"Why was the youngling sent to find me?" Taziem asked, more interested in this than in how thin the forest canopy had become. "Have we come to the place where the dragon corpse was discovered?"

"Not yet, Great One," Luke replied. "That meadow is still a half-day's ride from here. We are approaching Timberton, however, and Santana would like to stop there to pick up some supplies. He said Lathwi was curious about towns. He thought you might be, too."

Taziem rumbled, approving the gypsy chieftain's perspicacity. For he was right: if Lathwi wanted to know more about a thing, then she most certainly did, too. "Santana is smart," she said. "I will return to the caravan."

Luke nodded, acknowledging her decision, and then stretched a hand toward his cousin. "Come here, Mimsy, and ride back with me. We'll make better time that way."

But Mim gave her head a vehement shake and stood her ground. "I want to walk with the Great One, Luke. She was telling me about the days of Ever-Light."

Taziem had no interest in resuming the youngling's education at the moment. She had never seen a town close up, and her imagination was tugging at her like a strong wind at her wings. "Leave me," she told the child. "I have had enough company for now."

"But will you finish the story some other time?" Mim asked, as Luke hauled her up and into the saddle with him.

"Yes," she said. She did not realize until much later that the youngling had wrung a promise from her without even trying.

⁞⁞

The road to Timberton was broad and dusty, a rugged strip of impacted red dirt that ran straight through the much diminished forest. Stumps were as common a sight as full-grown trees now, and the reek of violated wood hung heavy in the air. Taziem was offended, but did not say anything until the sharp tangs of rotting pulp and sewage joined the miasma. Then she turned to Luke, who was riding alongside of her, and said, "Does the stink keep predators away?"

"No, Great One," he replied, looking equally revolted. "As far as I know, it serves no purpose."

A short time later, a clearing appeared to the left of the road. It was stacked high with denuded tree-trunks. The trees looked very sad and cold without their leaves and branches. The smell of sap was very strong. Taziem stared. She could not understand why anybody would want to cut down so many perfectly good trees.

"This is called a lumberyard," Luke said, as if *he* were reading *her* thoughts for a change. "People from Timberton will load this wood onto great wagons and haul it off to the south and west, places that have no timber of their own. The last time I came through here, this yard was busier than a broken anthill. Today, it's quiet as a grave. I wonder if someone has had an accident."

The lumberyard gave way to a collection of ugly, raw-boned buildings that hugged the sides of the road like fresh-water barnacles. Although it was still light out, there were very few people moving about the town. Indeed, the only noticeable activity was coming from a squat, ochre-colored shack that bore the likeness of a grinning dragon on its side. Several men had gathered around the doorway. They broke off their conversation as the caravan went rolling by. One of them spit at the ground and growled, "Stinking gypsies."

Taziem snorted. From where she stood, it was they who stank. Indeed, she did not know which combination was worse: that of fresh pine sap and decaying pulp, or that of beer, gish, and unwashed human bodies.

The wagons rolled to a stop in front of the general store. Santana and the other wagon-masters converged in the road outside of the building. Luke stood in their midst, but did not go with them when they went inside. Instead, he kept watch on the wagons and the children who came spilling forth from them in their fathers' absence. Brimming with pent-up energy after the day's long ride, they immediately began a boisterous game of tag in the road.

"Stay close," Luke told them. "We'll be leaving as soon as we have our supplies."

Taziem watched the younglings as they frolicked, for while she did not find their antics particularly entertaining, they were still the most interesting thing about Timberton. She had imagined an exotic, exciting place; a communal nest or warren filled with clever humans doing clever things. But there was absolutely nothing clever about this town. It smelled like a badger's hole. And its atmosphere was oppressive—like a storm on the horizon. The sound of gypsy laughter had drawn several people from their hidey-holes, but they were all hollow-eyed and grim-faced, as if they had all been sick for a long time.

"Look at them," she heard one woman mutter, "all smiling an' happy. You know they ain't got frights driving them crazy. It ain't fair."

"Fair?" someone else echoed. "Hell, it ain't natural. Damn gypsies. I'll bet you anything that the ghosts are their doing. I'll bet you they put a curse on us."

That tweaked Taziem's curiosity. She wondered if it was possible to curse an entire town, and how powerful a sorceress would have to be to accomplish such a feat. If only Lathwi had not extracted that promise about experimenting with magic from her! Timberton would have made a perfect subject.

The men from the tavern joined the crowd. Shortly thereafter, the word 'curse' began to circulate at a feverish pitch. Luke gave his lip an anxious nibble, and then tried to call the children back to the wagons. Caught up in their game, they ignored him.

Then someone shouted, "Stone them!"

Luke went racing into the store. A moment later, he came racing back out with Santana and the other wagon-masters on his heels. Their hands hovered near the hilts of their knives.

"Friends!" Santana said, forcing a note of false cheer into his voice. "What goes on here? Has one of our little scamps said or done something to upset you? If so, tell me and I will punish the culprit."

"We want the witch who cursed us," one of the gish-drinkers yelled. "We're gonna burn her at the stake."

The mob cheered at that. Santana raised his hands, palms outward, as if he were trying to ward off the sound. "There must be some mistake," he said. "No one from my family has cursed anyone here."

"Liar!" someone snarled. "We got eyes in our heads, we can see you ain't got the frights like we do. You *musta* sent 'em!"

"Believe me, my friends—" A stone went whizzing past his head. He stubbornly stood his ground. "We did no such thing. Nevertheless—" Another stone arced toward him. Through gritted teeth, he said, "I think we can help you."

"You've done enough already, you gold-toothed bastard!"

"Then good day to you." He waved his brother and cousins toward their wagons. As they retreated, he added, "And good riddance."

Rocks began to fly in earnest—a furious hail that first bloodied Luke's brow and then panicked the caravan's horses. The beasts bolted for the edge of town, dragging the wagons and their discomposed masters with them. When the dust settled a moment later, the only stranger left in Timberton was Taziem. One of the men from the tavern hastened to grab her by the arm. He had an abundance of facial hair, all of it matted. Instead of a shirt, he wore a hardened leather shell that made him look like a giant tortoise. She liked his looks, but not his smell.

"Looks like they decided to leave their witch with us after all," he said, and then bared his teeth at her. They were crooked and yellow—an unconvincing threat-display. "I've never seen a black gypsy. Someone must've given her a taste of the fire already."

His grip was causing a painful cramp in her arm, so she freed herself with a tug. He immediately grabbed her again. He was larger than most humans, but still no match for a dragon in strength. She extricated herself again, and then showed him what a threat display should look like.

"Do not touch me again," she said.

He mocked her with a laugh that reeked of beer. "Why not?" he retorted. "You gonna curse me or something?"

She shrugged, refusing to commit herself. He grabbed her arm and said, "C'mon, let's start the fire—"

He choked on the tail-end of the word, then started to turn red. A moment later, he let go of her arm and clutched at his throat like a man in need of air.

"What is it, Jarv?" one of the other gish-drinkers asked. "You swallow a bug or somethin'?"

But Jarv could not reply. Taziem still had her Will wrapped around his windpipe. As she squeezed, his eyes bulged in their sockets and frothy spittle gathered at the corners of his mouth. His face was now as red as raw meat. He tried to gasp. He tried to pant. The strangled noises that scraped past his mouth horrified the crowd.

"Stop it!" a woman cried. "You're killing him!"

He dropped to his knees, then plunged face-first into the dust. But while he did not move, he was not dead. She was not angry enough, or hungry enough, to go for the kill. The fool would have a sore throat when he woke up, nothing more.

"I am leaving now," she said, addressing all of Timberton. "If you wish to live, you will leave me alone."

One of the women in the crowd dropped the rock that she had been holding and made a sign to avert evil. Several others did the same. Taziem scorned them with a look, and then sauntered out of town.

Chapter 11

*T*_{*he*} common room at The Pig's Pizzle was crowded—an orderly mixture of woodsmen, travelers, and even a few borderland soldiers. The delectable smell of roasting pork was wafting into the room from the kitchen, but Jamus could not afford to buy supper—not yet anyway. That was why he was sitting in an out-of-the-way corner, searching for a likely sucker as he nursed his watered-down beer. He dismissed the woodsmen right away. As a rule, they had a lousy sense of humor even when drunk, and he was in no mood to argue with a man who swung an axe for a living tonight. He excluded the soldiers for much the same reason. Why take chances when they could get a body killed?

He scratched his chin, then scowled at the stubble that tickled his fingertips. He needed a shave. And a bath. And blessed Dreamer, some clean clothes! He had lost everything except his wallet and his sword when that damned dragon ambushed him. In the week or so since then, his traveling money had flowed from him like blood—a major hemorrhage on the pathetic excuse for a horse that he had bought in sore-footed desperation from some sharp-eyed shyster of a farmer, then a steady trickle on food and drink. Now, all he had left was dregs, a few coins of minuscule worth. In bygone days, that would not have been a problem. All he would have had to do was declare himself to the owner and ask for credit. Innkeepers were usually happy to accommodate important people. Unfortunately, he wasn't important anymore, only infamous. If he approached the innkeeper with a request for credit, the best he could hope for was a swift boot in the rear as he was being thrown out of the inn. The worse he could expect was—well, suffice it to say that he would not be hocking his sword anytime soon. If he wanted to eat tonight—and Dreamer, he was famished!—he would have to hustle coins from the unsuspecting and the drunk.

And he had the perfect candidate in sight.

The man was big, especially through the shoulders and arms. He looked like he could toss a yearling cow clear across the room. At the moment, though, all he was tossing was shots of gish, one after the next—and all of those were going down his throat. In between drinks, he would glance over his shoulder as if he were expecting someone to come through the door, then shake his red-thatched head and mutter to himself. Based on the amount of alcohol the man was consuming—and the rate at which he was consuming it—Jamus figured that he'd be unconscious within the hour. Which meant that the time to act was now. So he raked his fingers through his hair, then snatched up his nearly empty mug and set out to earn his supper.

"Greetings, friend," he said, as he closed in on the man's table. "Mind if I join you?"

The man gave him the briefest of once-overs, then gestured to the chair across from his own. There was a yellowing bruise beneath his right eye, and a healing cut on his lip. Up close, he seemed more distracted than drunk. This would have intrigued the old Jamus. The new one was merely disappointed. There was more risk involved in hornswoggling a sober man. Still, he had come too far to back out now.

"You look a bit out of sorts," he said, as he took his seat. "Is something troubling you?"

"Sort of," the man replied, and then poured himself another drink from the jug that sat at his elbow. As an afterthought, he motioned for Jamus to help himself. "S'on me."

"Oh, no, I couldn't," Jamus replied primly, and then appeared to have a change of heart. "Well, maybe just the one." He poured himself a dollop, then drank it down. The gish coursed through him like liquid fire. He smacked his lips, a crude expression of approval, and then said, "So what brings you to this little patch of nowhere, friend?"

"Gord," the man said. "The name's Gordyn." He glanced over his shoulder, then shook his head and muttered, "Behind me, he's right behind me. He said so and I believe him."

"What was that?" Jamus asked politely, just making conversation. "Who's right behind you?"

"A friend," Gord said, and took another drink. "We're on our way to Compara. We have a message for Jamus D'Arques."

At that, the whole room seemed to go quiet. Jamus felt blood rising in his face—a guilty, self-aware flush. He could almost see twenty-six ghostly fingers pointing his way. He leaned in close to shush the man. "Quiet, man! That name will buy you no friends in this place."

But it was too late. A pair of soldiers had already peeled away from the bar, and were now on their way over to Gordyn's table. Jamus stifled an urge to groan, then helped himself to more of the man's gish—without an invitation. Jamus figured that Gord owed him that much for getting him into this mess. As he knocked the drink back, he prayed: *Please, Dreamer, let me survive this night.* All thoughts of winning his supper by a sleight-of-hand were gone.

The soldiers converged on Gordyn. Their uniforms marked them as borderland regulars. Their grimy faces and tired eyes implied that they had been riding hard for some time now. One of them grasped Gord's shoulder as if he meant to put him under arrest.

"Gordyn?" he asked, in an incredulous tone. "Gordyn the horse-trader from New Uxla?" As Gordyn swiveled in his seat to get a better look at the speaker, he said, " By the Dreamer, it is you! What a huge coincidence. Ooh," he added, as Gord's face came into clearer view. "Sorry again about that eye."

Gordyn dismissed the apology with a swipe of his callused paw and then gestured for the soldiers to sit down. As they did so, he introduced them to Jamus. "Thomas, Ross, this is my friend—" He paused for a moment, grasping for a recollection that he did not have. "Well, he hasn't mentioned his name yet, but I'm sure he will eventually."

Jamus was hunched over his mug like a weary traveler might, trying to keep his face out of plain sight. Instinct urged him to mumble something about needing to piss and then making a break for the stables instead of the nearest tree, but he forced himself to remain still. A stranger had a message for him, he told himself, and he wanted to know what it was. That, and a hasty retreat now would surely attract unwanted attention.

"The name's Zak," he said.

It was hard to tell if anyone at the table heard him, though. They were already having a drink together. Jamus helped himself to another one, too—but only because he thought that not doing so would make him stick out.

"So what brings you to this place?" Thom wanted to know. "The last we saw you, you were looking for your friend."

Gordyn grimaced at that and then glanced over his shoulder. All of a sudden, he seemed very tense. "He found me a few hours later," he said. "We started out for Compara, but—" He blinked back a moment's confusion, then tried again. "But—" He tossed a shot of gish down his throat, then forced himself to go on. "He'll be along shortly. He sent me ahead with a message for some fellow named D'Arques."

"Really?" Ross asked. "How peculiar. We carry a message for him, too."

"About the commander?"

Thomas lowered his eyes like one ashamed of something, and then nodded. "Lathwi sent us after we broke into the dungeon. She said D'Arques would be interested in the information."

At the sound of Lathwi's name, the sip of gish in Jamus' mouth took on the sour tang of bile. "What?" he muttered to himself. "No dragons this time?"

"Then you don't know the worst of it," Gord said. He glanced over his shoulder, then lowered his voice. "Stone and his aide were Veeder's men. I say 'were' because they are no more. My boy saw to that."

Ross's hand went to his throat. "Maybe we shouldn't be talking about this."

Gordyn snorted. "You think this D'Arques fellow is going to care?"

Jamus didn't mind at all. In fact, he wanted to hear more, more, more. He had already put several bits of their gossip together. Something unpleasant was brewing in the borderlands—something nasty enough to make Lathwi take notice, she who didn't give a damn about anything but her own self. And unless he missed his guess, Pawl had assassinated a garrison commander. A *commander!* What sort of trouble had his old friend gotten himself into? The only good news that he'd heard was that Pawl and Lathwi were no longer traveling together, but even that wasn't as satisfying as he had thought it would be. Dribs and drabs be damned! He wanted the whole dish on everyone, friend and foe alike. So he took a deep breath and willed himself to be brazen.

"Gentlemen," he said, keeping his voice as well has his head low, "I regret to inform you that Jamus D'Arques is gone from Compara. He was banished from the city after an unfortunate incident—*his fault, his fault, his fault!*—with rioters. However," he added, as Gordyn's mouth fell open, "I know where he is." Then, because times were hard and the pork smelled so damned good, he said, "For a bit of supper, I'll tell you where he is."

The soldiers tensed as if stung, and the one named Ross reached for the hilt of his sword. But Gordyn shouted at the serving-wench. "You there," he said. "Bring me and my friends here some supper. We'll have another pitcher of gish as well." As the woman scurried off with the request, he turned a bloodshot eye to Jamus and added, "No man's going hungry in my company, mate. But I'll be glad to beat everything you eat right back out of you if I get the idea that you're lying to us."

"Trust me," Jamus said. "I know exactly where D'Arques is. But you must promise not to hurt or expose him to a crowd. If you cannot make such a vow, I'll take my leave of you now and no hard feelings."

"Hurt him?" Gord echoed. "Why on earth would I want to do that? Pawlie would have my hide just for thinking such a thing."

The Dreamer bless Pawl, Jamus thought, and took a moment of extreme comfort in the fact that his one friend left in the world was someone as splendid and true as Pawl. Then supper came steaming out of the kitchen and he forgot everything else. His belly crooned as the first bit of roast slid down his gullet. He nearly wept at the taste of hot, buttered yams. The food was so good, and he was so hungry, it didn't even occur to him to tap into the fresh pitcher of gish until his plate was empty. By then, everyone else was done eating, too.

"All right, stranger," the soldier named Thomas said, "we've been patient with you, this though our cause is urgent. Now tell us where D'Arques is, or suffer."

Poised on the edge of a very sharp, unforgiving sword, Jamus balked. If he had misread these men, he could die in the coming moments. And while he did not have much in the way of a reason to live, he was not in any particular rush to meet his death, either. Still, he'd made a deal. He *had* to declare himself. The small part of him that still cared about things like honor insisted on it. The admission swelled in his lungs. But as he opened his mouth to release it, a portly man dressed in traveling clothes bumped into him. The beer that he'd been carrying back from the bar sloshed all over the front of Jamus' shirt.

"Random's balls!" Jamus swore.

"So sorry, my friend, so very, very sorry," the fat man babbled, his fleshy face a caricature of red-cheeked distress. "The innkeeper should allow more space between his tables. Can I buy you a drink to make a—" He cut himself off with a cry of recognition. At the same moment, his apologetic expression hardened into a frown. "Don't I know you?"

Jamus feigned an all-consuming interest in wringing the beer out of his shirt—any excuse to keep his head down. "I don't believe so, no."

"But I do," the man insisted. "I know it." He snapped his fingers as if he were trying to command a trick from his brain. As he did so, Jamus ever so discreetly reached for the hilt of his sword. "I saw you in—That's it!" The man snapped his fingers again. "You're D'Arques, aren't you, The Butcher of Compara." His mouth shaped itself into a nasty vee. "Oy, fellas," he started to say. "Look who we—"

Gordyn grabbed him by the wrist, just hard enough to cut him off. "You must be thinking of somebody else," he said, with a smile like a scimitar, "because this here is my cousin, Zak, my mother's sister's son. He may be a little on the cranky side, but he's no butcher."

"But—"

"So don't be calling him by the wrong name. Rumors get started that way. So do *riots*."

"But—"

Gord's knuckles paled. So did the fat man's face. "You're not arguing with me, are you, friend? Because I wouldn't advise it. I have been known to lose my temper when I've had a few. And as you can see, I've had a few."

"I don't want no harm, friend," the man said. "I made a mistake. I'm sorry." He glanced at Jamus, then averted his eyes. "Now that I've had a good look at him, your cousin doesn't look at all familiar.

"Can I go now?"

Like a big cat playing games with a mouse, Gord held onto the man for a moment longer. Then, with a laugh as broad as his smile had been, he let him go and gave him a cheerful clap on the upper arm in parting. "You have yourself a nice evening, you hear?"

The man hurried off. In his absence, all eyes at the table turned to Jamus, who folded his arms across his now-soggy chest and tried to look nonchalant rather than vastly relieved. "I told you I knew where D'Arques was."

"Aye," Thomas said, looking none too pleased. "The question is, what are we supposed to do now that we've found you?"

"Why don't you do what you set out to do and give me my messages?" Jamus said.

"Why should we trust you?" Ross asked. "The fat one called you a butcher."

Jamus shrugged. "I'm just trying to survive a particularly nasty set of circumstances. As are we all, I think." He caught Ross's eye and added, "I'm willing to trust a pair of soldiers who deserted their garrison."

Ross strangled on a logjam of words. But his shieldmate remained unruffled. "It was a righteous desertion," he said, in a low, matter-of-fact tone. "Commander Stone is corrupt. He meant to hang two innocent people even though he *knew* that the only witness against them was lying. There have been other—irregularities—as well."

"Pawlie wanted me to tell you that the border's in jeopardy," Gordyn chimed in, without prompting or encouragement. He looked much more relaxed now, as if a great weight had been removed from his shoulders. "A southern warlord by the name of Veeder is preparing to invade, and the garrison's integrity has been compromised."

The hair on the back of Jamus' neck stood up at that. What desperate tidings! Wynn needed to hear them as soon as possible. And one of his loyal sub-commanders had to regain control over that garrison even sooner. Jamus thought about that for a moment, then concluded that he should be that commander. He was the closest to New Uxla at a time when every minute mattered. And nobody down there would know that Wynn had not formally assigned him to the post. A bitter voice in the back of his head wondered why he ought to put himself out for a man who had outcast him, but he refused to listen to it. His country needed him. And he was ready to serve.

And Wynn had never said anything about his never working again.

His mind began to reel—not from the gish, although he'd had plenty of that—but from excitement. He'd gone without a sense of purpose for so long now. In its grip, he felt restless, giddy, eager to get moving. He felt like declaring himself to the whole damned room. Instead, he went to work.

"Here's what you're going to do," he told his companions. "Come the morning, head straight for Compara. Once you're there, ride for the garrison and ask for Quartermaster Cross. Tell him what you told me. He'll get you in to see the governor. Oh," he added, as the soldiers absorbed the instructions, "I don't think you need to mention that you're deserters. If anybody asks who sent you, tell them it was your new commander. I'll testify to that after the dust settles down."

Thomas and Ross exchanged a look, then shrugged in the way of men who have resigned themselves to fortune's whims. "Like I said," Thomas said, "it was a righteous desertion. We'll say so before a tribunal."

Jamus shrugged. So long as they got the message through to Wynn, he didn't care what they said—although if it were him, personally, he would keep his mouth shut. A military prison cell was pure misery, and a sentence of hard labor made it even worse.

"As you wish," he said, and then turned to Gordyn. The redhead seemed to have gone from intoxicated to full-on drunk in the last five minutes. His eyes were unfocused. His head was wobbling on his neck. Part of Jamus envied the man. The rest hoped to take advantage of the man's condition—but only just a little bit. "Gordyn," he said, "I need your help, too."

"Howzat?" Gord asked.

"I need you to trade horses with me. Just for a while," he added, as Gordyn shook his head. "It'll take me a month to get to New Uxla on the nag I'm riding now."

But Gordyn continued to shake his head. "Sorry," he said. "Can't."

"Why not?" Jamus asked.

"Because I'm comin' with you." Before Jamus could object, or even think of objecting, he added, "This friggin' curse is driving me mad. I gotta find Pawl and bring him home."

"Curse?" Ross asked, glancing furtively around him. "What curse?"

"Lathwi did it," Gordyn moaned, and then pitched forward. His face landed in his empty plate with a muted thud. A moment later, he began to snore.

With that, he became as a brother to Jamus. As such, he was entitled to Jamus' help—especially if it meant thwarting the black-hearted bitch who had killed his true love. And, Jamus added, as he helped himself to more of Gordyn's gish, it would be nice to have company on the long, hard road ahead.

Chapter 12

*T*aziem strode down the darkened road, tracking the caravan by the moon's milky light. Although it was late, and her feet ached almost as much as her empty belly, she did not stop to rest or eat. She meant to find the gypsies so they could pamper her. She was not angry with them for leaving her behind. They had chosen to run away. That was their right, and their nature. She had simply chosen—otherwise. But maybe the gypsies would not know that. They were a cautious people. Respectful. Maybe they would try to curry her favor with offerings: gish, viands, a foot massage. That would please her very much.

Even as the thought crossed her mind, a soft nicker rippled out of the darkness. A moment later, the metered sound of a large, four-legged beast wading through brush grew loud in her ears. It did not occur to her to be alarmed. This was either a fellow traveler—or supper. She welcomed either possibility. The shadowy outlines of a man on a horse's back appeared in the road ahead of her. The horse bore no saddle. Its rider was tall and scrawny, a sub-adult male. He held his reins in one hand, and a brace of skinned hares in the other.

"I thought you might be hungry," Luke said, as she closed in on him.

She snatched the rabbits from him without a word and immediately began to feed. The sharp, salty-sweet taste of fresh meat unleashed her long-repressed hunger. As soon as she gobbled down the last bit of coney, she glanced around for something more to eat. Luke's horse broke into a nervous prance.

"Where is Gem?" she asked, thinking of the woman's tasty roast chooks. "Where is Tikka and her stew of goats?"

Luke gestured vaguely in the direction from whence he had come. "They've gone ahead of us, Great One. If we hurry, we can catch up with them by morning. Otherwise, they'll wait for us on the bluff overlooking Murdered Dragon Meadow.

"Shall we go?"

Disappointment gusted through Taziem like a desert wind. She wanted food and drink and a rousing game of dice; and she did not want to walk all night to get them. "My feet hurt," she complained, petulant as a diva. "I am tired of walking."

"My horse is quite strong," Luke told her. "It can carry both of us. Or, if you'd prefer, I can walk while you ride."

"I do not ride horses," she said. "I *eat* them."

Luke's mouth chasmed into a distressed 'O'. At the same time, his eyes turned shimmery, like a pair of mud puddles in the moonlight. But he swallowed his regrets in one hard little lump and then slid down from the horse's back.

"If you wish to eat her, Great One," he said, offering her the reins, "then do so. I would not have you go hungry."

Taziem rumbled, broadcasting annoyance rather than hunger. She had no doubt that the manling's offer was sincere. He was *always* giving her things, sometimes before she even knew she wanted them. But up until this very moment, she had not realized or even suspected that he would give her *anything*—even the things that he held most dear, even when the giving pained him. Such behavior was unnatural; illogical; and thoroughly undragon-like. And the peculiar thing was, the more he offered her, the less she wanted from him. She rumbled again, troubled by the observation. Being human provoked some very curious side-effects.

Luke was still staring at her with those sorrowing eyes of his. The hand with the reins was still extended. She rejected the entire package with a show of teeth.

"Horse meat does not agree with my digestive tract," she said, "especially this late in the evening. "I will eat when we rejoin the caravan."

"As you wish, Great One," he said, beaming now with boyish joy. As he vaulted back onto his horse's back, he added, "And thank you so very much for sparing my horse. I raised her from a filly."

She had no interest in the horse's history and so refused to discuss it. Instead, still peevish, she voiced another complaint. "It would have been more seemly for the caravan to wait for me here, however. Murdered Dragon Meadow has a most inauspicious sound to it."

"A thousand apologies, Great One," he said. "But we couldn't risk making camp so close to Timberton."

"No stone thrown from that disgusting place could fly this far," she argued. "The camp would have been safe. We could have been pitching dice and drinking gish at this very moment."

"That might have been the way of it if we were outsiders, Great One. But we are gypsies. Our safety is never a sure thing."

Her petulance disappeared beneath a wave of curiosity. "Why do you say that?"

He shrugged like a man in ill-fitting armor. "Outsiders have never liked the folk of the Wandering Tribe. We are a smarter, happier, and freer people, and they cannot bring themselves to forgive us for that. When all is well in their narrow little world, they tolerate us as vendors and fortune-tellers, vagrants to be despised or maybe pitied. But if a piglet goes missing while we're in the vicinity—aha! We become thieves. And if a child comes down with damp lung, it *must* be because one of us gave it the evil eye."

"Does such an eye exist?" Taziem asked, ever and always interested in different types of magical lore.

"I do not know," he said. "But it doesn't matter. Repeat a thing often enough in a fool's presence, and sooner or later, the fool will embrace it for the truth. And when that happens—" His voice caught on something in his throat. He swallowed hard to wash the obstruction away, and then went on. "I was not yet born when the last pogrom broke out, but I have heard The Little Mother speak of it many times. She says it started with a plague of pox. She says the outsiders brought it upon themselves by living in rat-infested towns like Timberton. But as the pox spread, so did rumors of gypsy-magic. And as the deaths mounted, so did the demands for vengeance. Then the governor's daughter died, and the whole province went mad for a time."

He paused to clear his throat again, and then began to chant in a tight-fisted voice.

"We shouted for peace;
"We sued for mercy;
"The outsiders laughed as we crawled.
"We died by the sword;
"We died at the stake;
"The outsiders watched, enthralled.
"We died in the dirt;
"We died on the run;
"Only our ghosts were appalled."

As the last of his dirge melted into the night, he turned to Taziem. In a voice now thick with bitterness, he said, "You saw how it was back in Timberton, Great One. They wanted our blood. And to make matters worse, there were several sons-of-the-south among them."

"What are those?" Taziem asked.

"Southerners, Great One," Luke said. "Members of some warrior-cult by the look of them. That kind doesn't even treat their own people well."

Southerners. Taziem recognized the term. Lathwi had used it in reference to the cowardly jackals who had pack-attacked her back in the days when she was studying with Liselle TrueHeart. She accessed the memories that her daughter had shared with her, then hissed as the image of a large, leather-shelled man with matted facial hair appeared before her mind's eye. The similarities were too numerous to ignore.

"After you left Timberton today," she said, "a man dared to lay his hands on me. I think he must have been one of these soldiers you speak of. He was quite stupid."

He sucked in a quick, suspenseful breath. "What did you do to him?"

She shrugged. "I did not let any air get into his lungs for a while."

He groaned. "Blessed Dreamer. What have you done?"

She shrugged again. "You need not fear for him. He did not die."

"No, but you humiliated him in front of a bunch of Northerners," Luke countered. "And in a cultist's eyes, that's even worse than death. Add that to the fact that they often kill gypsies for sport and perhaps you can see why camping in these woods tonight would not have been wise of us."

"Perhaps I can," she said, and lapsed into a thoughtful silence. She had learned many things about humans just now. But putting what she knew into context was going to take some time.

ဢ ♋

Shortly after sunrise, they came across a small heap of pebbles on the side of the road. Taziem thought nothing of it, but Luke knocked it down and then steered his horse into the woods. An hour later, they stopped for a rest.

"Where is the caravan?" Taziem asked. She was very tired and very hungry, and the thought of more walking made her very cross. "I have not seen any sign of it since we left the road."

"That is good," Luke said. "Perhaps no one else will, either."

"How is such a thing possible?" she asked.

"In times of trouble, our women travel on foot and erase the wagon ruts with a broom or tree branch," he said. "And our horses wear these—" He held up something that looked like an oversized burlap sock. "—to hide their hoofprints. The women pick up their droppings, too."

The part about handling dung revolted Taziem, as it would any dragon, but other than that, she liked the idea behind the trick. It was clever and fun—a powerless version of illusion. She decided to wrap her own feet and thereby disguise her tracks. And indeed, the only thing she left in her wake when they resumed their trek was the scent of crushed arrowood leaves.

Originally northbound, they were now heading west. The terrain grew steeper as the morning progressed, and the forest acquired a spindly, overgrown look. Indeed, the brushwood finally became so dense, Taziem could not imagine a wagon getting through it. But just as she was about to ask Luke if he knew where they were going, a bird's song caught her attention. Although it sounded quite like a ruby-throated nuthatch, its call was a half-pitch too high. She cocked her head, listening for a reply. To her surprise, it came from Luke.

A moment later, a wagon-sized gap appeared in the wall of bracken that they had been skirting. Luke urged his horse through the opening.

Taziem followed on the beast's heels. Once they were both inside, the gap closed up like a fast-healing wound. Taziem was impressed. Dragons did not have anything like this.

"What is this place?" she asked, as Luke dismounted.

Santana came striding out of the brush with the answer. "We call it a safe haven, Great One. It is one of several refuges that our ancestors created nearly a century ago so our people might have a ready place to hide. Regrettably, the Tribe still has need of such places."

With that, he turned to Luke and said, "Well met, nephew. Were you followed?"

"No, uncle," the manling replied. "And I laid an hour's worth of false trail for any who might come looking. It comes to an end in a bramble patch."

"Excellent," Santana said, although his expression remained dour. "Now go and find yourself some breakfast. It will have to be cold fare," he added, as Luke licked his chops, "for we cannot chance a fire. Even the slightest wisp of smoke could betray our location."

"I will eat, too," Taziem said. She did not care if her food came hot or cold. A hungry dragon would eat anything as long as it was not *too* rotten. And the night's walk had left her famished.

Luke went racing off. Taziem intended to find a sunny spot and bask in it until he reappeared with food, but it seemed that Santana had other things in mind for her. "Great One," he said, in a polite but insistent tone, "while you're waiting, there's something over yonder that I think you should see."

She held his gaze for a long moment, but weariness clouded her line of sight and she could not see through to his thoughts. What could possibly be so important that she had to see it *now*? Could he not see that she did not want to do any more walking? An urge to refuse him swelled like indignation within her. But even as she opened her mouth to give it voice, logic intervened. Santana was a sensible man. He would not vex a dragon, footsore or otherwise, for no good reason. If he thought she should see something, then she probably should.

"Show me," she said, a grudging rumble that made it clear that she was doing him a favor.

He bowed respectfully, then started on his way. She followed at a slower pace, taking in details as she went. The refuge seemed much the same from the inside as it had from the outside. The undergrowth was perhaps a tad less dense, and the trees were not quite as rangy, but even so, a thicket by any other name was still a thicket, brooding and claustrophobic. And while the caravan's mere presence was usually sufficient to liven up any given space, such was not the case here. Perhaps it was because the wagons were tucked here and there amidst the brush like newborn fawns, their brightly painted panels hidden from view. Perhaps it was the lack of cook-fires and their scented smoke. Or—perhaps it was the way the younglings clung to their mothers' skirts and stared at her as she passed, instead of flocking toward her like gulls as they had done at the gathering. Whatever the reason, it made Taziem uneasy. She had grown used to the ready cheer of gypsy society.

The ground sloped upward for a short while, then abruptly gave way to a thin line of moaning pines and patches of blue sky. Taziem was not happy to see the trees. They grew exclusively on exposed cliffsides, where Wind shaped their trunks into garish twists and stripped their branches of all but an outer tuft of long, greenish-blue needles which vibrated when touched. The resulting sound resembled a human moan. The stronger the wind, the louder the moan. On particularly blustery nights, the noise traveled as far as the next valley—a woeful, uneven chorus. She did not want to listen to that tonight, not after walking throughout last night. So she invoked the secret Name of Wind. In response, a puff of air ruffled the hair on her head. She bared her teeth, a friendly display, and asked her friend to stay away for the night. It fluttered her hair again, a playful assent, and then blew away. A moment later, Santana called to her from the edge of the cliff.

"Great One," he said. "Look here." As she hunkered into a crouch beside him, he added, "There lies Murdered Dragon Meadow."

She squinted down at the distant patch of field-grasses. It looked the same as any other patch of field-grasses she had ever seen—sunny and green, ringed by trees, a good place to drowse or hunt. She did not see any dragon bones, though. Indeed, she did not see *anything* that required her immediate, no-time-for-breakfast-and-a-nap-first attention. Irritation flared within her. She swiveled her head toward Santana, meaning to give him a taste of it. As she did so, she caught a hint of movement out of the corner of her eye. So. There was something down there after all. Her predator's instincts reckoned it for a fawn or pig. Her irritation acquired a ravenous edge. She hissed. The nearest pine shivered as if with fear or ecstasy.

"All I see is my breakfast," she told Santana, with more than a hint of menace in her tone.

"And a fine breakfast it is, too," he replied blithely, as if he were oblivious to his danger. "A plump, young bull-calf. But there is more to see than meets the unaided eye." Before she could snap at him for posing riddles to a hungry dragon, he handed her a long, reddish-metal tube capped with curved glass at both ends. "Here," he said, "put the small end to your eye and look again."

An instant after Taziem did as she was told, her irritation dissolved in a shower of wonder and surprise. Amazing! This tube made Murdered Dragon Meadow appear so close, she could almost count the blades of grass that the bull-calf had in its mouth at the moment. The sight made her dizzy, then triggered a desire to take wing and go hunting. But even as that primal impulse swirled through her, she could not help but wonder what such a tasty creature was doing so far from a farmer's paddock.

"An excellent question," Santana said, when she asked, and then repositioned the tube for her. "Now look there—among the trees. What do you see?"

At first, all she saw was green leaves fluttering in a breeze. Then she caught sight of a two-legged figure crouching in the shadows. She lowered the tube so she could meet Santana's gaze.

"I see a man," she said. "He is either hiding himself or voiding his bowels."

The ghost of a smile flitted across Santana's mouth. "I suspect he is hiding, Great One," he said. "And if you look hard enough and long enough, you will see that he is not alone. I know because I happened to spot the lot of them early this morning. They were tying the calf to a hunk of deadfall so it couldn't run away."

"Do you see why I wanted you to see this?"

"Yessss," she hissed, as a conclusion with Eldahzed's eyes took shape within her. "Yes, I do." Her hunger turned into a fire in her belly. Her weariness fell away. "I also see what must be done."

ഗര

Masque sketched a loop in the afternoon sky, then flattened out and went gliding on the back of a friendly thermal wind. As it sailed along, all sported out, it looked for a likely clearing in the treetops below. Now that it was done playing, it wanted to eat until it could not move and then snooze its bulging belly away. It wondered if any wild horses lived among these trees. Masque *liked* horse meat.

As it savored the taste that accompanied the thought, something hard and pointy clamped down on the tip of its tail. Masque honked, more from surprise than true pain, and then slung its neck around to bite back. But it was too late. A black and tan streak was already zipping past it, projecting mockery all the way.

"You are too slow, little dragon!" it crowed. *"Too slow! You cannot catch Pinch The Powerful."*

Masque rumbled, a dyspeptic sound. This tanglemate was *not* one of its favorites. Pinch bullied. Pinch bragged. Pinch was all body and no brains. Unfortunately, none of its other tanglemates had been in the area when

Masque returned to Taziem's caves; and Masque had *so* wanted to play. Now all it could do was rue its desperation.

"*Masque The Stunted,*" Pinch taunted, flying just beyond its tanglemate's reach. "*You are so small, you would probably be dead already if Lathwi did not protect you like she does.*"

"*And you are so stupid,*" Masque countered, "*you would probably forget your own Name if you did not shout it out after every other thought like you do.*"

Stung by the insult, Pinch roared and then flung itself at Masque. An instant later, they were locked together, tails and necks entwined. They snapped at each other. They slashed at each other. They hissed and spat and jeered. Then Masque happened upon a toe-hold that its larger tanglemate could not oppose. If Pinch wanted to escape, it would have to abandon their clinch and thereby concede the game. Masque let out a triumphant bugle, proclaiming supremacy over Pinch for the very first time.

"*Masque The Magnificent is the superior dragon!*"

But instead of admitting defeat, Pinch bared its teeth in a defiant grin. Then, still clutching Masque, it closed its wings and folded them against its back. The two of them fell for a moment, then bobbed to a stop in midair as Masque redoubled its wingstrokes. There was a desperate tang to its excitement now. It *knew* that it was not strong enough to keep two dragons aloft until such time as Pinch grew weary of being a lump. Even so, it was determined to win today's contest. Pinch had been a pain in its backside for much too long. Masque wondered what Lathwi would do in this situation. Something clever, it supposed. Something cunning. Something like—

Inspiration struck like a bolt of sorcery. An instant later, Masque folded its wings, too.

For one giddy moment, the two tanglemates hung motionless in the cloud-scudded sky. Then gravity reached out and began to drag them down. They fell slowly at first—a seemingly lazy spiral that abruptly flattened into a headlong dive. The sky became a blur. The wind acquired a whistle. Masque did not think itself so clever now. The ground was expanding at an astounding rate. The treetops that were rushing up to catch them looked solid enough to break a dragon's bones. Masque winced at the thought. But it meant to hold fast as long as Puff-Headed Pinch did, no matter what the cost. The trees were only a moment away now. Masque turned its head, bracing for impact. As it did so, it caught sight of a prey-beast of some kind grazing in the clearing below. Inspiration struck again. It relayed the image to Pinch along with a deceptively casual thought.

"*Hungry?*"

"Famished," Pinch replied.

"Then let us hunt."

"Yes, let us."

Two pairs of wings snapped open as one. Neck and tails untwined. Sharp-tipped branches clawed at Masque's soft spots as it skimmed away from the canopy's embrace, but Masque did not care. It was still alive, alive, alive! And better yet, it had proven itself to Pinch. That big blowhard would think twice before trying to dominate Masque again! It did a quick dance to celebrate its new status, and then began to circle the meadow with its tanglemate.

"I will make the first strike," Pinch said. *"If the beast gets away from me, you must bring it down before it escapes into the woods."*

Masque rejected the plan with a snort. Pinch was not likely to miss. And once it had the beast in its clutches, it was even less likely to share.

"I saw it first, so I will strike first," it countered, and went careening toward the meadow. Pinch followed, broadcasting fury. As Masque strained to keep its feeble lead, an emphatic Voice erupted in its head.

"The beast is bait, set out by dragonslayers. Stay away!"

With a startled honk, Masque broke off its attack. But Pinch kept on going as if it had not heard. In passing, it bugled, *"I am Pinch! I go where I will! If any man dares to trouble me, I will eat him, too!"*

Masque projected a troubled thought into the gathering gloam. *"Mother? Where are you?"*

Her reply contained an image of moaning pines that bore the setting sun in their branches. Masque swiveled to the west. A bluff spanned into view. It was fringed with skeletal-looking trees. Taziem confirmed the location with the mental equivalent of a nod.

"Come to me," she said.

"But what of Pinch?" Masque asked.

"Pinch was warned," she said—a thought as cold as a winter wind. *"Now Pinch will suffer."*

A combination of curiosity and uncertainty made Masque circle back toward the meadow. When it saw that Pinch was feeding on the beast's sweetbreads now, it pitched a complaint at its mother. *"If that is your idea of suffering, then I want to suffer, too!"* But before it had a chance to act on the thought, three men came racing into the clearing. As they ran, they twirled something long and ropey-looking over their heads. Masque's envy turned to alarm.

"Be aware, Pinch," it said. *"Men approach you."*

"Let them," Pinch replied, chasing the thought with an image of bloody teeth and claws.

At someone's shout, the men let go of their twirly things. As soon as they were airborne, they opened into giant spider webs that then landed on Pinch's back. Greedy Pinch looked up from its feast at that, but did not appear upset.

Then more men emerged from the woods. These bore long, barbed spears.

"*Pinch!*" Masque shouted. "*Come away from there!*"

At the same time, Taziem roared, "*Masque! Come to me. Now!*"

Unable to resist a direct command from its all-powerful dam, Masque wheeled back toward the west. Frantic moments later, it landed on the bluff. A tall, all-black, woman with golden eyes met it there, but it would have recognized Taziem in any guise by her magnificent aura.

"*Mother,*" it squawked. "*Those men are going to kill Pinch.*"

"*I know,*" she replied.

Just then, Pinch roared. Taziem raised a reddish metal tube to her eye. A moment later, Masque felt her pulse a thought off to someone else. Pinch roared again, a sound of outrage and pain. Masque squinted, but could not stretch its vision that far. The meadow and its occupants remained a maddening blur.

"*What is happening?*" it asked Taziem.

She relayed an appalling image: Pinch tangled in weighted webs, flailing wildly as men drove their spears into its soft spots again and again and again. Flecks of gore flew through the air. The trampled grass gleamed gold with blood. .

"*Slayers!*" Masque hissed, trembling with excitement. "*We must stop them.*"

"*Not yet,*" Taziem replied, and continued to peer through the tube. "*Knowing the who of this matter is not enough. We must know the why of it as well.*"

Masque shifted its weight from one hindquarter to the other and back again—an anxious dance. Taziem was wise, it told itself. Taziem knew all. Therefore, her reasons for waiting must make perfect sense. But while Masque trusted her motives, it suspected her methods. No dragon deserved that kind of treatment, not even insufferable Pinch.

An alien thought slunk into Masque's mind. Although it was desperately weak, it still possessed the power of Pinch's secret Name. "*I am in Need, Masque. Help me—*"

Masque's claws flexed. At the same time, its wings unfurled. But even as it sank into a crouch in preparation for take-off, Taziem issued another command.

"*Wait.*"

"*I must go,*" Masque said, glad of the Name-magic and its compulsive guarantees. "*Pinch Called.*"

"Pinch is gone."

Although Masque knew that dragons did not lie, it did not want to believe what it had just heard. So it Voiced its tanglemate's Name—once and then again. But it made no contact, no connection. The thoughts rippled across the void, and then quickly faded away. Masque retracted its wings and keened for the lose of a tanglemate. Taziem took him to task for that.

"Stupid dragons die every day," she said. *"If you wish to live to adulthood, you will be quiet and learn from Pinch's mistakes."*

Masque swung its head in Taziem's direction, meaning to exact a full explanation of this terrible, would-be lesson from her. Before it had a chance to express its demand, though, a sudden scrap of movement caught its attention. It squinted at that spot, then let out a surprised honk. There were men in the woods at the bottom of the bluff! Although they were wide-spread, Masque could see that they were converging on the meadow. It began to whip the ground with its tail.

"More men," it hissed. *"Do you see them?"* At its mother's nod, it hissed again. *"This countryside is infested with dragonslayers. Pinch never stood a chance."*

"Nonsense," Taziem scoffed. *"You listened to me and are alive. Pinch ignored me and died. Our choices define our chances, little one."*

She took one last look through the tube, then tucked the thing under her arm and focused her attention on Masque. Her golden eyes were hard like Oma-stones; and while the pupils were round instead of slitted, Masque could still see dragon-fire burning within them. It averted its gaze almost immediately, acknowledging her superiority. That drew an approving rumble from her.

"I am going to cast an illusion over us so we will not be seen," she said. *"Then you are going to fly us down to the killing field. The men you saw in the woods below are mine,"* she continued. *"You will meet them soon. Do them no harm."*

"No harm," Masque echoed meekly.

Taziem worked her magic. For those who could hear it, the sound was cold and bright, like icicles singing in a hailstorm. When she was done, she closed her youngling's forearms around herself and said, *"Let us go now. And land softly. I want this to be a surprise."*

ഔ ര

Pinch's corpse lay open from sternum to groin. The dragonslayers were rooting through its viscera like a pack of wild hogs. One pulled out the liver only to pitch it aside with a snarl. Another kicked at a loop of ichor-coated intestine.

"Lotta guts in these bastards," that one remarked.

Masque began to tremble again. These men did not even mean to eat what they had killed. How perverted! How vile. It wanted to charge into them, biting and clawing like fury itself. It wanted to hurt them as terribly they had hurt Pinch. But Taziem would not permit such a thing.

"You will stay here, away from their spears," she said. *"If the illusion crumbles and they come for you, you will not fight. You will fly away."*

Masque wanted to know what *she* was going to do if the illusion crumbled. For while its scales were not completely knitted yet, at least it had them. Taziem had nothing with which to turn aside a dragonslayer's spear. But she did not give it a chance to raise that issue.

"Remember what I said about choices and chance," she said, as she went prowling off. *"I have no desire to lose two younglings in the same day."*

Taziem approached the dragonslayers with purpose but not haste. The set of her shoulders was like a promise of violence and pain. But she did not unleash her fury when she finally reached the ring of gore-spattered grass where the men were going about their grisly work. Instead, she stood there and watched, just out of everyone's way, until the hairiest of the lot drew Pinch's bloody gizzard from its body cavity.

"Ah, here we go," he said. "Now let's see if there's a prize inside."

His companions wiped their bloody hands on their leggings, then closed in around him. Taziem drew closer, too, choosing a space directly to the gizzard-holder's rear. If he felt her breathing down his neck, he showed no sign of it—he was too busy examining the nuggets of acid-washed rock and bone that acted as grist in a dragon's digestive tract. One by one, he held these bits up to his eye. One by one, he cast them aside—all but the last, which he tossed into the air with a whoop.

"I think we got one, boys!"

Quick as thought, Taziem grabbed his head and twisted it sharply to the left. The neck offered her a moment's resistance, then yielded with a deceptively soft pop. As the slayer collapsed to his knees, she roared, "Now!"

Santana and the other wagonmasters sprang up from the tall grasses with knives in hand and fell upon the dragonslayers. The attack was so sudden, and so swift, the slayers had no chance to grab their arms and fight back. One after the other, they slumped to the ground. And one after the other, the gypsies cut their throats.

This turn of events astonished Masque. It had been so curious about Taziem's intentions, it had not noticed these other men stealing across the meadow. How cunning they were! How sly and bold! It wanted very much to meet one of them for itself. And now that the dragonslayers were all dead, it saw no reason to hang back. So it shivered, ridding itself of accumulated stress, and then went lumbering toward Pinch's corpse. As it drew near, it heard one of the good men address Taziem.

"Our thanks, Great One, for allowing us to assist you in this matter," he said. "My only regret is that we could not make those pigs suffer more for their crimes."

Taziem did not reply. She was standing stock-still over the man whose neck she had snapped. Her jaw muscles were taut. Her fists were clenched. Masque chanced a glimpse at her thoughts only to encounter a wall of uncompromising fury.

"Mother!" it blurted, stunned into ineloquence. *"Why are you so angry? The dragonslayers are dead."*

An image of a small, blood-red stone took shape in Masque's mind. A memory straight from the waning moments of Ever-Light followed. In it, The Dragonbane howled with pain and rage as a tentacle of primal might wrested that same bloody stone from the center of Her brow.

"I do not understand," Masque said. *"What has prompted you to think of such a thing here and now?"*

"The last time I saw that stone," she said, *"newborn Pinch was putting it in its mouth."* She paused to compose herself. *"And that was why the slayers cut Pinch and the others open. They were looking for—this."*

Her fist sprung open, revealing Galza's third eye.

Masque recoiled at the sight. Its nostrils went white around the rims. As it stared, too shocked to do otherwise, Taziem continued to share her thoughts. *"No human knew what happened to Galza's talismans after Her fall at Lathwi's hand. And no dragon would tell. Therefore, it must be that the dragonslayers are somehow in league with The Dragonbane."*

"But Galza is dead!" Masque said. *"I saw the knife plunge into Her eye. I watched Her die."*

"So it seemed, youngling." Taziem said, shading the thought with a wistful sort of regret. *"So it seemed. But all the evidence argues otherwise. I now believe that while having a body gives Galza certain advantages, She does not need one to exist."*

Dread bubbled to the surface of Masque's mind. *"How are we to prevail if That One cannot be killed? She will destroy us all and then dance on the mountain of our bones."*

Taziem hissed, a reproach as sharp as her claws. *"Your fear is unbecoming, Little One. And your logic is sloppy. We know that Galza's powers are sorely diminished so long as She is without a body. We also know that She cannot assume a new body without the aid of Her talismans. You have one of those in your gut; I have another in my hand. Therefore, it is reasonable to conclude that dragons are safe enough for the moment."*

"Tell that to Pinch!" Masque countered, punctuating the thought with an image of its tanglemate's eviscerated corpse. *"Galza may be nothing more than a sinister voice in the dark, but as long as She can find like-minded creatures to do her*

bidding, She does not really need *a body. Other dragonslayers will come, wait and see. More younglings will die."*

Masque's argument took Taziem by surprise. She had not expected one so young to harbor such sophisticated insights. Callow or not, though, the little one was right. As long as there were people willing to ally themselves with Galza, younglings were in peril. And a threat to the young was a threat to the future, for dragons were not a prolific race. She touched her tiny stub of a nose to her offspring's rounded muzzle, a gesture of pride and affection. But before she could compliment Masque on the excellence of its thought, the echoes of a distant moan distracted her.

"Moaning pines," she heard one gypsy say.

But that was not right. Wind had agreed not to play in those trees tonight. And Wind was never false. Another cry drifted down from the bluff. This one was harsher, a hunter's shout.

"Something is wrong," Taziem said.

The gypsies did not hear her, though. They were already racing back across the meadow and toward their hidden horses. As they ran, a thin curl of smoke rose up from the top of the bluff. Taziem stared at it for a moment, surprised at how well it stood out against the blue sky. Now she understood why Santana had said no fires.

"What goes on?" Masque asked.

"I do not know," she replied, and suffered a strange pang of anxiety. *"And that is not acceptable. Take me back to the headland at once."*

The urgency that had overcome her now infected Masque as well. The youngling drew her into its arms and then bounded into the sky as if its own life were at stake. As it sped toward the bluff, the shouting grew louder, harsher, and more frequent. One plume of smoke suddenly became three, and orange flickers appeared amidst the night-shrouded trees.

"Circle the area," Taziem said, as Masque closed in on the moaning pines. *"We will see more that way."*

And she was right. From up above, the haven's woes became all too apparent. Two wagons were smoldering; a third was fully ablaze. By its orange light, Taziem could see shadowy figures weaving in and out of the trees. One of those shadows took on the voluptuous curves of Santana's eldest daughter, Tikki. She was calling for help. A big, grizzled man was chasing after her. Taziem hissed—a sound of recognition and rage.

"Put me down," she told Masque. *"Now."*

"There are too many trees down there," the youngling said. *"I cannot land."*

But Taziem did not care about that. She was fixated on that dragonslayer—that *warrior.* He was Galza's ally, the same as krim, or worse. He had to die. Nothing else mattered or sufficed.

"There is no need for you to land," she said. *"Just get as low as you can and then let me drop."*

"As you wish," Masque said, a concession feathered with doubts. As it swooped toward the ground, it added, *"But do not blame me if you land on your head instead of your feet."*

The next thing Taziem knew, she was falling out of the sky. She plunged past a tree's leafy branches, then through a gauzy layer of smoke. By the time she decided that wingless flight did not agree with her, the ground was right beneath her. Her feet slid out from under her as she landed, spilling her onto her buttocks. As she hit the ground for the second time, she swallowed Galza's stone, which she had been safekeeping in her mouth. Her first thought was to cough the vile thing back up before it had a chance to get caught in her gizzard. Then it occurred to her that that was one place where Galza would never think to look and swallowed again for good measure. A moment later, she sprang to her feet and went hunting for dragonslayers.

But hunting as a human was different from hunting as a dragon. Her perceptions were off; her instincts skewed. The shouting and crying distracted her. A twig snapped to her left. She swiveled that way, thinking prey, only to see Luke come prowling out from behind a tree. His face was smeared with blood and grime. A grim blend of anger and worry had darkened his eyes. He started to say one thing to her only to go suddenly wide-eyed and blurt another.

"Behind you!"

She turned to see a red-faced townsman rushing out of the night and toward her. The axe in his hands was already arcing toward her sternum. She side-stepped the stroke, then grabbed the axe by its neck in passing. As she did so, Luke lunged past her and thrust a knife into the outsider's throat. Blood gushed. The smell made her hungry.

"Have you seen The Little Mother?" Luke asked, grimacing as he yanked his knife free of the corpse.

"No," Taziem replied.

His eyes rolled in their sockets. The ridges in his brow grew deeper. "I am sorry, Great One," he said, as he blended back into the night, "but I have to find her."

Taziem had no idea why the cub was apologizing.

She resumed her hunt, now armed with an axe, but had trouble setting her bearings. The ongoing hue and cry of mayhem made the refuge seem small, while the fluctuating light of the wagon-fires made the shadows seem unusually dark. She might have prowled the night away in vain if a furious rustling had not broken out in the bush to her left.

"Hold still, you stupid bitch," a man snarled, "or I'll kill you here and now!"

The voice was loud and guttural, not lilting like a gypsy's. Taziem recognized the accent immediately. She hefted the axe, then prowled into the brush. The ongoing struggle masked the sounds of her approach, but it soon became obvious that she could have ridden in on the back of another dragon without drawing the Southerner's notice. He was on his knees between Tikki's legs, attempting to mate. Tikki was screaming and scratching and kicking. He punched the gypsy woman in the face. As he did so, Taziem swung the axe at the back of his head. Had the edge struck him, she would have split his skull open like a fruit. But she got caught him with the flat instead and so merely knocked him over. He was back on his feet in an instance, spitting with pain and fury. A savage thrill raced through her as their eyes met.

"You!" he snarled. "I've been looking for you." He glanced at the spot where he had had Tikki pinned a moment ago. The woman was long gone, but he broke into a leer just the same. "You should have waited your turn," he said, as he hitched his trousers up. "The first one always goes too quick."

Taziem made no reply. She recognized this dragonslayer. He was the one whose life she had spared back in Timberton. She would not be so foolish twice. Step by step, she closed in on him. With each stride, she saw his life grow that much shorter. She had a better grip on the axe now. And his long-knife was on the ground. His eyes darted from her axe to the blade, once and then again. The third time, he lunged for the weapon—just as she had predicted he would. She swung the axe: a vicious, double-handed stroke. But he ducked beneath the sweep and stabbed her in the thigh with a dirk that he pulled from out of nowhere.

Pain shot through her like lightning, pain such as she had not known since she was a soft-skinned youngling. It burned; it blinded; it left her breathless. She dropped the axe and staggered backward. Her leg felt hot and cold at the same time.

"I always keep a spare for emergencies," Jarv gloated, as he jammed the dirk back into his boot-top. Then he picked up the axe and stalked after her. "Now it's my turn."

Her injured limb buckled, spilling her to the ground. The dragonslayer laughed.

"That leg bothering you?" he taunted, as he bore down on her. "Here, lemme cut it off for you."

He hoisted the axe over his head. She tried to scoot backward and out of his range, but a dense patch of brushwood blocked her avenue of escape. Disbelief added its voice to a chorus of astonishment and pain. In spite of everything that she had learned over the centuries, she was going to die a stupid, stupid dragon. The axe-head whistled toward her. She pulled her knees to her chest to protect her vitals. As she did so, the brake erupted in a shower of splintered wood and debris. The tail-end of that shower contained a dragon's snarling muzzle.

"What the—?"

Masque gave the dragonslayer no time to finish his question. It clamped its jaws around his throat, crushing his windpipe in the process, and then gave the still-twitching body a savage shaking. Meanwhile, Taziem rolled back onto her backside and tried to stand up. She did not want to show weakness to another dragon, not even the one who had just rescued her from her own stupidity.

"You can let go now, little one," she said, with feigned insouciance. *"I think he is dead."*

Masque gave the corpse one last shake for good measure and then tossed it into the night. *"Feh,"* the youngling thought, as it craned its head back in her direction. *"He tasted bad."* It touched noses with her, then sniffed at her wound. *"That smells good. Can I lick it?"*

"If you wish," she said, projecting a sort of weary, maternal indulgence. But in truth, she was glad that Masque had offered, for she would never have asked—this even though dragon's saliva aided the healing process. She had to be strong, strong, strong to maintain her dominance. But she slid back onto her backside just the same.

"Why did the dragonslayers attack these other humans?" Masque asked, as it lapped at her. Its saliva burned as it seeped into the wound, but it was a cleansing kind of fire. Her whole leg was already starting to go numb. *"Do they seek this territory?"*

"No, Little One," she replied. *"The attack was not about territory. The slayers are like krim—hateful creatures. They kill because they have no respect for life."*

Masque loosed a scandalized honk, then drew its head back and hissed a warning. A moment later, a man stepped out of the shadows. He was small and lean, but the set of his shoulders spoke of a terrible weight. Until he spoke, Taziem did not recognize him as Luke.

"Great One," he said, "forgive the intrusion. But the Little Mother has asked for you."

Taziem was tired, hungry, and sore. Since Katya-Queen could not remedy any of these things, Katya-Queen would have to wait to see her. "Tell her I will come later," she said. "Tomorrow, perhaps, or the next day."

"Please," Luke said, injecting a full measure of urgency into his tone. "You must come now. The Little Mother is dying."

Only then did Taziem notice how quiet the safe haven had become. The shouting had stopped, as had the fighting. No frantic footfalls rang out. All she heard now was the uneven crackling of several small fires, and an occasional groan. She had never regarded these as ominous sounds. But she did now. *Katya-Queen dying?* That seemed wrong, too, even though she knew full well that all things died in their time.

She pulsed a thought at Masque. *"Help me up."*

"The hole in your leg will heal quicker if you rest," the youngling said.

"I have been Called," she replied.

The youngling had no argument for that, and so nosed her to her feet. An instant after it withdrew its support, though, she collapsed. "Oh, no," Luke cried. "You are hurt, too. By all that is sweet and sacred! This has been an evil night."

Taziem was on her feet again, and clinging to Masque's neck with both hands. So long as she had a breath of air left in her body, she was going to answer Katya-Queen's Call. No other response sufficed. "Where is she?"

"This way," Luke said, and motioned for her to follow.

Taziem took one faltering step, then another. Before she could attempt a third, however, Masque loosed a disgusted snort and stuck the length of its neck through the space between her legs. The next thing Taziem knew, she was sitting on the youngling's shoulders.

"This is unseemly," she said. *"You are not a pack-beast."*

Masque shrugged. *"The sooner you answer your Call, the sooner we can eat. And I am hungry."*

Once again, Taziem bowed to expediency and her offspring's generosity. And once they got moving, she had to admit—sitting down was far less painful than trying to walk. She could see better from this vantage-point too, although none of what she saw was to her liking. A discarded sword came into view. Its face was bloody. A few steps later, she spotted a child's slipper dangling from a low-hanging branch. There was a dark stain on that, too.

Then she noticed the lump.

It was sprawled in front of a now-smoldering wagon, and at first she thought it was a bedroll that someone had saved from the fire. Then, as Masque went lumbering by, it let out a loud moan. Moments later, a gypsy woman came hurrying out of the shadows. Her steps were nimble with hope. "Yorgi?" she said. "Is that you?" She dropped to her knees alongside of the lump, then gently rolled it onto her lap—only to hiss at what she saw. "Timberton filth." A knife flashed. The lump went limp. The woman shoved it aside, then got up and resumed her search. "Yorgi?"

Luke was waving them toward the blackened, skeletal remains of a wagon now. A small bonfire blazed in front of it. Several gypsies stood in its light. They half-turned as Masque approached, but on this night, not even the sight of a dragon in its true form at close range could rouse them from their gloom.

"*Let me down,*" she said to Masque. "*Do not menace anyone who may come near.*"

Masque lowered itself to its belly, then slanted a shoulder so Taziem might have an easy slide to the ground. In truth, it was happy that she was getting down. She might not look like much in her human form, but she sure got heavy fast!

As soon as Taziem hit the ground, pain shot through her leg like lightning. Sweat beaded on her forehead. Her stomach started to churn. If Luke had not inserted himself under her arm like a crutch, she would have fallen on her face. She rumbled appreciation at him, but he did not seem to notice. His eyes were focused on a point beyond the fire. Intuition told Taziem what that point was.

"Take me to her," she said.

"This way," he replied.

Step by faltering step, they hobbled around the bonfire, and if he found her great weight burdensome, he did not let it show. As they put the blaze to their backs, Santana rose out of the shadows to meet them. His stubbled cheeks were streaked with salt. His shoulders were stooped like a very old man's.

"Great One," he said, in a devastated voice. "My thanks for coming—"

She was more interested in the bundle that he was cradling close to his body and so cut him off with an upraised hand. With that same hand, she then drew back the folds of the bundle's swaddling blanket. A small, bruised face came into view: Mim. She had been slashed repeatedly. One gash had barely missed her left eye; another traversed the underside of her jaw. The wounds had been stitched and salved, but the youngling would bear their scars for the rest of her life.

"She will survive," Santana said. "But I fear she will never be the same."

"She has the heart of a dragon," Taziem replied. "Those wounds that do not kill her will make her stronger."

"I am sure I will take comfort in that thought some day," he said. "But right now, my heart is too sore for such solace."

A feeble cough called their attention to a nearby pallet. Although its occupant was hidden beneath a heap of furs, Taziem knew that this must be Katya-Queen. She pulled Luke in that direction, then sank to the ground beside the old woman and pulsed a thought.

"You Called. I have come."

Katya turned her head toward the fire—a slow, pain-wracked process. Taziem wished that the old woman had not troubled herself. For she was a wretched sight. Her eyes were sunken; her lips, gray. One corner of her mouth was leaking blood.

"Great One," she said, a breathless whisper, and extended a hand in her direction. That had blood on it, too. "You—honor me. Although you have not been with us long—I know you for a—friend."

Taziem did not know what to say to this, and so said nothing. Katya did not seem to notice or mind. She coughed again, then wiped her chin and went on. "As you can see, I am—dying."

"Are you relieved?" Taziem asked, remembering an earlier conversation of theirs.

Katya snorted as if amused, but the effort left her upper lip red. "In a way," she said. "But—I did not ask you here—to talk about me." She gestured to Santana, who was hovering nearby. He hastened to her side with Mim in his arms. Katya brushed the sleeping child's cheek with her wrinkled, bloodstained fingertips, then looked at Taziem. "My granddaughter has the power," she said, "but not the knowledge. One without the other does not—suffice. That is why I now ask you—to be her mentor."

Taziem unconsciously recoiled.

"You did it for Lathwi," Katya went on, struggling not to gasp between words. "Now do it for Mim. And me. So I may die knowing that the future of the Wandering Tribe is in good keeping."

Again, Taziem remained silent. It was not that she had anything against Mim. Indeed, as far as human younglings went, she was more tolerable than most. But to *mentor* her? Did Katya-Queen have any idea what kind of a commitment she was asking?

"I do," the old woman said, projecting a much younger and less bloody image of herself. *"And if I had any other choice—"* She grimaced as something within her seized up, then managed a fragile half-smile as Taziem siphoned the pain away. *"But I have no other choice. So, please. Help us."*

But Taziem continued to balk. Lathwi had started out as a diversion to keep her entertained during that last month of pregnancy and then continued on as a case study in human behavior. There had been no promises involved, no formal commitments. And that was as it should be—

Another wave of pain crashed through Katya. She clutched at herself. Her face went slack. Her eyes began to glaze over. Even so, she willed herself to catch Taziem's gaze and hold it. *"Will you? Teach the girl?"*

Taziem could feel the woman slipping away, faster and further with each passing breath. She extended a tendril of power, a life-line to which Katya could cling if only for a while, but the queen of the Wandering Tribe refused it.

"Too late," she said, with that same fragile half-smile. *"Promise—"*

Her head lolled. Her breathing stopped. The psychic link between her and Taziem dissolved.

"She is dead," Taziem said, too stunned to say more.

Someone behind her let out a low moan. Luke and Santana started to cry. To Taziem's surprise, her eyes began leaking, too—great, salty drops that stung the scrapes on her face. She did not know why she was crying. She knew that everything died in its time. Perhaps it was the manner of the old woman's death that distressed her. No one's last moments deserved to be filled with blood and pain. Or perhaps this was just how the human body expressed its grief. But even as she considered these possibilities, truth paid her a visit. She was crying because she had denied an exceptional human being her dying wish. And she would carry that knowledge with her until *her* dying day.

She dashed the tears from her eyes with the back of her grimy hand, then turned to Santana. "When the youngling is healed," she said, "I will take her home with me."

Santana looked both relieved and aggrieved at the prospect. "Thank you, Great One. We will be forever in your debt."

But Taziem did not hear him. As soon as she claimed Mim for her own, her guilt began to transform itself into resentment and rage. She had had to commit herself to the child's education because Katya was dead. And that wise old dragon-heart had died at the hand of Galza's allies. Son-of-the-south, Timbertonsman—it mattered not. They ate together. They lived together. They killed together. Therefore, they were all the same. Earlier this evening—had it really been just a few short hours ago?—Masque had said that thwarting Galza was not enough, not when She had so many willing to serve Her. And Masque had been right. Something had to be done. *She* had to do something.

And she knew exactly where to start.

It was time to make men think twice about becoming The Dragonbane's allies. It was time to make them *afraid*.

Chapter 13

A band of leatherclad riders raced hard and fast across the dusty plain, trying to outrun the worst of the brutal summer sun. They numbered five in all: four warriors, and Lathwi. Although she loathed her new companions, she had sought them out of her own accord. Why waste time and energy avoiding her enemies, she had reasoned, when they could take her where she had to go? So she had barged into the southlands like a stag in rut—loud and proud and full of fight. A patrol had converged on her almost immediately. She remembered how smug its pot-bellied captain had been.

"Well, well," he crooned, as he and his men closed around her. "Who do we have here?"

"That is for me to know, and General Veeder to find out," she replied haughtily. "Take me to him at once."

The patrol hooted and jeered. The captain mocked her with a leer. "The general has no need of an arrogant Northern whore. But me and the lads here aren't so particular. Slide down from that pretty horse of yours and show us what you've got. If we like what we see, we'll let you live for a little while."

She paused for a moment as if weighing her options, then abruptly drew her sword and charged.

Caught off-guard by her aggressiveness, the captain died of a slashed throat before he had a chance to clear his own weapon from its sheath. She hacked the next man out of his saddle, then roared with pain and fury as someone struck her in the back with a sword. Such a blow would have cut anybody else in half. But she was wearing her dragon scales, and so escaped with nothing more than a bone-deep bruise.

"Random's balls!" someone swore. "We fight a demon here!"

Lathwi curled her lip at the mistake. What was it with these people from the south? They would probably call a mouse a demon if it did not fall over and die when they shouted at it. But while being taken for krim annoyed her, a wise dragon did not hesitate when opportunity popped up; and she saw how such foolishness might work to her advantage. She felled her next attacker with a Word and jag of lightning from her fingertips, then menaced the rest of the patrol with a look.

"You *will* take me to General Veeder," she said, reinforcing the command with subtle compulsions. "Otherwise, I will slay the rest of you here and now. Not only that, but when the general and I finally do meet,

I will tell him how you quailed before me, and your family names will be forever shamed."

The patrol's former second-in-command crooked his thumb and littlest finger at her—a peasant gesture meant to avert evil. Lathwi laughed at the irony. That seemed to frighten the fools even more. They turned their horses toward a chain of mountains in the distance and rode off without a thought for their dead. Still laughing, she followed.

Now, almost two days later, that mountain range dominated the horizon. Lathwi could hardly wait to reach its shadowed slopes—not because she preferred the highlands to these dry desert plains, but because she would then be one step closer to the end of her quest. General Veeder was camped somewhere up there. And he would know where his necromage was. One way or another, she meant to pry that information from the warlord. Then she was going to fulfill her promise to Liselle and go home.

Now, if only there were some way of making that course of events unfold faster! She was tired of these filthy outriders and their uncouth ways. She was tired of people in general. She craved green hills, a book of magic, and the enlightened society of dragons. But even as the ache took wing in her heart, her companions slowed their now-frothing horses to a walk. Without seeming to, she scanned the horizon for signs of trouble. All she saw was heat shimmering up from the horizon: a languid, hypnotic dance that evoked images of water and trees. She blinked, trying to banish the mirage, but it was no trick of the eye. They were approaching an oasis. No doubt the riders meant to shelter there until nightfall.

As much as she wanted to, she could not contest their decision. It was hot, even by dragon standards, and her horse's hide was drenched with sweat. An afternoon in the shade would leave it in better shape for a long run tonight. And she could use the time to go hunting for something to eat. She had not done so since taking up with Veeder's men, as they would have bolted like jack-rabbits an instant after she was out of sight, and while her compulsions would have eventually dragged them back to her, *eventually* did not suit her plans. Leastwise, it had not suited her yesterday. Today she was hungrier, and more willing to take chances. And the desert would see that they did not get far.

The oasis loomed ahead: a fair green island of date palms and reflected sunlight. Tantalized by the smells of water and shade, the horses broke into a run. Lathwi shared their excitement—until she got her first good look at the desert refuge. The date palms bore crudely carved graffiti on their trunks. Discarded bones and other garbage littered the fine white sand. Even the air carried humanity's taint: a faint but lingering stench of sweat and urine. Indignation swelled within Lathwi like a bee-sting. Leave it to humans to foul their own sanctuaries. Leave it to them to ravish a gift freely given. And no doubt they would complain most bitterly when the spirit of this place finally grew weary of such treatment and withdrew its life-preserving powers.

"Stupid creatures," she hissed to herself, as she stripped the tack from her horse. "Fools," she added, as she fed the beast a measure of grain. Then she turned toward the outriders. They were clumped beneath the palm trees like loose droppings. None of them dared to look her in the eye. "You had best be here when I return," she said, in a haughty tone. "Elsewise, you will spend the rest of your days looking over your shoulder for me."

Then she strode off into the desert.

⚮

The hunt did not go well.

She had a taste for something big and red-blooded, so she staked out a well-worn trail in the hope of catching a pronghorn or wild ass on its way to the watering hole. But her patience soon wilted in the hot summer sun, and all at once, she found herself craving jack-rabbit instead of big game. She spooked one out of hiding by beating at a patch of dry brush with her sword, but it dove into a thicket of spiny cacti before she could nab it. Birds, she decided then, eyeing the outlines of a nest in a nearby tree. She was definitely hungry for birds. Or eggs.

In the end, she settled for snake: a rock-viper that she found snoozing in the cool recesses of a stone outcropping. It was not very large, or all that tasty, but she gobbled it down as if it were a juicy tenderloin. Afterward, she allowed herself to lounge for a while in the outcropping's shade, solitude being her reward for enduring the company of brutes. Quite by accident, she fell asleep. By the time she snapped awake, the sun's last bloody rays were already a stain on the horizon. She hissed, berating herself for being so weak, then sprang to her feet and headed back toward the oasis in the small hope that her horse would still be there when she returned. She had no such hope for the Southerners. They would have bolted as soon as the desert started to cool down. But the nearest mountain was still half a night's ride away, so she had plenty of time to overtake them. And if they had taken her horse—well, they would have even more cause to fear demons when she finally caught up with them.

As if in response to that thought, her amulet pulsed. She froze in mid-stride, then listened for the tell-tale sounds of sorcery being worked. But all she heard were ordinary early evening noises: the rustling of tumbleweeds in a breeze, a tiny scrabbling across the sand, the leathery whisper of bat wings. Her amulet pulsed again—a low-grade warning.

From that, she concluded that there was some sort of magical artifact in the area, and that it was not aimed specifically at her.

The question now was—what to do about it?

She glanced toward the oasis. Her Southerners were growing further and further away with each passing moment. The longer she delayed, the harder it was going to be to track them down, especially if they made it to the mountains. But—she was curious. She wanted to know what sort of artifact she had stumbled onto, what it was doing here in the desert, and why her amulet had not reacted to it earlier. She tried to factor her horse into the balance, but its weight proved negligible. Losing a beast was *inconvenient.* Ignoring an unknown source of magic was unwise.

So, using her amulet as a sort of divining rod, she began to search for the artifact. When she was on the right track, the warning pulses came frequently. When she strayed off-course, they grew fewer and further between. She became so intent on the chase, she did not realize that she had doubled back onto her own trail until she saw the outcropping where she had caught the snake. There were two shadowy figures prowling around those rocks now. Neither of them resembled anyone from the patrol. She stole closer, taking such cover as she could find. The figures did not see her. They were stalking something else.

"It's here, I tell you," she heard one of them whisper. "Look, here's a piece of its hide."

The other snorted. "That's a snake-skin, you moron. Demons don't shed."

So, she mused, these humans were hunting for a demon—her, most likely. That would explain why they were following her trail. That might also explain why her amulet was reacting. It would make sense for demon-hunters to have some sort of demon-bane in their possession. She only knew of one such bane—The Spell of Unmaking—but her education was still far from complete. This, then, would be her next lesson.

The demon-hunters worked their way toward the far end of the outcropping. The larger of the two was the more diligent hunter. He poked his broad-sword into every hole and overhang that he saw. The other fellow seemed more interested in the stars overhead, even when his companion jumped back and said, "There it is, my lord—under that ledge! I saw its eyes!"

"It's probably just a rat, Dall," Milord drawled. "Or maybe a big spider."

Nevertheless, he went to investigate. As he sank to his knees beside the overhang, Dall raised his blade—not to watch and ward, but to chop Milord's head off. At the last moment, though, warned by a careless footfall, he swiveled around and blocked Lathwi's sword-stroke.

The man's supposed sighting had suckered the dragon in her. For if there was a demon loose in this world, then it had to be killed—regardless of the circumstances. So she had drawn her sword and gone rushing to Dall's aid. By the time she realized that his claim was a ruse, she was already committed to a head-on attack and so went after Dall instead. He hesitated for a moment when she engaged him—just long enough for her to shoulder past his guard and drive her blade into his groin. As he crumpled, white-faced with pain and shock, she turned to confront the other man.

Dall's would-be victim was sitting cross-legged on the ledge that had nearly been the end of him. Although he was not a handsome man, his appearance intrigued her. He was clean-shaven. His eyes were watery and blue. The silvering red hair on his head had been pulled back into a parade horse's tail. When she leveled the tip of her sword at his heart, he smiled. That intrigued her, too.

"You are from the north," she said.

"An accident of birth," he replied, with a shrug of his narrow shoulders.

"Your man was going to kill you," she said.

"I know." Although nothing about his smile changed, it suddenly seemed quite chilling as he glanced at his writhing companion. "He's been thinking about it for a while now."

"Because you are a Northerner?"

"I suppose that had something to do with it." His gaze shifted back to her. He was blasé, conversational even, as if there were no length of sharp-edged steel between them. "Why did you stop him?"

"That was not my intent."

His smile twitched at one corner—a show of restrained amusement, perhaps, or perhaps a nervous tic. "I see. Am I to be your next victim then?"

"I have not decided yet."

And that was the unadorned truth. She had no qualms about killing Veeder's men, for they seemed to respect nothing save violence and death. But this man was a Northerner, and seemingly unarmed—a peculiar combination in this part of the world. Not only that, but something about him was setting her amulet off. She was tempted to investigate further.

"There's an oasis not too far from here," he said then. "Might I persuade you to decide my fate there instead of here? I've been riding for several days, and would like to rinse the dust from my throat before I die."

"I do not believe such a move would be wise on my part," she replied. "Where there are two demon-hunters, there might well be more; and I am in no mood for more company tonight."

He snorted—the same mocking sound he had used on Dall. "Stranger, you might give a body a bit of a start at first sight, but you're definitely *not* a demon. And no matter what your intentions might have been, you *did* save my life, so I'll guarantee yours for the night."

"That is bold talk for a man who is staring at the wrong end of a sword," she said.

His only reply was a shrug.

The gesture pleased her. It spoke of hidden strength and confidence. It smacked of dragons. Her curiosity became an itch that would not be ignored. So she withdrew her sword from his throat, then motioned for him to climb down from the outcropping. As he did so, he glanced at Dall's now lifeless body.

"It would seem that I am in need of a new bodyguard," he said. "Would you be interested in the position?"

Would you be General Veeder?" she asked.

"Not quite," he replied.

"Then I am not interested."

They started back toward the watering hole. At Lathwi's insistence, he led the way. She followed on his heels, ready to spit him on her sword at the slightest whiff of treachery, but he went quietly, radiating composure, as if they were out for a night stroll. Her amulet continued to pulse at regular intervals. This was a confirmation as well as a warning, and it kept her on her guard.

When the oasis finally loomed out of the darkness, it was not as she remembered it. A small, white tent stood by the water's edge. A natty little campfire kept it company. Only three horses idled in the nearby shadows now. Amazingly enough, one of them was hers. She hissed Milord to a stop, and then caressed the great vein in his neck with the tip of her sword.

"Where are the men who were here earlier?" she asked, suspecting a trap.

"I sent them back to the border," he replied, as blasé as ever. "That's where they belong."

"How is it that they left my horse behind?"

"I told them to."

"Why?"

He shrugged—a daring gesture, given his circumstances. "It's a fine animal. Too fine for outriders. I thought General Veeder might like it."

"You know Veeder?"

"I am in his service."

"In that case, you will take me to him."

"Maybe tomorrow," he said. "If you decide to let me live that long. Tonight, I'm going to give myself a much-deserved rest." He eased the sword away from his neck with a ginger forefinger. "You may join me if you wish."

She rumbled, admiring the man's audacity. Now it was her turn to demonstrate the quality of her nerve. With a convincing flourish, she returned her sword to its sheath. Then she motioned him to go where he pleased. He headed straight for the tent.

"I'll be out in a minute," he said, as he ducked behind the silken tent flap. "Make yourself at home."

She rolled her eyes at the absurd suggestion, then went to check on her horse. It was resting quietly with the other animals. Neither it nor its tack had been harmed in any way, but someone *had* opened her saddlebags. She could tell by the knots that now held them closed—they were nothing like the ones she had tied. She wondered who the snoop had been, and what he had been hoping to find. Gold, she supposed, or maybe gish. But certainly not two bags of grain and a dragon's knuckle-bone. She picked up that nub and rubbed it between her finger. The Bone-Man had said that it would keep her well; and so far, she had come to no harm. She wondered if his other predictions had come true, too, despite her efforts to circumvent them. She found herself hoping that Pawl was well.

The sound of a tent-flap being swept aside called her back from her thoughts. She stowed the knuckle-bone in the leather pouch that swung from her belt, and then turned to rejoin Milord. He was on his way toward the water's edge, naked as a newborn except for the bracelet of brightly colored stones around his wrist. She studied his physique with scholarly detachment. Aside from Pawl, the few men whom she had seen undressed had all looked the same—ridiculously soft, and hairy. And Milord definitely adhered to this standard. His pale chest and belly were flabby. His backside looked like a rug.

"Care to join me?" he asked, as he dipped a toe into the pool.

"No," she replied, and sat down in front of the fire.

"Suit yourself." He waded in up to his knees, then submerged himself. When he surfaced a moment later, his face was to her. "Ah," he sighed. "Much better." He wrung out his sodden ponytail, then sat down in chest-deep water and scooped a handful of sand from the bottom of the pool. "So," he said, as he scoured his skin, "tell me why you want me to bring you to Veeder."

"I hear he is gathering an army," she replied, statements of fact that had nothing to do with the truth. "I hear he pays well."

Milord rubbed his teeth with a forefinger until they squeaked, and then said, "You don't know what you're getting into, stranger. So go home before you get hurt."

"Tell me what I do not know," she said.

"Well, for one thing, the general doesn't like northerners."

"He hired you."

The same supremely self-assured smile that had intrigued her earlier took hold of his mouth once again. "He tolerates me. And only because I have certain talents that he needs."

"I am talented," she said. "Perhaps he will find a reason to tolerate me, too."

"Perhaps." He stood up, then splashed his way to shore. As he did so, he said, "Hand me that robe, would you?" and pointed to a lightweight bundle that was sitting by the fire. She obliged simply so she would not have to look at his nakedness. "Thanks." He pulled the robe over himself, then stretched out on his back in the fire-warmed sands across from her. There was a canny quirk to his smile now. His gaze was probing. "But why risk it? Is it the man who draws you? Or his cause?"

"I care for no cause but my own," she said. Then, because she did not want him to delve any deeper into her reasons for being here, she sought to distract him. "Why do you wear that on your wrist?"

His expression avalanched as he glanced down at the bracelet. One moment, it was amused; the next, melancholy. "It belongs to my sister. She's been lost for many years now." He traced a finger over the stones, then added, "I've dedicated my life to finding her."

"Does the general know that?"

Just like that his melancholy was gone, swept away by a rogue wave of surprise and appreciation. His mouth quirked. His nostrils flared. "You're not what I expected."

Lathwi could have said the same of him. He was far more interesting than those border dullards—sharp-eyed and quick-witted, an audacious enigma. Under different circumstances, she might have found it easy to appreciate his company. But not in this particular time and place. Milord served Veeder. Therefore, no matter how intriguing he might be, Milord was not to be trusted.

"I am hungry," she said, and stood up. "I am going hunting."

"I have food," he said, gesturing toward his tent.

"I do not want your food."

His smile spread across his face and into his eyes. "I like your style, stranger. I like *you*. So even though it'll probably get you killed in the end, I've decided to take you to Veeder—if that's really what you want."

"That is what I want," she said.

"Then be ready to ride in the morning," he said. "And if you rise before I do, feel free to fix us some breakfast. I hate riding on an empty stomach."

"I do not fix breakfast."

Irritation flickered in his eyes, but it was a fleeting thing—there one instant, gone the next. "I believe you are going to be good for me," he said. "Oh, and by the way, my name is Seth—Lord Seth, when we're in the presence of knuckle-dragging Southerners. What shall I call you?"

"Lathwi," she said, because her use-name was no secret.

Then she strode into the desert.

₧₨

Seth stared after the big, armor-clad woman long after she had vanished into the night. *Lathwi.* He could not place the name—this, although he dabbled in languages. He could not place her accent or manner of dress—this, although he had traveled all over the continent on Ylana's behalf. He rubbed his sister's bracelet against his cheek.

"What would you think of this one?" he wondered. In a softer voice, he said, "I think you'd like her. She's *different.* I have a good feeling about her."

He had long since grown accustomed to being loathed. That was the necromage's lot in life. Most men feared what they did not understand. And Veeder's troops were no exception. They insulted him to his face, and made the hook-fingered sign for evil behind his back. No one wanted to do his bidding, but everyone did—because Veeder said they had to, and because disobedience could land them on a sacrificial slab. And while no one had come right out and challenged Seth to a duel to the death yet, several covert attempts on his life had been made. Dall's had only been the most recent.

Oh, the look on that buffoon's face when he turned and saw Lathwi there!

He still did not understand why she had come to his rescue. *Such was not my intent,* she had said, with refreshing bluntness. Then what was? He would have to ask. He was *so* curious about her. She did not kowtow. She did not sneer. And apparently, she did not want to see him dead. These were all good reasons for keeping her around, but she had offered him one better as well. Lathwi was intelligent.

Does the general know that?

No. No, he didn't. Indeed, the muscle-brained blowhard didn't even suspect, even though he *knew* Seth was a necromage, even though he had *seen* Ylana's coffin. What a pleasure it was to talk with somebody who could see beyond her own nose. And who gave a damn if that nose bore the marks of a disgraced whore?

Actually, Veeder was bound to give a rather large damn about that. He disliked northerners, women, *and* whores. Lathwi would offend him on sight. Had she rode into his camp with those border scum, she would've wound up in a holding pen in a heartbeat. Fortunately, she was riding with him now. He'd figure out a way to protect her—at least for a while. After that—well, he would just have to wait and see. There was no point in getting too far ahead of himself.

A yawn rushed over him like a tide, sweeping his thoughts out to sea. He got up, then headed for the bedroll in his tent. But as tired as he was all of a sudden, he still had an uncommon spring to his step. Something about it reminded him of Ylana.

"Soon, little sister," he whispered. "I promise."

∞ ∞

Shortly before dawn, Lathwi returned to the oasis. She had thought to catch Seth still abed and thereby give herself a small psychological advantage, but to her surprise, he was already awake and waiting for her. All three horses were saddled. His tent was down and packed. The only thing left of his campfire was a few wisps of fragrant steam.

"Well, there you are," he said, as she strode toward him. "I was starting to think that you'd changed your mind and left without me. Want some of this pemmican cake?"

"No," she replied. Pemmican was wretched stuff: shredded jerky mixed with lard and dried berries. At best, all it would do was spoil the memory of the tasty tortoise eggs that she had foraged for herself last night. At worst, it could pitch her guts into an all-day uproar. And that was *not* a pleasant way to spend a day in the saddle. "We must be on our way before the day gets too hot."

He pocketed the rest of the cake with a shrug. "I've been ready to go for almost an hour now."

They rode hard and fast through the desert's last leg. As the morning passed, the terrain grew ever more rugged. Spires of rock protruded from the ground like giant fangs. Stands of cacti gave way to vast bramble patches and the occasional stunted tree. By the time they came to the base of the nearest mountain, there was nothing gentle or soft left in sight.

"We should stop here," Seth said, "and give the horses a rest."

Lathwi wanted to press on. But before she could say so, a fast-moving shadow sailed overhead. She looked up to see a giant, cinnamon-colored dragon gliding through the sky. Even from a distance, she could tell that it was a sire: no female possessed such a spectacular wingspan. As she watched, the drake circled back around for another pass. She urged her horse toward the nearest shelter—an overhang crowded by boulders. But

Seth simply sat in his saddle and gaped. She hissed. Just once, she wanted to travel with a human who did not fall stupid at the sight of a dragon.

"Come here," she urged him. "Come quickly, but do not run. Dragon eyes are attracted to sudden movements."

His horse started toward her, but it was the beast's idea, not Seth's. He was still staring into the sky. His expression was vacant and confused. Lathwi hissed again. This dragon-foolish man was putting them both in considerable danger! She doubled back and grabbed Seth's horse by the reins, then led it and Dall's riderless beast back to her makeshift shelter.

"Get down," she said. When he did not respond, she pulled him out of his saddle and slung him toward the far corner. He landed hard on his backside, but did not protest his harsh treatment in any way—if indeed he noticed it at all. His attention was all for the drake.

He was flying directly overhead now, and low enough for Lathwi to see him in all of his glory. And what a magnificent sight he was: as big a dragon as she had ever seen, over ten times her size from nose to tail-tip, and a handsome, dusky-red color. Although she had never seen the sire firsthand, she recognized him from Taziem's memories. This was Bij The Mighty—her mother's Chosen. He was projecting hunger and chronic rage. But he flew over them and on without a hitch in his wingstrokes, which meant that he had not seem them.

"Give her back, you bastard!" Seth screamed. "Give her back."

The drake turned on a wingtip and started back toward them.

For one stunned moment, all Lathwi could do was gape at Seth and wonder what could have possibly possessed him to shout after a hungry dragon. Then she grabbed her knife from its sheath and cut the leather tie that bound Dall's horse to Seth's saddle. The horse pawed anxiously at the ground. She turned its back toward the approaching drake and then smacked it hard on the backside. With a surprised neigh, it bounded off. Lathwi pressed herself against the rocks and held her breath. For if Bij did not fixate on the beast as prey, he would surely see her and Seth, and he *hated* trespassers, especially the human variety. She would have to use magic to survive his challenge, and she did not want to do that unless there was absolutely no other choice.

"Stay still," she hissed at Seth, as Bij closed in on the alcove. "And if you let out so much as a peep, I will feed you to him personally."

He rolled his eyes, then huddled deep into the folds of his robe. As he did so, the world turned gray. Lathwi bit her lip—one moment, then two. The shadow continued on its way. A moment later, she heard a horse's terrified squeal and then a triumphant roar.

"No!" Seth wailed. "Please! Not Ylana."

Lathwi closed the gap between them in five angry strides, then grabbed him by the front of his robe and hoisted him to his feet. Tears were dripping from his eyes now. His breath was coming in shallow gasps. But he still had a lost look about him.

"What ails you, man?" she said, shaking him as if to break up the apparent logjam in his brain. "Do you want to end up as the lining in a dragon's belly?" When he did not respond immediately, she slapped his face out of sheer irritation, and said, "Is that what happened to Ylana?"

The sound of that name seemed to draw him out of his daze. He shook his head, then pressed his hand over the cheek that she had slapped and absently scratched the sting away. A moment later, he dragged a sleeve across his eyes and dared to peek at the sky.

"Is it gone?" he asked.

"Yes," she said. "No thanks to you."

"Sorry." Chagrin dominated his features now. The thin seam of his mouth looked like a stress fracture. "It's been a while since my last spell. I was rather hoping that I was done with them."

"Hope is not a reliable counselor," she said, and then pushed him out of her air space. Although it was the smallest of shoves, he stumbled backward and then flopped onto his backside again. He shot her a resentful look and started to get up again, but she would not allow it. "We do not want to be anywhere in plain view while that dragonsire is in the area. So use this time to relax and recover." Then, because she was curious and because she felt entitled to the knowledge, she asked, "Who is Ylana?"

"My sister," he said, and for a moment, his eyes grew distant again. "The darling of my parents's later years. A dragon—" He closed his eyes as if by doing so, he could either invoke the memory or block it out. "A dragon took her from me."

Lathwi was neither surprised nor shocked to hear that. Sometimes, for their own various reasons, dragons did indeed take people. Taziem had taken her. Her tanglemate, Shoq, had taken quite a number of dark-haired females. The question that begged asking was, *What had Ylana's dragon done with her afterward?* But she did not give it voice. If Seth wanted to believe that his sister was still alive after being nabbed by a dragon, that was his business. And she was living proof that such a thing actually happened from time to time.

But she certainly was not going to offer to help him in his search.

"A man with your sort of affliction should make a habit of traveling at night," she said instead. Then, as she replayed the encounter in her mind, she added, "But perhaps that would not have made a difference in this instance. Most adult dragons hunt at dawn and dusk, when it is cooler and the prey beasts are busy feeding. That sire was hunting under a hot, midday sun."

"That's probably because there isn't much game left in these parts," Seth said.

She cocked her head, an invitation to explain. He needed no further prompting.

"There's a gold mine on the far side of this mountain," he said, "a mine so rich, it could finance a dozen armies for a hundred years. But it's not doing the general any good because that crazy red drake keeps shutting the operation down. At first, Veeder tried to placate the beast with virgin sacrifices. Then he tried to kill it with poisoned meat. Now he's trying to starve it into going elsewhere. His troops have orders to kill anything larger than a rabbit on sight."

The policy outraged Lathwi. For in addition to being wanton and wasteful and a revolting abuse of power, such wide-scale slaughter was also futile. No wonder Bij had been so agitated. "Dragonsires do not abandon their territories," she said. "And so long as there are miners in the area, the red one will not starve."

"You seem to know quite a bit about dragons," Seth said, regaining more of his composure by the moment. He looked her up and down as if he were seeing her for the first time, then stroked his chin and added, "Veeder may have some use for you after all."

"Who are you to Veeder that you can predict his whims?" she asked, allowing her contempt for the general to spill onto Seth. He did not seem to mind, though. He was his former, inscrutable self again. The transformation fascinated Lathwi in spite of herself.

"I am his advisor," he replied. "Among other things."

"Is that an important position?"

"You could say that."

"Yet you travel alone and unguarded," she said, poking for soft spots in his pride. "In the north, important men travel with armed escorts."

He deflected the jab with a shrug. "I had Dall—until you killed him. And while it may appear otherwise, I am not defenseless."

She snorted, disparaging the claim. "A one-legged grandmother with milk-eye could bring you down, Milord."

His smile went taut. The canny lights in his eyes went cold. "You'd be wise to have a care about the way you talk to the men around here," he said. "Veeder isn't as tolerant of arrogant women as I am."

"My tolerance has its limits, too," she said, a simple statement of fact. Then she sat down in the alcove's scant shade and retreated into her thoughts.

Seth watched her through his lashes for the longest time. He had to admit, he was fascinated. And Ylana liked her, too.

Chapter 14

*S*tand fast and declare yourselves!"

Lathwi and Seth reined their horses to a stop, then looked for the speaker. There were plenty of places for him to hide along this narrow pass. The mountain stood tall and rugged on both sides of the gap. A smattering of alpine pines provided extra cover.

"I am Lord Seth, special advisor to the general," Seth said. "Will a demonstration of my abilities be necessary?"

A man dressed in camouflaged leather stepped out from a niche in the mountain's side. His crossbow was pointed toward the ground, but his scowl aimed at Seth. "No, my lord," he said, a surly pardon. "You may proceed. General Veeder is expecting you."

As he and Lathwi resumed their trek, she began to appreciate just how lucky she had been to encounter Seth when she had. They had been challenged three times on this road so far; and each time, he had gained them safe-passage with the mere mention of his name. She suspected that such would not have been the case if she had continued in the company of that border patrol.

Special advisor. She wondered what that meant. Seth would not tell her, even though she had asked several times. "You don't need to know," he had said. "And it's best if you don't ask." Which made her all the more curious. And speculative. Maybe *he* could help her find Veeder's sorcerer if the general would not cooperate. Maybe he would *advise* her. But she did not voice her hopes aloud. She did not know enough yet.

The pass leveled out, then began to slope downward. A short time later, a small valley came into view before them. Hemmed in on three sides by tall sandstone cliffs, it looked more like an oversized bear-trap than a rogue army's hide-out. Even so, there was no doubt that there was indeed an army based here. Even from this distance, Lathwi could see clusters of the white shelters that Pawl called tents. They stood out among the trees like giant fungi. And a fog-like haze of accumulated smoke hung low in the air, waiting to be blown away by a rare summer breeze. Seth took a deep breath through his nose, then expelled it again as an exaggerated sigh.

"Home sweet home," he said, and then turned his sardonic half-smile on Lathwi. "Last chance to change your mind and go home."

"Why would I want to do that?" she asked.

His only reply was a shrug.

Their descent into the valley passed without incident, but soon thereafter, Lathwi got a foretaste of what life with Veeder's army would be like. She and Seth were riding past a meadow that had been trampled to bare dirt. Two companies of men were taking weapon practice there. As they drilled, they hooted and sneered to each other in voices pitched to carry.

"Looks like the North-Man finally found a bodyguard worthy of him," one said. "A woman! Ha!"

A second yelled, "Hey, Maggot! Is that a woman or a demon?"

"Does that matter to a ghoul?"

Seth snapped a wrist at the men—a quick, abrupt gesture, as if he were throwing something at them. Many responded with the hook-fingered sign for evil. The heckling dropped to a diffuse, disgruntled mutter. Seth tossed his ponytail much like a horse trying to rid itself of flies, then sniffed as if he had just caught wind of a very bad smell.

"Veeder's vanguard," he told Lathwi. "They'll be the first in any fight—first to kill, first to die, first to stab you in the back. You should be glad that you saved my life. By doing so, you saved yourself from a stint with that scum."

She did not think much of them, either—not because they were Southerners, but because they had showed extremely poor discipline by talking during a drill. Pawl would have left the whole lot of them whimpering in the dust.

They rode on—through a rather scabrous-looking camp and toward an oversized tent that commanded the best overall view of the valley. As they approached, two guards came rushing over to take Seth's reins. Neither of them, however, seemed pleased to see him.

"The general is expecting *you*, North-Man," the younger one said, in a surly tone. "But no one said anything about a whore."

"She's not a whore," Seth replied, as he dismounted.

"But she bears the marks—"

"You had best tell me something I don't know already, Todd-stool," Seth said, in a voice that sounded like sweet reason and venom at the same time. "Otherwise, I might have you reassigned to a holding pen."

Both guards went quiet and pale. In the ensuing silence, Seth collected Lathwi's reins and then handed them along with his own to the older guard.

"Take these animals to the stable-boy," he said. "See that he keeps them separate from the common stock. And set my tent up in my usual spot."

"Yes, Milord," the man said, and then led the horses away. Todd-stool remained behind, scowling like a man caught in a homegrown patch of quicksand. With a reptilian smile, Seth presented him to Lathwi.

"She's going to wait right here until I call for her," he said, looking from the guard to her and back again to make sure they were both listening. "If she comes to any harm, any harm at all, I'll hold *you* responsible. Is that clear?"

Todd-stool responded with a sullen grunt.

"Excellent," Seth said, and then disappeared into the tent.

Lathwi sat down on the ground next to the tent, then shut her eyes as if she meant to catch a quick nap. But the tent was made of silk—the perfect fabric for eavesdropping. And there were so many things that she needed to know.

"Seth!" a deep voice boomed. "About bloody time. Is it true? Have your people recovered another one?"

"I believe so," Seth replied, in his usual, unruffled tone. "Let us see and be sure."

In the ensuing silence, Lathwi's amulet began to pulse like a bird's heart. By that, she knew that the two were discussing Seth's mysterious demon-bane, and that it had just gotten more dangerous. Her curiosity quickened. She wanted to know what it was—

"By the bones of Mighty Grange," Veeder exulted. "It's a match!"

—and why this Veeder was so pleased to see it. Under other circumstances, she might have tried to obtain that information by magical means. But not now, not while the general's mage remained an unknown to her. She did not want to do anything that might make him suspect that there was another sorcerer in the vicinity.

"The signs are converging," Veeder gloated. "My time approaches. Soon, the whole world will know my name."

"Soon," Seth echoed, "but not yet. In your vision, you possess all of Grange's tokens. As of now, you're still missing two."

"So hurry up and find them!" the general snarled, proving himself as mercurial in temperament as he was in tone. "My army grows restless in this chicken-coop of a valley. And that damned red dragon continues to wreak havoc with my payroll. I *must* begin my campaign *soon*, Seth, or heads will fly. Is that clear?"

"It is," Seth replied. "And believe me, my lord, I'm just as eager to find those tokens as you are. In fact, with that in mind, I've recruited another dragonslayer."

She snorted to herself. Taziem's chosen was one of the mightiest sires alive. The general could recruit a hundred slayers to his service and still lose his war against Bij The Red. Indeed, Bij would probably relish the odds. And the carnage.

"Thought you were being clever, ay, whore?" Todd-stool growled. At the same time, he grabbed her by the hair and hauled her to her feet. "Just wait till I tell the general you were spying on him."

With a menacing hiss, she pulled free of his grasp. "Touch me again, fool," she said, "and I will make certain you wind up in a holding pen."

The color drained from his face, just as it had when Seth had threatened him. She peeked at his thoughts, hoping for a glimpse of these mysterious pens, but all she saw was darkness swirled with faceless prisoners. An intense, doomsday foreboding accompanied the image.

"That bare-faced freak doesn't know you're a spy, does he?" he said, trying to keep his mind on more pleasant things. "All he knows is that you're from the north—just like him. Maybe the general will let me kill you both for his carelessness."

"I am no spy," she said, which was the dragon's truth. She had not come to sniff out Veeder's strategies. She had come to slay his mage. "And you could not kill me even if you had leave to do so."

He disputed that claim with a sneer, then gave her a contemptuous, one-handed shove. Although she could have stayed on her feet quite easily, she allowed herself to fall down. An instant after her butt struck the ground, she picked up a fist-sized hunk of rock. Todd-stool raised his forearm to protect his face. As he did so, she smashed the rock into her own cheek. Tiny spangles of pain danced across the field of her vision. Blood began to trickle down her face. She treated her would-be assassin to a dragon's merciless grin, then threw the stone into the distance.

For one stunned moment, all Todd-stool could do was stand there and gape. His eyes were locked on her self-inflicted injury, but they both knew that he was staring at his own freshly turned grave.

"You're demonspawn," he rasped. "Just like that damned wizard."

That snagged her attention. *Wizard?* That was another word for sorcerer. *Could this puerile fool possibly know something about Veeder's mage?* She thought to take another, more extensive look at his mind, but before she had a chance, Seth emerged from the tent. As soon as he saw her damaged cheek, he turned a furious shade of red and then rounded on the guard.

"You dared to defy me?" he asked, in a low, venomous tone. "You dared?"

"No!" Todd-stool blurted in reply. "It was her. She was spying on you and the general and when I caught her—"

Seth silenced him with an upraised hand, then turned to Lathwi. "Is that true?" he demanded. "Were you spying on me?"

"I *was* listening," she freely admitted. "No one told me not to until this fool—" She gave Todd-stool a scornful once-over. "—found me out."

"Then what happened?"

"He grabbed me by the hair and forced me to stand. Then he pushed me. I fell to the ground." She laid the facts down like paving stones and then let Seth jump to his own conclusions. "He said he hoped to kill me." That was true, too. "And you."

With a chilling little smile, Seth turned his attention back to Todd-stool. "Bad luck, old boy," he said, "for I'm more inclined to believe her than you. And that means I'm going to have to make an example of you."

"No, Milord," Todd stammered. "Don't—"

But Seth had already beckoned to a pair of passing soldiers. Neither man looked happy to see the northerner, but neither offered him any insult, either.

"Yes, Milord?" one of them asked.

"You are to take this man to the infirmary and shave him to the waist," Seth said, radiating authority and menace. "After that, conduct him to the holding pen. I'll look in on him later. If he's not there, well—" He narrowed his eyes at the two soldiers. "I guess I'll have to come looking for *you.*"

"He'll be there," Soldier Two said, and then dealt Todd-stool a resounding blow to the mouth for stammering a protest. "No one wants to hear it, dog. So keep your flap shut and come this way."

He and his mate led the disgraced guard away. When they finally moved beyond earshot, Seth turned to Lathwi with a milder version of his earlier scowl and said, "As for you, woman, this constitutes your second and last warning. Keep your nose to yourself. Otherwise, I'll have someone cut it off."

"How Southern of you," she said.

His eyebrows leapt up, becoming twin arches of surprise; and for one taut-fisted moment, he tottered on the brink of anger. But just as she thought he was going to plunge head-first into that abyss, he stepped back from it with a forced chuckle. A moment later, his smile filled out, and his eyes acquired an admiring gleam.

"You play dangerous games with dangerous people," he said. "I like that. But it will probably get you killed some day."

She shrugged. "Everything dies in its own time."

He answered her shrug with one of his own. "Just so you know. Now hurry up and disarm. General Veeder has agreed to grant you an audience." Then, as she undid her swordbelt, he said, "When you get within two sword-lengths of the general, you will drop to one knee and bow your head to him."

"Why?" she asked.

"Because he's the mightiest warrior alive," he said, with a tight little smile that showed too much tooth. "And because it's polite. And because he'll kill both of us if you don't."

Under other circumstances, Lathwi might have challenged all of those assertions. Pawl had slain krim with nothing but a sword. That made *him* the mightiest warrior alive as far as she was concerned. And what was so polite about showing somebody the top of one's head? That seemed rather ridiculous to her. And as for Veeder killing her, well—he would not be the first human to try. But she had nothing to gain by antagonizing Seth at this point in time, so she kept her thoughts to herself.

"Ready?" Seth asked, when she had shed all of her killing things. Before she could say yea or nay, he swept the tent-flap aside. "After you."

Although the tent was large enough to house a dozen men, it seemed unbearably small to Lathwi. The silken walls were partly to blame. They filtered most of the color from the incoming sunlight, leaving everything a mangy shade of gray. They also stopped the wind from blowing fresh air in and hot, skunky, human-scented air out. But even if the tent had been as airy and well-lit as a mountain tarn, it still would have seemed small; and that was because of the man who sat at its far end. He was the biggest human being she had ever seen: almost two heads taller than her and at least half again her weight. His bare shoulders and chest were those of a bull. His arms looked like ironwood trunks that had ruined many an axe-head.

"That's close enough," Seth said, softly, when she came within the prescribed distance of that mountain of a man. "Now do as I told you." As she dropped to one knee, he bowed stiffly from the waist and said, "General Veeder, this is Lathwi—the mercenary I was telling you about. She's an expert on dragons."

As Veeder studied her, so she studied him. His eyes were deep-set. His nose was flat and broad, with a curious, scar-like tattoo across the bridge. This, together with his overgrown hair, both head and facial, lent him the aspect of an aging lion.

"I see you've encountered one of my men already," he said, noting her bloodied cheek.

"I have encountered many of your men already," she replied. "Most of them are now dead."

The general did not react to that bald statement of fact. Instead, he continued to scrutinize her as if she were a heap of suspicious meat. As he did so, he absently rubbed at his breast-bone. At first, she thought he was flea-bitten. Then she caught a glimpse of something beneath his massive beard. She thought it was a tattoo at first, for it was oddly shaped, with thick, heavily blackened edges. Then he shifted in his chair, exposing more of his chest, and realization struck her like a miniature bolt of lightning. She was looking at a brand—no, *brands*! There were others under the matted carpet of his beard. She wondered if they were self-inflicted, and if so, for what reason? To prove that he could endure pain?

"The man who scarred your face was a son of the south, too, wasn't he?" Veeder asked. She nodded. "So you understand that men from the southlands expect females to know their place?" She nodded again. Irritation spasmed across his face. "Then why do you want to enlist with a southern army? Are you insane? Or just incredibly stupid?"

She drew herself to her full height like an insulted dragon. "I am neither mad nor addled," she said. "As for my place, I know it well. I belong among the mighty, not the weak. And I have heard that you pay well."

He sneered—a sound of frustration and rage that was all for Seth. "Oh, yes, I pay *very* well, don't I, Seth? Or I would, anyway, if you were any kind of a mage at all."

Seth deflected the barb with a gentle snort. "Now, general," he said. "You know very well that I'm doing all—"

"Shut up," Veeder snapped. "I've heard your excuses a dozen times already." He locked Lathwi in his sight again. "You. You're supposed to be the expert. Tell Seth here what he's been doing wrong."

But Lathwi did not hear the question. Her mind was a whirl of profound disbelief. She had come all the way over a mountain to find Veeder's sorcerer, and now it seemed that he had been within reach all along. Seth! She should have known. Power attracted power, and he had the demon-bane. But he did not look like a mage. There was no gold in his aura, no discernible reservoir of power—

"You!" Veeder boomed. "*Mercenary.*" At the same time, Seth elbowed her in the ribs. "I'm talking to you. How do you kill a dragon?"

She stuffed her astonishment into an isolated nook in her backbrain, then hastened to share some common knowledge. "The young ones have soft spots here—and—here," she said, pointing to her own armpits and groin while imagining Seth's. "The younger the dragon, the larger the spots. A sword thrust to any of these places can be lethal—."

"Yes, yes," the general said impatiently, "I know how to kill the little ones. But what about a big one? How would you slay a drake?"

"It cannot be done," she replied, speaking strictly from a human standpoint. "The old ones have no gaps in their scales."

His face turned a furious shade of red. The rest of him clenched like a fist. He strained a curse between his teeth, then spat the leavings at her.

"Useless cunt! You're no good to me. Seth, take her away and have her killed."

"As you wish," Seth said. "But don't you think you're being a bit hasty? After all, *she* does know how to kill the young ones. And as you know, we *do* have a use for such knowledge."

Lathwi added that last statement to the list of the mage's growing list of crimes.

"I don't care," Veeder said. "She's a woman, and a northerner to boot. No matter how talented she might be, she'll be more trouble than she's worth. Get rid of—"

Lathwi chose that moment to butt in. "I cannot slay the red dragon," she said, "but I can draw its attention. If you try to kill me, I will bring it to this camp, and it will eat you and your army."

The threat shocked Veeder out of his temper tantrum. For one amazed moment thereafter, all he could do was gape at her. Then he turned toward his advisor, who was trying valiantly to keep his mouth from crimping into a smile.

"Are you sure she's a woman?" he asked.

"As sure as I can be without having slept with her," the mage replied.

"All the more reason to kill her," Veeder said. "But since you seem to value her so highly, I'll hold off on deciding her fate till the morrow. Perhaps the proper course of action will come to me in my dreams."

"It often does," Seth said.

"Until then," the general went on to say, "she's to remain in your custody. Guard her well, for any problems that she might cause will be on your head."

"There will be no problems," the mage assured him.

The warlord stood up—an obvious dismissal. As he did so, the burns on his chest could be clearly seen. There were six of them in all: a small full moon at the top of the sternum; a larger crescent at the bottom; a pair of opposing handprints; and two inverted sickles. Lathwi stared. She could not help herself. Something about the pattern begged for recognition.

"So," Veeder said, inhaling deeply to expand his chest, "you marvel at the Brands of Grange, do you? Good. For it is my birthright—an inheritance forecasted by the stars. In the weeks to come, this pattern will become my standard, and the world will bow down before it."

As he stood there, basking in his projected glory, Seth urged Lathwi to her feet. "Come," he said. We've wasted enough of the general's valuable time." To Veeder, he said, "I'll return for a full debriefing as soon as I secure her. Do you need anything while I'm about?"

"Yes," Veeder replied. "I need a dead dragon." But for a rare change, his good mood held firm. Before Seth could make his excuses, the general laughed and waved him away. "Go on, leave me already. You Northerners have no sense of humor."

Seth was quick to act on those orders. Lathwi followed at her usual pace. "Well," he said, as they left the general's tent behind. "That went better than I thought it would."

"He wants to kill me," Lathwi said. But what she was thinking was: *Now? Now? Should she kill Seth now?*

"True," he conceded, "but he hasn't yet. And he won't, either, once he gets used to the idea of you."

She had vowed to kill the mage who had stolen Liselle from the Dreamer's Keep. And, unless her logic had taken a completely wrong turn somewhere, here that mage was, walking right next to her through a secluded strip of woods. All she had to do was reach out and snap his neck. No one except maybe Veeder would miss him right away. And by the time someone found him, she could be long gone.

"Did you hear what I said?"

Now? Now? Opportunity urged her to do it. But instinct held her back. There was something more here than met the human eye. She did not know what it was exactly, only that it had to do with dragons somehow. Further investigation was warranted.

"What's wrong with you?" Seth demanded. He had placed himself in front of her, and was now trying to daunt her with a steely glare. "You haven't heard a word I said."

"Now I know why Dall wanted to kill you," she said, trying to catch him off-guard in the hope of springing a secret or two from him. "You're a sorcerer."

A pang of guilty unease flashed across his face, but he chased it away with a scoff. "That twiddling fool. I wouldn't have wasted so much as a word on his flea-bitten neck. Or on yours, for that fact. So you can quit your scowling. I'm not going to harm you."

"Swear it."

"Sorry," he said, "but I swear to no one. You'll just have to trust me."

She continued to glower. It was part of the charade—as was seeming betrayed. "You should have told me what you were when we first met."

He shrugged. "You didn't ask."

"Do you answer every question posed to you?"

"Ask me one and find out."

"What was General Veeder's sorcerer doing out in the desert?"

His smile turned cold. So did his eyes. "I am not the general's mage," he said. "I am a mage in the general's service. And what I do for him is none of your concern. How come you're so interested?."

"It was merely a question," she said, "and I am curious by nature. If you do not believe me, look into my thoughts. I have been told that sorcerers can do that."

"Some can, some cannot," he said curtly, slow to shake off the pique which had seized him. "Few would bother over such a trivial point."

Which meant that he was probably one of the ones who could not, she decided, and then tried to coax another secret out of him. "What else can sorcerers do?"

He arched a mocking eyebrow at her, as if he knew exactly what she was trying to do. "Why do you want to know?"

"Because when one is traveling with a scorpion," she said, "it is safer to know the scorpion's habits. Or so my mother says."

"Your mother sounds like a smart woman."

She let his mistake pass uncorrected. "So may I not know what else a sorcerer can do?"

Her tenacity toppled the last of his grievances, and a disbelieving smile emerged from the rubble. "Damn, but you're a persistent one," he said, looking her up and down again and again as if he could not believe what his eyes were trying to tell him. "Sleep with me tonight and I'll tell you anything you want to know in the morning."

"No."

"Why not?" he asked. "I can give myself an appearance that pleases you."

"Maybe," she replied, "but you will still be a scorpion at heart. And I have no wish to be stung."

He laughed aloud, startling a flock of blackbirds that had settled in the canopy overhead. Lathwi tracked their flight, envying them their little wings and the freedom to fly away from troublesome situations. How much easier their lives must be. How much simpler.

"I thought you might prefer this spot to a holding pen," Seth said. "My tent's just over yonder." He gestured at a shaded knoll. She made a point of committing the site to memory. One never knew when such knowledge was going to come in handy. "If it were up to me," he went on, "I'd stay and keep you company, but I've got to get back to the general. And while I regret the necessity of it, you'll have to be restricted while I'm gone. It won't be bad," he hastened to assure her. "I'll just raise a few wards to keep you from straying too far from this spot. We'll both be safer that way."

She scowled at him—a show of unhappiness that was all bluff. For in truth, his precautions suited her. She wanted some time alone to contemplate the situation and its possible conclusions. If he wanted to guarantee her privacy for her, so much the better.

"Just leave me enough space to swing a sword," she said. "I need to practice."

He struck a dramatic pose: spine arched, head thrown back, arms open to the sky. She waited for the scintillating, psychic sound of a Will being gathered and worked, but it never came. Instead, Seth began waggling his fingers and spouting nonsense. A moment later, he lapsed back into a normal stance and wiped his brow with the back of his sleeve as if he had actually broken a sweat.

"There," he said, "you should have all the room you need. If anyone manages to cross these barriers, feel free to kill him. I'll be back before nightfall." He half-turned to leave only to glance back at her over his shoulder and loosed an afterthought. "Can you truly summon the red dragon?"

She did not reply. Indeed, she could barely look at him at the moment for fear of losing her composure. What a charlatan this man was! He had not raised any wards. He had simply pretended to do so. She had to admit, it was an elegant trick. A body who did not know better would have been spellbound by Seth's reputation, and his own fears. But as a rule, illusions only worked on the unsuspecting; and in this instance, that happened to be Seth. She intended to take advantage of that in the very near future.

Meanwhile, Seth mistook her silence for prudence and twitched an amused smile in her direction. "I suppose I'd keep that answer to myself, too, if I were you. But he'll have to know eventually, you know."

"Perhaps he will find out sooner than he thinks," she said, just to keep him and his employer guessing.

Seth chuckled, then started on his way. A few steps later, he laughed aloud and said, "I *love* a woman who plays dangerous games!"

As soon as he was out of sight, she set out to scout the area. She headed for his tent first, hoping to find a cache of demon-banes or its like secreted among his things, but if there was such a thing in that stuffy, room-sized shelter, it was warded *very* well. And after what she had seen so far of Milord's magic, she did not think he could manage such a feat. Indeed, she was not entirely sure that she had the right sorcerer. The mage whom Liselle had described was powerful enough to breach the barriers between life and death. Seth's power was so negligible, it did not even show up in his aura.

Still, Veeder's men feared him. And she knew from experience that Southern warriors feared very little—even when fear was called for. So Seth was either a fraud, or there was something about him that she was not seeing yet.

She prowled out of the tent and into the surrounding woods. As she explored the area, she wished that she had gotten a look at the bane that had attracted her to Seth in the first place. *"It matches,"* Veeder had said. And: *"Find the other two."* To which his so-called mage had replied, *"I'm as eager to find those tokens as you are. In fact, with that in mind, I recruited another dragonslayer."* She rumbled to herself—an eruption of frustration. Most dragons would not know a bane from a chicken bone. So why bother to kill them?

"After all, she does know how to kill the young ones."

Up until then, Lathwi had assumed that Seth's interest in dragon-slaying revolved around Bij. But with that statement, he implicated himself in Eldahzed's murder. For that reason alone, he deserved to die. For that reason, she would kill him. But she wanted to know so much more before then. Was he killing dragons because one of the skyfolk had abducted his sister? Or were his motives linked to Veeder's wishes? She rumbled again. There were too many unknowns here, and not enough facts to plug them all up.

She happened onto a trail that led further away from the camp. It was too broad and footworn to be a deer-run. She wondered if it led anywhere useful—like out of this valley. No doubt, she would have need of a lesser traveled escape route by the time her stay here came to an end. She started to follow it only to abandon it a moment later as a set of voices came racing up behind her.

"Come on, Kel," one voice urged, "let me go. I'm *begging* you. You can tell him that I overpowered you and escaped."

"Sorry, Todd," another replied, "but then we'd wind up in the pen. And I'd rather cut my own nuts off than find myself in there."

From the cover of a broad ironwood tree, she watched as three soldiers strode into view. One of them was naked to the waist. As he drew closer, she could see that he was completely hairless, too. Even his eyebrows and chest hairs had been shaved. He looked very, very odd—sort of like a pillar of dirty salt in trousers. The pair of guards who flanked him both looked supremely uncomfortable.

"Then slip your knife in my boot-top," Todd said. "I'll stick the maggot the next time he comes too close."

"That's been tried already," Kel said, lowering his voice to a near-whisper. "More than once. But it doesn't work, I tell you. He can't be killed."

"But—"

The trio tramped past her hiding place and into uncharted territory. But as much as Lathwi wanted to see where they were going, she dared not follow. The ground cover was not as lush ahead, and besides, the day was growing old. She needed to be back on Seth's proscribed turf before he returned. So, with a promise to resume her investigations in the very near future, she began backtracking. As she did so, she contemplated the one tidbit that she had picked up along the way.

At least some of Veeder's men believed that Seth could not be killed. *How interesting.*

She wondered if this were another of Seth's clever sleights-of-hand, or if he really *was* impervious to steel. He himself had hinted at such a thing back at the desert's edge: *"While it may appear otherwise, I am not defenseless."* Had he been trying to engage the power of suggestion? Or could he possibly be more than he appeared?

Or—maybe those would-be assassins had simply not been adequate to the task.

She drew her sword and assumed a fighting stance. As she began the first drill that Pawl had ever taught her, an unbidden image of the swordmaster took shape in her mind. He was bare-chested and sweat-slicked. She thought of that night in Markham's barn. He had taught her things on that occasion, too. She shook off the erotic chill that skated through her, then continued with the drill. When she was done with it, she moved on to the next. She slashed and parried, stepped and whirled. Her sword became a silver blur. She practiced until her arms grew numb and her legs felt weak. She practiced until she almost too tired to think.

Then her amulet pulsed, announcing Seth's return. Moments later, he emerged from the lengthening shadows, clapping his hands to show his approval. "It seems you weren't overstating your abilities after all," he said. "That was a remarkable display."

Lathwi was far less impressed. Her sides were heaving. Her vision was slightly blurred. Five years as a dragon had left her complacent. She had all but forgotten how hard a human had to work to mount a decent defense.

"My old master would have beaten me black-and-blue for all the mistakes I made today," she said.

"Well, he's not here, so you don't have to worry," Seth said. "Now stow your weapon and come with me. I've got supper."

At the mention of food, she became lightheaded. The last thing she had had to eat was a cache of eggs back in the desert. And all of a sudden, that seemed like a very long time ago. She was ready to eat *anything*—even a bowl of stew or porridge. But judging by the bloodstained sack that Seth was holding up, she was not going to have to make that kind of sacrifice to her hunger. She sheathed her sword immediately, then all but dragged him back to his tent. There, she stared at the sack while he started a fire.

"Were you bored while I was gone?" he asked, as he worked.

"No," she said.

"Did you miss me?"

"No."

The fire took to the wood with a greedy whoosh. Seth smiled at his handiwork, then hauled two thick, still-bleeding steaks from the sack. "You can thank the latest raiding party for this," he said cheerfully. "Tomorrow, it'll be hardtack and pemmican again."

"Do not put mine on the fire," she said. "I will eat it like that."

A peculiar smile curved across his mouth, a reptilian look of surprise and delight. He slapped the steaks onto separate plates, then handed one to her. When he sat down with the other one, she arched a wondering eyebrow at him. He responded with a shrug.

"I was only going to cook mine as a courtesy to you," he said. Then, as he drew a knife from a fold in his robe, he added, "You and I are more alike than you think."

"We are both mercenaries who prefer the taste of meat to that of char," she said, with just a hint of an insulted chill in her voice. "I believe the similarities end there."

"I wouldn't be so sure of that if I were you," he said.

"Why do you say that?" she asked. "Did you look into my mind?"

"I didn't need to," he said. "I can see it in your eyes."

"Ah," she said, much relieved. "Then it is no longer a wonder that Veeder's men dislike you. No one's secrets are safe."

"Remember that," he said with a wink, and then turned his attention to his meat. A moment later, she did the same.

She fed in typical dragon fashion: fast and messy, ripping the meat with her teeth instead of cutting it into polite little chunks with a knife. When she was done, she turned in Seth's direction with a mind to poach, but there was nothing worth the stealing left on his plate. Disappointment flowered within her. She would not have guessed that such a runt could choke down that much meat that quickly. She licked her plate clean, then her fingers. As she did so, the day's exertions caught up with her. She tossed the plate aside, then stood up and stretched. It was dark out now except for the fire's light. She thought to sleep for a few hours, then resume her investigations of that foot-path. But even as she was about to go in search of a cozy nest, Milord seemed to read her thought.

"You'll be sleeping in my tent tonight. Don't worry," he added, as she lobbed a scowl at him. "I won't try to force myself on you while you're sleeping. I prefer willing partners."

"I prefer to sleep in the open."

"Nevertheless," he said, switching to that sweetly reasonable tone of his, "I must insist that you stay inside tonight. If you were to walk off in your sleep, I could lose my head."

"I do not walk in my sleep. And even if I did," she added, unable to resist toying with him, "would not the wards that you conjured earlier keep me from straying too far?"

"They don't work as well at night," he said, straight-faced and without so much as a moment's pause. "Besides, Veeder wants you on a short chain. And as you know, the general gets what the general wants. So no more arguments."

She opened her mouth to press the issue only to realize what a fool she was being. What better place to kill a mage than in his own tent? And what better time than when he was asleep? Sharing his tent would provide her with definite possibilities—if not tonight, then tomorrow night or the next. And a wise dragon never turned her back on a chance.

"Very well," she said, emoting haughtiness instead of resignation. "I will sleep in the tent." She headed that way only to stop at the flap. "Can I choose any spot within? Or do you wish to dictate to me about that, too?"

"You may choose for yourself. Just bear in mind that I'll be sleeping in the cot—with or without you there."

She shrugged, then ducked into the shelter and curled up in the corner farthest from the cot. When Seth did not follow immediately, she heaved a ready sigh and fell into a doze. But something prevented her from slipping into a deeper sleep. Maybe it was her belly, complaining about the relative lack of food these days, this as it digested tonight's one small steak. Or maybe it was Seth sitting outside, mouse-quiet except for the occasional rumble from his gut. Whatever the reason, she was still semiconscious when someone walked into the campsite and said, "All is in readiness for you, Milord."

"Are you sure they all took the mythalmar?" Seth said. "The last time, one of them didn't, and made things—difficult. I wouldn't want that to happen again. Would you, Kel?"

There was no mistaking the menace in his tone for anything else.

"No, Milord," Kel replied, and now there was fear in his voice as well as loathing. "This time, I administered the mythalmar myself. There will be no more—difficulties."

"Good man," Seth said cheerfully. "You may go now."

Without another word, Kel hurried off. As he did so, Seth got up and poked his head into the tent. Although Lathwi's eyes were shut, she knew that he was staring at her. She could almost feel his gaze boring into her skull, trying to gauge her wakefulness. She let out a soft snark. A moment later, he withdrew from the tent and started after Kel. As soon as his footfalls faded out of earshot, she sat up. She was wide-awake now, and very curious. On any other night, she would have followed Seth just to see what all this talk of mythalmar and difficulties was all about. But tonight she had more pressing concerns—like finding a quick way out of this valley. Once that little matter had been taken care of, she could finish her quest and *go home*. So she summoned her Will and cloaked herself in illusion. Then she set out to investigate that trail.

A shiny, almost full moon hung in the clear evening sky, providing plenty of light for hunting and tracking. Her amulet pulsed once as she rediscovered the footpath, then again as she began to follow it. She scowled. *That* had not happened the last time that she had set foot on this trail. Therefore, either some new danger had sprouted up in the interim, or Seth was somewhere ahead of her. This unanticipated development did not dismay her. Indeed, she was pleased to think that fortune had acted to slake her curiosity. So she continued on her way. The trail—and the pulsings—led her through a pocket of forestland and up to a mountain's side. The rockface loomed tall and sheer, imposing in its ruggedness. Its only flaw was a large, onion-shaped opening that smelled faintly of the grave. She curled her lip at the odor, then tensed all over as the psychic residues of magic came spurting forth from the cavern's depths. The sounds were like nothing she had ever heard—harsh and discordant, extrasensory punishment, a fell, black cacophony that went on and on. She covered her ears with her hands, trying to block out the noise. As she did so, a finger of fog drifted into view. At first, she thought it was Liselle, for her former mentor had always had awful timing. Then it was joined by another, then another and then many more. In the span between two heartbeats, she found herself standing in the middle of a frigid cloudbank. A dainty, disembodied hand reached out of this haze as if to catch and hold her in passing. Scores of anguished eyes and mouths beseeched her as well.

"Help us. Stop him. Send us back."

She did not fear these ghosts, but their sheer numbers appalled her. What possible reason could *anyone* have for tearing so many from their afterlives? It was wrong. It was wicked. Liselle had been right to send her to end it. So even as the ghost-swarm churned all around her, she stalked into the cavern. The moon's light abandoned her after the first step. The earth's radiant heat forsook her after the third. But she had grown up in a place like this, cold and dark and underground, and would have felt quite at home if not for that ongoing psychic racket—that and the rotting meat smell that kept getting worse instead of better as she continued through the passageway.

A bubble of dim light appeared ahead. Lathwi could tell by its shape that it was an entrance to some inner chamber. A few steps later, she heard someone chanting, too. The voice, although hoarse, sounded familiar. But she did not want to think about that at this particular moment, and so extended her magical senses toward the chamber instead. To her vast surprise, there were no protective spells in place, not even the simplest wards. She wondered if this was a show of carelessness or arrogance, and then decided that it did not matter so long as it worked to her advantage.

"Please," someone in the chamber croaked. "No more. Mercy."

She slipped into the chamber like a wayward ghost, then hid herself in shadows so she could safely catch her bearings. She knew immediately that this place had been made by some long-gone underground river rather than dragons. The ceiling was high and the walls, smooth. A long, jagged crack ran alongside the far wall. A stone altar stood on the edge of that chasm. A well-muscled bald man was strapped to its surface. His intestines hung from him in loops now. Some of his other organs gleamed darkly by a ritual fire's light. Amazingly enough, though, Todd-stool was still alive.

"Mercy," he said, in little more than a whisper. At that moment, by some trick of the light, it seemed as thought he were looking right at Lathwi. But she made no move to save his life. As far as she was concerned, he had been dead since they met. Instead, she watched as a still-chanting, blood-soaked Seth raised a sacrificial knife over his head and plunged it directly into Todd-stool's chest.

The sound of his magic crescendoed: a sickening spike. The trickle of ghosts that had been rising out of the crevasse then became a despairing flash-flood. For one stunned moment, all Lathwi could do was stare at Seth's back and try to reconcile what she thought she knew with what she was seeing now. She would never have guessed that he was capable of such a prodigious act of magic. Indeed, although Veeder had named him as such, she had half-convinced herself that Seth was more of a mountebank than a mage. His aura had supported that theory. So had his fictional wards. But she saw how it was now. She finally understood. A necromage had no real power of his own. He had to get it from other people by stealing their life-forces.

Despicable!

She usually admired creatures who were bold enough to take what they wanted when they wanted it. But stealing life itself was—

Seth loosed a strangled cry, then cut Todd-stool's bonds and rolled him into the abyss. As the body plunged from sight, Lathwi's amulet began to pulse with heightened urgency. Before she could react in any way, the wards that she had not sensed earlier snapped into place, trapping her within the stronghold.

—wrong.

A voice rose up from the chasm's depths. It was soft but fell, the creeping stuff of nightmares. The sound of it stood Lathwi's hair on end. *"I am weak,"* it whispered. *"So weak. Blood alone no longer suffices. Before I can storm The Dreamer's Keep again, I must have the rest of My talismans."*

Seth made some reply, but Lathwi did not hear it. A single thought was spinning through her head at break-neck speed: it could not be! Could not.

"Make haste," the voice said. *"Dragon larvae grow like vermin. If you don't kill them before their soft spots disappear, you'll have to find another way into their bellies."*

A memory unfolded in Lathwi's mind. In it, a tangle of newborn dragons had just gobbled down Galza's tokens like a course of tender sweetbreads. "Nothing can survive a dragon's digestive tract, not bones or gold or Oma-stones," Taziem had assured her. But what if Taziem had been wrong?

"Did you see her this time?" Seth asked. "Did you find Ylana?"

Lathwi stole toward the blood-spattered altar, hoping to disprove her suspicions. Her amulet pulsed twice with each step, but she was not worried about Seth spotting her. He was too involved in his ill-conceived ritual to notice anything else.

"Yes," the voice whispered.

Seth's voice caught in his throat. For a long moment, he could not speak at all. In that moment, Lathwi got close enough to see the altar's adornments: two tiny golden fists, their thumbs opposed; and two obsidian spurs. The very same tokens that her younger set of tanglemates had gulped down.

The Dragonbane was still alive.

"So where is she?" Seth demanded.

Now everything made a terrible sort of sense—even the scars on Veeder's chest. They marked him for a dupe, not some Southern legend's heir. The Dragonbane and Seth were using the general and his self-deluding ambitions to recover Her tokens of power.

"I could not get to her fast enough," the voice confessed. *"She eluded Me."*

The last of Lathwi's shock burned off like wisps of morning fog, leaving her mind clear. Any doubts that she might have had about killing Seth were gone now. He was in league with the enemy. *The Dragonbane.* Therefore, he would die. No matter that she might have called him friend in another time and place.

"Then leave me!" Seth roared, a sound of disappointment and rage. "Go back to your bed of corpses. Imagine spending eternity there. For the next time you fail me, I'll feed your tokens to a volcano and be done with you for good."

The sound of his magic spiked again. Then, like a fever, it broke all at once. His wards dissolved. He collapsed to his knees. Moments later, he started to vomit into the abyss. Between spasms, he sobbed aloud as he had after their encounter with Bij. This breakdown came as no surprise to Lathwi. Ritual magic consumed enormous amounts of energy, oftentimes more than a human body could stand to lose. A ritual involving blood and Galza would probably leave him incapacitated for *days*.

Not that he had that long to live.

She prowled toward him—the only shadow with a sword. He was a dragonslayer, Galza's stooge. He had to die. Her one regret was that he would not be able to appreciate the irony attached to his death. For she was going to invoke Shadow with his blood. And when She finally showed Herself, Lathwi was going to kill Her for the third and last time. The thought gave her a savage thrill.

Seth was still spewing bile into the chasm when she reached his side. If he knew she was there, he did not show it. The only name he called was Ylana's—over and over again. It was then that she realized that he was at least half-mad, driven there by loss and guilt and years of dabbling in black magic. But that did not excuse him from his fate. He had allied himself with The Dragonbane. The reward for that was death. She raised her sword like an executioner. But before she had a chance to strike, a Voice sounded in her head.

"Lathwi! I am Masque. Where are you?"

She responded instantly, projecting a self-image and a vague impression of her location into the ether. *"I am here, little one,"* she said. *"What ails you?"*

Moments later, Masque Called again. This time, the thought was more emphatic. *"Lathwi! Where are you?"*

"Here!" she replied, but to no avail. Something about this chamber was blocking her response. She scowled—an urgent, disturbed grimace. If Masque did not hear from her soon, it would think she was dead.

And the youngling was in Need. Otherwise, it would not have Called.

Her gaze darted from the back of Seth's neck to the passageway and back again. Desires clashed like swords within her. She knew what Pawl would do if he were here in her stead: he would strike now, while he had the chance, because the north's security was in jeopardy. But she was a dragon, not human. The whole of mankind could not compete with a single tanglemate's Need.

But Galza could.

Galza the Corrupter. Galza the Scourge. Her death would delight all dragons—past, present, and future. Killing Her took precedence. She had the chance. She had to take it. But even as she made up her mind to do the deed, Masque Called again.

"Lathwi! If you are playing with me, stop at once! I do not like this game."

The youngling's desperation overruled her decision. A tanglemate Called! She was not capable of ignoring its need, not even for Galza. For good or for ill, Seth's neck would have to wait.

So she went racing out of the chamber. As soon as she hit the passageway, she pulsed a thought to its tanglemate. The youngling did not reply, and she could only hope that this was because it had not heard her. She broke into a headlong run. The cavern gave way to forestland. She abandoned the foot-path, then Called the youngling again.

An image of an undersized calico dragon immediately popped into her mind. It was sky-dancing for joy. The accompanying thought was both a celebration and a rebuke.

"Lathwi! Where were you? I Called and Called, but you did not answer! It was not a good game to play."

"It was no game, Little One," she said. *"But never mind about that for now. Tell me why you Called."*

"Taziem sent me to find you," Masque said, flashing an image of a magnificent black dragon. *"She said to look for you in the southlands, but the south is a very big place and I could not find you. Finally, I grew desperate and Called."*

"Why did Mother send you?" Lathwi asked, trying to hide her impatience.

"She has news."

"Let me have it."

A series of images came to her: a pack of Southern soldiers; Pinch's eviscerated corpse; a small, red stone covered in golden ichor. The accompanying thoughts bristled with outrage. *"I have found the dragonslayers,"* Taziem reported. *"They were killing younglings on Galza's behalf. She is still alive, and eager to have her talismans back. As soon as I have punished the fools here for the crimes that they committed in Her service—"* Another image intruded: an old woman's face. Katya. Her eyes were closed; the seams in her face, lifeless. *"—I will join you in the south, and we will rid the world of the rest of Her minions. Until then, ward Masque well. It harbors a talisman in its belly."*

As soon as the message came to an end, Masque withdrew its thoughts. Lathwi did not appreciate its politeness, though. She was too busy fuming. By all that was shiny and sharp! Both Galza and Her chief follower could have been well on their way to being dead already if Taziem had not distracted her with a handful of old news and a bewildered youngling. What had she been thinking? But even as she bemoaned her lost opportunity, logic came to the she-dragon's defense. Taziem had no way of knowing that her daughter already knew about the dragonslayers and the talismans. And if the news had come just a few hours earlier, she would have been extremely grateful for it. As for Masque, well—it was a tanglemate. If anyone had to ward it, it might as well be her.

"*Come to me,*" she told the youngling, re-casting the image of Veeder's valley. "*But take care as you draw near. I am surrounded by dragonslayers.*"

"*You keep strange company, Soft One,*" Masque said, a thought fletched with awe and disapproval. "*But I am more concerned about dragonsires. I heard a great drake in the distance this afternoon. He sounded very angry. And very hungry.*"

"*He is both,*" Lathwi said. Then, because sires had no qualms about killing their own offspring, she added, "*So do your best to stay away from him.*"

"*I will,*" the youngling promised, and then severed the link.

In the ensuing silence, Lathwi considered her options. She could either go back to the cavern and try to pick up where she had left off, or she could return to Seth's tent and wait for another opportunity. She had no doubt that Seth would still be suffering from the debilitating aftereffects of ritual black magic. The question was: did she still have enough time to accomplish everything that needed to be done? From past experience, she knew that killing Galza was no quick or easy trick. If she was found out before she could finish her work, death might well be the least of her worries. Still, she hated to turn her back on something that was already there. A wise dragon did not count on fortune striking twice.

The sound of footsteps disrupted the debate. Moments later, a man's voice rang out in the night. "Nah, they're not here, either. He must've taken her to his hidey-hole."

"To show her his magic wand?" another man sniggered.

"Something like that." The speaker paused as if to marshal his thoughts, and then heaved a long-suffering sigh. "Come on, Davor, let's go and get 'em."

She could see the men now. Although they were following the trail, they were not paying much attention to it or anything else. "What's the rush, Kel?" the taller of them asked. "I hate going into that place. It's a fuckin' chamber of horrors, is what it is."

I know," Kel said. "But General Veeder told us to find that northern whore's son and his bitch, and that's exactly what we're going to do. Elsewise, we'll wind up just like Todd."

Jaxe shook his head and shuddered. "That poor bastard." In a lower voice, he added, "Think we'll see him there?"

"I'm not going to look."

They strode past Lathwi's hiding place and on toward the cave. She waited until they were out of sight, then headed the other way. A few minutes ago, she had regarded Masque's Call as one of fortune's meaner tricks. Now, however, it seemed like an act of pure providence. If those guards had happened into Seth's stronghold when her powers, both mental and physical, were focused on The Dragonbane, she probably would not have been able to save the situation—or herself. As it was, all she had to do was bide her time and wait for another opportunity. Dragons were good at that.

Seth's tent rose out of the darkness. Lathwi did not want to go back into it, for it was hot and stuffy and cramped, but she had no choice. If she was not there when Seth returned, he would lose faith in her—and that would complicate matters. No doubt she was already under suspicion for not being there when the soldiers came calling. With that in mind, she relieved herself. Then she returned to her corner in the tent.

Sometime later, the flap snapped back. The silhouette in the opening belonged to Seth. Although it was dark, she could see what a toll his necro-ritual had exacted on him. His eyes were red-rimmed and swollen. His cheeks were slack. He stood hunched over himself, as if he were carrying all of his weight in the pit of his stomach.

"Where were you?" he croaked, in a ravaged voice.

"Why do you ask?" she asked.

"There are two men waiting outside," he said. "They said you weren't here when they came looking a little while ago."

"They simply did not look in the right places," she said. In response to the doubts that slumped across his face, she added, "One man has an old scar where his left eyebrow should be. The other is missing his front teeth."

His reservations hardened into a scowl. "I told you to stay in the tent. You could have cost me my head."

An image spun out of Lathwi's memory: her standing over his spewing body with her sword in hand. She dismissed her regrets with a shrug, and then offered him a dodge disguised as truth. "I have a bladder. From time to time, I need to empty it."

He grumbled—a resentful, only half-mollified sound. "You had best be telling the truth, woman. I'm in no mood for games tonight."

"Read my mind if you do not believe me."

He cast her a bilious look, and then rejected the proposal with a shake of his head. "Perhaps later. Right now, the general wants to see us."

"At this hour?"

"At this hour."

"Why?"

"I don't know, damn you," he snarled. "Just shut up and get going."

Given the paucity of her choices, Lathwi opted to do as she was told. She got up, then strode out of the tent. The two guards whom she had seen earlier were waiting there, but she did not say a word to them. Indeed, she did not say anything to anybody until she and Seth were admitted to Veeder's pavilion. When she saw the man bound to the center tent-pole, a name spurted past her lips before she could stop it.

"Pawl!"

Chapter 15

*H*is head was bowed, his braid in disarray. Judging by the grass and dirt stains on his pants, and the streaks of dried blood on his jerkin, Lathwi reckoned that he had put up a rather spirited fight before being subdued. As she gaped at him, questions crowded into her mouth. But she would not give them voice, not while Seth stood right here beside her and Veeder waited ahead. The general was already smirking at her like a cat who has just swallowed a tasty canary.

"You know this man?" he asked, in a tone that was both incredulous and pleased.

"I do," she said, too stunned to try and dissemble. "He is Pawl of Compara. He taught me the ways of a sword."

Seth whistled through his teeth. Veeder looked from her to Pawl and back again. "And why is he here?"

"You had best ask him," she said, although it was the *how* of it rather than the *why* that was gnawing at her. The compulsion that she had set upon Gordyn had been a strong one. "I entered the southlands alone."

"I *have* asked him," Veeder said. "Several times already." He rubbed his meaty left fist with his right hand, then added, "So far, he's declined to answer me." He shoved that fist into Pawl's gut—a seemingly effortless punch that made Pawl cough up air and a thin spool of blood. "But the both of you should know that I'm just warming up."

Lathwi was not concerned for herself. Nor did she feel sorry for Pawl. She had done everything in her power to keep him away from this place, and here he was anyway. She was so aggravated at the moment, she wanted to hit him a time or two herself. Were all men fools? And sons of fools?

He should be in Compara now!

"So," Veeder said, "what will you, swordmaster? I can beat you to near-death in front of your old student. Or—I can beat her in your stead. Or—we can skip all the fun and games, and you can just tell me what you're doing here."

Pawl raised his head to glare at the warlord. The right side of his face was a mass of lurid bruises. That eye was swollen shut. "We were lovers some time ago," he said, in a voice thick with bitterness and blood. "I wanted us to be married, but she wouldn't hear of it. When I pressed her to reconsider, she stole a horse and ran away. I never expected to see her again. Then she turned up in New Uxla last week. As soon as I set my eyes on her, I knew I had to try and make her mine again." At that, he turned his scowl on Lathwi and added, "But I had no idea that she'd developed a taste for the sort of men who like to carve up women's faces."

Veeder mocked Pawl with a laugh. "Imagine! A warrior chasing after a woman. It could only happen in the decadent north." Then, like a great cat that has just sighted its prey, he went suddenly straight-faced and still. "Now answer me this, Pawl of Compara: what was Wynn Rame's swordmaster doing in New Uxla in the first place?"

"I was visiting Gordyn the Horsetrader," Pawl replied, and then spit out a bloody nub that Lathwi belatedly recognized as a molar. "He's a former shieldmate of mine. He wants me to go into business with him."

"I see," the general said. "And during the course of this visit, did you happen to relieve the garrison commander of his head? I only ask because I received a description of the assassin two days ago, and you fit it rather closely."

Despite his bindings, Pawl managed a small shrug. "What is one northerner more or less to you?"

"Plenty," Veeder said, "if the northerner in question belongs to me. And Trevor Stone was mine." He rammed his fist into Pawl's midsection again. "It took me months, and a mound of gold, to buy that bastard. Then you came along and lopped his damned head off." He struck Pawl again, harder this time. "Were you ordered to assassinate me, too?"

"I am *not* an assassin," Pawl said, a denial flecked with bloody drool.

"No? Then you must be a spy. And here in the southlands, the penalty for spying is harsher than the penalty for murder." The warlord half-turned to face Lathwi. "You—*mercenary*," he said. "Here's your chance to prove yourself."

"What would you have me do?" she asked.

"Execute the spy," he replied.

Without a moment's hesitation, she reached for her sword. But the blade was not in its scabbard. One of Veeder's personal guards had taken it and her knives away at the door to the pavilion.

"I will get my sword," she said, and turned toward the flap only to be called back by the general.

"Wait," he said. "I've got a better idea."

"Do tell, general," Seth said. His face was a pasty shade of white, all but the dark half-moons under his eyes. If he had not discreetly positioned himself against a tent-pole, he would have fallen down a long time ago.

"The troops are restless," Veeder said. "A little entertainment would boost their morale. So come the morrow, we'll turn both of these northerners loose on the practice field and let them fight—to the death.

If the woman wins, I'll put her on the pay-roll. If the spy wins, I'll grant him safe-passage to the border."

"Is that—prudent?" his mage asked, scowling as he looked Pawl up and down. "He is, after all, a swordmaster. And who knows how much he's seen since he left New Uxla."

"Do you doubt your champion's abilities?" Veeder asked, arching his tone as well as his eyebrows.

"No."

"Then prudence shouldn't be an issue, should it?"

"I was a fool to even suggest it," Seth said.

If Veeder heard the hint of sarcasm in that concession, he showed no sign of it. He clapped his hands together as if to applaud his victory and said, "That settles it then. We'll hold the battle directly after morning mess. Until then, our friend Pawl The Spy will stay here with me—just in case I happen to think of more questions to ask him. But you and your champion may go back to whatever it was that you were doing when I sent for you."

"As you will, general," Seth said, and then shambled out of the pavilion. Lathwi followed in his wake. On their way back to his campsite, he half-turned to her and said, "If you lose to that man, Veeder will make me suffer for acting as your advocate. And if I suffer, you will, too. That, I promise you."

She dismissed the threat with a shrug. "If I lose, I will be dead. What could be worse than that?"

"If you lose," he warned, "you'll find out."

∞ ∞

Eventually, Veeder returned to his bedroll. Moments later, he began to snore like a man with a conscience as pure as snow. Pawl listened to the rogue's night noises with a mixture of fury and frustration. His ribs ached. His mouth tasted of blood. And his arms and hands had long since gone numb. Even so, he tried to free himself from his bonds. If he was still here when the new day dawned, he would have to cross swords with Lathwi. And there could only be one outcome to such a duel—an outcome dictated by his own bungling.

If only he had known that she had infiltrated the camp!

But even as he scourged himself with that guilt-spangled lash, a tiny, indignant voice in the back of his head did its best to shield him. She was a lone woman from the northlands who bore the scars of a disgraced whore. Who would have guessed that she could just saunter into a camp full of Granger-thugs and make herself at home? The few scraps of news that he had gleaned from her trail had certainly suggested otherwise.

The first tidings had overtaken him in the hills beyond the border. He had been out hunting for a late-night supper when he saw a glow in the distance. Although Lathwi did not make fires of her own, she was not averse to sharing someone else's on a cool, summer night, so he decided to investigate. The glow led him to a camp. Four haggard, hard-bitten Southerners were huddled around a meager cook-fire. They were drinking gish, and talking about a black-scaled she-demon.

"No one's to say anything about this to anyone when we get back, you hear?" one of them growled. "Otherwise, they'll say we're cursed and cut our throats in our sleep."

A second man glanced over his shoulder at the great, sandy plain that Pawl had yet to cross and then licked his lips. "You don't think she's really following us, do you?" he asked, in a deserter's nervous whisper. "She said she'd eat us."

"Oh, quit your twitching," a third grumbled. "We set that clean-shaven prick of a sorcerer on her, didn't we? He probably had her bound to his Will before she even knew we were gone."

The first one snorted—a bitter exhalation. "That maggot gets a slave till the end of time, while all we reap is saddle-sores. Random rot the both of them, I say."

It never occurred to Pawl that they might *not* be talking about Lathwi. He knew from hard experience that krim would have killed all four of them on sight. And who else in these naturally hellish parts was apt to be mistaken for a demon? But as glad as he was to finally have word of her, he did not appreciate the news. Assuming the worst—and he had found that it was usually wise to do so when Lathwi was involved—this *clean-shaven prick* was the rogue who had wrested Liselle's ghost from The Dreamer's Keep. A mage who could manage a feat like that would surely be powerful enough to turn Lathwi to his Will. The thought of her enslaved stoked the furnaces of his concern.

He had to find her. Help her. Save her.

So he resumed his hunt. It took him through the foothills, across the desert, and into the mountains beyond. There, he encountered his first foot-patrol: a pair of soldiers more intent on a good gossip than watching for intruders. Pawl sneered at their lack of discipline. Had they been his recruits, he would've given them a souvenir or two for their carelessness. As it was, he merely followed along and listened to what they had to say.

"You seen the sorcerer's new whore yet?" one asked.

His companion loosed a nasty chuckle. "Scary-looking bitch, ain't she? I don't get what that freak sees in her—aside from the fact that she's northern."

"They say she's a demon. They say she'll do *anything* for him."

"Not for long. Veeder don't like her."

"Neither do I. I hear she's the reason Todd wound up in the pen."

"Poor bastard."

Pawl shadowed the Southerners for a while longer, but they said nothing more of use and anxiety soon demanded an about-face. He was convinced now: the sorcerer was holding Lathwi captive. *They say she'll do anything for him.* But that wasn't Lathwi's nature. She always served her own best interests first. Therefore, she had to be enslaved or ensorcelled or probably both. And although he had no idea as to how he was going to counteract those conditions, he could not have stopped himself from trying even if he had wanted to.

And look where his efforts had landed him!

He slumped against the tent-pole, allowing it to support his weight. He was tired, battered, and heartsick: a shipwreck of a man. Not only had he failed to rescue the love of his life, he'd gotten himself caught, too—this, after successfully infiltrating this devil's butt-crack of a valley. For at least the hundredth time, he berated himself. He should've been more careful, in less of a rush. He should've been looking for pitfalls around such a large camp. But it was dark out, and his thoughts were all for Lathwi. The next thing he knew—*whoosh*! He was hanging from a tree in a cat-net like the rawest of recruits. He almost wished that the responding patrol had killed him then and there.

Almost.

He strained against his bonds again. It would be dawn soon. He did not want to start the day here.

෨෬

Lathwi stormed toward the practice field with the bellicose acuity of a crossbow bolt. She had gone to sleep in a savage mood, and a half-night of tossing and turning had done nothing to improve her frame of mind. *Stupid Pawl*, she thought. *He was not supposed to be here.* She wanted to whack him on the shins until he learned how to stay away for his own good. She wanted to thump him in the nose, just like she used to thump Shoq when he was being especially foolish.

She did not, however, want to kill him.

"Slow down, damn you!" Seth growled, as he struggled to keep up with her. Still exhausted from last night's ritual, the sorcerer was in an even blacker mood than she was. "You're still in my custody, you know."

She allowed him to think what he would. But she did not alter her pace.

Mountain fog had rolled into the valley overnight, a blanket thick enough to leave the morning gloomy and gray. Even so, the atmosphere was unquestionably festive. The smell of breakfast beer hung in the air. Laughter and good-humored shouting rang out in the near distance.

"Pin him!"

"Stick him!"

"A copper scrittle says Raf holds!"

"What goes on?" she asked, wondering if the commotion had anything to do with Pawl.

Seth twitched her a half-hearted shrug. "Sounds like wrestling. When there's no one else to fight, these savages cheerfully twist each other into knots."

Shadows emerged from the foggy foreground, and then thickened into clusters of soldiers. They had tankards in their hands and knives in their belts. Their excited clamor sheered off into silence as Lathwi and the mage came within hearing range, then resumed as a hostile rumbling in their wake. Lathwi did not notice. Her attention was centered on Pawl. He was standing in the middle of the practice field like a prize bull on display. His hands were tied, his ankles hobbled. He had a rope around his neck, and a trio of armed guards at his back. She rumbled with displeasure. Seth arched an eyebrow at the sound.

"It's a little too late for second thoughts," he said.

"I have not changed my mind," she replied.

"Good," he said, and then parodied one of his own sly smiles. "Because it's time to start this spectacle."

At that, he gestured at Pawl's guards. They hastened to undo his restraints. As they did so, Veeder's troops formed a deceptively loose circle around the two would-be contestants. Seth strode to its center, then raised his scrawny arms for attention.

"As you know," he said, "this is to be a fight to the death. Anyone who interferes without permission will be flogged. Anyone who tries to plunder the deceased afterward will be shaved." In a more jovial tone, he went on to say. "General Veeder wagers a gold scrittle on the spy. I'll take three to one odds on the woman. Is anyone game?"

A roar shattered the grudging silence that had settled over the field—the voice of a crowd eager to bet. A moment later, a self-appointed bookie started calling for markers and names. Seth legitimized him with a nod.

As meager as it was, Lathwi was grateful for the delay—anything to postpone the moment when she and Pawl faced off. Because if the hard truth be told, she did not know what she was going to do yet. She was not so naive to believe that Veeder would actually let the swordmaster live if he killed her. Nor did she think that her own life would be that much longer for killing him. Under almost any other circumstances, she would have used sorcery to resolve the problem. A Word here, a spell there, and her worries would all be behind her. But there was a quest involved here, a quest whose resolution meant more to the world than any one man's life. If she used magic today, she would lose the advantage of surprise over Seth and Galza. And if, in her absence, they went into hiding, she could spend the rest of her life trying to find them.

As that thought crossed her mind, Seth clapped her on the back. "Time to start earning your keep," he said, with a gaiety that was not reflected in his eyes. He gave her a tiny shove toward Pawl. At the same time, in a much lower voice, he said, "Do *not* fail me."

Lathwi studied her erstwhile companion for a moment, taking in details. His face was swollen and bruised around the eyes and mouth. His wrists were rubbed raw around the bones. She wanted to touch him. She wanted to taste him. Instead, she drew her sword.

"My marker's on you, Northerner," one of Pawl's guards said. He sliced through Pawl's hobble, then handed him a sword and shoved him in Lathwi's direction. "Eternal shame on your father's house if you lose to that wizard's whore."

Lathwi began to circle Pawl like a wary fire-dancer, unwilling to start the duel. In almost no time at all, the crowd's excited rumblings took on an ugly, menacing note. "*Do* something!" Seth mouthed at her. But it was Pawl who made the first move—a jab to the heart. She parried the stroke, then went on the offensive just as he had taught her. Their swords sparked and clanged. She suppressed a grin. Even now, surrounded by an army of enemies, she loved sparring with this man.

"Your form's not bad," he told her, as they squared off again.

In reply, she feinted right and then stabbed at his thigh. It was a beginner's move, predictable in every way, and yet she somehow managed to strike him. As blood welled up in the gash, those few spectators who had dared to bet on a woman cheered. She bit back a wave of disbelief. Good as she was, she should not have been able to score on a swordmaster so effortlessly. Fearing that Veeder had hurt him in places that she had not thought to look, she took a step back and gave him a quick once-over. Only then did she realize how narrow his stance was. And how *sloppy* his guard was. A child with a butter knife could get past such defective defenses.

Comprehension broke over her like heavy surf on a beach. Pawl was forfeiting this match—and his life—to her. For her. So she could complete her quest.

Crazy human. He was always giving her things that she did not want. And things that she could not refuse.

೮೦ ೦೪

Pawl let his grip on the sword go soft. A moment later, Lathwi's sword bit into his thigh. Pain ignited within him, side by side with a bittersweet pride. She had learned her lessons well. Her strokes were powerful and clean. Given the right openings, she'd make fast work of him.

If only he were in more of a hurry to die!

He hated the thought of giving up his life to an overgrown cut-worm like Veeder. . He wanted to hope! Fight! Win! But the plain fact of the matter was, they were in this predicament because of him. And eager or not, he knew what he had to do. He adjusted his stance, creating a subtle opening in his defense. None of the audience noticed it. But Lathwi did. Surprise flashed in her eyes. Her oft-scarred face darkened. Twice.

Then a reddish-black blur came roaring out of the foggy sky.

"Dragon!" someone shouted.

Veeder's troops broke for the trees like a herd of panicked deer. At the same moment, the reddish-black blur snatched Lathwi up in its arms and soared back into the fog. For one stunned moment, primal instinct held him frozen in his tracks. Then reason kicked in—*dragons liked Lathwi*—and it occurred to him that this might be his chance to escape. He began running for the woods: an awkward, lopsided lope that favored his wounded leg. Somewhere behind him, he could hear Veeder shouting.

"Come back here, you fools!" he raged. "It's not the red! It's *not* the red." Then, a few moments later, he changed his tune. "The spy! Grab him! If he gets away, I'll feed the lot of you to that dragon myself. Seth, damn your eyes. Where the hell are you?"

One Granger reined himself in, then another and more. Then, like cattle dogs on a runaway bull, they worked to cut Pawl off and hem him in. As soon as the swordmaster realized that he couldn't win the footrace, he limped to a stop. His thigh was burning and bleeding and threatening to give out. He intended to stand his ground while he could, and go out fighting.

೮೦ ೦೪

"Lathwi," Masque crooned, as it whisked her into the sky. *"It is very, very good to see you again. I was afraid that dragonslayers had taken you."*

"It was a near thing, little one," Lathwi said, and then flashed the youngling an urgent image of Pawl. *"Circle back for this man."*

"Why?" Masque asked, punctuating the thought with an impression of staggering weight.

"Because he is with me," she replied.

The youngling chirped—a sound that was, for some strange reason, accompanied by gypsy images. Then it dropped its shoulder and turned on a wingtip, taking them back into the fog. As they punched through the cloud-cover, they both roared for all they were worth. A goodly number of men scattered.

"Not as many as last time," Masque noted, a thought laced with disappointment. Then it zeroed in on Pawl. He was fending off three Southerners. Two had swords. The third wielded a whip. Lathwi heard it crack, once and then again. The third time, Pawl's blade tumbled from his hand, and the two swordsmen rushed in. Lathwi flung them back with a Word. An instant later, Masque plucked Pawl up from the ground.

"Where now?" it asked, even as it strained to regain altitude.

"I do not know yet," Lathwi replied. *"Just fly us away from here."*

The youngling flapped its way toward the tree-line. As it did so, Lathwi spotted Seth. He was standing alone in the open field. His hands were knotted in his hair. Their eyes met for the briefest of moments. He looked distraught, traumatized; betrayed.

"Give her back, you bastard!" he screamed. "Give her back."

A spear thunked into the span of Masque's chest, then bounced away without leaving a mark. Another went whizzing past Pawl's nose.

"Shit," was all he said.

"Fly higher," Lathwi urged her tanglemate, more concerned about its soft spots than her own. *"Climb above the fog so they cannot see you."*

"I cannot," Masque replied, panting the thought. *"I have not eaten or slept for two days. And you two are heavy.*

"Which way do you want me to go?"

They were flying over the valley's treetops now, if only just barely. Through the canopy, Lathwi caught glimpses of Veeder's troops. Some were on horseback. Many carried spears. All of them were hot on Masque's trail. She might have dismissed their headlong efforts if the mountain which housed Seth's stronghold had not been coming up fast. But her undersized tanglemate would not be able to clear that peak with them in its arms. Indeed, it was struggling to stay aloft already. They needed to find a place to set down soon. But which way to go? She rejected the western pass. That was too heavily guarded. And Bij The Mighty lived to the south. That left them with one choice.

"Head east," she said.

The youngling veered in that direction.

"Where are we going?" Pawl asked.

She swiveled her head around so she could look at him. He was dirty, disheveled, and bruised. His thigh was bloody, as was his nose. Yet despite his sorry condition, there was a ferocious gleam in his eyes. It took her a moment to recognize the look, but when she did, she laughed aloud.

Pawl of Compara liked to fly!

"You laugh at the oddest moments," he told her.

"We are heading east," she replied.

"What's there?"

"I do not know."

The eastern tip of the valley loomed into view: two mountains standing hip to hip. There had been a pass between them at one point in history. She could tell by the land's conformation. But over the course of the last century or two, a progression of landslides had turned that gap into a landlock.

"I smell water," Masque said. *"Lots of water."*

"Me, too," she said, and then wondered, *"Can you clear that bank?"*

"Maybe."

Masque aimed itself at the ridge's lowest point and redoubled its efforts. And what an effort that was. Its wingstrokes became labored and ragged. Its sides began to heave. But, by slow degrees, it gained altitude. The tree-line receded, then gave way to a steep upper slope of earthen rubble. A short time later, an astonishing slip of deep blue water came into view.

"I have never seen such a big lake," Lathwi said. "It is beautiful."

"Your eyes are exactly the same color," Pawl said—and then let out a surprised yelp as Masque let go of him. Lathwi made a grab for his outstretched hand only to find herself falling, too.

"If Taziem can do it, so can you," Masque thought, as it half-flew, half-caromed toward the lakeside. *"I have no more strength."*

By then, Lathwi had already landed with a breath-robbing "Woof!", and was tumbling down the dam's rubbled backside. She tried to check her slide by grabbing onto a bush in passing, but its shallow root system was no match for her weight in motion, and it went careening down the slope in her hand. By the time she finally rolled to a stop, she was scratched and bruised and vaguely nauseated. But how terribly fun! She would have to come back here some day and try that descent again. It was much more exciting than simple free-fall. She picked herself up, then went hunting for Pawl. He was farther down on the slope, sprawled in the rubble like a piece of debris. Fresh blood trickled from his mouth. His thigh wound was encrusted with dirt.

"Well," he rasped, as she helped him to a sitting position, "I don't think Veeder's men will be coming down that way."

"No," she agreed, "but I am sure they will find a ready alternative. We must be away from here by the time that happens."

He scrabbled to his feet, clutching his left side with his right hand. Although she knew that he could have broken ribs or worse, she said nothing because neither of them could do anything about the problem at the moment anyway. But as they half-shinnied and half-slid their way down the rest of the grade, she lent him a shoulder for support.

A small, rock-strewn beach waited for them at the bottom of the dam. It stretched perhaps a quarter-mile to the north, and less to the south. Beyond those points, all Lathwi could see was sheer cliffs and water.

And Masque.

Her tanglemate was floating belly-down in the lake. Its wings were half-open. Its head was submerged. Lathwi could not tell if it was breathing or not, and so broadcast a frantic thought.

"Little One! Are you well?"

Masque's calico head broke the surface with an elaborate splash. It had a large, tail-flapping fish in its jaws which it swallowed whole. *"Lathwi,"* it said, *"I am Masque. I am feeling much better. This lake is as warm as summer rain, and full of tasty fish! Shall I catch one for you?"*

"Only if you have already eaten your fill, little one," she replied. *"Otherwise, you must hurry up and feed yourself. You will not be able to stay here much longer."*

"Why not?"

"We are being chased by dragonslayers," she said. *"They will kill you if they catch you."*

The youngling smacked the water with its calico wings, creating a sound far larger than itself. *"Let them try! I will feast on their livers."*

"Another time perhaps," Lathwi said, wringing all traces of amusement from the thought. *"Today, there are simply too many to challenge. But I know of something else that you could do if you are strong enough to fly again."*

"So long as I do not have to carry anyone," it said, *"I could fly to the—"*

A furious clamor erupted overhead—Veeder's men piling up on the ridge. Some of them hurled curses at them. Others cast spears. Most of those fell short of their mark, but one came close enough to prompt Pawl into hiding. From the cover of a boulder, he said, "Lathwi, where to next?"

She did not reply. She had already gone back to communing with Masque. *"Find Taziem. Guide her back to yonder valley as quickly as you can. Tell her I have found a whole army of dragonslayers."*

Masque hissed at the image of Galza that sprung out of its memory, then began to paddle ashore. *"Mother will want to hear this message,"* it said. *"I will leave now."* As it came splashing onto the beach, it added, *"You will have to catch your own fish."*

Lathwi caught the youngling's pretty, calico head in her hands and drew it toward her so they could touch noses. As she did so, Pawl said, "Lathwi, we don't have a whole lot of time before we're overrun here. So if you've got a plan, I'd really like to hear it."

As a matter of fact, Lathwi did not have so much as an inkling as to how she and Pawl were going to proceed from here. But she did not want the youngling to know that, for then it would not want to leave. And she very much wanted it safely on its way. So instead of answering the swordmaster, she finished touching noses with Masque and then urged it on its way.

"If you are in Need," she said, *"you know my Name."*

The youngling echoed the sentiment, then flung itself into the air.

"Wait!" Pawl cried after it, and then turned to Lathwi. The look on his face was one of confusion and dismay. "Where's it going?"

"I sent it away," she said. "It was not strong enough to carry us to safety."

"I see," Pawl said, and then glanced back at the dam. Dozens of Veeder's men were climbing down the longer but less precipitous flanking slope now. Many more lined the ridge-top. "So, I guess you're going to Change into your dragon-self and fly us out of here. Right?"

She dismissed the idea with a shake of her head. "It would not be wise of me to attempt a transformation while I am this tired and distracted. I could forget myself. The quest would be lost."

"It's going to be lost anyway unless we get out of here in a hurry." He looked the dead-end beach up and down, as if he were hoping to find a means of escape washed up on the shore. "Can you swim?"

"No."

A spear whizzed by, close enough to flutter her hair with its tiny wind in passing. He grabbed her hand and started hauling her toward the beach. "I think it's time for you to learn," he said. "Unless, of course, you can walk on water."

"The water is not cold enough for that," she replied, and then hissed as inspiration snuck in through the back door. Smart Pawl. Clever Pawl. He was a rare dragon's jewel among men. She tightened her grip and broke into a lope.

"What is it?" he asked, trying to glance over his shoulder even as they splashed into the lake. A volley of arrows chased after them, skimming the surface like emaciated flying fish.

"Just come with me," she said. "Do not let go of my hand, no matter what."

They went from ankle-high water to thigh-deep. Then, as the water level rose over Pawl's hips, he began to grind his thoughts like teeth. Lathwi pressed on without a word. Waist-high, water began pouring into her scales through the seams. Chest-deep, Pawl half-turned to gauge their lead on Veeder's men only to learn that they did not have one anymore. A handful of warriors had already reached the base of the dam, and were now heading for the beach.

"If you've got a particular trick in mind," he said, feeling for a sword that he had lost earlier, "*now* would be a good time to play it."

Lathwi agreed. In up to her neck now, she invoked the secret Name of Water.

The lake's surface grew suddenly choppy. Happy little waves lapped at her face. Their breath smelled of algae and fish.

"Lathwi—" Pawl said, infusing her name with urgency. But she silenced him with a hiss.

A large comber was rolling toward them now. As it drew near, the likeness of a drowned man's face appeared in its foamy underside. At the same time, an alien thought popped into her head. It was curious, but clear and calm: *Why do you Call, when I am already all around you?*

"Because this man and I are being chased by humans who are to us as Fire is to you," she replied. *"I Called in the hope that you might help us escape their malice."*

Water sputtered at the mention of Fire. An instant later, the wave rolled over their heads and toward those Southerners who were charging through the lake. Those unlucky men screamed as the comber crashed down on them and were not seen again. The foamy avatar that had remained in Lathwi's presence let out a watery chuckle.

"I think the rest of those Fire-people will stay on dry land and wait for you to wash ashore," it said. *"I will give you what you need if you wish to disappoint them."*

"I wish that very much," Lathwi said.

The avatar blessed her with its dead-man's smile, and then abruptly disintegrated. An instant later, something came bobbing to the surface. At first, Lathwi thought it was a giant jellyfish, for it had that domed, translucent look about it, but then it expanded to the size of a bathing tub. She poked a finger into its side. It dimpled like a full bladder, then engulfed her wrist without breaking. She waggled her fingers. The bubble redoubled its size. Confident now of its nature, she stepped into it and then pulled Pawl in after her.

"What the hell?" he sputtered, as the bubble closed around him.

"Water has consented to share its air with us," she said. "Now we can make our way to safety at our leisure."

"If you say so," Pawl said, looking supremely unsure about the whole situation.

She pulled him forward: one step, then another. He sucked a deep breath into his lungs as water closed over their heads only to express it as a shout as the lake bottom fell away beneath them. As they plunged into the dark blue depths, unreasoning fear gripped him. He had to get back to the surface. *Had to.* He flailed at the bubble, trying to claw his way through it. His heart threatened to burst through his ribcage. *They were going to drown!*

Then Lathwi's voice called him back to reason. "Just relax and breath," she said. "No harm will come to us. I promise."

He ceased his flailing. A moment later, his breathing became less ragged. And while he remained a bit wild-eyed, at least he was focusing again. Lathwi was glad that he had calmed down, and not just because all of his thrashing about had been annoying. She *liked* the sensation of falling through water. It was a lot like flying, only not as fast. She was sure that Pawl would like it, too, once he got used to the idea.

Her ears popped. Her mouth went dry. Then the lake bottom came into view. It was flat and sandy, an underwater meadow of dark green corkscrew grasses and pink anemones. An instant after they landed, Pawl's stranglehold on her hand eased up.

"I had no idea," he said, as he looked around. "It's beautiful down here."

"So it is," Lathwi said, and then half-turned to her right as something in the murky distance caught her eye. Pawl turned that way, too. As they watched, seven silver-sided scarimund came swimming into view. They were large, powerful fish—veritable kings of the lake. But an instant after they started toward the bubble, they shifted course in unison and went shooting out of sight.

"Guess we scared them aw—" Pawl began, only to cut himself off as he caught a glimpse of an enormous, streamlined *something* weaving its way in and out of the murk. His grin capsized. His voice dropped to a whisper. "Did you see that?"

"I did," Lathwi said.

"What was it?"

"I do not know," she replied. But there it was again—a fleeting shadow in the distance. This time, it was closer. Much closer. "But I believe it is heading our way."

Chapter 16

*L*uke reached the outskirts of Timberton just as the sun was starting to set on its shabby facade. He was dressed in a scorched vest and bloodstained trousers: the same clothes that he'd been wearing the night of the attack. He'd added another gold loop to his left ear since then—Santana's gift to him for defending the Dowager Queen. But while he had accepted the token to avoid insulting his uncle, he felt like a consummate fraud for wearing it. Because defending was not the same thing as *saving*.

Every time he closed his eyes, images assailed him: The Great One stopping an axe-blow in mid-swing; a blur of shadows, trees, and smoke; then streamers of bright orange flame leaping from the windows of Katya's wagon. The Little Mother was huddled against the back of a tree. Mim was standing in front of her, trying to ward off a swordsman with a willow switch. Blood was streaming from a pair of deep cuts on her forehead.

"Stay back," she cried, cracking the switch like a whip at her attacker's face. "Stay back or you'll be sorry."

Luke was already running to his cousin's aid when the Southerner laughed and slashed at Mim. Her cheek split open like a fruit. As she screamed, he went to cut her throat. That had been when Luke buried his knife into space between the bastard's shoulderblades—all the way up to the hilt. The would-be child-killer arched his back, dropped his sword, and then pitched forward onto Mim. His body muffled her howls.

"Quiet now, Mimsy," Luke said. "You're safe under ther—"

Even as the words left his lips, a pair of outsiders converged on them. One was Southern; the other, a fat, backwoods fool armed with an axe. "Look here," that one said, pointing at Katya, "that's their witch! Stick her! I'll take care of the boy."

But the townsman was no match for a fleet-footed gypsy. Luke danced past his swinging axe and stuck a knife into his side in passing. Then he threw himself on the Southerner's back and bit down on an unwashed ear with all of his might. The warrior bellowed his rage and pain, then seized Luke by the back of the neck and slung him off like a dirty nightshirt. Luke hit the ground tumbling—and spitting out bits of ear. A moment later, he was on the Southerner's back again.

"Stay away from her!" he snarled. "Stay away, or I'll feed you to a dragon."

"Stick around, boy," the man growled in reply. "You're next."

Then, despite Luke's frantic efforts to immobilize his sword-arm, the Southerner stabbed Katya in the belly. The blade made a horrible sound going in. Katya whimpered just a little as he pulled it out. Blood appeared on her lips a moment later, shiny and dark and wrong.

Luke screamed something then, he did not remember what. The next thing he knew, he was driving a furious elbow into the murderer's temple. The man staggered backward from the blow. Luke hit him again, in the same place, with the same force. He felt something crack—his elbow perhaps or perhaps the man's skull. It did not matter. He was so mad, he could not stop himself from lashing out, over and over and over again. The murderer fell down. Luke began to kick him. Indeed, he'd probably *still* been kicking that battered corpse if Santana had not pulled him away from it.

"Don't blame yourself," the gypsy leader urged him later. "You did your best. And the bitter truth is, our best isn't always good enough."

But Luke *did* blame himself—not only for the Little Mother's death, but for leading the outsiders to the caravan's safe haven as well. He should have been more careful; more cunning; more wood-wise. And once there, he should have mounted a closer watch. But he had been so caught up in the Great One's doings! Oh, how he had ached to be one of the men who had gone down to Murdered Dragon Meadow to avenge the young dragon slayings. And oh, how he had resented being left in camp to watch over the women and babies. After all, *he* was the lucky one. *He* was the one who had introduced the Great One to The Wandering Tribe in the first place. His place was with her.

All this and more he thought—this instead of watching the back door for treachery. And so the outsiders poured into the haven, unexpected and unchallenged. And so The Little Mother died.

Now all he had left was the hope of revenge.

That was why he had come.

He shifted in his saddle so as to sit a little taller, then urged his horse toward the center of town. People stepped out of their houses and shops as he rode down the street. He could tell by their expressions that they were expecting to see someone else.

"Look, Jo," one woman shouted to another. "It's one of those filthy gypsies." She shook her fist at Luke. "What have you vermin done with our husbands?"

Luke kept on riding. Like rats after a fabled piper, the people of Timberton followed in his dust. He could feel their ill-will boring into the back of his skull, and wondered if they could feel his in return, radiating outward like a steamy, airborne poison. *What had they done, indeed.*

He reined his horse to a stop in front of the general store. A crowd had gathered there: a few surly-looking men, but mostly women, snot-nosed children, and graybeards. He did not see any Southerners. *But he kicked the one in his head again and again and again.*

"What do you want?" the woman named Jo shouted. "You know we don't deal with your kind."

"He's come to put another curse on us," someone else yelled.

"You're right," Luke said, in a deceptively mild tone. "I have."

ಬಿ ಚ

Taziem circled over the forest, trying to manage her anger. Her injured hind leg throbbed to the beat of her wings. Her thoughts pulsed with a craving for violence. She was Taziem, The Learned One, a dragon of great wit and reason. She usually preferred to be in control. But not today. Today, she wanted to forget herself and go wild. Today, she wanted to be an unthinking beast.

Ironically, that was the human side of her talking.

She had, she feared, stayed human too long. Her thoughts were jumbled. Her logic was conflicted. Everything seemed to have two sides now, even her anger. Everything was more intense. Taziem the woman liked life like that. Taziem the dragon did not.

Below her was the village of Timberton. She meant to raze it tonight—*burn it to the ground like a gypsy wagon.* Its destruction would serve as a lesson and a warning for the rest of mankind: dragonkind would no longer tolerate those who aided Galza's cause. It was a righteous action, long overdue, and yet there was that craving, too: *dark as the blood on Katya's lips.* The old one's death was not supposed to matter. But it did.

She circled back around, then dipped lower in the sky. She could see Luke now. He was riding toward the town's mid-section, drawing the residents out of their holes and into the street as he went. Even from this height, she could feel their malice curling toward him like murderous tentacles. Or maybe that was her, too, broadcasting a desire to do more than just punish these fools for their misdeeds. The human in her wanted to make them *suffer.*

The gypsy reined to a stop, signaling his readiness to begin. She waited for a seemingly endless moment, then angled herself toward the town.

ಬಿ ಚ

"Ha!" a graybeard cried. "So you admit it. Your witch put a curse on our children."

Luke flushed, a fiery display of fury and grief. But he kept his tone level, as a messenger should. "She did no such thing," he replied. "Indeed, she would've helped you if you had given her a chance. And so your menfolk and their Southern friends *butchered her in her bed.*" He paused to let the accusation sink in, then added, "They died for that."

A collective gasp rose up from the crowd, then flattened into an angry buzz. But before anyone could put that buzz to words, Luke went on. "And now it's your turn to pay."

"Pay for what?" the woman known as Jo asked. "We done nothing wrong."

"Yeah," her neighbor added. "If anyone's gonna pay for something around here, boy, it's gonna be you, you cheeky shit." She stooped to pick up a stone, then added, "Now tell us what you did with our men."

"As I said, they are dead," Luke told her. "They allied themselves with the Southerners, who serve Galza Dragonbane—She who is known to you as The Dreamer's daughter, Shadow. From here on, all those who traffic with Her, directly or not, will be punished."

The graybeard scoffed. "Shadow, Shmadow. Let's stone the little turd."

The crowd responded with a ragged cheer. But before anyone had a chance to throw the first rock, an enormous shadow blotted out the sunset's pink-and-gray light. A moment later, the shadow disgorged an ear-shattering roar. The townspeople looked up as if they could not believe what they had just heard, then dropped their stones and ran for the safety of their cracks and holes like roaches.

"Remember," Luke called after them. "All those who side with The Dreamer's Daughter and Her allies side against dragonkind. And dragons will tolerate that no more."

His horse squealed and reared as if to second the decree, but it was only expressing its fear. For The Great One had just landed in the middle of the road. Her final wingstrokes stirred up a dust-devil that went gusting through the town. Luke stared at her for a long moment, trying to commit her magnificence to memory. For after tonight, he never wanted to see her again. She made him forget who he was, and what was supposed to matter most. When that happened, the people whom he loved died.

But oh, how it grieved him to give her up. She was like a drug that would always be in his blood. He touched his good luck piece for strength, then waved goodbye as she turned her golden eyes his way.

"I have delivered your message, Great One," he said. "Now, with your leave, I will rejoin my family."

Taziem dismissed the manling with a rumble. Now that he had served his purpose, she had further more use for him. Now that he had served his purpose, Timberton was going to die. She sucked in a righteous breath, then released it again as a stream of Fire.

The general store ignited with a whoosh. Moments later, a woman within screamed for help. Taziem ignored the plea. Gypsies had screamed, younglings had bled, and old Katya had died because of these people. There would be no mercy tonight. She loosed another stream of fire, then another and more. The town began to burn in earnest. It had never looked better in her eyes.

A small phalanx of wild-eyed men came shuffling toward her, brandishing swords and spears. In another time and place, these nervy fools might have amused her. But tonight, they just fanned her fury. She lashed out at the wedge's leader with her tail. The bones in his legs snapped on impact. He collapsed into a screaming heap. A portion of his followers rushed to his defense while the others tried to whisk him away. Taziem mocked their efforts with a roar, then set fire to another building. As she did so, someone jabbed something sharp into her left nostril. She swatted at the annoyance like Katya might have swatted at a bee. The man she hit fell down, then started crawling for safety. Human-cruel, she waited until he was halfway across the street before she stepped on him. His back broke like dry kindling beneath her weight. She roared again—a gust of primal hate.

Most of Timberton was on fire now. People were swarming out of the doomed buildings like panicked rats. A fat, milk-eyed woman bolted for the safety of the nearby woods, clutching a bundle to her sagging breasts. The she-dragon clawed her in passing. Her quarry crumpled with a shriek. The bundle tumbled to the ground and began to cry. The noise offended Taziem's ears. She bore down on the child, intent on shutting it up. But even as she opened her jaws to bite it in two, a small, wiry human with flowing, black hair appeared from out of nowhere and scooped the child into his arms.

"No, Great One," he said. "Not the children. These we will take and raise as our own. In that way, Timberton will replace what it took from The Wandering Tribe."

Taziem stared at the man for a moment. He was either the bravest person on the face of the planet, or the dumbest—she could not decide which distinction fit him best. Did he not know how unwise it was to thwart a dragon? Did he not understand his danger? Part of her wanted to savage both him and the baby. Part of her wanted to punish him along with the rest of the vermin in this town. But something was holding her back—something that she could sense but not quite name.

"Katya would have wanted it this way, don't you think?" the man asked then, and flashed her a fleeting smile laced with gold.

His mention of Katya-Queen blew the fog from her thoughts like an offshore breeze. All at once, she knew who and where and what she was again. She was Taziem The Learned One—an avenging dragon. The man in front of her was the gypsy, Santana. She was very glad that she had resisted the urge to kill him. But she still didn't know whether he was brave or dumb.

Not that that mattered at the moment.

She glanced at her surroundings as if seeing them for the first time. The townspeople were all gone now, scattered like mustard seeds in a wind, and Timberton was one big blaze. The sight appeased her craving for violence, but did not extinguish it. A very vocal part of her wanted to continue rampaging. That was wrong, un-dragonlike. She needed to Change back to her human form—not because she was any less savage as a woman, but because she lacked the capacity to do as much harm.

So she focused her Will, and then set it on the path to transformation. Her vision blurred. Her body began to shrink in all directions. As she Changed, the baby in Santana's arms clapped its hands and laughed.

Chapter 17

*T*he forests of Tryssa province were daunting by night—a dark, looming presence full of ghosts. Every now and again, one would catch Jamus' eye as it wove its way through the trees. They looked the same: slips of gray mist that glinted silver when they happened into a puddle of moonlight. And—they were all northbound. He wondered if Liselle was there among them only to wish that he hadn't. Every time he thought about her, a tiny piece of him died. Seeing her just accelerated the process.

Damn. He was getting morbid again. High time for a drink.

"How much further?" he asked his traveling companion.

Gordyn sat easy in his saddle, even after a long day's ride and way too much gish the night before. The easy smile on his face made it clear that he was looking forward to more of the same tonight.

"Half hour at the most," he said. "And I swear, you won't regret the press. Timberton is much more fun than a night out in these woods. You can get a decent ale at the tavern there, and a good figh—Mother of pearl!"

They had just rounded a bend in the road, and were now looking at an orange glow on the horizon. It was so big, and so bright, Jamus could see individual trees that were at least a quarter mile away. "Looks like one helluva fire," he said. "Think it's the forest?"

"Actually," Gordyn said, "I think it's Timberton." He reined his horse to a stop. Jamus did, too. "What do you wanna do?"

"I don't know," Jamus replied. He stared at the conflagration for a moment, wondering how it had started. What on earth could set an entire town on fire?

The answer came to him as an image: swarms of armed men with torches. *Maybe Veeder had launched his invasion. Maybe his troops had already gotten this far.* If so, then maybe a change of plans was in order. The garrison at New Uxla would have long since been overrun. But first things first. *What to do here and now?*

"Do you think Ross and Thom have reached Compara yet?" he asked.

Gordyn glanced skyward as if the answer were written in the stars, then shrugged. "It's possible. But I'm guessing that they're still a half-day away." He jerked his head in Timberton's direction and said, "Do you suppose our boy was involved with that?"

"Anything's possible," Jamus replied. Then, because he did not know what else to do, and because Gordyn probably would not be able to resist anyway, he urged his horse forward. "I guess we'd better go and find out."

As they rode, the smell of hot, resinous woodsmoke thickened in the air. Little by little, the glow on the horizon resolved itself into a patchwork of separate fires. Then Gordyn pointed to a great, smoking blaze in the near distance.

"That used to be the lumberyard," he said. A moment later, he added, "Maybe we ought to leave the horses here and have a look around on foot."

That sounded like a good idea to Jamus, but before he could say so, a voice pealed out of the darkness. "And what would you be looking for?"

They swiveled toward their right and squinted into the trees. But Jamus could see was shifting shadows. More ghosts, he thought at first. But then two golden eyes winked into view. They unnerved him more than he cared to admit.

"Who are you?" he asked in reply. "Are you hurt? Are there any survivors besides you?"

"My Name is my own to give or withhold," the voice replied. "But for now, at least, you may call me Taz. Do not ask me about survivors. I am *not* of Timberton. Now tell me you are looking for."

"We seek a friend of ours—Pawl of Compara," he said, admitting this because the voice had had no tell-tale accent. "Have you seen him tonight?"

"No."

"No offense," he said, "but how would you know?"

"I have met Pawl of Compara. He is very well-made."

Jamus opened his mouth, but no sound came out. Taz's statement had taken him aback. It was a promising and somewhat amusing surprise—*very well-made indeed!*—but a surprise nonetheless. He glanced at Gord, soliciting ideas on where to go from here, but the horsetrader bounced the matter back into his lap with a shrug. So he fell back on an old mainstay of intuition and charm.

"Any friend of Pawlie's is a friend of ours," he said. "So why don't you join us? Don't worry," he hastened to add, "we won't hurt you. We only want to know what happened here."

Laughter rippled out of the darkness—a feral sound that both disturbed and excited him. "I did not say that he was a friend. And you are in more danger of being hurt than I am."

A chill skated down his spine. An instant later, a woman came striding out of the brush. She was tall and brawny and black as a moonless night.

Her hair was close-cropped and curly. Jamus had never seen anyone like her—and he was something of a connoisseur when it came to women. He found himself wondering what she would feel like beneath him, and then sneered at the reflex. Here he was, staring at a disaster of unknown cause and extent, and all he could think of was sex. Would he never learn?

"My name is Jamie," he said, "and this is my friend, Gord. If you wish us gone, just say so. We want no trouble."

She continued to bear down on them. As she drew nearer, he noticed a fat, cracking scab in the meaty part of her left thigh. It had to be painful, because despite her efforts not to, she was favoring that leg.

"Ouch," he said, grimacing in sympathy. "How'd you get that?"

"A man stabbed me," she replied, with just the slightest hint of rancor. Then she gave him a critical once-over. "I like your hair. Do you have a wife?"

Jamus flushed. He usually appreciated a forward woman, but there was something about this one that gave him pause. It wasn't her size, or her coloring—he liked that kind of variety. It had more to do with her eyes, and the intensity of her gaze. He tried to stay focused on important matters.

"Tell me more about this man who hurt you, sweetling," he said. "Does he have friends? Did they start the fires?"

She cocked her head at him—a look both amused and predatory. "What will you give me in return for speaking of him?"

"Name your price," he said.

She did so without a moment's pause. "Spend the night with me."

Gord snickered and then muttered under his breath. "You are such a *lucky* bastard."

"As you wish," Jamus said. "Now speak to me. Is the man who hurt you still in the area?"

"He is dead. So are his friends," she said, and then held out her hand. "Now come with me. The night grows no younger."

"Not so fast. I want to hear more."

A wicked smile took possession of her mouth. Reflections of firelight danced in her eyes. "I promised to speak of the man. I did not promise how much I would say."

For one stunned moment, all he could do was gape at her audacity. It reminded him of—well, he didn't know what, exactly, but it was something that rubbed him the wrong way. But as ill-at-ease as he was, he had to admit that he had indeed struck a rather bad deal. The good thing was, she hadn't been as clever as she could have been, either. And one way or another, she was going to tell him what he wanted to know.

"You're right, you didn't," he said, in a wondering tone, as if he were as witless as she seemed to think he was. But when she reached for him again, he batted her hand away and then wagged his finger at her. "And I only promised to spend the night with you. I didn't say how or where we'd spend it. Did I?"

Taz's nostrils flared. At the same time, her mouth and eyes narrowed into hard-to-read slits. "Now you've done it," Gord whispered, but then she made a noise deep in her throat. It was part-rumble, part-chuckle, and thoroughly erotic.

"Handsome *and* witty," she purred, recovering her wicked grin. "How delicious. Climb down from that beast's back."

That wasn't a question or a request, but an outright command. And although Jamus had no intention of obeying her, he suddenly found himself dismounting. From the ground, Taz was even more imposing: taller than he by almost two hands, well-muscled but slightly plump. His fingers twitched with a desire to touch her. He crammed his hands into his armpits. But before he had a chance to do anything else, she pulled him to herself and gave him an open-mouth kiss that left his thoughts reeling.

"The man was from the south, and he had many friends," she said, breathlessly, as if such divulgences were a form of foreplay. "Some of those friends were southerners like him. The rest were from Timberton."

Collaborators! The possibility made him dizzy, then slightly stomach-sick—the same as Taz's kiss. But he did not want to believe that Northmen would conspire against their homeland.

"Maybe they were part of a trade delegation," he said, trying to think of legitimate reasons for a large group of Southerners to be in Timberton. "This province is famous for its lumber, and the south has a big thirst for wood."

"Do trade delegations steal into gypsy havens at night and murder everyone in sight?" Taz asked.

"No-o."

"Then they were not a trade delegation."

Once again, he found himself reluctant to believe what she was telling him. Southerners wouldn't come north just to kill gypsies. Would they? What advantage could they hope to gain from such a persecution? Perhaps Taz had simply gotten her information wrong.

"Where did you hear about this attack on gypsies?" he asked.

"The Great One did not *hear* about it. She *saw* it. She was there."

Jamus pivoted toward the sound in time to see a man striding out of the woods. He was small and wiry, with jet-black hair and caramel-colored skin. The hilt of a long knife jutted from his waistband. Sooty smudges obscured his face. Although he wasn't smiling, Jamus could see his front teeth. They were gold—the same color as Taz's eyes.

"You know me, Jamus D'Arques," he said. "You shared my family's campfire one night a few years back. My daughter, Tikki, danced for you and your friends."

"Yes, The Dance of the Flying Dragon," Jamus said, as the memory from another lifetime clicked into place. "I remember. You're Santana, son of Katya, the Dowager Queen. I—" So many things were cropping up here, one right after the other. His head was starting to feel like a merry-go-round at full speed. "I would not have expected to find you in such a troubled place."

"If we could all choose our own fortunes," Santana said, "there would be no such thing as bad luck. And Katya would still be alive."

"Ah," Jamus said, a sound of regret and sympathy. "I hear you." His own if-onlys came bobbing to the surface of his thoughts: they all wore Liselle's face. He weighted these down with fresh sandbags of bitterness and grief, then sank them again. "I'm very sorry for your loss. Your mother was a great woman. But—" He scowled, trying in vain to make a complete picture from these ill-fitting puzzle pieces. "Forgive me for asking, but why are you here? Were you camped nearby? Did the southerners come back and do this—" He gestured at Timberton's still-burning remains. "—after they attacked you?"

Santana shook his head. "The Southerners and their allies the townsmen attacked us two days ago. They have been dead since then."

That crazy, merry-go-round feeling was back again. He pinched the bridge of his nose in hopes of stopping the spinning. "If that's true, Santana—and I'm not saying it's not—then who's responsible for all this destruction?"

"I am," Taz said, in a matter-of-fact tone.

Gordyn backed his horse up a step. Jamus went very, very still. "You do know that arson is against the law, don't you?" he asked.

She shrugged. "The fools who were living here aided and abetted Galza's minions. Such behavior will no longer be tolerated."

"And who might this Galza be?"

With a roll of her eyes and a rumble, she scorned him for a fool, too. Santana hastened to educate him. "To outsiders, she is known as Shadow or the Dreamer's Daughter. The Great One believes that the Southerners are in league with Her."

Disbelief blew through Jamus like a blast of hot wind. He knew damn well that Shadow was five years dead. Liselle had been the instrument of

Her death. He narrowed his eyes at the gypsy chieftain as if he were trying to look right through his skull and into his thoughts.

"Are you mocking me?" he asked, in a tone that wavered between wonder and warning.

Santana expression went blank. "Not at all, my friend. That is truly what The Great One believes."

"And what about you?" Jamus said. "What do you think?"

"I believe the Great One is right."

"Well, you're wrong. The both of you. Wrong, wrong, wrong!" Shadow was dead. She had to be. Otherwise, everything that he had been told over the years was a lie. *She had to die. There was no other way. Some day, you'll get over it.* "You don't know what you're talking about." To his surprise, there were tears in his eyes. He scrubbed them away with the back of his hand and then shouted, "Do you hear me?"

"What ails him?" Taz asked Santana, not bothering to lower her voice.

"I don't know, Great One," the gypsy said.

Meanwhile, Gordyn got down from his horse and went to comfort Jamus. "There, there," he said, slinging a friendly arm around his companion's trembling shoulders. "This ain't nothing that a long night and a lot of gish can't cure. C'mon, let's mount up and get out of here. Maybe there's a tavern somewhere up the road."

"Ours is not much of a camp at present," Santana said, with just a pinch of bitterness in his regrets, "but you are welcome to stay with us if you so choose."

"Well," Gordyn said, glancing from the gypsy to Jamus and back again. "We wouldn't want to impose—"

Taz seized Gord by the wrist, then slung him toward Santana as if he were a child rather than a full-grown mountain of a man. "This one is yours for the night," she told the gypsy. "The other belongs to me."

A fresh round of surprise tugged Jamus back from despair's acid shores. Nobody ordered a gypsy around like that, or rather, nobody but Taz. He studied her for a moment, trying to guess the relationship between her and Santana. She wasn't a tribeswoman. She was too flamboyant, and too domineering. Yet she wasn't an outsider, either. Santana consistently addressed her as *Great One*. And gypsies *never* deferred to non-gypsies—not even when a little deference could make life much less grievous. But if she wasn't a gypsy, and she wasn't an outsider, then what the hell *was* she? He felt like he should know, like the answer was tottering on the very tip of his brain, just out of reach. All he could do was hope that it would eventually fall the right way.

Gordyn collected his horse's reins. As an afterthought, he grabbed Jamus' as well and said, "I guess I'll be seeing you in the morning, partner. Don't do anything I wouldn't."

Santana snorted as if there were something funny about that, then motioned for Gordyn to follow him. As they headed into the woods, Taz let out an erotic rumble. "Have you decided the how and where yet?"

He turned toward her. She was grinning that wicked grin again. Its meaning was quite clear. His first thought was: *why the hell not?* After all he had endured lately, he could stand a good romp. But something about this woman put him off. It could've been her almost predatory intensity, or that preposterous talk of Shadow. Or maybe it was her complete indifference to the destruction that she claimed to have wrought that bothered him. Whatever the reason, he found himself resisting her considerable charms. He wanted to take the high road for a change.

"I'm going to have a look around," he said. "You're welcome to join me, if you must."

Taziem raised her eyebrows, shaping them into twin arches of surprise and wonder. This human was resisting her! This, when he was obviously a man who enjoyed women. How novel! How intriguing! She wanted him even more now. So she consented to play his game in the hope that she could turn it into one of her own.

"You are mine for the night," she said. "Wherever you go, so shall I."

Jamus shrugged, and then started toward town. Even with a limp, Taz had no problem keeping up with him. They strode past the lumberyard, which was burning like the mother of all bonfires. The building groaned like a living thing as it burned. Every now and again, it coughed up a comet-tail of sparks and blew it into the now-gray sky. The heat from the blaze brought a sweat to his brow. The smoke brought tears to his eyes. He shucked off his shirt and draped it over his head.

"Does this mean that you have changed your mind?" Taziem asked.

"No," he said, filtering his breaths through his sleeve. "It just means that I don't care for smoke."

Then he saw the corpse.

It was sprawled on its belly in the middle of the road, untouched by the fire. Jamus could tell by its long skirt that it was a female. The ground beneath her face was dark and damp. Over the reek of smoke, Jamus smelled blood—and worse. He cast a baleful look at Taziem.

"Would it have killed you to let the women go?" he asked.

"It could have," Taz said, without a shred of regret or remorse. "For these people served Galza, and Galza wishes me dead."

He slammed the doors of his mind on that name. Shadow was dead. Deceased. Defunct. No other possibility sufficed. If Taz wanted to believe otherwise, that was her business. And if she felt driven to kill for those beliefs well, that was her business, too. He could hardly condemn her for doing so, not with his body count. Maybe *that's* what bothered him so much about her—that sneaking suspicion that they were two of a kind.

They passed through the center of town. The fires here had died down already, leaving a network of charred planks and glowing red cinder-heaps behind. He saw more corpses, one of them burnt to a horrible, blackened twist, but said nothing. He did not want to know. On the far side of town, with the ruins of Timberton at her back, Taz made another play for him. She kissed him again—a raw, wild assault that transcended pleasure and included pain. At the same time, she ran her fingernails down the length of his bare chest and maybe an inch or two past his waistband. For one over-stimulated moment, he thought about taking her right then and there: a fast, hard ride to hell and back, just so he could say that he'd seen hell. Then the memory of the corpses that he had just seen rose up to kill his desire. The high road, he urged himself. Stick to the high road. Wearing a tight smile, he pushed her out of his air-space.

"Thanks," he said, "but I'm not interested." She made a noise deep in her throat. It could have been doubt. It could have been amusement. Jamus was inclined to think that it was both—a thought that left him feeling exposed. He folded his arms across his chest, then said, "I tell you truly—"

A tendril of mist appeared in Taz's out-sized shadow. The sight of it made Jamus forget what he had been about to say. As it drifted toward them, he prayed that it was just a shift in the wind, that all he was seeing was smoke from the lumberyard. But his prayers went for naught. A heart-shaped face materialized in the midst of the fog. Its eyes were desperate, and all for Jamus. Although he had not so much as touched Taz, shame coruscated through him anyway. Just being in the presence of another woman was sin enough.

"Have you seen Lathwi?" the ghost asked.

The question ignited a fury which turned his shame to ash. "Damn your dead eyes, Liselle! Why must you plague me about her? You know I despise her."

"She is my one hope of returning to the Dreamer's Keep," Liselle replied, answering his anger with despair. "But I cannot find her. Or Pawl. I fear they are both dead."

Taz went completely still. A moment later, in a voice that sounded both strained and distant, she said, "How curious. I can sense her, but not link with her."

Liselle's heart-shaped visage flickered, turning worm-eaten and frightful. A moment later, it reoriented itself, focusing on Taz to the exclusion of all else. "Who are you?" it asked. "And what do you know?"

A sly smile spread across Taz's ebony face like a crack in unfired clay. "You know me, TrueHeart. And you have already heard what I know. Lathwi is alive."

The ghost stared at Taz for a long, hard moment, as if it were trying to look through her skull and into her thoughts. Then comprehension dawned, bringing a rare flash of delight to her ethereal face. "Learned One!" it said. "Forgive me. I did not recognize you in that form." Its gaze flitted from her to Jamus and back again. As it did so, its delight gave way to wryness. "I see you have overcome your dislike of soldiers."

"Some please me more than others," Taz said, and gave Jamus a playful swat on the butt.

A few moments ago, that lap-dog's slap and its intimate implications would've appalled Jamus. But not now. He was too busy trying to get over the fact that his beloved's ghost seemed to know the woman who was trying to seduce him—and that they were discussing the one person in the world whom he truly hated. Sweet, suffering mother. If this wasn't the strangest night of his life, Dreamer take him now!

"How do *you* know Lathwi?" he asked Taz, phrasing the question like an accusation.

She cocked her head at him. Amused lights danced in her golden eyes. "I believe you would refer to me as her mother."

"But Lathwi's mother is a—"

His voice cut out on him like a trapdoor, leaving the rest of the sentence to fall through the stunned, dark spaces of his mind. *A dragon.* Lathwi's mother was a dragon.

Random forfend and have mercy!

But everything made sense now: Santana's deference to Taz, her callousness toward her victims, Liselle's comment about not recognizing her in that form. A dragon, a dragon, a dragon. The dragon-bitch's mother. He wished he had known that earlier. He might've taken her up on her offer then, taken all she had to offer and then some just to spite her she-demon of a daughter. But even as the thought of rape crossed his mind, he found himself rejecting it. The fact was, he didn't hate *anyone* enough to hurt even a not-so-innocent bystander in that way. The realization relieved him.

Meanwhile, Liselle continued to press Taz for information. "How do you know Lathwi is still alive?"

"I can sense her life-force," Taz said. "But she is so far removed from this place, I cannot touch her thoughts."

"I must find her before she kills the necromage," Liselle said, growing wild-eyed again. "There are things she must know."

"If I see her," Taz said, "I will tell her that you are looking for her."

The ghost flickered like a fatty candle, and then swooped into the space just beyond Taz's nose. "Find her for me, Learned One," it begged. "Promise this to me on the life that I sacrificed to protect your folk as well as mine."

Jamus would've promised. He would've done anything to ease Liselle's distress, if only for a moment. But not Taz. She shook her head of close-cropped hair, an oh-so-human gesture full of a dragon's regrets. "I cannot make such a promise, TrueHeart," she said, trying hard not to think of Katya. "You will have to trust me to do what I can for you."

And that was more of a commitment than any other dragon would have made in her stead. Being human had some *very* strange side-effects. She shuddered as if to shake off some of those irregularities, and then watched with interest as the phantom began to dissipate. The extremities disappeared first, then the torso. But even as Liselle threatened to vanish entirely, Jamus blurted out a word.

"Wait!"

"I cannot," the ghost whispered.

"But—" He groped for the right words, but they would not come. "This—" He gestured at the space between himself and Taz. "We're not—I didn't—" Finally, he gave up and moaned the one thing that was always on his mind. "I still love you, you know."

A pair of ghostly eyes stared at him from a patch of swirling mist. A disembodied voice said, "Love is for the living. Enjoy what you have while you still have it."

An instant later, the mist dissolved. He and Taz were once again alone.

"I did not know that you were the TrueHeart's chosen," she said.

"Some choices weren't meant to be," he muttered.

Taz reached out as if offering him comfort, but while he ached for just that, he could not accept it from her. Every fiber in his body screamed against it. So he pushed her away yet again.

"No," he said. "Thanks."

She cocked her head at him. Now that he knew where to look, he could see the dragon in her. "Did you not hear The TrueHeart?" she asked. "She said to enjoy what you have while you still have it. That is sound advice."

He shrugged as if he didn't give a damn about anything his beloved had to say. But the truth was, he simply didn't want to take the advice. Not in this instance. If he could not thwart the daughter, then at least he'd deny the mother. The thought gave him some small satisfaction.

"Nevertheless," he said, "I must decline your offer of company, madam. I've ridden long and hard today, and desire naught but—" A large, triangular head went snaking past him. "What in all hell?" The head swung in his direction. Its eyes were the same color as Taz's. Its calico markings triggered a memory. "Hey! I know you."

The dragon narrowed its eyes at him, then swiveled its head back in Taz's direction. She cupped its tri-colored head in her hands and went nose to nose with it, then began to scratch the underside of its chin. The dragon crooned—a surprisingly content sound. Taz caught Jamus' gaze and held it.

"The little one bears a message from Lathwi," she said.

Hope and hatred flared within him in equal measure. He did not want to know where she was. *Did not, did not, did not.* But he could not go on being haunted by Liselle. The ache that her visits inspired was stronger than all the hate in the world. He resented that, too.

"Where is she?" he asked, through gritted teeth.

"The little one does not know," Taz said. "The last it saw of her, she was alive and well on the shores of a great lake. An army of Galza's minions has gathered in a valley near this lake. Lathwi refers to this place as Death's Door."

"I've heard of it," he said. "It's in the mountains south of the border."

"I must go there."

"Why?"

"Galza's minions are there," she said, in a tone like a shrug. "They must be destroyed."

Contempt curled Jamus' lip into a snarl. Leave it to Lathwi to demand the impossible—from dragons as well as people. "Look, Taz," he said, "armies are enormous things. You can't just pop in and destroy one by yourself, no matter *what* you are. You'll need help, and lots of it."

"Then help I will have," she said, without a moment's pause. "I will Call my tanglemates and their offspring and perhaps their offspring's offspring, too. We will fly south together. Then the world will see what happens to men who embrace The Dragonbane's cause."

She gave the calico's head a last caress, and then sent it away with an affectionate swat. "Go and find yourself something to eat now, Little One," she said. "I must begin Calling dragons to our cause."

But the little dragon did not withdraw. Instead, it swiveled its head back toward Jamus and gurgled. Taz responded with a chilling smile. Once again, he found himself wondering how he got into these kinds of predicaments.

"What did it say?" he asked, trying hard not to look concerned.

"It wanted to know if I was done with you, and if so, if it could have you," she said. "It thinks you look quite tasty."

"Oh, it does, does it?" He turned to look the calico in the eye. It bared its teeth at him. Jamus responded in kind, then said, "I'm not afraid of you, you overgrown lizard." On impulse, he punched it squarely on the nose and added, "That's for eating my horse."

The young dragon hissed, a hair-raising sound, then went for Jamus like a striking snake. At the last moment, though, it stopped short and snapped its jaws in his face. An instant later, it was gone.

"That was well done," Taz said, just as his guts began a belated buck-and-quiver. "It will respect you more for having stood up to it."

"How can you tell?" he asked.

"That is the way of dragons," she said, and then dismissed him with a flick of her wrist. "Leave me now. I have dragons to Call."

It should have been easy for him to walk away and leave her to her dragon-sized folly. It should have been easy for him, but—it was not. For in one splendid flash of insight, he had seen what would come of pursuing such a course of action. And he could not live with the outcome—no matter that he'd be able to blame it all on Lathwi in the years to come and not be all wrong.

"Wait," he said, and grabbed Taz's arm only to let it go again in a hurry as she rounded on him. Her teeth were bared. The lights in her eyes snapped and danced like those of a hungry fire's. He held out his hands, palms up, to show that he meant no harm. Her snarl softened into a sulk.

"Be gone," she said. "Your change of heart comes too late."

"You cannot turn an army of dragons on an army of men, Taz," he said.

She arched her neck at him. A distinct hint of menace crept into her hunter's-moon eyes. "Cannot? *Cannot?* Do you think to forbid me?" He sputtered a denial, but she remained testy. "Why do you care what happens to those men anyway? They number your people among their enemies."

"Too true," he conceded. "But you have to understand, Taz—most people are *afraid* of dragons. It's pure reflex. As soon as word gets out that you and yours attacked Veeder's army—and trust me, that kind of news will spread faster than a butt-rash at a bath-house—the first thing most folks are going to do is forget that the men you attacked were rogues and murderers. Soon thereafter, they'll start demanding protection against 'the dragon scourge,' and some self-deluded hero will start setting traps for your weak and defenseless. One or more of your kind will return the favor, and the next thing you know, it will be people versus dragons, and the killing will start in earnest."

Taz stared at him for a long moment. Suspicion gleamed hard and cold in her eyes, but it was tempered by a pinch of self-doubt. At last, she asked, "Is that really how it would happen?"

He nodded, a gesture laden with chagrin. "More or less. You saw how it went with the gypsies."

"Yessss." The gleam in her eye narrowed into something more dangerous. "But dragons are not as soft as humans."

"True," Jamus countered, "but humans are more numerous. And we breed faster. In a war of attrition, dragons would suffer more, faster."

Taz fell still for a time, so still that it seemed like she had fallen asleep. Jamus was not fooled, however. He could almost hear her turning his arguments over and around in her mind, looking for soft spot into which she could sink her teeth. Unfortunately, his position was entirely too solid—frightened people were frighteningly predictable. She must have realized that, too, because all at once, she loosed a frustrated hiss.

"Galza's minions must be destroyed," she said. "How am I to accomplish this without assistance? How am I to do what must be done?"

Now it was Jamus' turn to crack a sly smile. "You weren't listening, Taz. I didn't say you couldn't have help. I said you just needed to rethink your plan a little. And as it happens, I have a few suggestions for you."

Chapter 18

S_{eth} stood at the edge of his stronghold's abyss, straining to locate Lathwi and her detestable lover by magical means. But while he had just sacrificed two of Veeder's most able-bodied men and made himself strong on their life-forces, the hunt wasn't going well. Indeed, it could not possibly get any worse. Not only could he not get a fix on Lathwi, he could not even sense her. It was as if she no longer existed.

Bring her back, you bastard.

A part of him thought it a pity that that calico dragon hadn't eaten her—everyone concerned might have been better off if it had. Just ask the two men whose throats he had slit. Their only crime had been in telling Veeder that she and the swordmaster had up and vanished off the shores of Lake Random. A rogue wave had taken them, they said—them and a dozen mates who had gone into the water after them. Shortly thereafter, however, a new report came in. Twelve bodies had been recovered. Lathwi's and Pawl's were *not* among them. That's when the general gave the first two messengers to Seth along with a command: *"Find her."*

Now Seth was staring his employer's unspoken *or else* squarely in the face.

Maybe she really *was* dead, he thought—this, even as he cast his Will toward the waters of Lake Random again. Maybe she and that gods-rotted lover of hers had drowned along with the others. Most people couldn't swim. He couldn't. Veeder couldn't. Why should Lathwi be any different?

Because they hadn't found her body, dammit.

He kicked at the corpse at his feet, wishing that it were the woman he had been so keen to trust. Every time he allowed himself to think about her for more than a heartbeat, he almost choked on the logjam of memories and emotions that stuck in his throat. There was agony: standing out in that practice field, suspended between past and present as the calico dragon carried her away. And betrayal: the dragon returning to snatch Pawl out of danger's way with Lathwi not only still alive and well in its clutches, but *grinning* like a devil as well. And, humiliation: standing out in that field, powerless to do anything as she and her lover disappeared over the ridge. He wanted to howl. *Bitch! Was that any way to treat a friend?* If she *was* alive, and he *did* find her, he was going to make her very, very sorry that she hadn't wound up as food for the fish.

As he trawled the shorelines of Lake Random with his Will, one of the aides that he shared with Veeder entered the stronghold. Although Seth was immediately aware of him, he pretended otherwise. If he didn't, the man might get the wrong idea, and tell the general that he was slacking. And *that* would never do. Veeder was furious enough with him as it was—and for good reason for a change. Not only had he befriended a traitor, he had acted as her advocate. No one was going to be quick to forgive such a colossal mistake, not even himself. So he continued to act distracted until the aide began to fidget. Then he made a great show of retracting his Will and returning to ordinary consciousness, even chuffing with feigned surprise as he set eyes on his visitor for the first time.

"Kel!" he exclaimed. "I didn't realize I had company. What brings you here?"

"The general wants to see you," Kel replied.

"Of course he does," Seth said, all bluff and bravado. "Tell him I'll be with him as soon as I've finished up here."

"Tell him yourself," Kel said. "He wants to see you *now*."

Seth shrugged as if to make light of the general's prerogative, but inwardly, he was struggling to stay calm. For a sense of doom had just visited him, a sense so strong, it left his heart banging against his ribcage. He did not know if it was a true premonition or not, but in a way, that was irrelevant. What really mattered was that it had made him afraid. If Veeder saw that, he would eat him alive. That was his style, and his nature.

"Very well," he said, playing for time. "I'll go and *you* can clean up." He glanced at the bodies at his feet. "You'll have to be careful, though. If these aren't disposed of in the prescribed manner, they'll come back to life and kill you in your sleep."

Kel swallowed hard as he eyed the corpses. Beneath his beard, his complexion paled. "How long?" he asked.

"An hour at most," Seth said.

"I'll tell the general that you'll be there within the quarter-hour. If I have to come looking for you after that, I can promise you that you'll regret it."

Almost by accident, Seth drew Kel's attention to the blood on his hands. "I don't take kindly to threats. And those who come to this place uninvited don't always go away again. Tell the general I'll be there within the half-hour."

The color returned to Kel's face—a flash of frustration and fear. "Not a minute later than that, you hear?" he said, and then stormed toward the passageway. "I mean it, wizard. You've already caused enough trouble. If I suffer for your delay, so will you."

Seth waved him away like he might wave away an annoying blow-fly, then raised his arms over the corpses only to drop them again as Kel went scooting out of the cavern. He shook his head, thinking: *Some fools believed anything they were told.* Then, as he unceremoniously rolled the two bodies into the abyss, he added, *He ought to know.* He was the biggest fool of them all.

And for that, Veeder was going to make him suffer.

The only questions were: how much? And: did he want to stick around and take it? Unlike these half-witted Southerners, he was not good at ignoring pain. Even a small shaving cut caused him undue distress. Veeder's ministrations would put him right out of his mind, if not his life. But the only alternative was to flee. Now. He could get a decent head start in a half-hour's time. He even had a little power left to help him along the way. And it wasn't as if he would miss Veeder's company.

Excitement sparked within him, inspiring or perhaps merely unleashing a more audacious thought. He could run away from it *all*: Veeder, his mentor, the blood that wound up on his hands. Surely, Ylana would not fault him for wanting to leave such dark things behind. He strode over to his sister's coffin, swept the accumulation of what-nots from its surface and pushed the lid aside. As he did so, the sharp smell of preservatives stung his nose: Ylana's perfume. He stared at her cloth-wrapped body, so small and so frail, his parents's baby, the millstone around his neck. Surely he had done everything he could have—and more than he should have—to get her back. He stroked her forehead as if she were feverish beneath her winding cloth.

"What do you think, baby girl?" he whispered. "Shall I run away? Will you set me free?"

She made no sound. She never did. But an answer floated up from the depths of his mind nonetheless. *All he had to do was find those last two tokens. Two more, and they would all be free.* He sighed, a wistful exhalation. He did not remember what being free was like. *Puppy dogs and pine cones and suppers by the fire.* Simple Ylana. She liked simple things. He wondered if she would've liked Lathwi.

No-o.

He wondered if he should go after her.

No-o. Stay. Finish what was started.

An image of his sister's sorrowing eyes came to him then, begging him to do right by her and the promise that he had made to their parents. His heart sunk. His excitement drowned. As much as he wanted to, he could not leave little Ylana. He had let her down once already. He would not be able to live with himself if he did so again. He bent over and kissed the slight mound of her mouth—an apology and a promise.

"Don't worry, little one," he said. "I'm not going anywhere."

High-pitched laughter pealed through his head—the sound of a young girl running away from her nursemaid. He murmured, "See you soon, Ylana," then closed the coffin. For a fleeting moment afterward, he smelled wildflowers and meadow grasses instead of embalming fluids. The memory of it buoyed him all the way to Veeder's pavilion.

ଧ ଓ

True to Seth's expectations, the general was *not* in a pleasant mood.

"What do you mean, you can't find them?" he bellowed at his adviser. "What in Random's name have you been doing in that stinkhole of yours?"

"I've used every procedure I know of," Seth said, trying to lull his inquisitor into a better frame of mind with a soft, reasonable tone. "But so far—nothing. I think we need to consider the possibility that they're actually dead."

"I won't believe it," Veeder said. "Not until I see the bodies. Until then, I have to assume that they're headed north to raise the alarm." He paced a few steps, then slapped the tent-pole to which Pawl had been tied. The whole pavilion shuddered from the blow. As it did so, he turned to snarl at Seth again. "This is all *your* fault. You *swore* she was a mercenary. You *recommended* her to me."

Seth was tempted to point out that he had advised against the battle which had facilitated the duo's escape, but decided that that might well provoke the general into doing something rash. And rash was definitely not in Seth's best interests. So he stayed quiet while Veeder ranted on.

"Not only did you lead a spy into my camp," he said, "you showed her all around. Now she knows *everything* about us, you stupid bastard: headcount, location, passwords. You compromised my campaign." He drew a hunting knife from his belt, then angled the blade so it caught the filtered light. "The question now is—how shall I repay you for your folly?" He turned the blade toward Seth. "Gutting you seems too quick."

Seth's innards tensed at the mere suggestion. His underarms went slick. But he had expected this turn in the conversation, and knew exactly what to say to his would-be butcher. "I know you're pissed," he began. "Believe me, so am I. But if you think about it for a moment, I think you'll see that your plan hasn't been compromised yet. It's going to take those two Northerners weeks to make their way back to Compara with the news. And even if they get there sooner, what's Wynn Rame going to do? His entire territory is half-mad from its plague of ghosts. It will take him *months* to put an army together. You can be on his doorstep in a fortnight."

Veeder arched an eyebrow at him. "You're advising me to launch the invasion?"

"Why not? The troops are ready. And you still have the element of surprise on your side."

"But in my dreams, I always have all six of Grange's tokens in my possession before I begin my conquest."

Seth knew exactly how those dreams went, for he was the one who had sent them. What better way of ensuring Veeder's commitment to recovering the talismans than to tie them to his own success? But the general didn't need them to wage his war: none or two or four would serve him as well as all six. And at the moment, the possibility of war was the only thing standing between Seth and a very long knife. So he hastened to reinterpret his own lies.

"Perhaps that's why you bear their Grange-given likenesses on your chest," he said. "They symbolize the six, and thus, Lord Grange's desire for you to begin your holy campaign. When you didn't do so in the days after your branding, he sent the red dragon to force your hand. When the drake failed, he sent Lathwi."

Some of the menace drained from Veeder's face. He narrowed his eyes like a near-sighted cat, then loosed a loud, "Hmm," and began to absently scratch at the scars on his breast. After a while, he said, "I hadn't thought of that. But it makes sense. My Lord Grange was a man of action. He would want his heir to be the same."

"Then call your men to arms and lead them forth to glory," Seth said. "The north is yours for the taking."

A smile crept across Veeder's hair-rimmed mouth. Fell lights began to dance in his eyes. "Yes," he said. "Yes, I believe you're right. The time has come."

Seth allowed himself to breath just a little easier. They had turned an important corner just then. Now he needed to re-establish his position. "Splendid! As soon as I find the last two tokens, I'll join you on the road."

Veeder's smile took a sinister twist. "What's this, Seth? No stomach for a little open blood-letting? Or are you planning to run off as soon as my back is turned?"

"You know what I have to do in order to work my magic," Seth said, trying to match the general smile for smile. "And you know where my loyalties lie. If you want me to march with you, I'll march. I'm merely suggesting that I could serve your interests better by staying here and overseeing the recovery of the rest of your inheritance."

"As long as you remember that it's *my* inheritance, right?"

Seth willed himself to remain straight-faced as he lied. "I'm only interested out of intellectual curiosity. Besides, you're the keystone. The tokens won't work if you don't handle them first."

The warlord hmmed again, then shaved his thumbnails with the tip of his knife. A moment later, he said, "Sorry, Seth, but we're going to have to resume this conversation at some later date. I've got something else on my mind that I need to take care of."

"As you wish," Seth said. "Shall I leave?"

"Oh, no," Veeder said, and then shifted his grip on the knife. "Your presence is definitely required."

Chapter 19

*T*he shadow was circling Pawl and Lathwi. With every pass, it came closer and closer. Lathwi had a fair sense of what it looked like now: sleek, sinuous, *big*. It had no legs—front or hind. A ridge of shark's-fin spines ran from the back of its skull to the tip of its rounded tail. It had a long, boxy face, yellow eyes, and a score of catfish whiskers on its chin.

"What is it?" Pawl whispered—as if they had not already drawn its attention.

"I do not know," she said. On impulse, she reached out with her mind to find out. Curiosity welled up at her touch. At the same time, hunger receded. An instant after she made contact, the shadow abandoned its circling and came speeding toward them. As it approached, it peeled back its lips to reveal a formidable mouthful of teeth.

"Shit," Pawl said.

The creature glided to a stop less than an arm's length away from Lathwi, then flared its nostrils for a moment and blew a stream of air bubbles at her face. The watery membrane that contained her and Pawl absorbed the tiny, silver spheres. An instant later, the air within acquired a fishy tang. Lathwi bared her teeth at the creature in greeting and then pulsed it a thought.

"I am most pleased to meet you, cousin."

Its eyes narrowed. Another spray of bubbles escaped its nostrils and went belling toward the surface. *"How strange,"* it thought at her in reply. *"You speak as Spree do, and the lake makes you welcome. Yet you have the look of humans. What manner of creature are you?"*

"I am Lathwi," she replied, and flashed it a self-image of her as a dragon. *"I have many distinctions."*

"Are you tasty?" the Spree asked.

"I do not think so."

"That is the only distinction that matters to Splash," it said, and blew another barrage of bubbles at her. *"Away with you now. This is Splash's territory."*

"We cannot turn back," she said.

"You can go no farther, either. "Unless," it added, turning suddenly coy, *"you give me something that will make me forget you are here."*

Any doubts that she might have had about Spree and dragons sharing a common, if far-removed ancestor were gone now. And she was pleased to humor this most distant relative.

"What's going on?" Pawl asked, as she patted herself down for a suitable token.

"It wants us to pay a toll for our passage through its territory," she said.

He snorted—an incredulous, almost amused sound. "Jamie will never believe me when I tell him that we were robbed by a giant water serpent at the bottom of an unnamed lake."

"Then why say anything?" she asked.

"Who could resist?" As an afterthought, he added, "I have gold if you need it."

"Keep it ready," she said. But she did not think that she was going to need it. For she had her good luck charm in hand now. As soon as she touched it, she knew it was the right thing to give the Spree. She held the piece of bone up to her eye and peered through its hollow center. She put it to her lips and made it whistle. Then she held it out for Splash to see.

"This came to me by way of an old man," she said, sharing the memory of that encounter along with the thought. *"It has kept me well."*

"Wonder of wonders," Splash said, as the Bone-Man's wizened image formed in its head. *"You are The Chosen One."* It shivered as if frightened or appalled, and then pulled its body alongside their bubble. *"You must come with me."*

"Where to?" she asked, not at all sure that she wanted to humor the Spree that far.

"I cannot say," it said, blanking its thoughts.

"And if I refuse to go?"

"I will eat your companion."

"Why is it looking at me like that?" Pawl asked, scowling as the Spree grinned at him.

"It wants us to go somewhere with it," she said, "but it will not name the place. It says it will eat you if we do not comply. What say you on the matter?"

He glanced from her to the Spree's wicked-looking bite and then back to her. His expression was emphatic. "I say we go with it."

That was her thought, too, so she gestured him toward the Spree's back. "Do not worry about the bubble," she said, when he balked. "It will hold."

So they scrabbled onto a space between two of Splash's foremost dorsal spines. The Spree's back was perhaps a bit less yielding than a horse's, and perhaps a bit more precarious-seeming, but overall, it was not that much different from what they were used to. As she shifted to adjust her seat, the water dragon let out a happy rumble.

"*My brothers and sisters will not believe me when I tell them,*" it said.

"*Tell them what?*"

"*That I found The Chosen One nosing around the bottom of the lake like an overgrown muck-feeder.*" Before she could ask—chosen for what?—it went on to say, "*Hold on. I swim very fast.*"

And that was not an idle boast.

In no time at all, the lake became a murky-gray blur. Its denizens became fleeting streaks in the distance. Lathwi enjoyed the ride at first, for she had a dragon's affinity for speed. But as time went by without variance or respite, her pleasure yielded to boredom. She wanted to breathe fresh, warm air again. She wanted to walk on dry ground and then take a nap on a sun-warmed rock. She did not express these wishes aloud, however, for Water was a touchy element. And it tended to drown those who displeased it. Hoping for distraction, she touched Splash's mind again.

"*Can you tell me the purpose The Chosen One is supposed to serve?*"

"*It is not my place to say,*" it replied. "*But fear not. All will be made clear to you soon.*"

"*How do you know?*"

"*I was born with the knowledge.*"

With that, the Spree changed course and began swimming toward the surface. As it ascended, the water grew sunnier by degrees. And as the light changed, so did the color of Splash's scales—from black to green-gray to a handsome silver-blue. By the time the water-dragon broke the surface, it and the lake were the same color. Lathwi marveled at that, then yelped aloud as twin plumes of superfine mist shot past her ear and into the air: a half-day's breath expelled.

"*Ah,*" Splash thought, as the vapors drifted back down to earth. "*that felt good.*" It flared its nostrils and added, "*I like breathing.*"

"Where are we?" Pawl asked, with a bit of an edge to his tone. Their bubble had dissolved as soon as it touched fresh air, and at first glance, there seemed to be no land in sight. "This thing isn't planning on dropping us off here, is it?"

"I will ask," Lathwi said, and tapped into the Spree's thoughts again. "*Can you tell me where we are going yet?*"

Splash dipped its head beneath the water, then blew another blast of mist from its nostrils. A rainbow formed within the sun-spangled spray, then turned into a tiny strip of sand on the horizon. "*Your final destination remains a mystery,*" it told her. "*But that is your next stop.*"

"*What am I supposed to do once I get there?*"

"*I do not know.*"

"*Then how will I know when I should leave?*"

"The Lord of The Lake will guide you. That is his island."

"So?" Pawl asked. "What goes on?"

She pointed to the islet that Splash was fast approaching. "We will be getting off there, for reasons that the Spree cannot or will not make clear."

"Well, at least it's dry ground."

The islet's shoreline expanded, becoming an inviting stretch of clean white sand. A small patch of forestland stood beyond the beach, a deep green clump against a clear, blue sky. The Spree glided to a stop, then looped its head in Lathwi's direction.

"This is as far as I may go," it said. *"Tell the Lord of The Lake that it was Splash who found you."*

"I will do that," she replied, and then turned to tell Pawl that it was time to take their leave of the Spree. Before she could get a word out, though, the water-dragon rolled over, pitching both of them into the drink. As they flailed their way back to the surface, it swam away. Its chortling echoed through Lathwi's thoughts for quite some time.

"Praise the Dreamer for making the water shallow here," Pawl said. "I don't think I could've swum all the way to shore."

She remembered his sore ribs then, and the abuse that he had taken from Veeder. But she did not feel the least bit sorry for him. Indeed, now that they had put the general behind them, she felt free to revive her gripe with him for following her.

"You would not have had to worry about such a thing," she said, "in Compara."

"You never know," he said, and started wading toward shore.

She splashed after him, wanting to press the issue, but could not think of anything to say. Her thoughts were suddenly lead-footed, hobbled by exhaustion. And the malaise quickly spread to the rest of her body. By the time she splashed ashore, all she wanted to do was flop down in the sand and sleep. So that's exactly what she did.

☙ ❧

She was curled up in a cozy nest of clouds when a voice chimed in her head. *"I see you, Dragon's Daughter. Come and play a game with me."*

She blinked. The clouds disappeared. The next thing she knew, she was standing on a warm, white-sand beach with the sun in her eyes. A stooped old man in a dirt-brown robe was standing next to her. He had merry eyes and a crooked, gap-toothed smile. He motioned for her to follow, and then began strolling along the shore. He left no footprints in his wake.

"I see you survived the little dog's bite," he said. "Congratulations."

She shrugged, then stooped to pluck a shiny bit of glitter out of the sand. To her wonder and amazement, it turned out an Oma-stone the size of a cherry. How delightful! And how auspicious. Fortune was smiling in her direction again. She held the diamond up to the sun, admiring its many facets. As she did so, the old man asked, "If you could have anything you wanted, what would it be?"

"Clear skies and good hunting," she replied. Almost as an afterthought, she added, "And an end to The Dragonbane."

The diamond pulsed white in her hand. At the same time, power surged through her—a startling spurt that burned away her fatigue. She felt energized; revitalized; ready to resume the journey. Beside her, the Bone-Man cackled.

"What if you could have more than that?" he asked.

An image formed in her head—herself and Pawl lounging on a mountain of diamonds while humans worked nonstop to make it ever larger. A nest like that was every dragon's dream. But she was not interested in a nest built by humans. Finding the stones was part of the fun for her. So were the associated memories.

"I am content," she insisted.

The Oma-stone flashed again, pumping more power into her system. The influx swept away the limits that had previously defined her abilities; and unexplored potential began oozing into the void. Her fists knotted. Her nostrils flared. She felt mightier than the mightiest dragonsire; more potent than a city of sorcerers. She laughed at the feeling. The sound of her voice shook the whole world. She turned toward the Bone-Man. The sparkle in his eyes had burned out, giving him a desolate look.

"What is happening?" she asked.

"I am sorry," he replied. "But you have been Chosen."

With that, the diamond flared like the first Oma-stone: a bloom of power beyond any that she had ever experienced or imagined. It swallowed her up, then filled her to the brim. All she could do was marvel at its composition. Most of the power was elemental, the unnamed cousin to Earth, Wind, Water, and Fire. But laughter accounted for part of it, as did love and hope and joy. Pain contributed, too. Birthing pains, growing pains, the pains of dying, defeat, and death—she knew them all now, in intimate profusion, and they made her strong as the world.

Chosen for what?

Although she did not voice the question aloud, the Bone-Man answered it as if she had. "For better or for worse, fortune has tapped you as Shadow's nemesis, Daughter of Dragons. The time has come to put that age-old wrong to rest."

"But—" She raised her hands. The aura surrounding them was so intense, all she could see was a white-hot glow. "So much power—" She could not put her thoughts into working order. "Why?"

"I cannot tell you outright," he said, "for The Chosen must follow her own path to its unique conclusion. But I *will* say this: if, at some point, you should decide to invoke the potential that has been bestowed on you, remember to look beyond the obvious first." He paused to let her absorb that advice, and then added, "Remember, too, that those who do not learn from their mistakes will repeat them until the end of time."

He raised himself onto the tips of his toes, then framed her head in his hands and kissed her brow—this despite the fact that she was at least twice his height. "Fare well, Daughter," he said. "Choose your path wisely."

Then, without another word or warning, he vanished.

"No! Wait!" she cried, grabbing at the spot where he had just been standing. "I do not—" *Understand*, she wanted to say, but even as the word took shape in her mind, an unseen something seized her by the forearm and instinct kicked in. She let out a snarl, then pulled away—and woke up to find herself on her back. Pawl was crouched next to her. One side of his face was encrusted with sand. His eyes showed bleary concern.

"Are you well?" he asked. "You were shouting in your sleep."

She scooted into a sitting position, then ran her fingers through her tangled tresses just to reorient herself. She could not believe that her encounter with the Bone-Man had been a dream. It had been so vivid. So real.

You have been Chosen.

"Lathwi?" Pawl pressed.

"I am well," she said, and that was the truth. Her fatigue had given way to a sense of profound refreshment. And she felt as loose and limber as an otter's pup—this despite that headlong tumble down the escarpment. "How long was I asleep?"

"I don't know," he replied. "I was dead to the world, too. I'd probably still be out if you hadn't started shouting. What was that all about, if you don't mind my asking?"

The Bone-Man's scrawny image popped back into her mind. His gap-toothed grin was that of a trickster's. "I was—" The old man's words echoed through her head: *Look beyond the obvious.* "I was dreaming." With a cackle and a pop, the image disappeared. "Did you dream?"

"I did," he said. "But only about you. And that's not unusual."

The thought of him dreaming about her unsettled Lathwi, but in an oddly pleasing way. On an impulse, she reached out and brushed the sand from his face. His whiskers tickled her fingertips. The feel of his firm, warm flesh excited her. Taziem was right, she thought. He was very well-made for a human. She wondered if that was the reason she did not want to stop touching him.

"The bruises that Veeder gave you are gone," she said. She stroked those places, then moved on to the back of his sunburned neck. From there, she moved on to his torso. "How fare your ribs?"

He tensed as if stung by the memory, then let out a laugh. "Believe it or not, they feel as good as new. But—" He tensed again. His expression went intense. He grabbed her hands as she ran them down his back. "If you keep that up, something else is going to snap."

Then he pulled her close and pressed his lips to hers. A kiss, he called this. It was not a thing that any dragon would do, but she enjoyed it just the same. Perhaps it was the feel of his warm breath caressing her face. Perhaps it was the taste of his mouth. All she knew was, it made her feel whole, complete. And that was why, suddenly, she shied away from his embrace.

"What's the matter?" he asked.

"I must return to Death's Door," she said.

"Now?" At her grim little nod, he glanced toward the lake. "Are we going to take the Spree-Express again?"

"Not *we*, Pawl," she said. "*Me*. I am going alone."

"Think again, Lathwi."

All at once, she remembered why she had been angry with him earlier. And all at once, she was angry once again. She loosed a hiss that made him recoil. "Do you live to contradict me?" she asked. "This is my path to fly, not yours."

Pawl's eyes narrowed. His jaw grew taut with purpose. The next thing she knew, he was kneeling in her breathing space once again. This time, however, he did not kiss or embrace her. This time, he held her with his gaze.

"I know this isn't the time or the place for what I'm about to say," he said, "but I figure I'd better say it anyway—before you compel someone else to crack me upside the skull." She opened her mouth to protest the statement's inaccuracy, but before she could get a word out, he pressed on. "I've been going your way since the day we met. And I don't intend to stop now. You have my heart—"

She glanced down at her hands, then hissed at the lie. "I do not."

"And you have my spirit—"

She hissed again. "I would do no such thing!"

"So you might as well come to terms with the rest of the man. Because I mean to stay with you until my dying day, Lathwi. Life is entirely too dull without you."

In her younger days, she had dismissed love as a word for poets and fools. But in the wake of that declaration, she knew otherwise.

The dream had been right, she thought. There *was* power in such human things as laughter and love. Because she could feel Pawl's plainspoken passion resonating through her like a bell's peals—finding and then binding with kindred potentials whose existence she had only begun to acknowledge. The irony was that it only strengthened her resolve to leave him behind. But where she would have simply stranded him here on the isle for his own good yesterday, today she would explain her reasons first. *You have been Chosen.* He deserved that much.

"A soothsayer told me that someone entwined in my life would make a wish and perish for it," she said. "I do not want that someone to be you, Pawl. Therefore, I would have you stay here while I finish my quest. It will be safer for both of us that way."

"That won't work," he said. "Because the only occasion I have to do any wishing at all is when we're apart, and then, all I wish for is you. So the way I see it, the thing for us to do is stay together."

It was, she admitted, a delicious bit of reasoning—logic fit for a dragon. It was also permission to quit her solitary lifestyle—if she chose to take it. She was not without her reservations. Companions could be such a nuisance. She would have to learn how to share. And compromise. Was any kind of power worth that kind of aggravation? She peered at Pawl through her lashes. Hope radiated from every seam in his weathered face. The sight plucked at the newly forged bonds between them; and for better or worse, her decision was made.

"If you want to join me," she said, "I will not refuse you. But we must leave now, for it is a long flight from here to where we need to be."

His face went blank. "Flight?"

She cast him a sly, sideways smile. "I cannot ask Water to aid us again, for we are in no immediate danger. And Splash did not share its secret Name, so I cannot Call upon the Spree for help. Therefore, to return to the mainland, we must either swim or fly."

"And you don't know how to swim," Pawl said wanly. At her nod, he swallowed a lifetime of reservations in one conspicuous gulp only to belch up one of them right back up. "Are you sure you're strong enough to carry me all that way?"

A corner of her mouth twitched—an inscrutable spasm. "I am not going to carry you."

"Then who is?" he asked, sweeping the skies with his dark brown eyes. "Not that little calico, I hope. I never thought I'd say this about a dragon, but it's not big enough."

"I do not have time to Call another dragon," she said, and that corner of her mouth twitched again. "And besides, there is no Need."

"What do you mean by that?"

"Just remember who you are, Pawl," she advised him, "and all will be well."

She shifted, meaning to climb to her feet. As she did, her left hand folded around something hard in the sand. An instant after she palmed it, echoes of vast power skirled through her like a heady desert wind. Even before she laid eyes on her find, she knew it was the Bone-Man's diamond.

"Mother of pearl!" Pawl exclaimed, as she held the stone up to the light. "If that's the kind of flotsam you can find on this beach, then maybe I *will* stay put."

She tucked the diamond into the pouch that held her lucky knucklebone. She knew that finding the Oma-stone was no coincidence, but beyond that, nothing was clear. Was it a token from Splash's Lord of The Lake, his way of letting her know that she was good to leave the island? Or did it perhaps pertain to a different aspect of her quest? If only the Bone-Man had not swaddled his thoughts in conundrums and riddles. If only he had favored her with a rare bit of plain talk. She immediately mocked herself for such a thought. Complaining about the Bone-Man's riddling was like complaining about water being wet. It was nothing more or less than his nature.

"All right, Lathwi," Pawl said. "If we're going somewhere today, let's get started. Otherwise, the suspense is going to drive me crazy."

And that, she thought, was Pawl's nature: always ready to go forward in spite of his fears. He should have been born a dragon. "You are right," she said. "It is time for us to go."

"What do I need to do?" he asked, in a less insistent tone.

"Just stand there," she told him, "and remember who you are. You may feel a little pain during the Change, but it will pass."

She stared at the swordmaster for a moment, imagining his new form down to the last details, and then began his transformation. His aura thickened into a haze which then swallowed him up. That magical cocoon began to shift and warp. Everything was going according to her Will and her Way—with one tiny exception. Everything was happening much *faster.* He went from two-legged to four-legged in the blink of an eye. His neck grew like a blade of grass beneath a midnight sun. This, with no extra effort on her part. Indeed, she was so relaxed, it felt as if she were working dream-magic.

In almost no time at all, the Change was complete. Pawl the man was gone, and Pawl the dragon stood in his place. As she watched, he shook off a load of stress with a shudder. An instant later, he swiveled his head toward his backside and touched his nose to the tip of his tail. The tail twitched. He stared. Lathwi smiled.

"Close your mouth, Pawl," she said. *"Dragons do not gape."*

He craned his head toward her, then rumbled a greeting. His eyes were the color of honey. The rest of him was bronze. *"I know you,"* he said, his first tentative attempt at dragon-speak. *"You are Lathwi."*

She nodded approvingly. *"How do you feel?"*

"Bigger," he thought at her. *"Everything else seems smaller. You have the most amazing eyes."* He flashed her an image of a cloudless azure sky. *"It would be very easy to get lost in them."*

Although Lathwi did not usually care for flattery, it gave her a small, unexpected thrill today. Handsome *and* charming, she mused to herself. What a pity that she would have to Change him back some day. But all she said was, *"This form suits you."*

"Really?" His chest puffed out. His wings snapped open. As he preened for her, muscles rippled beneath his scales. *"I think I like being a dragon."*

"Who would not?" she wondered, and then shooed him back toward the beach. *"Give me some room so I can work my transformation."*

But there was no work involved. An instant after she visualized her dragon-self, it became a reality. The Change happened so fast, it was virtually painless. And the fatigue that usually followed on the heels of such a significant expenditure of power never kicked in. Indeed, she could not recall a time when she had felt stronger or more energized. She had the sense that, in a pinch, she could turn everybody in Compara into dragons.

What was going on here?

"Lathwi," Pawl said, as he lumbered toward her. *"The form suits you, too."*

She extended her neck, then touched noses with him. *"I am glad you are coming with me,"* she said. *"Now into the sky with you. We must be off."*

With a Word, she summoned a friendly breeze. It filled her wings, then lofted her into the sky. A moment later, she was soaring over the lake with Pawl in close pursuit.

"How are you faring?" she wondered. *"Are you afraid?"*

In response, he trumpeted his joy. She answered with a roar of her own. At that moment, they were a pair of dragons in flight; and for that moment, nothing else mattered or sufficed.

෨ ෬

They flew throughout the day—nonstop, because they could not find so much as a sandbar on which to land. Now, as dusk loomed on the horizon, spilling its colors across the lake, they hitched a ride on the back of a friendly thermal wind and searched for land. They needed to stop and rest for the night. They needed to eat. Leastwise, Pawl did. To Lathwi's amazement, she still felt as fresh as she had back on the Bone-Man's isle, even after managing *two* transformations *and* a day's flight. If she'd been traveling alone, she probably would not have even thought about stopping this early in the evening.

But she had to consider Pawl, too.

He had come a long way on his first day as a dragon, farther than she would have asked him to under normal circumstances. He had made no complaint over the miles, but such a sustained effort was starting to take its toll. His triangular face was taut with focus and fatigue. His wingstrokes were floppy instead of crisp. If they did not find land soon, he was apt to fall asleep in mid-flap and do a nosedive into the lake.

Even as that half-comic, half-upsetting image took shape in her mind, she caught her first glimpse of Lake Random's western shoreline. It was a welcome change of sight after a day of nothing but water: a rugged, twilight-tinged ribbon of glacier rubble. Lathwi directed Pawl's attention to a patch of isolated beach.

"We can sleep there for the night," she told him.

"I thought we were bound for Death's Door."

She responded with the mental equivalent of a shrug. *"It will be easier to find by day. Besides—"* She projected a tasty-looking image of a scarimund at him. *"Are you not hungry?"*

He sent her a stark image of emptiness that killed any lingering doubts she might have had about stopping. She angled herself toward the ground and began her descent. He followed on her tail. But this was his very first landing, and weariness had rendered him clumsy. So while she touched down on the beach with barely a sound, he splashed down in the shallows and then hissed a warning when she rumbled with amusement.

"At least I do not punish you when you make a mistake," she said, chasing the thought with the memory of her first lesson in swordplay. On that occasion, and on many others afterward, Pawl had cracked her in the shins with his stave every single time she failed to do *exactly* as he said.

He curled his lip at her, then flopped on his belly in the sand. He looked so tired, and so comical, she could not help but take pity on him. *"Stay there and rest,"* she said. *"I will find you something to eat."*

Thinking of Masque and all of the fish that it had caught just off-shore, she turned toward Lake Random. It looked almost sinister in the waning moments of twilight, like a great pool of liquid darkness. But it wasn't the water's appearance that gave her pause, but rather, a reluctance to get her feet wet. She was warm and dry. She wanted to stay that way.

So she baited a tendril of her Will with a morsel of power and then cast it into the lake.

Something struck almost immediately. With a thought, she hooked it by the gills and then gave her Will a tug. A fish as big as a yearling bull came arcing out of the water and toward the beach. A heartbeat later, it was flopping for its life under Pawl's nose. If he found anything peculiar about that, he did not let it show. Indeed, he barely batted an eyelid before crushing the grouper's skull with his jaws. After that, all he showed was his appetite. Lathwi rumbled at that, then cast her Will into the lake again. Although she did not feel hungry, she knew she had to feed to maintain her body's well-being.

Her second catch of the day was a smaller steakfish. She did not care for its rich, dusky pink flesh, or the low-tide smell, but she ate as much of it as she could stomach just the same. Every bite that went sliding past her teeth seemed to immediately convert itself into energy. By the time she was done feeding, she felt bloated and too large for her skin. She had rather enjoyed the feeling this morning. But now it was starting to alarm her. Of a mind to discuss her newfound puissance, she rejoined Pawl. He was curled up in a ball now, and looking much more relaxed.

"Something is happening to me," she said, as she curled up alongside of him. *"I am becoming more powerful by the minute."*

"I cannot say the same," he replied, slurring the thought as if he were drunk. He yawned, and then nestled his chin in the hollow between her shoulder-blades. The image he was giving off was cozy and dark. *"Sorry."*

An instant later, he was asleep.

It was such a dragon-like thing to do, she could not even hold it against him.

℘ ○ ℘

Morning dawned, cool and overcast. Fog from the lake cloaked everything in a fleecy, gray haze. Lathwi woke first, with the abruptness of a firecracker going off. After an entire night's rest, she felt as potent as a small sun. She nosed Pawl, then nudged him out of his dreams with a thought.

"Lazy dragon."

"Tired dragon," he countered irritably, and pulled himself into an exclusive knot. *"Let me sleep."*

"I am leaving now," she said. *"I will not be back. If you do not leave with me, you will probably spend the rest of your life as a dragon."*

A month ago, that threat would have had him on his feet in an instant. Today, it was a much slower goad. *"Worse fates could befall me,"* he told her, as he rolled onto his back. *"Like dying before my time. Or living without you."*

This time, his hybrid charm provoked a different reaction from her—playfulness instead of pride. So, without another word, she unfurled her wings and launched herself into the sky. The fog engulfed her immediately. As she winged her way toward the open sky, she strewed a thought in her wake.

"Call me if you need help getting off the ground. Lazy dragons often do."

An offended roar welled up from the fog. She bared her teeth in a dragon's grin and kept on going. As she ascended, the fog thinned into a delicate mist that gave rise to a garden of rainbows. Lathwi was so enchanted by the sight, she did not notice the great, winged shadow that had closed in over her head until a Voice boomed like thunder in her head.

"Do you seek to challenge me?"

She veered to her left to avoid flying with the dragon who had positioned himself in her flight-path. He was huge—a rust-colored dragonsire of awe-inspiring proportions. Although this was the first time Lathwi had seen him in person, she recognized him as Bij The Mighty from her mother's memories. She had forgotten that this was his domain.

"No, Magnificent One," she said, offering him an exaggerated image of himself because she needed his good will and he had always responded well to Taziem's flattery. *"I know I am no match for your—"*

Before she had a chance to finish the thought, Pawl broke through the fog-bank like an overgrown crossbow bolt. And before she had a chance to stop him, he inserted himself between her and Bij, and struck an aggressive pose. She hissed, highly annoyed. Just when human intelligence was called for, Pawl had succumbed to pure, dumb, dragon instinct. She hissed again. At times like this, she almost missed the man who used to fall faint at the mere thought of dragons.

Almost.

"Stand down!" she urged him, and then hastened to placate Bij. *"We have not come to challenge you, Mighty One. We are hunting a human who is in league with Galza."*

"Galza is dead," Bij said. *"My chosen, Taziem The Learned One, told me so."*

"I believed so, too," she said. *"But—"*

Once again, Pawl let instinct overpower his common sense. *"Let us by, Old One. Our business is urgent."*

The dragonsire scorned him with a look, then flicked him in the nose with the tip of his tail. The blow was meant to be insulting. So was the thought that accompanied it. *"You are a stupid runt. Your mother should have eaten you at birth. Since she did not, it falls to me to put you out of your misery. I do not think you will be much of a challenge."*

Roaring defiance, Pawl launched himself at the dragonsire. Bij danced away from the attack, then slashed at Pawl's underbelly in passing. A golden welt rose up on Pawl's inner thigh: first blood, the price of inexperience. Moments later, Bij drew second blood, then third. The wounds were minor, mere tokens of contempt. But Lathwi knew that the sire would soon tire of its game and then tear his smaller opponent to shreds. She did not want that to happen. But she was not sure she ought to intervene, either. Bij had issued a formal challenge; Pawl had responded to it. That was the way of dragons. Interference in such matters was not. Maybe, despite all her maneuvering, the Bone-Man's prediction was about to come true.

Maybe. Maybe not. All she knew was that he did not stand a chance against Bij. He was scored in a half-dozen places now, and his wingstrokes were growing frantic. If she did not do something soon, he was going to die.

And that something would have to be magic. Nothing else about her was going to have any impact on a dragonsire as mighty as Bij. But while she was nearly bursting with potential, she felt a curious reluctance to invoke it. A part of her worried that she was too powerful now, a danger to all instead of a select few. Another part feared that once she tapped into it, it would spill from her like once-dammed waters until it was all gone. She did not want that to happen.

But it looked like she was going to have to take that chance. Pawl was oozing blood from a dozen scratches now, and starting to lose altitude. Bij was circling him like a famished vulture. She scowled, poised on the brink of decision. But even as she made her mind up to go to Pawl's aid, a Voice impinged on her thoughts. It was fringed with surprise and relief.

"Lathwi?"

"Taziem?" she replied, equally amazed. At her mother's mental nod, she asked, *"Where are you?"*

"Look to the north."

Lathwi craned her neck in that direction, but for a long moment, all she could see was a thick band of heat undulating on the horizon. Then a fast-moving speck appeared above the haze. It was joined by another, then another, and then many more. She could not contain her amazement. Such a swarm had not been since the last days of Ever-Light.

"I tried to Call you some time ago," Taziem said, *"but I could not form a link. Where have you been?"*

"It is not a story quickly told," Lathwi replied, *"so I will tell it later. Can you tell me what goes on here?"*

"I have gathered an army to destroy an army," Taziem said, with just a hint of smug triumph. *"Where are the dragonslayers hiding?"*

An image of Veeder's valley leapt to mind. But even as she transmitted it to her mother, Pawl let out a pained roar. She looked his way to see him spiraling toward the ground with Bij in close pursuit. The sire had given up his game at last, and was going in for the kill.

"Mother!" Lathwi said, suffering a stroke of desperate inspiration. *"Call Bij. He will not let us pass."*

The presence in her head withdrew only to re-insert itself a moment later. *"I have Called. He comes to me."*

And so it was. Bij was winging his way toward the specks in the distance, leaving Pawl to live or die on his own. Because the challenge was over, and because he was still falling out of the sky, Lathwi disregarded her fears and Willed Pawl a bit of her newfound potential. An instant later, he pulled out of his nosedive. She turned her thoughts back to Taziem.

"What will you do when Bij gets there?" she asked.

"I do not know," Taziem said. *"Perhaps I can talk him into joining my army."*

"Perhaps," Lathwi replied, lacing the thought with doubts. *"While you try, I will be on my way. I will meet you in the valley of the dragonslayers as soon as I am done with Galza and her mage."*

"Good hunting to you," Taziem said.

"And to you as well."

The swarm was taking on size and details now. Huge wingspans, long necks, tails trailing in the wind: it was a sight to gladden the eye and heart. She roared to celebrate its existence, then rounded on Pawl as he came flying toward her. Judging by the ease of his wingstrokes, he had his strength back. His wounds were all healed as well. An hour ago, she would have marveled at her potency, for she had accomplished far more than she had intended with that tiny pulse of Will. But at the moment, she was too furious to care how powerful she had become.

"What were you thinking, challenging a full-grown sire on your first day with wings?" she demanded.

"You are my Chosen," he replied, a thought chocked with infantile pride and male bravado. *"No one may threaten you, not even the mightiest sire."*

She hissed at him. *"Instinct is a handy thing for a dragon to have, Pawl, but do not let it rule your every move. Otherwise, you will forget who you are, and go wild."*

"Would that be such a bad thing?" he asked, grinning at her like a mischievous youngling.

"Wild dragons are stupid dragons," she said scornfully. *"I do not keep that kind of company."*

His nostrils flared as if he had finally caught a whiff of his danger in the air. At the same time, the playfulness drained from his eyes. The next thing she knew, she was glaring at one very self-aware—and very contrite—dragon. *"You are right,"* he said, *"I was starting to forget myself. It will not happen again."* He paused as if he were not sure if he should go on, and then added, *"I was seized by a need to impress you."*

"I know."

He flashed her an image of Taziem's army. *"Are we going to join them?"*

"No. Our fortune awaits us elsewhere."

"Good," he said. *"I have no wish to be anywhere near that sire ever again."*

"Smart dra—" she began, only to cut herself off with a scandalized hiss. *"Pawl! Are those* people *I see with those dragons?"*

She squinted, trying to see past the ridiculous illusion, but her eyes had not been fooled. At least a score of dragons were carrying men with them. Even little Masque had one. And it was clear that these men were passengers, not a snack. She shook her head, trying to rid herself of the disbelieving buzz in her ears. Men and dragons—cooperating? Taziem obviously had a rich tale to tell as well.

A roar followed on the heels of that thought—a terrible, furious sound. Both she and Pawl instinctively shied away from it even though it was not aimed at them.

"Why is he so angry?" Pawl asked.

"He must *have seen the humans,"* she said. In response to Pawl's continuing puzzlement, she added, *"Bij* hates *people."*

"I wonder what he will do."

"As do I. But as I said, our fortunes lie elsewhere. So let us go."

They went.

Chapter 20

*T*aziem was tired. Her wounded leg ached. And the sun was beating down on her back in a most unpleasant way. Under ordinary circumstances, she would've given in to her complaints and gone aground in the hope of finding a patch of shade where she could rest and wait out the hottest part of the day. But there was nothing ordinary about today's circumstances. Today, she had an entire swarm of dragons at her back: her two surviving tanglemates, Rue and Ruin; a score of their offspring; and a score more of her own brood, including Haqqaq, Zephyr, Brystle, and Masque. All of them had answered her Call. All of them had seen the need to join together and destroy Galza's dragonslayers.

And—all of them had agreed to bring humans with them.

There were significantly more dragons than men. Indeed, the majority of her army was empty-handed. But those dragons who *did* have passengers did not seem to mind them. Haqqaq carried Santana like a trophy. Luke could hardly be seen against Ruin's massive chest. Taziem glanced down at her own passenger: Jamus. After an initial bit of distress, he had settled down quite nicely—so nicely, in fact, that he was drowsing in her arms at the moment. She supposed she should be carrying her new fosterling, Mim, in his stead, for while she was in dragon form, the child was the only one who could speak with both races. But the human side of her wanted Jamus—just in case another opportunity to seduce him presented itself. For she was not used to being rebuffed. It was a curious, not entirely pleasant experience, like an itch that was just beyond reach. She wanted to see if she could get this sad-eyed, golden-haired man to scratch that special place. She wanted to test his limits.

Besides, this joint expedition had been his idea. It was only right that he co-lead it.

A Voice intruded on her thoughts. The self-image that accompanied it belonged to Masque. *"Mother,"* it said, *"we are approaching the lake where I last saw Lathwi. Shall we stop and look for her?"*

The tail-end of that thought was fringed with weariness—and for good reason. The youngling had been carrying Mim since Timberton. *A little one for a little one*, it had said, and would not pass her on to another dragon. And Taziem had to admit, they seemed to be getting along quite well. She toyed with the thought of sending them to the lake. They would be safer there, far from the slaughter. And if they *did* find Lathwi, so much the better. But even as the idea took shape in her mind, a distant roar disrupted it. All of a sudden, every dragon in the swarm was thinking the same thing.

Who was that?

Sharp-eyed Masque was the first to see the trio of dots in the distant sky. One of them was enormous. The other two—were not. Taziem strained her eyes, trying to force more resolution out of them, but they refused to cooperate. Once again, Masque came to her aid.

"It's Lathwi, Mother!" it exclaimed. *"Lathwi and two drakes. I think they are fighting over her."*

Without a moment's hesitation, Taziem made contact. *"Lathwi?"*

"Taziem?" her fosterling replied, sounding equally amazed. *"Where are you?"*

"Look to the north," she said. Then, as Lathwi's perceptions shifted, she added, *"I tried to Call you some time ago, but I could not form a link. Where have you been?"*

"It is not a story quickly told," Lathwi said, *"so I will tell it later. Can you tell me what goes with you?"*

"I have gathered an army to destroy an army," Taziem said. *"Where are the dragonslayers hiding?"*

An image of a narrow, wooded valley took shape in her mind only to disintegrate as a pained roar rolled across the sky. An instant later, Lathwi blurted, *"Mother! Call Bij. He will not let us pass."*

Reacting to the urgency in her fosterling's Voice, Taziem immediately did as she was told. *"Bij!"* she said, flashing an image of herself to her long-time mate. *"I require your presence. Come to me."*

His responding thought was rife with confusion. *"Taziem? What are you doing here? Is it your Season? Why did you not Call sooner?"*

"Come now. I will answer your questions when you get here."

He did not deign to acknowledge the obvious. Instead, he got his bearings from her thoughts and went streaking toward her.

"What will you do when he gets there?" Lathwi asked.

"I do not know," Taziem admitted. *"Perhaps I can talk him into joining my army."*

"Perhaps." The thought was riddled with doubts. *"While you try, I will be on my way. I will meet you in the valley of the dragonslayers as soon as I am done with Galza and her mage."*

"Good hunting to you," Taziem said.

"And to you as well."

Bij was closing in on the swarm already—and growing larger and angrier-looking by the wingstroke. As he closed in, Taziem had both time and cause to worry. By now, her Chosen would be half-crazed about all the dragons in his territory. And when he saw what the dragons had with them—

A roar shook the air like a monstrous thunderclap—a definitive completion of the thought. And Bij's already furious mindset went soaring into the realm of the truly wild.

"Humans?" he raged. *"You have humans with you? Tell me you are going to eat them."*

She made no reply. But in the innermost compartment of her mind, a place where she alone had ears, she grumbled at fortune's capriciousness. In a territory as vast as this, it should have been easy to avoid one semi-stupid dragon.

"Did I hear thunder?" Jamus asked, stirring back to wakefulness. A moment later, he sputtered a curse. "Sweet, suffering Dreamer! Who's that big red bastard? Please tell me he's on our side."

Even if she could've somehow told him who that big red bastard was, she would not have done so. Because what she had to say about Bij would only frighten him, and a frightened man was the last thing she wanted on her hands just now. She shifted her grip on him, trying to keep him out of Bij's sight. If she had just a little bit more time, she would have set him on the ground before Calling Bij. Or, if she had been quicker-witted, she would have given him over to some other dragon. But there had been no time, and she did not think as fast when she was weary, so she would simply have to deal with the situation as it had unfolded.

Bij was only a few dragon-lengths away from her now. His musk was a blend of fury, confusion, and a sulfuric need to dominate.

"Drop that thing," he demanded, picturing Jamus as a lump of dragon droppings. *"Drop it now, or I will disown you as my Chosen."*

"This man is under my protection," she said, turning so her own substantial mass separated Bij and Jamus. *"I may not drop him for all the Oma-stones in the world."*

"Then you are my Chosen no more."

He slammed into her—a hard but glancing blow that forced her to swerve toward the ground. Jamus tensed like a newborn prey-beast whose one chance of survival hinges on its ability to stay perfectly still. Bij doubled around and sideswiped her again. Taziem rumbled her displeasure.

"It would appear that your Chosen bears you some ill-will," her tanglemate, Ruin, observed. *"Shall I challenge him for you?"*

"No," she said. For while she had no further use for Bij, she did not want to see him—or her tanglemate—come to harm. *"I have been able to talk some sense back into him in years past. It may be that I can do so again. If*

nothing else, that will keep him occupied while you and the rest of the swarm to continue on to the valley."

"As you wish," Ruin said, and then veered westward just as Bij bumped her again.

"Shit," Jamus said.

Had she been able to, she would have agreed. As it was, though, all she could do was snap at Bij in passing and then manage her descent. She cut through a decaying layer of fog, then followed the scent of water to a lake as blue as Lathwi's eyes. The shoreline spanned as far as the eye could see in both directions. Most of it was too rocky to permit a landing, but she spotted a small strip of beach in the near distance. She set down there, then dumped Jamus like a sack of feed and hastily scratched a message into the still-cool sand.

SHOW NO FEAR. AND DO NOT DO ANYTHING STUPID.

Jamus swallowed hard, then got behind her. Moments later, Bij's landing churned up a sharp-toothed blizzard of sand and water. He was all but frothing at the muzzle now. His eyes were the sulfurous color of dragon blood. It was all too easy for Taziem to read his thoughts. They were all violent, and they all involved images of a pale, golden-haired man.

"Where is it?" he demanded. *"Give it to me now, and I will consider taking you back as my Chosen."*

"Bij," she said, slapping him with his own Name, *"did you not hear me earlier? I have guaranteed his safety."*

He roared with fury and frustration. In his mind, he had Jamus by the neck, and was shaking him into gory parts and pieces. *"How did he trick such a promise out of you?"*

She hissed, offended by the suggestion. *"He played no trick. I made the offer of my own free will."*

He roared again. *"Why would the Learned One do something so stupid?"*

"Stupid?" she huffed, even more offended now. *"You think me stupid? He is an enemy to Galza. And the enemy of an enemy is a friend."*

"Galza is dead. You said so yourself."

"I was wrong, Bij-ling," she said, straining for patience that was slow to come. *"Look, here are my memories. Try to see beyond your obsession."*

She opened her mind to him, just as she had so many times in the past. Back then, she had done it gladly, out of a desire to share. Now she was doing it out of pure desperation.

∞ α

Bij waded into his once-Chosen's thoughts with little regard for her comfort. He was furious with her—so furious, he could barely think. Not only had she befriended one of those smelly, land-wasting vermin, she had carried it into *his* territory. And her excuse was laughable. Galza, indeed. How dumb did she think he was?

Through her eyes, he watched as humans gutted one of his spawn. Its death did not rouse him. As far as he was concerned, one less youngling in the world was one less competitor. And as for that pebble that the dragonslayers had pulled out of its gizzard—well, what of it? Maybe it *was* Galza's. But maybe—it was not. The world was full of ugly red stones. The only thing that connected it to Galza was Taziem. And if she could be wrong once, she could be wrong again. And again. And again. Maybe she had some sort of brain-sickness. That would explain her unwholesome affinity for humans.

"There is nothing *wrong with my brain,"* she said.

A desire swelled within him then, the desire to play with her just as he had played with that bronze runt earlier. So he peeled his lips back in a display of sweet reason, and said, *"So you say. But I saw no army of dragonslayers among your memories. That suggests that one does not exist."*

Taziem hissed at him—a familiar sound. *"Your logic is sloppy, Bij-ling. You did not see the army, because* I *have not seen it yet. But not seeing a thing does not mean that the thing does not exist."*

Her frustration triggered a jolt of visceral satisfaction within him. He enjoyed the feeling so much, he hastened to experience it again. *"Very well, let us say that Galza is* still alive. *And let us also say that this army of dragonslayers* does *exist. That still does not explain the humans. Did you bring them along so you could drop them on Galza's minions?"* He rumbled, appreciating the image of bodies falling on bodies that came to his mind. *"That would almost be a sight worth seeing."*

"These men serve as a symbol of unity between our two races," she said, and he could tell by the sharpness of the thought that she was struggling to keep impatience at bay. *"If we did not have them with us, people would mistake our attack on Galza's army for predatory behavior."*

He rustled his wings, a show of unconcern. *"What of it?"*

She rewarded him with another spike of frustration. *"Like it or not, Bij, men are part of this world. And like it or not, they are here to stay. If we do not find a way to co-exist, we dragons may eventually go the way of the Ever-Light."*

The images that accompanied the scolding were of abandoned nests, empty skies, and vast territories left undefended. Bij refused to take her forecast of extinction to heart, but he could not completely ignore it, either. Taziem was the Learned One. It was her lot in life to know things that others did not. He rumbled, a thwarted sound, then snapped at her nose like a petulant youngling.

"You think you are so smart," he said, *"but you do not know everything yet. And you should have asked me before bringing humans into my territory."*

"You are right," she said. *"I should have asked."* As he savored that surprising admission, she went on to add, *"Therefore, I am asking now. Will you, Bij the Mighty, allow me to transport humans into battle against the dragonslayers? I promise by the power of my Name that I will take them back to their own lands as soon as the battle is won."*

Disbelief exploded within him, touching off a private firestorm of bitterness and rage. In all the time that he had been her mate, Taziem had never once made a promise with such little regard for her own convenience. That she had done so now, on behalf of a race that befouled every little thing that it touched, offended him to the very core of his being. It was perverse. Outrageous. Utterly unacceptable. Instinct urged him to strike at his treacherous once-Chosen, but he was smarter than that. She had been full-grown for centuries now, and had no soft spots left—

Leastwise, not on her body.

A new game sprung to his mind. Without a second thought, he put it into play.

o

"Let me see your man," Bij said, projecting earnestness. When Taziem balked, he went on to say, *"I won't hurt it. I promise. I am curious, is all. I have never seen a man from this distance, leastwise not one that was still alive. I believe the experience will be good for me."*

His request dumfounded her. She would never have expected him to ask such a thing—or make to such a promise. *Let me see your man.* She snuck a peek at his mind, suspicious of his motives, but all she sensed was an excited sort of expectation—as if Bij did indeed believe that he could get something out of the encounter. The possibility made her giddy. Could it be that she had finally convinced him to reject his obsession? It must be so! He had promised, had he not? And because of that promise, she could not rightly refuse him. That would be an insult of immense proportions, one that would precipitate a challenge. Where would Jamus be then?

"Stay there," she told Bij. *"I will fetch the human."*

≈ ≈

Jamus' bowels were squirming like a sack of fresh-caught snakes.

Just a few minutes ago, he would have sworn on his mother's grave that dangling above the clouds while two of the biggest dragons that he had ever seen confronted each other was *the* most terrifying experience that a man could have. But now he believed that being stuck on the ground with nowhere to run while those same two dragons confronted each other again was more terrifying still. He felt so helpless cowering in

Taz's shadow, like a toothless pup with human memories. Every time she shifted, he damn near jumped out of his skin. And every time that big red bastard made a sound, he came a little closer to shitting himself.

Sweet, suffering Dreamer! How did he get himself into these predicaments?

Taz shifted again, spooking him out of his thoughts. The next thing he knew, she was standing nose to nose with him. Her amber eyes were unreadable. Her bearing was equally vague.

"What's he want, Taz?" he whispered.

She erased the first message she had scratched for him with a swipe of a forearm, then replaced it with a second communication.

BIJ WANTS TO MEET YOU.

"Great," he muttered to himself. "Just great."

Apparently, she mistook his sarcasm for consent, for she nudged him in the other dragon's direction. He swallowed a hard lump of fear. As it went down, it turned his feet to lead weights. She nudged him again, more insistently this time, making it clear that the matter had already been decided for him. Faced with this stunning lack of options, all he could do was put on his bravest face and venture forth to meet this pain in the ass named Bij.

The drake hissed as he stepped into view. A moment later, its head came snaking toward him. Its jaws were open. Its dagger-like teeth were surprisingly white. It snapped at him, once and then again, coming within mere inches of his nose each time. His breath caught in his throat like a sliver of bone. At the same time, he recalled his encounter with the calico dragon, and what Taz had said afterward: *it will respect you more for having stood up to it.* So he balled his trembling hand into a trembling fist; and when the drake struck at Jamus a third time, he punched him hard on the nose.

Bij roared. Taz roared, too. An instant later, Jamus' world became a bottomless pit of rich, red blood and pain.

☙ ❧

Bij gloated to himself as the human stepped into view. What a puny, ugly thing it was. He was going to enjoy scaring it into losing control over its bowels. Taziem would know what a truly loathsome thing it was then and realize just how wrong she had been to befriend it. Once she came to her senses, she would want him to accept her as his Chosen again. Indeed, he could barely wait for her to ask. Because sex was her soft spot. And that was how he was going to make her suffer. He was never, ever going to dance for her again.

The first time he menaced the human, it turned deliciously pale. The second time, he heard its guts loosen and knew that it was on the verge of humiliation. So he snapped at it a third time, never thinking that it would lash out and box his nose in return.

Fury blazed to new life in Bij—an inferno so hot and wild, it consumed all reason and restraint. All that remained was pure, unfettered hate. He struck again. A roar filled his ears. Red blood filled his mouth. Yet even as he gloried in the salty-sweet taste of it, he returned to reason and realized what he had done.

An instant later, he could not move.

ЄОСЯ

"Bij!" Taziem roared. *"No!"*

But she was too late. He was already drawing back from his strike. Jamus' right arm and shoulder were mangled—a ragged mass of hemorrhaging flesh. For one stunned moment, disbelief held her spellbound. Then panic slung her into action.

With a vicious crack of her Will, she froze Bij in his tracks before he could strike again. Then she Changed herself to her human form and rushed to Jamus' side. Blood was pumping from his wounds; his lips were starting to turn blue. She clasped his hand. It was limp and cool. Even so, she refused to accept what common sense was telling her. He was going to live. She was going to see to it.

Fortunately, Lathwi had taught her many tricks.

ЄОСЯ

Jamus was dying. He knew that. Some last fragment of his shattered awareness told him so. The process was not as traumatic as he had imagined it would be.

There was surprisingly little pain. He had gone numb almost immediately—from shock, he supposed dreamily. Now everything was growing cold in a comfortable sort of way. He shut his eyes, or at least it felt that way. He could still see things. There he was as a boy, playing soldier games with a gangly country-lad named Pawl. And over yonder stood his mother, weeping for pride and joy as Wynn Rame sang his praises at a banquet that was being held in his honor. He saw the faces of women whom he had bedded: Julia the chambermaid, his first; Fleur, the baker's daughter who smelled like warm bread; an entire procession of others. But even as these appeared to him, they were eclipsed by an image of the only woman whom he had ever truly loved.

Ah, Liselle.

Her heart-shaped face was hovering above him now. Her hand was reaching out of the sky to stroke his cheek. In his day, he had done more than his share of things that no decent man could take pride in. But the only mistake that he thoroughly regretted was never openly declaring his love for his quick-witted, sharp-tongued sorceress. So he did it now, over and over and over again.

Love you, Liselle. Love you.

He was out of breath now. He gasped, trying to fill his lungs, but only caught the tail-end of an feeble sip. He tried again, harder this time. His chest refused to rise.

Sweet Dreamer. This was it. The end.

A spasm of sheer animal instinct urged him to try and claw his way back over the threshold that he had just crossed. At the same moment, the image of Liselle that he had been embracing in his thoughts became a tangible presence. Her hand was outstretched. Her eyes were brimming with ghostly tears.

"Come to me, my poor, dear love," she said, in a tone as bittersweet as her smile. "We will go to the Dreamer together."

The thought of being with his beloved again smothered the panic that had welled up within him. He stopped fighting for air that would not come and reached for her hand instead. As he did so, the bonds between him and this world began to unravel—a soft, painless process like a worn cotton seam finally giving way. He grew lighter, then lighter still. Liselle's aura began to gleam bright white. But just as he was about to float into her waiting arms, something caught him from behind and hauled him back into his body. He tried to escape this unseen hook, but it held fast. And when he tried to beg Liselle for her help, he learned that he still had no breath.

She did not seem to notice his distress. She had gone perfectly still, as if she were trying to eavesdrop on a conversation between two fleas. And when, at last, she abandoned that pose, she turned wide-eyed and fluttery with alarm.

"Hurry, Jamus," she said, thrusting her hand at him like an impatient mother with a dawdling child. "We do not have much time."

"I cannot," he replied, hoping that she could read his thoughts. *"Go without me."*

"No-o!" she howled, and then abruptly disappeared.

Now Jamus was alone in a slow-spreading darkness. It was very cold now, and he could not breathe. And yet he would not die.

Chapter 21

*V*eeder's valley was deserted when Lathwi and Pawl got there. The rows of tents were gone, the animal pens empty. The only thing stirring was the wind among the trees.

"I was afraid this might happen," Pawl said, as they circled overhead. *"Veeder must've broken camp as soon as he found out we got away. My guess is he's heading north to start his campaign while he's still got surprise on his side. It should be easy enough to track him, though. A mob like that tramples everything in its path."*

"I do not need to track him," Lathwi said, veering north toward a flat-faced mountain. *"The one I am looking for is still here."*

"How do you know?"

"I can hear him."

Indeed, the residues of Seth's magic were so vile and discordant, she would not have been surprised if Pawl had sensed them, too—him and every other creature unlucky enough to have ears. The space right behind her eyes ached because of it. And it felt like her nose wanted to bleed. But Pawl swore he heard nothing but the wind.

They spiraled down to a small, forest-hemmed clearing near the mountain. There, with little more than a thought, she Changed into her human form. One moment, she was comfortably perched on four legs and a tail; the next, she was pitched precariously upright on two. She had been taught—and taught well—that sorcery should not come easy. But she had to admit, such facility made life *very* convenient.

"You next," she said, flashing Pawl an image of his former self.

He deflected the thought with a shake of his head. *"I will stay a dragon for now. I can protect your back better in this form."*

"But if something goes wrong—" She deliberately let the thought trail off into nothingness. *"No one else can restore you to your former self."*

He shrugged. *"I'll take my chances."*

She was not inclined to argue the matter further, for he was right. A dragon *was* better protection than a man. So she gave the underside of his muzzle a fond scratch, and then went searching for the onion-shaped opening in the mountain's side. It was not hard to find. The passageway's graveyard reek had grown much stronger in her short absence. She would have been able to track it at night, with her eyes closed, just by using her nose. And those with more delicate sensibilities only had to look for ghosts.

Pawl saw them before she did: a river of milky-gray shadows streaming from the mountain's side like breath on a frosty morning. At first, he thought it was smoke or even steam from a lava tube or hot springs. But he did not smell smoke. Or water. Or sulfur. Then he realized that the river was streaming against the wind. And then he realized that the river was made of spirits. He shook his head, amazed by the sheer numbers.

"So many unhomed," he said, tingeing the thought with pity. *"And for no good reason. I am glad you are going to punish the person responsible."*

"I am not going to punish him," she said. *"I am going to kill him."*

The entrance to Death's Door loomed ahead of them. Lathwi narrowed her eyes at the darkness beyond and said, *"If a slight, red-haired man emerges from this place before I do, bite his head off."* The accompanying image was graphic. *"If my mother arrives, point her in Veeder's direction."*

He acknowledged her instructions with a rumble, and then touched noses with her. *"Maintain proper balance,"* he said, which was one of the very first things he had taught her about swordplay.

"Call me if you have need," she said, and then she continued on her way.

The passageway was as pitch-black as she remembered it, but this time, she did not have to feel her way along its cool, damp walls. She could see in the dark now, just like a cat. And Seth's psychic profanities drew her ever forward, like fish-hooks in the brain. If nothing else, his death would put an end to those appalling sounds. And at this point, that was not the least of her reasons for wanting to kill him.

A gap in the darkness loomed ahead. Ghosts were rushing forth from it as if in panic. Within, she could hear Seth screaming in a raw, almost strangled voice. "I don't care *how* weak you are. Find her, or we're finished for good."

A ghost brushed against Lathwi's face. It felt like a cobweb—gossamer soft and slightly sticky. She batted it aside with a negligent wave, then stepped into the stronghold like an invited guest only to gag at the smell. Fresh blood, burning torches, rotting flesh: the combination was enough to turn even a grave-robber's stomach. She did not know how Seth could bear it.

The necromage was standing before the altar that he had erected on the edge of the chasm. The altar bore a body wrapped in shabby linens. The ground beneath it was littered with Seth's victims. As Lathwi watched, he grabbed one of these by the hair on its head and abruptly slashed its throat.

"There!" he howled, as blood spurted into the abyss. "Is that what you needed? Find her, damn you! And bring her back."

Ghosts continued to stream out of the chasm. One trailed its insubstantial fingers through Lathwi's hair and cried, *"Hurry, hurry!"* as it passed. And indeed, she saw no reason to delay the moment any longer. Seth had done more than enough to deserve his death and anything else that that feckless Dreamer cared to impose on him for plundering her Keep. The atrocity must stop. She grabbed the hilt of her sword only to release it again because Seth had claimed that he could not be killed by steel. And while that might well be another of his non-magical illusions, she made a habit of assuming the worst. That left less to chance. And there was more than one way to kill a man. So she marched right up to the still-ranting mage and seized him roughly by the scruff of the neck.

"Wha—?" Seth sputtered. The slipstream of ghosts froze for a moment, and then began to decay. He tried to re-establish the link between himself and the Door, but it had slammed shut because of his lapse in concentration. As soon as he realized that, he let out a howl that filled the chamber with despair. "No-o! Oh, Ylana!" A moment later, he went as stiff as a plank in her grip. In a cold, quiet voice that contrasted sharply with his earlier ranting, he said, "That was my last hope of getting her back, stranger. And you're going to die for ruining it."

"I think not, Milord," Lathwi said, and spun him around to face her.

"Oh," he said, as he set eyes on her, and his voice flattened like a mad dog's ears. "Look who's here." He glared at her for a long moment, allowing her to get a good look at his face. Two long, parallel gashes scored the flesh beneath each of his eyes now. The tip of his nose was gone, too. That made him look very peculiar indeed. "Do you like the new look?" he asked. "Veeder gave it to me for shepherding a spy into his camp." Then he locked eyes with her and said, "Do you have any idea what I'd like to do to you right about now?"

An instant after he posed the question, he sent a mass of ill-gotten power her way. She deflected it with the merest of smiles. His eyes widened with surprise only to narrow as comprehension set in.

"I knew there was something extraordinary about you from the moment we first met," he said, in the flippant tones of a man who has nothing to lose. "I just couldn't put a finger on what that something was." He tipped his head back as if he were trying to see her better. "However did you manage to hide the fact that you're a sorceress?"

"Sometimes, the best hiding places are right out in the open," she said. Then she hoisted him up by the front of his robe and held him over the abyss. "Can scorpions fly, I wonder?"

"Not the last time I checked," he said, striving for his usual half-dry, half-mocking tone. "But before you drop me, answer me this: Why am I the one dangling over oblivion instead of Veeder? He's the one who's on his way to rape your homeland."

"The general intends to challenge other people for their territory," she replied. "I can understand that, for that is the way of dragons. But you—" She curled her lip at the horrors she had seen here. "You do terrible things of your own free will."

"That's not true," he blurted, and then waxed sullen. "I had no choice."

She shook him as if to jar the truth loose. "No choice, Milord? You could have turned a deaf ear to Galza when She first started whispering at you, but you did not. You could have abandoned Her teachings when they called for sacrifices of blood and life, but you did not. Instead, you went further and further down that path, knowing all along that it was going to get darker and darker still—"

"It was the only way," he shouted, and then glanced at his sister with a desperate, not-quite-rational, yearning in his eyes. "It was the only way to get Ylana back."

Lathwi followed his gaze back to the shrouded body on the altar. That was the last bit of the puzzle—and the final horror. He had spilled an ocean of human blood and murdered at least two of her tanglemates in the misbegotten hope of reanimating a corpse. The wrongness of such an ambition made her feel as if she were wallowing in excrement. She lost all desire to hold him aloft. But even as she decided to let him drop, a fluttering in the space above the chasm distracted her. An instant later, that fluttering took on faint substance: Liselle. Her ghostly eyes were the embodiment of urgency.

"No," the ghost cried, "you must not kill him yet!"

Lathwi hissed, highly perturbed. Leave it to Liselle to complicate a matter at the very last moment. First, she wanted the mage dead. Now she wanted him alive. What new whim could she possibly be entertaining?

"It is not wise to leave a live sorcerer dangling over an abyss," she said, through gritted teeth. "So if there is a reason behind your request, state it quickly."

"You must call the unhomed back to this place first. For when the necromage dies, he will take our only link to The Dreamer's Keep with him. Those of us who were taken from The Dreamer's arms will be trapped here forever—unless the necromage takes us home. You can make that happen, Lathwi. I know you can. I can see it in you."

"Truly, Liselle?" Lathwi asked, seething with resentment. First, she wanted Seth dead. Then she wanted Seth alive. Now she wanted to use him as a channel back to the feckless Dreamer's Keep. Had it not occurred to her that Seth might resist being used in such a way? "Truly?" She thrust the necromage in the ghost's direction. "Can you see it in him as well?"

"No, I cannot," it replied, in a voice as cold and fetid as a grave. Her face melted then, becoming a hollow-eyed fright's head. "But make it happen anyway. Otherwise, I will haunt you for the rest of your days."

Now *there* was an argument worth considering. A living, breathing Liselle had been a colossal pest at times. A Liselle who could pass through walls had the potential to be much, much worse.

"I'll do it," Seth told her, all humility and rue. "I swear. Just promise not to drop me."

Lathwi snapped her teeth just inches away from his mutilated nose. "I will make no promises to one of Galza's disciples. But you will do as I bid you nonetheless."

She slung him at the altar's feet and then pinned him there amidst his own victims with an effortless extrusion of Will. When he made no effort to test his bonds, she loosed a satisfied grunt and returned her attention to Liselle. The ghost once again wore its heart-shaped face. A corner of its mouth flickered as if from a nervous tic as it waited for its former student to speak.

"I have no wish to be haunted," Lathwi said. "Tell me what needs to be done."

A rare smile flitted across Liselle's face. It made Lathwi think back to the ghost's flesh-and-blood days. At times, she had indeed been a colossal pest. But there had been other, better times as well—times of learning and sorcery. The recollection banished her lingering resentments about having to keep Seth alive. If her old mentor said it had to be done, then so it would be.

"First, you must collapse the wards that protect this place," Liselle said, slipping into her old half-haughty, half-pedantic teacher's cadence. "Otherwise, the unhomed will not hear you when you call them."

Lathwi turned to Seth, thinking to scry the nature and disposition of his safeguards from his thoughts. Before she could do so, however, his wards became visible to her as if of their own accord. There were only a few—and all of them had been sloppily wrought. She wondered if this was arrogance or carelessness on Seth's part, or simply a lack of the right kind of power. Whatever the reason, it made her task ridiculously easy. She bound the constructs to her Will with a thought, and then crushed them into cosmic dust with a Word.

"Now what?" she asked, as her vision returned to normal.

"Summon the unhomed," Liselle said. "Then open the door to The Dreamer's Keep and send us through it."

As soon as Liselle said this, Lathwi knew exactly how it had to be accomplished: she had to call the ghosts back with a song of power. That bit of out-of-body inspiration confounded her for a moment, for she did not know how to sing. She had never learned, and indeed, until this very moment, had had no inclination to try.

But she tried now.

The first note fell from her lips like a brick. The second flattened in her throat. Then she was overcome with feelings not her own, and music came flowing out of her. It was beautiful and compelling—a melody of sorrow and might. It filled the chamber with a promise of redemption, and then infiltrated the ether. Meanwhile, Liselle's ghost grew more substantial. The ache in its eyes gave way to hope. Yet even as it began to float toward the chasm and Death's as-of-yet unopened Door, it tensed as if stung. A moment later, it went streaking out of the chamber. In parting, it cried, "Wait for me!"

Lathwi did not appreciate being deserted, especially in the midst of an unfamiliar procedure, but no hint of annoyance crept into her voice. The song remained strong and true. And in response to it, the unhomed came drifting back into Seth's stronghold.

They constituted a trickle at first: a timid gray haze that refused to go anywhere near Seth's altar. Then, as Lathwi continued to sing, that trickle thickened into a stream that thickened into a river that overflowed its banks. Soon, the chamber looked as if it had been thoroughly fogged in.

She looked down at Seth. He was shivering now, chilled nearly to the marrow by the presence of so many ghosts, but he did not seem afraid. Indeed, when she nudged him with her toe, he was quick to flash a smile at her.

"Not bad for a beginner," he said.

"I am ready to open the Door," she said, refusing to banter with him. "I can and will do it without your help if I must. But I will show you mercy if you cooperate. How will you?"

He stared up at her for a long moment. She could feel his thoughts churning in his head. Hate tangled with regard. Regret snarled with resentment. He was confused, tired, and in pain. He ached for things that he could not have. But the madness that had driven him to such dark extremes was gone.

"That was my last chance," he said, more to himself than to her. "Poor Ylana is gone for good." His eyes came back into focus. His half-smile was more sweet than bitter. "I wouldn't mind helping you, whether you grant me mercy or not," he told her. "The only problem is—I can't find the Door unless I make a sacrifice. Only the dead are permitted to know the way."

She scorned his chosen form of magic with a curl of her lip, then gestured at their surrounds. "The dead are all around us, Milord. Pick one for your guide and let us go."

"Easier said than done, I'm afraid," he said, and it was so. None of the ghosts would go near him, not even for the chance to go home. "For some reason, they don't trust me."

"They are dead, not stupid," she said, and then looked around for Liselle's ghost. Since it wanted to return to the Dreamer's embrace so badly, it could serve as her guide. But the heart-faced phantom was nowhere to be seen, and when Lathwi Called its secret Name, she got no reply. She rumbled to herself, venting annoyance. The one time when she could have used the pesty ghost, it was off pestering somebody else. She sought out another of the unhomed, hoping that it would volunteer, only to hear more bad news.

"Fool! Do you think we would be waiting here if we could wait by the Door?" the unnamed phantom asked, hissing contempt. "You only know the way to the Keep once."

So. The easy way had been barred to her. And yet she had to go forward. She had promised Liselle. And that new, out-of-body instinct of hers worried about the rest of the unhomed. A solution occurred to her, one that she would never have considered if the situation had been any less dire. But Seth needed a sacrifice and she needed a guide, so—she Called a Name.

Minutes later, Pawl came charging into the chamber. *"I am here. Where are you? Are you well?"*

"I am," she assured him. *"But I need your help."* He cocked his head at her, urging her to continue. *"I cannot get to Death's Door without a guide. And if I cannot get to it, I cannot open it. And if I cannot open it, the unhomed must stay that way."*

"And you are telling me this because—"

"Because I need you to be my guide."

Pawl consented to such an easy-sounding task with a thoughtless snort. The next thing he knew, he was back in human form, and Lathwi had her left hand pressed against his chest. A slight, red-haired man in a grimy Guzzini robe was standing beside her. His mutilated face was hard to read, but his eyes were open pages of surprise.

"I'm impressed," Seth said to Lathwi. "But what's he doing here?"

"He is going to be our guide," she replied.

Seth choked on clot of air. "You'd do that to your own lover?"

"Do what?" Pawl asked.

"And you thought *I* was made of hard stuff? Mother of pearl, woman. You're the hardest stuff that was ever born."

She silenced him with a hiss, and then said, "Pawl will guide you to Death's Door. There, you will catch the Door and hold it open while the unhomed return to their beds. I will shunt the power necessary to accomplish this into you through a link. If you try to abuse that power, I will kill you where you stand. Knowing that, are you still of a mind to do this?"

"What if I say no?" Seth asked.

Lathwi shrugged. "It matters not to me. If you do not volunteer to take an active part in righting one of your own wrongs, then I will compel you to do it."

"Do what?" Pawl asked, now sporting a puzzled scowl. "What's going on?"

She leaned against him, for no other reason than to be close. "Do you trust me?"

"With my life," he replied, surprised that she should question the obvious.

"Then do not fear," she said. "I will be with you throughout."

Then, before he could ask *throughout what,* she stopped his heart with a Word.

ເ∞ ⊂ຂ

Seth gasped—not because he had just witnessed a spectacularly cold-blooded murder, but because an awful, almost orgasmic bolt of power coruscated through him immediately afterward. His thoughts soared. Every nerve ending in his body came alive. He spotted a tiny white mote just as it plunged into the abyss. His vision tunneled, then whisked him off in pursuit of it.

"Do not fall too far behind," a Voice warned him.

That was Lathwi. They were linked now, although he could not say exactly when or how that had happened. One moment he had been alone in his head; the next moment, not. She was investing him with the power he was going to need to hold the Door—huge gouts of it by his standards, but apparently only the merest bits by hers. For even as she was attending to him, another tendril of her Will was shooting after Pawl. Seth could see it out of the corner of his mind's eye: a scintillating streak of pure purpose. He had never even imagined that *any* human being could be that powerful.

The darkness at the end of his vision-tunnel paled, becoming a muzzy sort of gray. Moments or eons later, the door to The Dreamer's Keep appeared. To Seth, it seemed like a garrison's heavy, iron-reinforced gates. Only The Dreamer and Pawl knew how it seemed to Pawl.

"You'd better hurry if you want to catch him," he said, but thinking that it could not be done. *"Things happen rather quickly from here on."*

And indeed, Death's Door was already swinging open to admit the spark that was Pawl's spirit.

"Just do what you came to do," she said. *"Everything else is my concern."*

The spark bobbed toward the threshold. Chameleon-quick, that other extension of her Will lashed out and snapped it up like a wayward lightning bug. Seth gaped, stunned by the display. He had tried to do that back in the early days—tried and failed, again and again, until that part of him broke down and gave up.

Who was this woman?

The door was swinging shut now—a disappointed closing. With a pulse of his Will, Seth surged forth and inserted himself in the opening. In times past, he had always had to struggle to maintain this position. The door pushed on him, threatening to sweep him aside; and power bled from him as if from a wound. But today, he barely noticed the pressure that the door brought to bear on him. He felt as strong as the earth. And clean.

"I am ready," he told Lathwi. *"Send them."*

Moments later, the first of the unhomed came flitting down his vision-tunnel.

∞ ∞

An instant after she stopped Pawl's heart, Lathwi plunged an offshoot of her Will into his body to keep it alive. At the same time, she sent another scion racing after Pawl's spirit, and still another after Seth. She would not have been able to manage a three-way split a week ago. It would have been too complicated, a drain on her concentration *and* her power. But today, it was as easy as breathing.

She caught up with Seth first. Pawl's death had engaged the mage's potential. Now she energized it with power from her own vast reservoirs. As she did so, Death's Door phased out of the blackness and then swerved open to welcome Pawl. The bright, white spark of his spirit instinctively headed for the entryway. A moment's panic gripped Lathwi then, for Seth was right. Things were happening much faster than she had thought they would. And once Pawl's spirit crossed into the Keep, the bonds between it and its body would break down, and he would be lost to her forevermore.

That was unacceptable.

So she grabbed for the mote with more force than she might have otherwise. Her lightning-like strike caught it right at the threshold. It broadcast confusion as she pulled it away from the door, and then abruptly fell silent. That alarmed her, but before she could do anything, Seth flashed her a thought.

"I am ready. Send them."

She scowled, begrudging the moment that it would take her to start the ghosts on their way. The only thing she wanted to do right now was find out what was wrong with Pawl. But—she had made a promise. And that promise held. The part of her that was still standing beside the chasm broke into a Song. As she sang, she made her link with Seth accessible to the unhomed. And as she sang on, they inserted themselves into that sorcerous slipstream and began the journey home. The bravest went first, by ones and twos. Others followed in skittish clumps. Lathwi looked for Liselle, but did not see her and so Called out.

"TrueHeart! Make haste. The time has come."

A faint Voice replied. *"Wait—!"*

Annoyance flashed through her only to sheer off into alarm. For the once-shining mote in her grip was growing as muzzy and gray as a ghost. Even as she realized this, she diverted the rest of her ongoing concerns to a tiny, self-regulating corner of her awareness and concentrated on Pawl. With one thought, she returned the spirit to its body. With the next, she Willed the two to meld. The spark settled into its usual place. Pawl twitched as if he had been poked in his sleep. But when she withdrew the scion of Will that had been keeping him alive—nothing happened. His heart refused to start beating on its own. She hastened to reassert control over that part of him, then rifled through her mind for reasons as to why this could be happening. Had he crossed some portion of the threshold before she got to him? It *had* been a near thing. Perhaps she had nudged him over that boundary even as she snatched him back from it. Only one thing was certain: she was nowhere near as clever as she had supposed. Not then. Not now.

Nevertheless, she meant to do everything in her power to keep Pawl from dying.

৵ৎ

The unhomed were a great, gray river of spirits flowing back into The Dreamer's Keep now. They streamed over and around and through their doorman; and like a river, they broke things down and carried them off. Away went the madness. Away went the hate. Away went the darkness that Seth had embraced but never come to love. He had been deceived, defeated, and cast into despair of late, and yet—he was curiously content. Performing this tiny act of expiation had lent him a sense of peace that he had not known in years.

And that was a mercy that he had not expected from Lathwi.

He could still sense her through their link: a reservoir of power so vast and clean, it boggled the mind. But her presence was nowhere near as imminent as it had been when she had first sunk her Will into him. He wondered at the change, but made no attempt to find out what had caused it. For he had no doubt that she was going to kill him sometime in the very near future, and he had no particular desire to hasten that moment's arrival.

"Why do you not kill her instead?" a familiar voice whispered. *"Strike now, while she is distracted, and claim her power for yourself."*

The thought of that amazing reservoir rushing through him triggered a sharp pang in his loins. But his lust was short-lived, a condemned man's last fantasy. He accepted his death sentence, even agreed with it. He deserved to die for what he had done.

"What about your sister?" that darkling voice asked. *"Did she deserve to die, too?"*

He flashed back to the body on his altar: little Ylana, waiting so patiently. He had failed her so many times. He wondered if Lathwi would bring her back if he asked—the smallest of boons in exchange for *his* life. Surely that was a better solution than murder. He did not want any more blood—or ghosts—on his hands.

But his mentor scorned the suggestion with a delicate sniff. *"That one,"* it said, picturing Lathwi, *"will give you nothing but pain."*

"That's not true," he insisted—this even as his mutilated face began to burn. "If not for her, a dragon would've gotten me. She's a decent sort."

"She is a dragon!" the darkling countered, in a blistering tone. *"If she saved you from some other lizard's belly, it was only because she wanted you to line her own."*

Shockwaves rolled through Seth: great, psychic combers that caused Death's Door to shudder. An instant later, panicked ghosts began to rush the entryway. Seth wanted to reassure them, but his thoughts were stuck on Lathwi. She couldn't possibly be a dragon. Could not. He would have sensed such a thing somehow.

His mentor chuckled—a hair-raising sound. *"But it is possible, sweetling. I know her. Yes, I do. She claims kinship with the one who took your sister."* A moment later, it chuckled again and added, *"It probably killed Ylana to please her."*

"Shut up," he said, struggling to block terrible images from his mind. "Just shut up."

But the darkling went on and on in its black-honey voice. *"Kill the dragon-bitch, Seth. Do it for Ylana."*

"No."

"Do it for yourself."

"No!"

"Then let me do it for us all."

The turmoil in Seth's heart reached a frenzied pitch. Just a few moments ago, he had had a sure new grip on right and wrong. Now everything had turned slippery on him. He wanted to kill the dragon and save his sister. Or was that the other way around? He was so disconcerted, he did not notice that he had lost his hold on Death's Door. Inch by inch, it was creeping shut—and sweeping him toward the Keep in the process. Those few unhomed who had yet to pass through the gate were now frantically scrabbling to do so.

"Come away from there," the darkling said, waking him to his danger. *"Come away and do what must be done."*

A jolt of panic burned his confusion off, then abruptly receded. In the fresh-swept moments that followed, his vision ran clear. He saw the path that his mentor wanted him to tread: it started out black and grew worse with time. And while he no longer wanted to go that way, he saw too that he would—if not now, then later, in a fit of grief or guilt. He was weak. It was a failing.

He knew what had to be done.

So he stayed where he was, and let Death's Door sweep him into the Dreamer's Keep. In the instant before they were disconnected, he slung a last thought at Lathwi.

∜∝

"Sorry...."

The thought impinged on Lathwi's awareness. A moment later, the link between her and Seth disintegrated. She knew immediately that he was dead. He would not have been able to escape her Will any other way. She forced herself to check the chamber for assassins. Seeing none, she then returned the bulk of her attention to Pawl. For while she had tried just about every trick she knew, his heart *still* would not beat on its own. It was beginning to look like she had killed him with her arrogance.

But looks could sometimes be deceiving.

So she continued to infuse him with power—as if she could compel his body and spirit to merge. As she did so, a hint of dissonance encroached on her awareness. It was a subtle presence at first, a sense of creeping unease. Then it began to grow. Bit by bit, it wormed its way into her awareness. Bit by bit, it crowded her other concerns aside.

Then her amulet let off a sharp warning pulse.

She snapped back to the waking world to see a blackened corona of poisonous might coruscating toward her. All she had time to do before it struck was raise her Will like a shield. The impact blasted her from her feet and then bowled her heels over head. But—she was still alive when she skidded to a stop on the chamber's floor. And all that remained of the corona was the stench of scorched ozone. She bounced back to her feet, ready for whatever came next. A palsied movement urged her eyes toward the altar. To her amazement, it was Seth. He had dumped Ylana's body onto the ground, and was now sitting where the corpse had once lain.

But that could not be. Seth was dead. She had felt him die. Moreover, he could have sacrificed a thousand men and still not have been powerful enough to manage a blast like the one that she had just repelled. She scowled at him, trying to tap into his thoughts. As she did so, he leered and then aimed something in her direction. An instant later, that something belched another clot of blackened might.

Understanding caught up with her an instant before the barrage did. This was not Seth. This was *Galza*. The Dreamer's Daughter had possessed the mage's body, just like She had once possessed Liselle's. And now She was tapping into the power that She had shunted into Her talismans back in the days of Ever-Light.

The salvo splashed against Lathwi's defenses like a giant gob of corrosion. With a Word, she converted it into foul-smelling steam. Then, before Galza could attack again, she reached out with her Will and plucked the blackness that was The Dragonbane out of Seth's corpse. Shadow struggled like a crazed thing, but She was little more than a spirit now; and without the full complement of Her talismans, she could not hope to win free of the magical holding pen that Lathwi conjured for Her.

A savage sense of triumph welled up within Lathwi. At long last, the world was going to be rid of The Dragonbane—and she was the one who was going to make it so.

Even as the thought crossed her mind, a flicker of movement caught her eye. She glanced in that direction to see the Bone-Man crouched beside Pawl. The old man looked unhappy.

"This was not well done, Daughter," he said.

"I know," she replied. "I would undo the deed if I could. Is he still alive?"

He nodded. "Your magic sustains him. But sooner or later, you will have to let go."

"I know. I think it will be later rather than sooner, though. I may yet find a way to rectify my mistake."

"I know of a way," a Voice whispered then. *"Let Me go and I will tell it to you."*

For one out-of-body moment, Lathwi actually considered the offer—anything to get Pawl's heart beating again. Anything to right the wrong that she had done. But even as the thoughts crossed her mind, she was reminded of Seth. This, no doubt, was how it had started for him—with desperation and a crust of hope. But she knew better than him. She knew that no amount of magic, black or white, could change so much as a moment of the past. And believing otherwise was simply a way of avoiding responsibility.

"Your poisoned honey will not work on me, Galza," she said. *"I know You. I will not serve You."*

The Dragonbane sneered. *"Is it so much better to serve The Dung Queen and her rapist instead?"*

"I serve no one but myself."

"Prove it," Galza said. *"Keep the power that you have been given for yourself. Use it to bring wonder back to the world."*

Images of singing fish and talking clouds bloomed in Lathwi's head. Knowledge sweetened the water. Wisdom sprang from the dirt. There was no strife left in the world, no hunger, bad luck, or disease. *"Men would live in peace,"* Galza whispered. *"And dragons would reign supreme."*

Lathwi snorted, refusing to believe that Galza would wish such good fortune on the skyfolk. Galza had always hated dragons first.

"I am no threat to you or your kind now."

But Lathwi was not tempted. She knew that strife was part of the natural order. So were hunger, disease, and misfortune. Tampering with such things would only lead to other, unforeseeable problems. For the world was not meant to be a perfect place. And dragons were not made to reign supreme.

"Nor will You ever be again," she said, in a tone that signaled the Dragonbane's impending extinction.

The problem was, she did not quite know how to go about the process. Even with her newfound powers—and Galza's sorely reduced state—she could not assume that The Dragonbane would be easy to destroy. That mistake had been made twice already.

The thought triggered a memory, something that The Bone-Man had told her back on the Isle of Dreams. *"Those who do not learn from their mistakes will repeat them until the end of time."* She glanced at the old man. He was pressing a piece of bone to Pawl's brow.

"Am I about to repeat a mistake?" she asked. "Or rectify it?"

"I cannot say," he said, but something in his bright monkey eyes made her think of something else he had told her: *"Remember to look beyond the obvious first."*

Had he been telling her *not* to kill Galza?

The dragon in her roared, venting ancestral hatreds: *Galza had to be destroyed! Otherwise, She would return to wage war on the skyfolk again.* But the more rational parts of her could not help but consider the idea. Every time dragons tried to destroy that noxious creature, She came back to attack them from behind. Perhaps it was time to try a different approach.

But what?

Setting The Dragonbane free was *not* an option. No part of her was prepared to show that much leniency. But if she could not kill Her, and she could not let Her go, then what was left? Exile had not worked. Shadow knew Her way home all too well. But—what about confinement here on this world? As far as she knew, that had not been tried. She made up a list of requirements for such a prison. It would have to be escape-proof. Sorcery-proof. And inaccessible to men. It would have to be monitored by dragons.

As Lathwi reviewed these specifications, an image took shape in her head. It was hard, flawless, and fraught with magic—just like the Oma-stone that she had found on the Isle of Dreams. She drew the diamond from her pouch. It seemed to grow heavier in her hand. Getting Galza in there would be easy enough, she thought, as she studied the stone. The trick would be keeping Her there—if she decided to make the attempt.

"I am not going to kill Her," she shouted at the Bone-Man, hoping to startle an incriminating reaction out of him. When he failed to react at all, she finally accepted the fact that he was going to be of no help. She would have to determine Galza's fate alone. But just before she dismissed the old man from her thoughts, she said, "By the by, it was Splash who found me in the lake. It wanted you to know."

At that, he started laughing—a rolling, rumbly-tumbly, belly cackle that sounded like water bubbling from a spring in this bleak, death-soaked place. It was so infectious, it even drew a half-smile from Lathwi. Only Galza remained unamused.

"Do not do this," She said, as Lathwi prepared to confine Her within the stone. *"Keep the power for yourself. Do what the Dreamer dares not—"*

"I am," Lathwi said, and then transported Her into the Oma-stone. Galza hurled Herself at the diamond's matrices like a bottled bumblebee, but to no avail. The gem was too strong for Her.

And Lathwi worked to make it stronger still.

Layer by layer, she wove a cocoon of protective wards and forbiddings around the stone. Layer by layer, she made it impregnable. It was slow, painstaking work. It should have been draining as well. But such was not the case. Her energy levels remained stable throughout the weaving. Her focus stayed steady, too. Indeed, she felt as strong at the end of the ritual as she had at its beginning.

With a last Word of forbidding, she sealed the cocoon shut. No lightning flashed in the moments that followed. No thunder sang out. It seemed wrong that dragonkind's long-lived feud with its first and only enemy should come to an end with so little violence or fanfare. So she roared to get her ancestors' attention, then popped the Galza-Stone back into her pouch and said, "It is done."

"Is it?" the Bone-Man asked. A moment later, he disappeared. This time, he took Pawl with him.

She started to roar a protest only to cut herself off. Although it seemed otherwise at times, the Bone-Man did not play senseless games. If he had taken Pawl, he had done so for a reason. And she had no cause to believe that he harbored any ill-will against her Chosen. So she decided to ignore Pawl's abduction for the moment—this, so she could consider the old man's parting riddle instead.

Is it?

But she had done everything she had set out to do. Had she not?

She glanced at Seth's body, wondering if he could have somehow tricked her into thinking that he was dead. He was good at illusions, and she had certainly been distracted enough to make such a ruse fly. But a closer inspection disproved that theory. The body was cold now, and turning blue. No illusion was *that* good.

Then she realized that it had something in its hands.

She prised his left fist open first, then hissed as she recognized the blackened twist within as the spent remains of an obsidian spur. She found three more untapped tokens in his other hand. If these had been mere symbols of Galza's power, she would have tossed them into the abyss with a cheerful good riddance. But they were also repositories of Her power—and therefore an incentive. Twice now, She had corrupted humans in an attempt to get those tokens back. As long as they existed, She would surely try again.

So. The Bone-Man was right. Her quest was not quite done yet. It would not be done until she destroyed the talismans.

She examined the three that Galza had not depleted. They were obscene things, but cleverly wrought. The sorceries that Galza had used to prevent would-be poachers from stealing the powers within were terribly complex. Dismantlement would not work. Neither would displacement. She would have to use pure, unmitigated force. And even then, she was not sure what would happen.

To be safe, she erected a Sphere of Containment around the three talismans. That would restrain the energies that Galza's ruptured tokens were apt to release. As an added precaution, she suspended the completed Sphere over the chasm. Then, because she was still ill at ease, she raised protective barriers around herself. For a moment thereafter, she gazed upon the construct as it bobbed in the air. It looked more like a stray soap bubble than the end of an age. That struck her as an auspicious sign. So without further thought, she coiled her Will around the Sphere and began to squeeze it with her newfound might.

Nothing happened.

She squeezed harder, then harder still. Sweat beaded on her forehead. A muscle in her jaw began to twitch. The Sphere constricted—but only ever so slightly. It felt as if she were trying to crush a dragonsire's skull with a pair of soup spoons. Still, a thing that yielded once would eventually do so again. All she had to do was keep on bearing down. She reached deep within herself for more power. Her heretofore inexhaustible supply was dwindling fast. As it disappeared, her breath grew ragged, and her vision blurred.

The Sphere shrank again—again by a mere degree. Lathwi could scarcely believe her eyes. Nothing else in the whole world could have withstood the pressure that she was imposing on those talismans. She was dizzy now, nearly drained of strength. She had the sense that her nose was bleeding. Without realizing it, she had pushed herself to the brink of her physical limits. To go on was to court her own destruction. Even so, she could not quit. The path was clear, and Galza's final defeat loomed ahead.

She dropped to her knees. But in her mind, she stood tall and dragon-proud as she invoked the only power she had left. *She was Lathwi, The Soft One. She had no regrets.* Then, with what felt like her last breath, she added her Name to the balance.

A handful of heartbeats passed. The Sphere remained intact. Lathwi gaped at it, dully amazed to think that she had come so far only to fail at the very end. Then, even as her Will began to unravel, the Sphere imploded, pulverizing the tokens within.

For one stunned moment, the whole world went still. Then the Sphere expanded again, blown out by forces beyond the scope of Lathwi's imagination. She grinned like a dragon at the sight, then let out a pained roar as the magical construct burst.

Shockwaves from the blast knocked her across the chamber. They also made the mountain shake, harder and faster than any earthquake. Stalactites shattered. Stalagmites toppled. The chasm began to widen. Ylana's body disappeared into its maw, then Seth's. The altar tumbled in after them. Lathwi watched all of this from a red-rimmed daze. She knew the chamber was collapsing. She knew, too, that she ought to leave before it came down on top of her. But she could not bring herself to move so much as a fingertip. She was spent, an empty husk. Everything had been sucked out of her. All she could do was watch as chunks of rock rained down all around her.

Then something struck her on the head and she watched no more.

Chapter 22

*M*other! *We have found them. We have found the dragonslayers.*"

Taziem did not respond to Masque's excited thought. The whole of her attention was focused on Jamus. His breathing had stopped. So had his heart. Nevertheless, she hung on to his essence, entombing it in its own body while she groped for a way to repair the damage that had been done to him.

"*Look!*" the youngling gloated. "*They see us. They are going to try and fight. Oh, this is going to be so much fun.*"

The problem was, he had lost too much blood. The smell of it, so sweet and salty and rich, was everywhere: in her nostrils, on her skin, in the sand. She had to correct that. She had to make him as good or better than he had been before Bij's attack. Had to.

"*Our humans are aground now—all but little Mim. Rue says I am to keep her safe with me.*"

She slung a venomous look at her once-Chosen. He was still locked in mid-strike, with eyes narrowed and teeth bared. His mind was a morass of disbelief and shame. He tried to share a thought with her, but she deflected it. He had broken a promise. He had lied. Isolation was the very least he deserved.

"*Mother, the battle is joined!*" The thought was accompanied by an image of dragons descending on a confusion of shoulders, swords, and shields. "*Mighty Ruin has drawn first blood.*" A moment later, it added, "*Our humans are fierce!*"

A thin, gray mist shimmered into being in front of Taziem, and then shaped itself a face. She recognized the ghost immediately, and indeed, was glad to see it. If anyone knew how to save Jamus, The TrueHeart would. But before she had a chance to ask, the ghost let out an urgent cry.

"Let him go!"

"I cannot," Taziem said. "He was under my protection when Bij betrayed him. I must make him right and well."

"That is beyond your power. Release him before his link to The Dreamer's Keep decays."

But Taziem was dragon-stubborn, and did not want to take the ghost's advice. She would find a way to repair him. She had to! Her reasons for not wanting to keep Jamus alive were not personal. She liked him well enough for a human, but she knew that all creatures died in their own time. It was just that his death here and now would create a perpetual black mark on dragonkind's collective memory.

"Such a smudge will teach the skyfolk humility," Liselle said, reading the thought. "If you are as wise as you claim to be, you will accept that and release him—"

"Look! Some of the dragonslayers are riding back toward the valley. Mim and I will follow them. They will not get away. Masque is hungry. And Masque likes horsemeat."

"Otherwise, you will shame dragonkind further by condemning a man's spirit to eternal exile. Believe me," the ghost went on, when Taziem continued to balk, "if there were a way to save him, I would tell you. I have loved him from the moment we met, and want nothing but happiness for him. But I tell you truly, dragon: he is already dead, and you are holding him where he no longer belongs. Is that your idea of protection?"

At that, the last of Taziem's denials crumbled like so much sand underfoot. The TrueHeart was right. She could not undo what had been done here. And hanging on to such a wrong-headed hope was like failing him twice. Dragonkind would simply have to learn to live with the memory of Bij's perfidy. And she would have to lead the way. She shifted Jamus' head in her lap, as if to make him more comfortable, and then stroked his cool, blue cheek.

"I am sorry," she said—the first time she had ever apologized to anyone. It was not a dragon ritual, this expression of regrets, but being human made her do weird things. "I meant you no harm."

Then she retracted her Will.

The corners of his mouth quivered as if with relief and then turned ever so slightly upward. An instant later, he went completely limp. Although she knew that he was gone now, Taziem continued to cradle his head in her lap. She had never had the opportunity to look a human in the face at the very moment of death. She wondered if they all smiled like that, or if it was just a quirk. It occurred to her that Liselle might know, but when she went to ask, she found that the ghost was gone now, too.

"Is it dead then?"

She arched an eyebrow in Bij's direction. He was radiating distress like the desert radiated heat. She could not resist the urge to compound his anguish.

"Yes," she said, all blistering contempt. *"Yes, he is. Are you proud of yourself, promise-breaker? How does it feel to be dragonkind's first liar?"*

If Bij had been able to squirm, he would have done so now—anything to relieve the pressure that accompanied those two new unsavory distinctions. But her stasis spell held him to his incriminating pose, and that was the way she wanted it.

"I did not mean to hurt it," he said. *"I only wanted to scare it a little. But then it hit me and reason fled and the next thing I knew, the taste of its blood was in my mouth."*

"I believe you," she said, convinced by the memory rather than the words. *"And that is the only thing standing between you and extinction at the moment."*

Bij bristled at that. He could not help himself. No one talked to a dominant sire like that: not a youngling, not a Chosen, and especially not a once-Chosen currently in human form. Even so, it made her wonder what else he might not be able to help. If he could not control himself, he could not be trusted. And if he could not be trusted—well, appropriate measures would have to be taken. So she eased Jamus' head out of her lap, then stood up and set out to test the depths of Bij's self-restraint.

At first, she just circled him, flaunting her human form and scent and sensibilities. His chagrin acquired a slightly sour tang. Then she struck up a cocky gypsy pose right in front of him, and the mental equivalent of his ears went back.

"So what is it about humans that threatens you so?" she asked. *"You do not know exactly, do you?"* Agitation began to churn within him—a dust devil of resentment and wrath that blew into a full-fledged funnel cloud when she jabbed a finger into the soft part of his muzzle. *"Is this where that puny little man hit you?"* she asked. *"He must have been very strong to make you break a promise with one blow."*

He would have lunged at her for that, if he had been able to move. As it was, all he could do was hurl a furious thought at her. *"Enough of your games, Taziem. If you are wise, you will let me go and—"*

She cut him off with a scornful hiss. *"Do not speak to me of wisdom, Bij-ling. For a dragon of your great age, you possess too little of it. And I am not of a mind to let you go after what you have done."*

Disbelief soared within him. *"Why are you raising such a flap over one little human?"*

"Because you lied, Bij-ling. Because you broke your promise and hurt him. It would not be unjust to kill you for that."

He doubted her ability to do so with a mental snort. In response, she sent a bolt of pain ricocheting through him. *"Make no mistake here,"* she said, as the pangs leveled his disdain. *"I could tear your life from you as easily as you tore Jamus' from him. But killing you outright would only teach future generations what they should know from birth—that stupid dragons die every day. They need to learn that they cannot break promises without suffering dire consequences. And so, Bijling, do you."*

He thought to argue with her. He thought to mock. But she closed her mind to his bluster and summoned her Will. She knew what to do now. More importantly, she knew how to do it.

She transformed herself first, an easy reversion to her dragon form. Then she went to work on Bij.

His mind went blank as her magic surged into him only to cloud again as that magic began to pinch and pull at him from every possible direction. She caught a stray thought—intense pain coupled with equally intense confusion. That pleased her, for the human in her wanted him to suffer for his crimes. Meanwhile, he continued to Change. His body warped, then compacted. His instincts reconfigured themselves, too. She directed his transformation down to the very last detail. Then she sealed his fate with the power of her Name.

For one long, windblown moment thereafter, all Bij could do was stand and gape at Taziem. His thoughts reeled as if from fever. His perceptions did not yet make sense. He could not understand why she seemed so much larger all of a sudden. He thought to take a closer look, but when he went to extend his neck, it remained stubbornly set on his shoulders. His confusion acquired a dreadful edge.

"What have you done?" he asked.

She studied her handiwork for a moment, taking in details—his flat, blunt-nosed face, the broad span of his shoulders, the apprehension in his beautiful amber eyes. She had tried to make him look like Jamus, but the laws of conservation had interfered. His skin was a rich, cinnamon color. His body was more massive, and more powerfully built. And she had declined to give him any hair, simply because she found it attractive and did not want him to have that advantage. Still, fortune had been kind to him. He could have looked much worse.

"You are a human in every way and respect now," she told him. *"Your skin will tear if it is scratched, your blood will run red from your veins. And once you are gone from here, no dragon save myself will be able to hear your Voice."*

He recoiled, mentally and physically. Unused to standing on two feet, without so much as a stub of a tail for balance, he fell down. His hindquarters were quite bony now. It hurt when he landed on them. He tried to roar his surprise, but it came out as a watery squawk. All at once, he began to feel very small. And very exposed. But he tried to hide that behind a dragon's haughty facade.

"I suppose you will kill me now as I killed your little pet," he said. *"You always did like to go out of your way to make a point."*

"Did you not hear me say that killing you outright would serve no useful purpose?" she asked, returning his insult on a subtler level by implying that his faculties were inferior to hers. *"I would rather you wandered the world in search of wisdom and perspective. So that is what you are going to do."*

Horror danced into his amber eyes, hand-in-hand with comprehension. Another watery sound spilled from his mouth. *"You are going to leave me like this?"*

Taziem grinned—a show of teeth that had nothing to do with mirth. *"If and when you find enlightenment, you may seek me out and try to convince me to return you to your former self. Until then, however, you had best avoid dragons lest you meet one who feels about humans as Bij The Betrayer did."*

With that, she unfurled her wings and took to the sky. He shouted after her, but she never once looked back.

Chapter 23

*L*athwi came awake with the dry, bitter taste of sulfur in her mouth and a roaring pain in her brainpan. The sun's light brutalized her eyes. The prominent aromas of grass and dirt made her stomach churn. She snorted to clear the smells from her nasal passages only to jar a memory loose. In it, she was slumped against a stone wall, too exhausted to move. The forces that she had just released were smashing Seth's stronghold into rubble. Hunks of rock rained out of the darkness. The crack in the cavern floor grew wider. Then came a red-fringed flash that should have spelled the end of her existence.

Yet here she was, sprawled out in the open air with the sun on her back and grass beneath her belly—in dragon form. She could not remember that happening, either.

These mysteries incited a low-grade itch in her, but at the moment, she lacked the drive to scratch them. All she wanted to do was bask here in the sun—and eat. She was so hungry, she would have even eaten a bowl of cold porridge if it had popped up in front of her. But the only thing likely to pop up under her nose at the moment was grass. And at the moment, she was in more urgent need of food than rest. So she heaved to her feet, meaning to catch and consume the first thing that happened across her path. As she did so, she caught sight of the pouch that had been trapped beneath her. She had no trouble remembering what was in it: the Galza-Stone. But the strange thing was—she could not sense it, not even when she made a conscious effort to do so. It was inert, unresponsive; as if it were no different than any other stone.

That confused her. Could it be that she had *imagined* confining The Dragonbane to the diamond and sealing Her up afterward? Could this be another of the Bone-Man's epic riddles? If so, then why was she so fatigued?

Hungry or not, this was one mystery that she could not dismiss. But just as she was about to dump the diamond onto the ground and have a closer look at it, a winged shadow soared overhead. Her first thought was: *Bij!* She went perfectly still, like prey caught in the open. For if the dragonsire caught her here, he would surely challenge her; and she could not count on Taziem to provide another timely distraction. The shadow made a second, lower pass. She stole a glance at it as it flew by. Much to her relief, it was not Bij at all, but a smallish, bronze dragon.

And it had just let go of something.

As that something fell, it separated into two distinct blurs. She blinked—once to clear her vision, and then again to brush back her disbelief. For those blurs were pigs! An instant after the first one slammed into the ground, she was on it like a meat-bee. The fall had broken many of its bones and tenderized its flesh. It was tasty and juicy and easy to eat. As she tore into it, she greedily eyed the second pig.

Then the bronze dragon landed in the clearing.

She bared her gore-flecked teeth at him—a warning to stay away from her meat. He rumbled as if amused by her threat display, then strode over to the other carcass and began to feed. He was a delicate eater, and very slow. She gobbled what was left of her pig down, then went over to steal a few bites from the stranger. To her surprise, he made no effort to drive her away. He simply went on eating at his leisurely pace until there was nothing but bare bones left. Afterward, as they rolled in the grass to clean themselves off, he extended his neck and touched noses with her.

"Your appetite encourages me," he said. *"I was worried."*

The self-image that accompanied the thought was one of a man with long brown hair and piercing eyes: Pawl! But that could not be. She had Changed him back into a man back in Seth's stronghold. And then—she had stopped his heart.

The memory shamed her. She had had no right to do such a thing, with or without his consent. That had been sheer arrogance on her part. And it had almost cost Pawl his life.

"How is it that you are as you are?" she wondered. *"When I last saw you, you were—human. And—"* She groped for a way to portray that estrangement between body and spirit, but settled for a spurt of embarrassment and regrets instead. *"You were dead. By my hand."*

"I don't remember that," he said. *"I don't remember anything except an old man with a fox's sly eyes. He came to me in a dream, and urged me over and over and over again to make a wish. When I finally did so, he disappeared. The next thing I knew, I was as I am now, and Liselle was begging me to fetch you from the mage's stronghold before it collapsed."* He cocked his head at her, a gesture of simple curiosity, then added, *"So how are you? You were unconscious when I found you. And the cave-in came near to crushing us both."*

She stared at him for a moment, while trying to digest everything that Pawl had told her. But there was so much to absorb, and she could not concentrate over the throbbing in her head. It churned her thoughts into a confused emulsion. Were Liselle and the Bone-Man working in collusion now? And why did that possibility bother her so?

"Lathwi?" Pawl pressed. *"Are you unwell?"*

"Not exactly," she replied, offering him the unadorned truth. *"My head aches, and I do not understand many of the things that have happened here. But the thing that pains me most is the thought that I almost killed you."*

"That'll pass," he assured her, *"along with the bumps and bruises."* When she did not respond, he nosed her again and said, *"Everyone makes mistakes, Lathwi—even blue-eyed dragons. So long as you learned from yours—and I believe you did—I bear you no grudge."*

His largesse surprised her. It was so enlightened, so evolved. So dragon-like. She nuzzled him, a gesture that a lesser creature might have construed as thanks, and then curled up against his sun-warmed belly. He let out a rumble that radiated satisfaction. A moment later, they both began to drowse.

"Was I a dragon when you found me?" she asked, as she drifted toward a dream. *"Or was I a woman?"*

"You were both," came Pawl's sleepy reply. *"As always."*

A pang of irritation tugged her back toward the waking world. Leave it to Pawl to manage a brilliant bit of dragon-speech when all she wanted was a simple, human answer. *"Very clever,"* she said. *"Now tell me plain. Which was I?"*

He rumbled, protesting the imposition on his nap, only to snap fully awake as the sound of many feet on the run thrashed its way into their clearing. Heartbeats later, they heard a familiar voice snarl, "Come on, you lazy bastards, keep moving. Seth's bolt-hole is just ahead. We'll be safe there."

"We'd better be," somebody else panted, "or I'll have that maggot's heart on a stick."

They exchanged a look that contained a name: *Veeder.*

The general's arrival came as an unpleasant surprise to Lathwi. She was so tired of men and their ill-conceived affairs. She would have been quite willing to sit back and let fortune decide Veeder's fate, but fortune had already tapped Pawl as its instrument. A vengeful grin had curved across his mouth. Eagerness now danced in his eyes.

"I am going to enjoy this," he said, as he glided out of their tangle.

"Where are they?" the panting man asked. "Do you see any of 'em?"

"Nah," someone else said. "They went after our horses, just like the general said they would. Now shut up and run."

Pawl was stalking the party now. Lathwi trailed behind. It was clear to her that his dragon nature was beginning to dominate again. If she did not Change him back to a man in the near future, the swordmaster of Compara would be lost. She could not allow that, not after having almost lost him once already. But since he stood a better chance of surviving a clash with warriors as a dragon than a man, she left him as he was for the time being.

They arrived at Death's Door ahead of Veeder and his men, but it was not as she remembered it. The onion-shaped opening was gone now, covered up by a steep bank of scree. A layer of superfine rock dust coated the nearest bushes and trees. Pawl swiveled his head around to grin at her.

"Those men are going to be very *surprised,"* he said.

She could see a handful or ragged blurs thrashing, crashing, and stumbling along the footpath now. The foremost one hazed into view only to skid to a stop at the treeline. "Damn you, Veeder!" he cried. "You said we'd be safe here!"

"What now, Kel?" the general snarled, and then shouldered past his aide. His hair and beard were slick with sweat and blood. The symbols on his chest had been defaced by a dragon's claws. He snarled again when he saw Pawl and Lathwi, and then said, "There are only two of them, you miserable excuse for a man. And judging by their size, they're still young. So quit crying and kill 'em."

Lathwi peeled her lips back, daring the men to go ahead and try. That prompted one man to snarl, "You want 'em dead, you kill 'em. I'm getting out of here." He turned and bolted back into the woods. Several others followed. But the general brandished his sword and stood his ground.

"By the blackened balls of Grange!" he said. "I am sick to death of dragons." He thrust his blade in Pawl's direction. "Come on, runt, try and get me. I've had bigger ones than you for breakfast."

Pawl was more than happy to accept the general's offer.

He approached the big man at a deceptively casual pace, like a curious youngling. But there was nothing curious about his thoughts. Those were firmly focused on Veeder. He anticipated the general's first strike—a thrust to the underarm, a would-be soft spot—and shifted at the last moment, deflecting the blow with a shoulder. Although his scaled hide remained intact, the stroke dented a bone nonetheless. Pawl roared, then snapped at the warlord's face. Veeder side-stepped the strike with a fearless laugh, then made a stab at Pawl's eyes. With a flick of his tail, Pawl knocked the man's feet out from under him.

"Without a proper stance, one cannot achieve proper balance," he thought at Lathwi, as Veeder went tumbling to the ground. *"Without proper balance, one cannot hope to survive."*

She loosed an amused snort only to tense as the general bounced back to his feet. Was his guard hand clenched now? She squinted. Yes, yes, it was. And a thin spray of dust was trickling from the cracks in his fist. She hissed. Veeder was going to throw dust in Pawl's face! She knew that trick—knew it and despised it. Only a coward stooped to such tactics during a challenge.

Until that moment, she had been content to remain in the background and menace the few men who had not bolted back into the woods. But in light of Veeder's treachery, she felt free to indulge in some trickery of her own. So even as the general began to fling the rock-dust at Pawl's eyes, she invoked a Word.

It should have stopped him. Indeed, it should have frozen every muscle in his big, hairy body. But—it did not. Pawl roared a protest as the dust blinded him. At the same time, Veeder ducked in and drove his sword toward the underside of his throat. When the scales there turned the thrust aside, the Southerner sputtered a curse and then went for the eyes. And those were a full-grown dragon's only unprotected organs.

Lathwi roared a warning. Pawl reared instantly, pulling his head out of Veeder's reach. A moment later, she flashed him an image of the general's exact location and said, *"Now! Strike now!"*

Pawl lunged forward, catching the general in his jaws. Bone splintered as he bit down. Blood fountained. General Ferman Veeder screamed once as his spine snapped, and then went decidedly limp. Pawl slung the body into the woods with a good riddance grunt. That prompted the few men who had chosen to stay with the general to bolt. Pawl scowled after them, and then said, *"We should run them down before they get too far."*

Lathwi was more inclined to let them go. But before she could say so, she was distracted by the appearance of a thin, gray mist in their midst. It rose up from the dusty ground like a wisp of morning fog, then shaped itself a face. The ghost's expression was bereft. Its spectral eyes were bleak.

"Liselle!" Lathwi blurted.

"I would urge you to spare those men," the ghost said. "You need them to carry the news about this campaign back to their countrymen. Otherwise, they will never know the truth about what happened here."

"Is that why you have come?" Lathwi asked. *"To give us advice? Or are you here to haunt me as you promised?"* For she now knew why it had bothered her to hear that Liselle had played a part in her rescue. The ghost should have been home by then. *"I held the link open as long as I could, you know."*

"I know," Liselle said, a hollow absolution.

"She overstayed because of me," another voice whispered.

Within the span of a blink, there were two faces in the mist. The new one looked haggard, as if it were wracked with pain or guilt, but it had an innate handsomeness about it nonetheless. As soon as Pawl saw it, he let out an aggrieved roar.

"Jamie! What happened?"

"I died of a dragon's bite," the ghost said. *"Taziem tried to preserve me, and in doing so, trapped me in this world."*

Now it was Lathwi's turn to vent her surprise and distress. The outburst attracted Jamus' attention. For the first time in over five years, he looked at her with something other than hate in his eyes.

"I know now how badly I wronged you," he said, "and so I ask nothing for myself except your forgiveness. But for Liselle, I will dare to ask a boon." Before Lathwi had a chance to respond, yea or nay, he said, "Send her back to The Dreamer's Keep. *Please.* She has done too much for too many to be denied her final rest."

It was, Lathwi thought, an honorable request. And she was not without her own reasons for wanting her old mentor gone. So despite her bone-deep fatigue, she decided to do what she could for the ghosts. She cleared her mind, then turned her focus inward. But something was wrong. She could not See the bright, white filaments of her Will with her mind's eye anymore, or feel them gathering into a whiplike cord within her. And the reservoirs of power that she had always taken for granted now seemed like nothing more than a false memory. She strained to exert her Will nonetheless, but to no avail.

"Send her back," Jamus urged. "You can do it. I know you can."

Before Lathwi could disillusion him, Liselle raised an ethereal hand to his cheek and smiled like the ghost of bittersweetness. "You ask the impossible of her, my dear," she said. "Lathwi's powers are no more."

"This happened to me one other time," Lathwi said, struggling to make sense of her situation. *"A blow to the back of the head started it. I was hit in the same place earlier today, so perhaps the same thing is happening again. Perhaps I simply need some time to recover—"*

Liselle cut the theory short with a tiny shake of her head. "This time, there will be no recovery."

"How do you know?"

"I can see the change in your aura. There's no gold in it anymore."

"But how can that be?" Lathwi wondered, more intrigued than alarmed. *"A few hours ago, I was powerful beyond reckoning."*

"That was The Dreamer's doing," the ghost said, flickering with sudden agitation. "She gave you a part of Her own essence. I saw it in you in the necromage's stronghold, and heard it in your song. But in the process of doing everything that needed to be done, you depleted your own powers even as you used up Hers."

Pawl rumbled, a disgruntled sound. *"That hardly seems fair."*

"The Dreamer *always* takes more from Her highest servants than She gives," Liselle said. "But—" Longing gusted across her face like a desert wind, sandblasting the bitterness away. "But her reward in the afterlife will be great."

"As yours must have been," Jamus said, radiating misery. "And I kept you from returning to it. Blessed Mother, I will never forgive myself for that."

Liselle cupped his cheek again. There was grief in her eyes, but tenderness, too. "I alone made that choice," she said. "So I alone will bear the blame for it. And if there is any solace for being exiled from The Dreamer's Keep, I'm sure we'll find it together."

The pain in Jamus' eyes spiked, then suddenly softened. He covered Liselle's spectral hand with one of his own. As he did so, the mist that embodied them began to dissipate. A moment later, Lathwi and Pawl were alone. Pawl shuddered, shedding a load of stress.

"Poor Jamie," he said. *"I would not want to die of a dragon's bite."*

Lathwi made no reply. She was still coming to terms with being an ex-sorceress. The change did not concern her overmuch—she was who she was, as always. But it had already had a huge impact on someone else. And she was not sure how she was going to break the news to him.

"Pawl—" she began. But he hissed her to silence.

"Someone's coming," he said.

His senses must have been keener than hers, however, for several minutes went by before she detected anything out of the ordinary. Then, to her wonder, snatches of a song came drifting out of the woods. The singer had a frail, lispy voice.

"Come out, come out, wherever you be,

"There's no one here but my dragon and me."

Now Lathwi could see a large, mottled shadow weaving through the trees. As it drew closer, it resolved itself into a dragon with calico markings. Masque! But what was that curious, singing lump between its wings?

"We will eat you, yes, we will.

"And that will teach you not to kill."

She squinted, trying to wring more sight from her eyes. The lump became a tiny, wild-haired human dressed in brightly colored rags. Doubly curious now, she reached out and touched her tanglemate's mind. The youngling bugled glad tidings in reply.

"Lathwi, I am Masque," it said. *"And I am very glad to see you. There are dragonslayers in these woods."*

"I know," Lathwi said. *"Are you hurt?"*

"No, just tired. And look, I have my very own human. She is little like me."

"I see," Lathwi replied, unsure if she should be amused or concerned. *"And what are you two doing here?"*

"We were hunting, *Great One."*

She did not recognize the Voice, and the accompanying self-image of a dark-eyed, olive-skinned gypsy girl gave her pause, too. For as far as she knew, the only gypsy who had the ability to mind-speak was Old Katya.

"Katya was my grandmother, Great One. I am Mim."

"Where are the rest of your people?"

"I do not know," Mim replied. *"We left them behind to chase after the horsemen who broke away from the rest of the slayers. Then we caught one of their horses and—"* She projected a loud slurp. *"—and lost track of where we were.*

"But I am sure they will be along sooner or later."

The two younglings were closing in on the clearing now. Both had bulging bellies and blood-spattered faces. Masque was so weary, it was almost staggering. It touched noses with Lathwi in passing, then curled up in a waning pool of sunlight. Mim stretched out across its backside. A moment later, they both began to snore. Lathwi rumbled—a dragon's chuckle.

What fun these two must have had!

"I think they have the right idea," Pawl said, pitching the thought over a massive yawn. But even as he began to cozy up next to Masque, a woman stepped into their midst from out of nowhere. She was all black except for her hunter's moon eyes. And although she was limping slightly, she still managed to carry herself like a queen.

"Interesting," she said, as she gave Pawl a critical once-over. Then she glanced at Masque and Mim. "Very interesting." At last, she touched her flattened stub of a nose to Lathwi's. "You have been busy, Soft One.

"Did you find the mage yet?"

Lathwi nodded. *"He is dead."*

"And Galza?"

Lathwi nodded again, and then dumped the contents of her pouch onto the ground. Taziem sucked a breath in through her teeth—once as the diamond spilled onto the grass, and again as Lathwi said, *"That is Her new home."*

Taziem made a wondering noise, then picked the diamond up and studied it from every conceivable angle. When she was done, she gave it a vigorous shake. The image that she shared with Lathwi was of Galza bouncing up and down within like a worm in a dried jolla bean.

"If I were you," she said, "I would rattle this stone at least once every day." Then, as Lathwi chuckled, she turned serious again and said, "I cannot see what you did to bind Her within the stone. Tell me how it was done."

"Later perhaps," Lathwi said. *"I am too tired now."*

Taziem glanced at the miniature tangle that Pawl, Masque, and Mim had formed, then seemed to wilt on those great, stalky legs of hers. "Come to think of it, I could use a nap, too." The urge to curl up spread across her face like a smile. She dropped the stone back into its pouch and then tried to hand the pouch back to her daughter. "Here. Guard it well."

But Lathwi had other ideas. She could not sense the Galza-Stone; therefore she was not a suitable keeper. And even if she had been the most suitable creature alive, she still would not have taken the pouch back. For a thought had come to her a moment ago, and it was growing louder and louder like an echo in reverse.

"From here on," she said, speaking as if she had been divinely inspired, *"you are to be the Keeper of The Galza-Stone. The rest of dragonkind is to be its guardian. I have done my part."*

Her mother arched an eyebrow at that. She could have been amused. She could have been impressed. Lathwi suspected that she was a bit of both. Nevertheless, Taziem looped the pouch around her wrist without an argument.

"It will make a nice addition to my nest," she said, and then tensed as a dragon's roar rippled across the darkening sky. A moment later, she vented that tension as a sigh. "That was Rue. He says the dragonslayers are all dead now. He says he and the others are going to feast on horsemeat, then head home with the gypsies."

Lathwi cast a look in Mim's direction. *"What about her?"*

"She's in my keeping now," Taziem said. "Katya asked me to teach her the ways of power." She stretched out against Pawl's backside. "But we are not going *anywhere* until I get some sleep." As she made herself comfortable, she slapped Pawl on the flank and said, "This one is really very well-made, you know."

"I know."

The last glimmers of twilight were fading from the sky now. A chorus of cicadas began to warm up in a nearby tree. Lathwi wished them elsewhere—not because they threatened to keep her awake, but because their high-pitched buzzing masked the homey wheeze of dragon snores. She looked upon the tangle in front of her with great fondess. It was, perhaps, the oddest tangle ever formed or made, but it was hers for the night and she was glad.

She settled down against Masque. The youngling smacked its chops in its sleep, then nestled closer. A moment later, Pawl extended his neck so he could rest his chin on the little one's back. Although his eyes were closed, she could tell that he was not asleep. His mind was too active.

"*I thought you were tired,*" she said.

"*I am,*" he said. "*But I am curious, too. Why did you did not tell Taziem that you are not a sorceress anymore?*"

"*Eavesdropper,*" she said, trimming the thought with mock-reproach.

"*I learned from the best,*" he said, but refused to be sidetracked. "*Will you tell me why?*"

Lathwi shrugged. "*She did not ask. And a wise dragon saves its secrets for the right moment.*"

"*Will you not miss having such power?*"

She shrugged again. "*Being a sorceress was fun, Pawl, and often convenient. But knowledge is the truest form of power, and I have not lost my capacity to learn.*"

"*But—*"

"*I am what I have always wanted to be—a dragon first and foremost. I have only one regret.*"

His eyes popped open, sprung by either wonder or surprise. She caught and held his gaze like a woman might catch and hold her man's hand. "*I am the one who Changed you into a dragon. No one else can Change you back. You will never be human again.*"

She expected him to be shocked; angry; aggrieved. She half-feared that he might reject her, too. Amazingly enough, all he did was project contentment at her.

"*Do you remember me telling you about the old man who came to me in my dreams?*" he asked. At her nod, he said, "*I told you that he urged me to make a wish. But I didn't tell you what that wish was. Shall I tell you now?*" She nodded again. "*I wished to be like this—so I could be with you.*"

For one astonished moment, all Lathwi could do was stare at Pawl and marvel at fortune's peculiar ways. As she did so, a tension that she had not even known was there dissolved in her belly. Its leaving made everything seem right in the world. She rumbled, savoring the feeling. Then she touched noses with her Chosen and went to sleep.

Made in the USA
Lexington, KY·
01 June 2010